PRINT EDITION

Sex, Bugs & UFOs © 2022 by Mirror World Publishing

Edited by: Robert Dowsett and Justine Dowsett
Cover Design by: BookCoverZone

Published by Mirror World Publishing in July 2022

Mirror World Publishing

Windsor, Ontario, Canada
www.mirrorworldpublishing.com
info@mirrorworldpublishing.com

ISBN: 978-1-987976-89-2

SEX, BUGS
& UFOs

WARREN A. SHEPHERD

mirror world
publishing

For Mum. You lit the first spark of my childhood imagination and encouraged a sense of wonder that launched a thousand dreams.

For Mr. Bawa, wherever you are. As my Grade 7 teacher, you inspired my nascent talent — for better or worse — and urged me to ponder the question: what if.

And most of all, for Poppy. Your combination of unwavering love and unflinching support is the only fuel I need for my journey to the stars. Without you, I'd never have gotten off the ground.

THEN

Explosions sparked the midnight sky, strobing the darkness with a frantic glow. Fireworks, the humans called them and for some reason, saw fit to employ them in their year-end celebrations. A curious use of pyrotechnics to be sure, but Chendra Vaziil had been on enough worlds to know that every species had its idiosyncrasies; Earth was no exception. It was a primitive planet populated by a race not much more sophisticated than the animals they kept as pets; a race so bereft of vision they'd yet to break free of their solar system to any great purpose; a race so seething with violence that it existed in a constant state of war with itself. In essence, Earth was the perfect place for him to hide.

Vaziil was in the last stages of his transformation cycle. Within days his genetic pattern would be set, and his alien physiology would become virtually undetectable to the uninitiated, save for an archive of his core matrix. Certainly, it would pass the scrutiny of these intellectually stunted simians. He stroked the length of his arm, admiring his handiwork, though he hadn't quite gotten used to

7

the sponginess of the human epidermis. How these beings had endured for so long with such a fragile shell was beyond him.

The Earth woman, at least, seemed pleased by his appearance. She slept soundly at his side, satiated by their lovemaking, as she called it. He knew humans were often led by their primal urges, the drive to copulate amongst the strongest. Cohabiting with her provided a suitable cover while he acclimated to his new home — and his new body. Besides, the activities they shared weren't altogether unpleasant. He flicked absently at the flaccid object dangling between his human legs, amused by its versatility. It was an adequate tool and the physical release it provided was surprisingly invigorating. There were worse things in the universe to endure.

Sounds in the hallway disrupted his thoughts. The woman's living accommodation unit was one of six in the old building so ambient noise was to be expected. But something about the nature of these sounds pricked Vaziil in disturbing ways, ways he couldn't quite put his newly human finger on.

As he pulled on his clothing, the realisation chilled him. He was on a strange world, interacting with a strange species. His senses thrummed with new experiences at every turn. Everything around him was alien to him. Everything around him *seemed* alien — except those noises. The weight of their footfalls, the rhythm of their gait, the simmering energy that surrounded them; it was all too familiar. Which could only mean one thing…

Too late. The door burst inwards, the sonic charges blowing the hinges away like dry leaves. Vaziil drew his arm up instinctively, protecting his delicate form from the shattering debris. The woman woke in panic, calling out the human name she knew him by. The room filled with smoke and noise, clouding his senses, but his attackers were no better positioned. Amateurs. In their attempt to catch him by surprise, they'd lost precious seconds waiting for the dust to settle. Vaziil used the confusion to his advantage, leaping over the screaming woman. He jerked her up from the bed, pulling her close to shield him.

Three figures poured through the doorway, their heavy weapons tracking mechanically toward him. They wore the distinctive cobalt body armour of the Thon Pahl Special Forces; not amateurs after all. Vaziil dragged the woman to the kitchen, grabbing the first weapon he could find — a spiral of metal she'd used to open a bottle of alcohol the night before. She squealed, the sharp sting of the tool piercing her throat, ever so slightly.

"Roger — what's happening? What are you doing?"

But Roger was no longer there. Vaziil was operating on one hundred percent Holrathon instinct.

The soldiers moved to within metres, steadying their weapons for a clear shot. The middle soldier's opaque helmet visor shimmered to a translucent sheen. "Chendra Vaziil. My name is Captain Sha'an and I am placing you under arrest for the crimes of genocide, mass murder, and terrorism. Surrender yourself and accept the consequences of your actions."

Vaziil knew of Captain Sha'an by her reputation only; the Thon Pahl were serious, indeed, about his capture. "Terrorism — really, Captain? I suppose that's one way to look at it. I much prefer the term Freedom Fighter. It has a much more noble ring to it, don't you think? It's a matter of perspective."

"Facts don't have a perspective. Be warned: this is the only offer you're going to receive that doesn't result in your immediate termination — and rest assured, no one would shed a tear if your life were to end at this very moment. Now, release your hostage and surrender yourself."

"Or what? You'll shoot through this human to get to me? I think she might shed a tear or two if she were caught in your line of fire. What do you think, Human? Would you mind being a victim for this soldier's cause?"

"Roger — I can't...I don't understand what you're saying. Who are these — what are these things?"

Vaziil clamped his hand over the mewling woman's mouth. "My dear Captain, I appreciate your tenacity, respect it even, but this human's life is inconsequential to me. If, as you say, I've killed these thousands of beings, then what's one more. Especially one of these." He shook his petrified hostage for effect.

"We've chased you across the cosmos, following the trail of blood to every planet you've ravaged, every species you've morphed into — but always one step behind. Do you really think we're likely to give you up now?"

"Well, that's the funny thing," he said calmly, "you don't really have a choice."

Captain Sha'an cocked her head toward her unwavering weapon. "We have all the choices in the world."

"Then you'll want to choose very wisely. You see, my dear Captain, I'm not just here on a sightseeing tour. My work here is at a very delicate stage and if it's interrupted, well, who knows what might happen. You need only remind yourself of the eighty thousand of your brethren who perished the last time."

Captain Sha'an seemed to choke on her words. "You mean the Thon Pahl colonists you butchered?"

The ripple of sorrow that betrayed the soldier sent a wave of exhilaration charging through Vaziil's soul. "Once again, it's all about perspective," he said, poking judiciously at the Thon Pahl's emotional wounds. "Semantics aside, all you need concern yourself with is that at this very moment, I have a device poised within striking distance of this pathetic rock — a weapon of sorts, if you will. Suffice it to say that this…device has a rather potent bite — potent enough to shake this world to rubble and scatter its ashes across the stars."

The two flanking soldiers shifted awkwardly; colour flushed from Captain Sha'an's already pale mauve skin, but she remained undeterred. "That's impossible. There is no weapon that can destroy a whole planet. The energy required would be more than — "

"Please Captain. You're thinking like a Thon Pahl, it's embarrassing. You might want to check your scanners."

Captain Sha'an nodded to one of her soldiers who checked the vibrant string of data pumping from his tactical module. "I'm detecting an object pushing through from hyperspace approximately 100,000 kilometres from the planet's surface," he said. "The object is roughly five hundred metres in diameter and giving off powerful energy readings. The pattern is unrecognisable but growing steadily. I've never seen anything like it, Captain."

Sha'an twitched. "There is no hyperspace window that close to this system, let alone this planet."

"Then imagine the havoc when my weapon punches through into normal space. Any planet caught in the blast wave of such a hyperspatial rupture would be pulverised to atoms and blasted across the light years without even leaving a stain on the universe."

Vaziil pushed the metal spiral deeper into the woman's skin; a dark trickle of blood snaked down her neck. "Maybe you're willing to sacrifice the life of one human but are you prepared to sacrifice the lives of billions? Billions. What kind of butcher would that make you?" He twisted his human mouth into a smile of sorts. "I can see that is a difficult question for you, Captain. So all you need to focus on is that the weapon is keyed to my biological triggers and is set to activate if I'm under threat. And between you and me, I'm feeling a little threatened at the moment. Therefore, I'm going to make you a counter-offer — one that doesn't involve blasting me with holes or blasting this world to…well, to nothing.

"You're going to let me leave this world, unhindered and unharmed." Vaziil raised a hand, holding back Sha'an's unspoken protest. "I know, I know. It seems like a drastic concession on your part. But once I am free, I can disarm the weapon directly at its source and we'll never have to speak of this matter again. Wouldn't that be nice? You and your friends need only put down your weapons and walk away."

Captain Sha'an thought long and hard. Almost too long for Vaziil's comfort. "And if we do, what assurances do I have that you'll keep your end of the bargain?"

"I offer no assurance, but it is a simple enough equation. No tricks. No subterfuge. Quickly, Captain. Time is ticking. By now, the weapon is already waking, warming, getting ready to kiss this world goodbye."

Sha'an checked with her subordinate again who nodded gravely at the readout. She turned back to Vaziil. "Then I should kill you right now," she said. "I'm willing to bet that if I eliminate your biological triggers there will be no detonation."

"An interesting bet, Captain, but the humans have a term for something called a dead-man's switch. Not a new concept but I think you can guess its function. What if killing me accelerates the detonation? Are you really willing to take that risk?" Vaziil chuckled, the sound like grinding glass. He knew this Thon Pahl would be fuelled by vengeance and bloodlust, a dangerous and clumsy mix in a soldier. It was only a matter of time before her mistakes consumed them all. But as the room sizzled with tension, he began to seriously wonder whether he'd misjudged the captain's obsessive commitment to bring him to justice.

Finally, Captain Sha'an deactivated her weapon and slowly secured it about her waist, her subordinates following suit at her signal. The human woman sobbed.

"You see," said Vaziil, "we're cooperating already." He scoffed at the Thon Pahl capacity for compassion, noting that it would ultimately be their undoing. With one arm tight around his hostage's

11

neck, he reached into his carry-bag, tracing the butt of his pistol with hesitant fingers. For the briefest of moments he considered engaging the soldiers, his human heart stuttering at the thought. But this Sha'an was a wily one. Though her weapon was holstered, her hand had not left its heel, ready to draw at a split second's notice. He could probably splash one of them before he fell but the stakes were far too high to take the risk. Instead, he retrieved a small disk and secured it to his belt. He thumbed it to life.

"Don't be so glum," he said. "Did you really think I wouldn't have an exit strategy? Besides, you've done a good thing here, Captain. You've saved billions of lives. You'll be a hero to the people of Earth and, indeed, to your own people. You do still have some people left, don't you?" Vaziil laughed, enjoying the human sensation.

"We tracked you down this time, Vaziil. We will track you down again, no matter how long it takes. It doesn't matter what colour skin you wear, there won't be a planet you can hide on where you'll be safe from us. We have many allies in the galaxy."

"That's where you're so very wrong. There are an infinite number of planets on which to hide. And Captain, I too have allies. But I wish you the best of luck in the hunt, nonetheless."

And then the strangest thing happened, causing Vaziil to question his understanding of the human will. The woman went silent and stiffened in Vaziil's arms. Her focus burned into Captain Sha'an's eyes and she spoke — calmly, coolly, one single word. "Shoot," she said.

The Thon Pahl captain's eyes twitched briefly and then, in one smooth motion, she drew her rifle into a firing position and let off a blast. The bolt seared through the right side of the woman's neck before exploding into Vaziil's shoulder. Captain Sha'an fired again into his chest as he stumbled backward, forcing his hostage loose. The woman collapsed to the ground, grasping at the world around her as her neck wound sizzled like bacon. She looked hopefully up toward Sha'an, mumbling incoherently. Vaziil tried desperately to vault for cover, but another blast took him in the stomach.

"That's enough Vaziil," said Sha'an. "You will yield, or you will die, here and now."

Vaziil gulped at precious air, dark purplish blood bubbling at his human lips. "No, Captain…I shall do neither." He clamped down on the disk at his belt; an angry energy cracked the room, engulfing him in a sphere of vibrant light. Sha'an and her soldiers unleashed a final barrage of weapons fire which splashed harmlessly against the shimmering shell; Vaziil's image flickered within. Then in one final burst of blinding energy, he evaporated into nothingness.

PART ONE

CHAPTER 1

Morrissey was seven when he first suspected that the world didn't fit him quite right. Two sizes too big or two sizes too small, he couldn't be sure. All he knew was that planet Earth pinched him in all the wrong places. Discovering this uncomfortable truth wasn't like when you learn there is no Santa Claus, or that In The Beginning, Man created God and not the other way around. No. The truth had hit him very much like the tight, smelly fist of a schoolyard bully called Norman Riley.

The fight, if you could call it that, didn't last long; a three against one attack rarely does. Why do thugs always travel in threes? But Morrissey managed to get off one good shot that seemed to make his point. After that, he spent most of the time blocking Norman's punches with his nose while his henchmen pinned Morrisey's arms.

Later that night, he sat at the dining room table, silently pushing peas around his plate while his mum sat patiently opposite. She was too good at mothering to force him to talk before he was ready, but he knew she couldn't go on pretending he didn't have an entire tissue box bunged up his nose to stop the bleeding.

"Do you want to talk about it?" she said softly.

Morrissey shrugged the question away without meeting her gaze. Finally, he answered. "Norman Riley is a wanker."

His mum suppressed a grin. "Davey! You can't call him that."

"Well he is. He's a bully and a wanker."

"But he's never picked on you before." A twitch of worry flickered across her face. "He hasn't, has he?"

Being the new kid in town made Morrissey easy prey in Norman's book, having only recently moved to London from a small town south of Sheffield. Up until now, he'd been able to avoid the brunt of Norman's torments; there were plenty of other victims further down the food chain. "No. I can usually stay out of his way."

"But not today?"

"Not today." Today, Norman had come at him with a full-on purpose. Kids can be horrible to one another, and Norman excelled at horrible. "He said…he said things."

His mum tried to defuse the situation with one of her tender smiles. "People say things all the time, Davey. Doesn't mean we have to start fights over them."

Morrissey glared. "Does it look like I started the fight?"

"No, but — "

"It was about you." The words came rushing out, unbidden. "He said things about you."

She stiffened. "What…sort of things?"

Morrissey replayed the scene over in his head, complete with Norman's malicious glee at having spread the poison. "He said you and his mum got into an argument at the Co-Op. Didn't you just say that we can't go around starting fights?" His mum looked away, sheepishly. "He said the fight was about whether or not UFOs are real. How is that even worth fighting about? He said you told her you'd seen one, that you'd even seen an alien." His mum's fascination with extraterrestrial phenomena was no secret to him; they'd often make a game of it as they looked up at the stars. Sometimes, when they were out in public, they would play a game of spot the alien, playfully pointing out likely candidates who could be extraterrestrials amongst the passersby, making up fantastic planets complete with complex races and civilisations. But that was a game. Their game. Norman had turned it into something vile and twisted. "He said you were a crackpot. A freak. A mental case." Morrissey turned his eyes up from his plate, fighting the well of tears. "Is it true? Did you see one — an alien?" His words felt sour and accusatory on the way out.

His mum blanched. Morrissey could tell she was struggling for just the right answer. "That's silly, Luv. Why would I say that?"

"Why would Norman say that? He's not smart enough to make something like that up. Is it true?"

She took too long to answer. "I'm so sorry, Luv, I really am. It's something I don't like to talk about."

"But you could talk to Norman's mother."

"Well, we weren't exactly talking." She clenched her napkin in her hand. "We were standing in the checkout line, flicking through the tabloids as you do. They had a story about a UFO sighting and she — well, she's just so stubborn!"

"That's not really the point, is it? So, it is true then, what Norman said?"

His mum plucked absently at the thumb-sized knot of scar tissue that rippled her neck, something she often did in moments of anxiety. "Would it be so bad if it was? I mean…a lot of people see unidentified objects in the sky. It doesn't mean they're mental cases, as Norman put it. It's not a big deal. Is it?"

Normally it wouldn't be. But there had been something in Norman's tone, in his outpouring of vitriol, which had burned through Morrissey's gut. "He made it sound like it was a big deal. He said that you and his mum got into a right slanging match — that you shoved her into a magazine rack."

"Erm…yes…I might've overreacted. A little. Okay, a lot. But she was being completely ridiculous. She had no idea what she was talking about, babbling on about things she couldn't possibly understand — "

"Mum! Stop it."

She took a deep breath. "You're right, Davey. It was a long time ago, another life ago. What's important is us, that we're okay. Are we okay?"

Morrissey didn't have an answer. Nothing seemed okay at the moment. "Norman said that it's why I have no dad — that my father couldn't stand being with a UFO crackpot." He pushed his dinner plate away and looked deeply into his mother's faltering eyes. "Is that why dad left us?"

She reached for Morrissey's hand, but he pulled it away, unsure if she was worthy of his affection. She was older than most mums in

Morrissey's circle of friends but never before had she looked so worn down. "Your dad — your father — he and I didn't see eye to eye on many things. And yes, that was one of them, to say the least. I really am sorry, Luv. I thought this would stay in the past where it couldn't hurt us, where it couldn't hurt *you*. I certainly never thought it would come out like this. Does that make sense?"

"Mum, I'm seven. How can any of this make sense to a seven-year-old?"

Morrissey felt her reach for him again, pulling him close, holding him tightly. This time, he didn't put up a fight; he had none left in him. "This isn't something a little boy needs to deal with," she said. "Not a little boy."

She rocked him gently and spoke in tones only a mother can. Morrissey didn't let go until sleep took him.

The next day she was gone. The only thing she left behind was her silver pinky ring wrapped in a note declaring her love for him with the hope that he would one day understand why she had to leave.

He never did.

Morrissey shivered. For years, he'd felt to blame for his mum's abandonment, that if he'd just kept quiet about Norman's taunts, they would have lived a full life together, facing whatever challenges came their way *together*. But a child's magical thinking can concoct all manner of justifications for trauma; in Morrissey's case, none of them were all that appealing. He'd even imagined that she had been abducted by the same UFO that had haunted her past. It was easier than accepting that she just couldn't be his mum anymore. The resulting chasm of doubt and yearning had chased him into adolescence and beyond, charting his life toward the inevitable path of UFO investigation. He'd never been quite sure whether he'd joined the Ministry of Defence's UFO Hotline to give credence to his mother's claims or debunk them, but in all his years with the department, he'd never found one shred of extraterrestrial proof that would salve his tortured conscience.

Long after his departure from the M.O.D., he'd carried his search into his private life, holding weekly informal support meetings for victims of UFO phenomena in his pub, The Crooked Crow, in an attempt to ease their troubled psyches. It was a haven — for them, and for him. He'd told the story about his Mum's disappearance many times in the group. Sometimes he told it to break the ice, to coax some of the newcomers out of their reticence. But sometimes, he just needed the catharsis, each time hoping he would find new meaning in the cold memory. There had been no such relief.

This week's session had been nothing out of the ordinary, a few new attendees along with the handful of regulars. But it had come to an abrupt end at old Mrs. Beasley's insistence on showing the group where the aliens had inserted her tracker. Morrissey tried to assure her that such a viewing was best held privately and anyone who wished to see it would contact her directly. So far there were no takers, and the group disbanded, each quietly going their own way.

As he stood at the bar, mired in his thoughts, he was suddenly struck by a woman sitting alone in a two-seater booth. She had ordered a Bacardi and Coke with the Coke on the side and sipped absently at the liquor while leaving the mix untouched. She watched the local patrons as they drank and talked, taking an almost sociological interest in their behaviour. Morrissey had never had occasion to use the word smitten in a sentence before but felt sure that this was, indeed, the right context.

The woman was out-of-the-box, no-assembly-required gorgeous. Though technically, her face shouldn't have worked. In a serendipitous mix of Asian and Slavic features, her chocolate-almond eyes were just a little too widely spaced and set above impossibly high cheekbones. Her aquiline nose charged boldly down the sharp angles of her face toward a set of lips that stretched rather cheekily across a delicate jawline. But somehow, she managed to fudge the numbers to achieve the sublime.

His bar manager, Suki, sidled up to him, catching him off guard. "You could always go and talk to her, you know. You do own the place."

"Very funny, Suki. Didn't you know that the expression 'to be out of one's league' was minted specifically for occasions like this. And she is well and truly out of my —"

And then it happened. The mystery woman sealed his fate with a simple smile; it was all the encouragement he needed. He knew that any romantic overture could spiral off in any one of a million horrible directions; even with her wonky math, she was truly greater than the sum of his parts. Not that his parts were without their own appeal. With a playfully sly grin and cheeky gleam in his eye, he was by no means a stomach-turner. But he wasn't necessarily a head-turner, either. Yet there's an incredible sense of freedom you got from not being God's gift to women.

Morrissey shifted his charisma into first gear and casually made his way to her table. He decided to start with something from The Classics. "Hello," was always a good icebreaker, followed up with a splash of honesty. "You know, I've been rehearsing what I'd say to you if I ever managed to work up the courage."

An eternity passed before she spoke. "Really? And what have you come up with?" Her voice was honey.

Morrissey shook his head nonchalantly. "A few platitudes, some faint praise, but most of it is absolute gibberish. I'm usually completely intimidated by beautiful women."

Self-deprecation was a tricky manoeuvre, one if not performed artfully could result in complete emasculation. Luckily enough, she seemed to be playing along. "Then I must not be trying hard enough since you are, in fact, talking to me."

"Don't get me wrong — you're a passably handsome woman, to be sure," he said, taking refuge in the cocoon of sarcasm.

"Is this what you call flirting?"

"It's what *I* call flirting. Others may beg to differ. In all honesty, I'm secretly hoping that you're already attached."

She eyed him quizzically. "Why would you go to all the trouble of approaching a strange woman only to hope she's unavailable?"

"It all comes down to pressure — and the art of avoiding it. That's one of the things you're either going to love about me or absolutely detest. Rejection I can handle — rebuilding my self-esteem is sort of a hobby of mine — but if a beautiful woman accepts your overture, well, that's when the performance anxiety really kicks in."

"You are a peculiar fellow, aren't you."

"It's best you know upfront."

"And this technique, it works with women?"

Morrissey leaned in closer. "You tell me."

The woman smiled. As if it couldn't get any better. "You do have a certain…charm about you." She extended her hand, her touch warm and electric. "My name is Kiki. Kiki Pashmina."

"I'm Dave. Dave Morrissey."

"Alright then, Dave," she said as she tossed back the carafe of Coke in one gulp. "Do you think you can handle the pressure of buying me another drink?"

He gave her a sly wink. "If you play your cards right, I could probably get us a staff discount."

"You are a smooth talker."

Morrissey nodded, somewhat proudly. Sometimes he surprised even himself.

Morrissey almost never passed out during sex. It was a trait he prided himself on, along with good hygiene and impeccable punctuality — both of which had come in very handy over the past several hours. The sexual heights they'd achieved were worthy of study in most branches of science, including zoology — and possibly even criminology. Indeed, of the top twenty sexual manoeuvres known to humankind, they must have checked off at least the top ten and added several exclamation marks to the top three. And yet he couldn't believe his luck. According to all the laws of physical attraction currently on the books, this shouldn't be happening.

He wasn't a prude; he wasn't averse to the occasional one-night stand. It was just that the occasion never seemed to pop up. And when it did, emotion often clouded the mix, competing with his male programming. As a rule he wore his heart on his sleeve which, true to the metaphor, tended to get a little messy. The romantic in him always hoped that if a woman chose to share such intimacy with him then she might possibly want more. But this exquisitely crafted beauty lying beside him was a tough one to read. He found himself both startled and aroused by her boldness. During their bouts of sexual acrobatics, she'd exhibited a curious mix of animalistic abandon tempered by a naive sense of wonder. There was even the oddest of moments when she'd gently cupped his genitals, gazing at them as one might look upon a new species of flower. Had Morrissey not been so impressed by her displays of carnal prowess, he might have thought it was her first time. And things had gone far too smoothly for that to be the case. Smooth as the skin on her —

"Are you looking at my bum?" Kiki stirred from her sultry slumber.

As it happened, he was. "Amongst other things." He traced a finger along the delicious curve of her back and took one more playful bite of her buttock, eliciting a soft, liquid moan of pleasure.

She rolled onto her side to face him, her expression both intense and curious. "What's the look for?"

Morrissey wasn't aware that he had one. "Nothing. Really. It's just that…"

"Go on, Dave. Spit it out."

"Well, I don't normally like to look a gift horse in the mouth — not that I'm calling you a horse, or anything." Kiki's curiosity was twisting into concern. "It's just…well…what the hell are you doing here?"

Her face flushed, as if she'd been caught with her hand in the biscuit tin. "What do you mean, here in your bed?"

"Sort of. Yes. Don't get me wrong. I'm really glad you are here. But I mean…look at you, look at me. The numbers just don't add up."

"Don't sell yourself short, Dave. You're a passably handsome man." Kiki winked.

Morrissey smiled at the call-back to his earlier tongue-in-cheek comment. "I guess I just can't believe my good fortune."

She leaned in close, triggering a buzz through his nether regions. "But you're right, it's more than that. I do have a confession to make."

"Don't tell me, sleeping with me was part of some sort of sex addict's twelve step program."

"What? No. Actually…I caught part of your meeting last night, the support group that you hold, for victims of alien phenomena, is it?"

"You were eavesdropping? I knew it! You're a UFO groupie! That explains everything. Thanks for shattering an otherwise perfectly serviceable fantasy."

Kiki poked him playfully in the stomach. "Seriously, I'm not a groupie. Let's just say that I've always had a…fascination for the subject matter."

"You should have joined us, the more the merrier. I could have gotten to know you a bit sooner."

"I wanted to see what you were all about first — there are a lot of charlatans out there. But you seem to be pretty genuine. You really know how to handle people in that situation, a natural, you might say. How did you get into it?"

"Now that's a long story." Morrissey didn't know how much he should — or could — tell this relative stranger, but he began to explain as best he could. It seemed another life ago that Morrissey had worked for the Ministry of Defence, where he'd single-handedly fronted the UK government's UFO Hotline. On paper, he was supposed to have acted as a buffer between the government and the British public, investigating everything from peculiar lights in the sky, to mysteriously butchered cattle, to oddly behaving spouses. In practice, the position had been a lot less glamorous, basically that of a glorified customer service rep, vetting panicked calls from the sad, the lonely, and often, the desperate. Certainly, there were a fair number of attention-seeking crackpots and charlatans out there, but for the most part they were largely rational, insightful, sensitive people, just seeking to be understood. They just needed someone to listen. "Mostly I just let them vent. These people need to know they're not alone and that they're going to be okay. If the best I can offer is a friendly ear, then so be it."

"That's very…noble of you."

Morrissey kissed her softly, firmly, drinking in her warmth. "I'll take noble," he said, "but it's more than that. Sometimes I think I need them more than they need me."

"So…the story about your mother — that's true?"

"Ah. You heard that bit. Yes. I'm afraid it is."

She reached out to the chain dangling from his neck, a small ring hanging from it; his mother's ring, the last gift he would ever receive from her. Morrissey flinched, physically and emotionally. He wasn't sure if he was ready to let Kiki in that deep. Finally, he yielded to her gentle touch as she carefully draped the chain along her hand. Maybe he was feeling just the right amount of vulnerable.

"This is hers? The one she left you?"

"That's it. That's my Mum." Morrissey found the lump in his throat made speaking awkward. Even now, after all this time, the small symbol of his past life was tied straight to his heart.

"It must have been very…difficult for you."

"You have no idea."

Kiki stroked his cheek, more tenderly than he expected. "No, but I'm learning. Now why don't you make yourself useful and put some coffee on," she said. "Then we'll see about something to eat."

"To be honest, I'm not all that hungry."

She gave him a sly smile. "I wasn't talking about food."

Morrissey gave her nipple a gentle tweak before padding into the kitchen, grateful for the distraction. As he assembled the coffee, the gentle buzz of his mobile phone tap-dancing across the counter stole his attention. It was the main line of The Crooked Crow. Suki would be the only one in at this hour, doing the bottling up. "Hey, Suki."

"Hey, Boss."

"Look, can this wait? I'm a little...tied up at the moment."

"I've been told that it can't wait."

"Told by who?"

"A gentleman. Or, at least, that's what he'd like me to believe. Between you and me, I have my doubts."

"What gentleman? What does he want?"

"He won't tell me. He flashed some Ministry of Defence ID. Said he's an old colleague of yours — says he has some old business to discuss."

M.O.D.? Speak of the devil. "Did he give a name?"

"Whitchurch...or something. I didn't get a good look. Wiry fellow. Thinning sandy hair. Bit of a rat face, if you ask me."

"Whitchurch? Yeah...I know him. Ask him — "

"Look, Boss, I'd love to play translator for you all day but you pay me to do a lot of work and I'd just as soon get to it. So if you could pry your new friend off your knob for five minutes..."

"Okay," said Morrissey, suitably chagrined. "Tell him I'll be right down." One of the bonuses of living above your workplace was that it didn't take long to get there. It was also one of the drawbacks.

Morrissey found his jeans piled behind the couch where Kiki had tossed them the night before. He pulled them on and then tracked down his t-shirt hanging from the lamp. He poked his head into the bedroom; Kiki was purring softly under the covers. With any luck, he'd be back before she knew he was gone.

CHAPTER 2

Morrissey entered the pub through the kitchen to find Suki fake-polishing glasses behind the bar.

"Thanks for keeping an eye on him," he said.

"And me, such a delicate flower." She plopped the towel down on the bar top. "That's enough excitement for one day. I'll be in the cellar if you need me."

The man sat in the snug at the back of the bar, his reedy hands folded crisply across a leather briefcase. The full overhead lighting bounced a solar flare off his forehead — he'd certainly lost a lot of hair since Morrissey last saw him. They knew one another from the M.O.D. where Whitchurch had functioned in a supervisory capacity at the UFO Hotline but seemed mostly interested in throwing a wet blanket over the truth rather than uncovering it.

Whitchurch rose to greet him, his handshake as cold and limp as a dead fish. "My dear David, how very good to see you."

They both knew it was a lie. Some of Morrissey's friends called him Dave. Most of them called him Morrissey. But of the ones who called him David, none of them did it with such punch-me-in-the-face aplomb. With pretensions far beyond his station, Whitchurch imagined himself next in line only to James Bond because he'd signed The Official Secrets Act. If he appeared friendly, it was only to further his own agenda, of this much Morrissey was certain.

"This is a surprise, Graham."

"Isn't it just. Thank you for seeing me."

"I gathered I had little choice."

Whitchurch tittered. "Do forgive my impertinence. By the way, I love what you've done with the place. Very...shabby chic. I bet the locals love a bit of rough."

Whitchurch forced a smile through his crooked overbite. Morrissey fought the impulse to force it right back down again. Despite his mum's sudden disappearance, she'd still had the foresight to secure his financial future by leaving him the pub in trust. It had her stamp. It had her touch. It had...her. The locals loved it just fine. "Can I get you a drink? Tea? Coffee? It's a little early for anything stronger."

"Thank you, no. I'm here on official business."

"So I've been told," said Morrissey with a shrug.

Whitchurch's pinprick eyes flicked furtively around the empty pub, building drama where there was none. "Actually, I'm here on a matter of unfinished business, an open case from your old department."

Now that did come as some surprise. There was no justification for the existence of a UFO Hotline in the modern world. Prevailing sensibilities saw little value in the pursuit of such frivolous endeavours as the investigation of extraterrestrial threats, choosing instead to focus their resources on the more tangible and realistic terrors looming locally. Eventually, important people who knew important things saw fit to strip Morrissey's department of one down to a department of zero.

"There are no open cases, Graham. I made sure they were all wrapped up before I left."

"Well, not all of them, it seems." Whitchurch snapped open his briefcase and withdrew a red file folder. He slid it slowly across the distance toward Morrissey. "Not this one."

Morrissey eyed the folder warily without touching it, as if doing so would taint him with Whitchurch's stench. "That's not one of mine. Can't be."

"Actually, it can. And it is, technically at least. It's been lying dormant for over twenty-five years. The subject of the file — a

25

woman called Ruth Small — passed away three days ago in a nursing home."

"Is that so unusual? People die in nursing homes every day."

"She was classified as Red Flag 5."

Morrissey's shrugs were becoming a habit. "Should that mean something to me?"

"It's an old classification system used to denote the subject as someone with suspicious connections to activities of an extraterrestrial nature. Never put much stock in it myself. Nevertheless, Ruth Small was a person of interest. Someone to be monitored. Unfortunately, with all the cutbacks over the years, there weren't exactly a lot of people to do the monitoring. None, as it happened."

"Still don't see what it has to do with me."

Whitchurch tried his best to crack a smile but instead looked as if he'd just smelt his own breath. "Come now, David. This sort of thing clearly plays to your strengths and I'd be a fool to let your talents go to waste. Besides, I know you've kept your finger on the pulse of this business, such as it is."

Morrissey was surprised Whitchurch was so well-informed. "This business is in the public domain, now. All I do is monitor any strange events. I haven't violated any confidentiality agreements."

"And I wouldn't suggest otherwise. But let's be honest, you've done more than monitor strange events. Am I wrong? You're weekly crying sessions with the victims of UFO phenomena, for instance?"

"They're support meetings, Whitchurch. These people need a place to feel like they belong, that they're not crazy." Just like me.

Whitchurch slapped the table. "You see! That's exactly the spirit with which I'd like you to approach this task."

Morrissey slowly shook his head in a way that suggested Whitchurch go fuck himself. "You're off your nut if you think I'm going to help you."

"David, I know we were never the best of friends, so don't do it for me, do it for The Old Man. You know you were always his favourite."

The Old Man in question was Archibald Smythe — Sir Archibald Smythe, Morrissey's former mentor at the Ministry. Old Archie had recruited him right out of university and had taken a distinct, albeit arms-length, interest in his professional development, forging an almost grandfatherly relationship with him. But they hadn't spoken since the dissolution of the hotline. "Smythe was the one who nailed the coffin shut on the department in the first place. Why the hell would he want my help now?"

"Ah…Actually, he doesn't. Look, I really shouldn't be telling you this — all a bit hush-hush until we've completed our investigation."

"Spit it out, Whitchurch."

"I'm afraid your old friend Archie is a bit…well…deceased, actually. Four days ago. In his home. Aneurysm, apparently, but as I say, we're still looking into it." Whitchurch gestured to the red folder. "In point of fact, this file was found in his personal home safe. Highly irregular, hence the investigation."

Morrissey's stomach shrivelled. They may not have parted ways on the best of terms, but Old Archie had been good to him over the years. "You might have led with the fact that The Old Man was dead."

"Well, as I said, it's all a bit hush-hush. I shouldn't even be telling you."

"Then why are you telling me — any of this? You never did have much regard for our work." And then the penny dropped. "Oh, I get it. The body's not even cold and you're hoping to grease your way into Smythe's office chair. You want this investigated by an outside player so there's no stink attached to you. You're a real piece of work, Whitchurch."

"Government, my dear David, is like nature — it abhors a vacuum. And we can all imagine how perilous it would be to step out into a vacuum without the proper protection." Whitchurch tapped the Red File. "I just want to protect myself from this. Besides, have you forgotten that shit rolls down?"

"What's that supposed to mean?"

Whitchurch reached into his briefcase again and placed a small sheaf of papers in front of Morrissey. "Do you recognise this?" He gave him a moment for it to sink in. "It's your application for planning permission to restructure the loading zone of this…establishment. I understand you've been having some logistical problems with your deliveries."

Morrissey felt a tightening pressure at his temple as he realised the full scope of Whitchurch's sour scheme. "Are you threatening to bugger up my rezoning plans if I don't help you with this case?"

"David, David, David, why must the glass always be half empty with you? What I'm saying is that if you do agree to help me with my problem, then I can facilitate your rezoning application. You see, glass half full."

"I just don't appreciate you drinking from my glass in the first place. You know, I don't think I ever told you what a shit-stain you really are."

"Be that as it may, what I'm asking is relatively painless in the grand scheme of things. The file is light on substance and heavy on redaction. I need you to fill in the gaps, as it were. Probably just a matter of dotting a few 'i's and crossing a few 't's." He flashed his best version of a friendly smile, too little, too late. "You scratch my back, et cetera, et cetera."

Morrissey eyed his rezoning application, sickened by the deal on the table. "Whitchurch, you may think you've got me by the short hairs, but if you think I'm buying into whatever twisted scheme you've got cooking, you are more deluded than I gave you credit for."

"My dear David, I think we've gotten off on entirely the wrong foot. I thought you might respond to a more...practical incentive, but it seems I was mistaken. So I will appeal to your more personal sensibilities. If you're not willing to undertake this endeavour for old Archie's memory, perhaps you'd do it...for your long lost mother."

Whitchurch's words sunk in slowly, like an icepick to the chest; the damage done before you even know it has pierced your heart. "What are you talking about? What's this got to do with my mother?"

Whitchurch feigned mild shock. "Oh, didn't I mention it? The funniest thing: your mother's name appears in this very file." He tapped the red folder with his grubby finger. "Unless it's referring to another woman who just happens to be called Marion Morrissey."

"Whitchurch, I've just about had it with your games — "

"Oh, this is no game, David. Her name only appears once but it is most certainly there in stark black and white."

Son of a bitch. "Why couldn't you have told me this from the start?"

"And spoil the surprise? Come now, David. Where's the sport in that."

Morrissey could tell Whitchurch was enjoying twisting the knife and found himself sickened, partly by the fact that Whitchurch had invaded such a personal and intimate part of who he was, and partly because he was right. He'd spent a lifetime searching for clues as to her disappearance, yet he daren't let hope wheedle its way into his heart again; he wasn't sure if he could withstand the inevitable disappointment. But if what this little weasel was telling him was true, he couldn't pass up the opportunity to at least try to learn more about why his mother left him, oh so long ago. In the end, he had little choice.

"Okay. I'll do it." The words tore at his throat like sandpaper.

"That's my boy! Just close your eyes and think of dear old mum!"

Morrissey was actually closing his eyes and thinking of throttling Whitchurch until his head popped. "But I swear, if you're holding anything else back from me, you'd better get it out now." It was his turn to look furtively around the bar. "As you can see, there are no witnesses. Who knows what might happen to you in this shabby chic pub."

Whitchurch paled, if that was even possible for such a pasty git. "Now, now, there's no need for threats. I'd have thought you'd show some gratitude. In any case, you can start with the nursing home where this Ruth Small lived. Talk to the staff, ask the requisite questions — you know the drill. Put a button on this as quickly as possible so we can all move onward and upward with our lives. Report only to me when you're done." Whitchurch placed his business card on the table and then skulked out the door.

Morrissey's heart pounded as he eyed the folder on the table, both thrilled and terrified at what he might find inside. His first pass through the document was a marathon race to find if Whitchurch had been telling the truth about his mother's involvement in this mystery. One thing was certain, the vile little rodent certainly wasn't lying about the redaction. It was a desert of black, dotted with oases of cryptic phrases and vague innuendos. Finally, he found the hidden treasure in the wasteland, his mother's name, Marion Morrissey. Unfortunately, he found himself shattered by the lack of context.

His second pass through the file was more methodical, hoping to attach meaning to his mother's inclusion somewhere amidst Ruth Small's history. The document hopscotched through the dead woman's life from an alleged childhood alien abduction to the bombing of a fertility clinic that resulted in the tragic deaths of two employees. A terrible crime, to be sure, but not one that would warrant a posting to the M.O.D.'s Red Flag 5 watchlist.

The resultant criminal charges were too much for her to bear and caused a significant mental shutdown. Deemed unfit to stand trial, Ruth Small spent her subsequent years being shunted from one institution to another, a place called Meadowbrook Estates being the one where she finally met her end.

Morrissey shook his head grimly. In his experience with the alleged victims of alien encounters, he found they mostly coped in one of two ways. The subject could either blank it out and try to get on with their lives the best they can, or they could become obsessed with not only finding proof of their encounter, but making others see the truth through their eyes. What Ruth Small's truth had to do with a fertility clinic was absent from the file, but it seemed the poor woman had taken the latter course to its most extreme — and deadly — limits.

He scoured the remainder of the document for any further clues amongst the scant facts. A couple of things jumped out immediately. First, there was something odd about the dates, more specifically, the date the case file was originally opened — ten years before the fertility clinic bombing. That meant that whatever had placed Ruth Small on the M.O.D.'s radar likely comprised the bulk of the redacted material. How his mum might be involved in that, he dreaded to think.

More curious was the name of the case officer who'd originated the file: A. Smythe. As in Archibald Smythe. AKA The Old Man. Since he oversaw the UFO Hotline, Morrissey shouldn't have been surprised that his name would pop up somewhere in this case. But that it would be front and centre on a file that had been kept hidden in his personal safe was something that felt just a little bit off-side and created enough of a mystery to push Morrissey beyond Whitchurch's remit. And none of the loosely strung together facts in the file gave him any sense of his mother's connection to the case in general or to the dead woman. Were they friends? Enemies? Lovers? All of the above? The possibilities were endless and the rampant speculation brought him absolutely no measure of comfort. Part of him wished he could talk to old Archie, to ask him what the hell it all meant. And part of him wished that he'd just stayed in bed. Bed...

Kiki!

He took the stairs two at a time back up to his flat, clutching the Red File tightly under his arm. Whitchurch's visit may have soured his mood and sapped his libido, but his pulse still thrummed at the thought of returning to his new bedmate. Unfortunately, she was no longer in his bed. She was standing stark naked in the centre of his living room.

"You are possibly the worst manservant ever," said Kiki. "I'm still waiting for my coffee."

"Sorry," said Morrissey sheepishly. "I got a little...sidetracked."

"I'll say. Where've you been?"

"Visit from an old work colleague. He needed my help with a...special project of his."

Kiki eyed The Red File warily. "And they say romance is dead. He must have been a very sexy old work colleague to drag you away from *this*." She forced Morrissey to the couch, spreading her nakedness across his most sensitive parts.

Morrissey felt the tightening of arousal shift his focus but the thought of the enigmatic investigation that lay ahead was just too powerful. "Look, Kiki," he said, halting her pelvic grinding, "I really like you. I mean *really*. And under normal circumstances it would take a very large restraining order to keep me away from you right now. But I need to get to work on this...special project."

"Is it more special than this?" She reached between his legs and cupped his genitals with just the right amount of tease.

"No-ho-hold on, there. I'd love to let your hands do the talking but I've got to jump in the shower and get going."

"I rather thought we might take a shower together," she said, resuming gyrational control.

"Erm...there is nothing I'd love more, but if we get into that shower together I may never come out."

Kiki leaned back, eyeing him curiously. "You do seem a bit...preoccupied. Is everything okay? Is there anything I can do to help?"

Morrissey clutched the file just a little bit tighter, as if it held the secret to all his dreams. "No, really. Thank you. This is something I need to do on my own."

"Will I see you again?"

"Trust me. What happened last night doesn't happen to me all the time. I don't intend on wasting the momentum. I will call you. Just let me take care of this first."

She pouted playfully, then walked slowly to the bedroom in the exquisite way that naked women tend to walk. "Don't leave it too long."

Morrissey eyed her longingly, grim reality taking a firmer hold on him with each article of clothing she put back on. They kissed deeply as they said their goodbyes. As intoxicating as Kiki Pashmina was, he was addicted to a far more powerful drug: Hope.

CHAPTER 3

Gaining access to Meadowbrook Estates had taken some deft subterfuge on Morrissey's part. Whitchurch had neglected to provide him with the necessary government identification, so he'd been forced to rely on the sympathy of strangers. He'd spun the charge nurse, a kindly Jamaican woman called Lorna, some flannel about how his family used to know Ruth Small but had lost contact. Upon hearing of her death, he'd now come to pay his respects. It was a clumsy ruse but seemed to tug the required heartstrings.

Nurse Lorna led him to one of the spare rooms where Ruth's meagre possessions were being stored. All that she was, all that she'd accomplished, all that she'd ever dreamt of being, had been crammed into two unmarked plastic bags and left at the mercy of the charity bazaar. Morrissey gently spread the items across the cold vinyl surface of the surplus mattress, trying to attach some meaning to each of the scant objects. He stared until his eyes watered, finding nothing unique, nothing odd, nothing overtly out of place — and certainly nothing flashing an extraterrestrial beacon.

Aside from the few articles of clothing, there was only a hairbrush — a tangle of yellow-white hairs matted in its bristles — a few toiletries, and a small wooden jewellery box containing a variety of hair clips. Whoever Ruth Small was, she'd apparently managed to skate through her life without dragging any record of it behind her.

"I don't suppose she had any photos?" The Red File certainly didn't contain any.

"Why yes, there was one. Isn't it in the bag?"

Morrissey fished through the items again but found nothing.

"Isn't that strange," said Nurse Lorna. "I know she used to have a photo of when she was young sitting on her dressing table. In a beautiful silver frame, it was. I always tell her how pretty she look." She tut-tutted. "Some of these cleaning staff got long fingers, you know. I bet one of them took it."

"That's a shame," said Morrissey. He always liked to put a real face to his investigations. He went back to filtering through Ruth Small's life. The most curious item of the collection was wrapped tightly in a faded woollen blanket; he only noticed it because one of its limbs was poking awkwardly through a fold. He unfurled the blanket and out rolled the saddest, rattiest, dirtiest little baby doll he'd ever seen; it was literally hanging on by a thread. Morrissey picked it up delicately, careful not to sever its head. The poor thing smelt vaguely of mildewed fabric and stale vomit.

"That was Miss Ruthie's baby," said Nurse Lorna. "She love that baby, so. Took fine care of him, too, though you wouldn't know it to look at him."

"No," said Morrissey, "but you can tell it — he — certainly got a lot of...attention." He placed the doll carefully back on the bed and poked absently at the rest of the items, searching for some hidden treasure that didn't smell of sick. "Did Ruth talk much about her past? Ever mention anything out of the ordinary?"

"Mister, these folk aren't always strong in the mind. Most of what they say be out of the ordinary." Nurse Lorna hesitated. "Of course, there's always plenty of rumours in a place like this and Miss Ruthie certainly come with her fair share."

"Such as?"

"I no like to gossip, Mister," nonetheless, "but some say that Miss Ruthie done something real bad when she be young, like criminal."

Morrissey feigned shock. "You don't say." He figured she meant the bombing of the fertility clinic. "That's terrible. Any idea how…or why?"

"No, Mister, but some say her mind too fragile to deal with it, you know, that she crack up. That why she come here. All I know is that whatever she do, she suffer long and hard for it until the day she die."

"So you're saying she wasn't happy here?" He may have been lying about his connection to the old woman, but he wasn't lying about his interest in her life.

"Miss Ruthie was a fine lady. But was she happy? No. She had a big heart, you know? But I think it was broken. No. Not broken — empty, maybe. Like, incomplete, you know? Like something deep in her heart be missing."

Morrissey felt a twinge of melancholy, sorrow for a woman he never knew. "Any idea what caused the sadness?"

"I don't know for sure, Mister, but I think it have to do with that baby," she said, nodding toward the limp doll splayed across the bed. "Sometime she cling to him like her life depend on it, even pulling him to her bosoms to feed. And then sometime, in the middle of the night, I hear her sobbing so much it break my heart. 'Where my baby at? They take my baby!' So sad. I come into her room only to find that poor dolly tossed into the dustbin. I take him out and clean him up. By morning, she forget all about the troubles in the night and she clutch that little mite all over again."

"Did she have any children — any real children?"

"She never mention and none ever come and visit. There's no next of kin listed in her file, neither."

"So maybe this doll is some sort of surrogate for something she wished she'd had — or a link to a painful memory of something she did have." Morrissey picked up the doll again, absentmindedly forcing the stuffing back into its body. Some of it was fabric, some of it foam pellets. But some of it was…paper? He fished out a small rectangular card from the doll's neck-hole. It was a business card, creased and worn from so much cuddling. On its front, a simple and unassuming font was etched in bold type:

> Help wanted battling aliens.
> Experience preferred.
> Bring own weapons.
> Sandwiches and tea provided.

As if things couldn't get any weirder.

The bottom of the card had held a telephone number, but it had been worn away to a ragged fringe, almost determinedly so. Morrissey handed the card to the nurse. "Know anything about this?"

Nurse Lorna eyed the card suspiciously, as if it were going to bite. "I never seen this before," she said, handing it back. "Maybe somebody try to help her deal with her devils. Lord know she need it."

Alarm bells jump-started his brain and a working theory began to develop. If his mother was somehow involved with the Ruth Small case and if she really had had an alien encounter as she'd claimed, she might very well be this mysterious Alien Hunter, which seemed like the right line of work for a UFO survivor.

"Did she have many visitors?"

"No, Mister. So sad. Like nobody even care. In all the years she was here, nobody ever come to see her — at least, not until a week before she pass. First, come a man. I don't know his name. They supposed to sign in but nobody does. He was tall fellow. And old — older than Miss Ruthie. A thick shock of grey hair. And he hunch over when he walk. I thought he was a friend, he seem nice enough. But when he leave, Miss Ruthie be so sad. I don't think he such a nice man, after all."

"Could he have left this business card?"

"I suppose. But I don't know how long that card been stuck in that doll."

She had a point. "You said the man came first. There were others?"

"One other. The day she die. A lady."

Morrissey's stomach knotted. He'd been putting off asking the question that ruled his thoughts, probably for fear of being disappointed, but this seemed like the perfect opening. "I don't suppose the woman's name was…Marion? Marion Morrissey?"

"Like I say, Mister, they never sign in."

"Was she an older woman?"

"I hear the voice, but I never see. She sound young, though."

Shit. Not a concrete disappointment but certainly leaning that way. "Did the police investigate?"

"No police. The woman long gone before anyone find Miss Ruthie dead. But there was a reporter snoopin' around after. Funny looking. Bulgy eyes, like a frog."

"I don't suppose you got his name? Or the name of the paper he was working for?"

"Now him, I do remember. Not his paper but his name: Skinner. I remember because he be so skinny — tall strip of a man. Barry Skinner, that's it. He keep asking me to call him Baz, or some such foolishness, but I too busy shooing him away. Gotta have some respect for the dead, you know."

Morrissey thought about the sad, lost woman who'd apparently lived a lonely life of desperation. But if a newspaper reporter was snooping around, chances were there was still some meat left on that bone.

CHAPTER 4

To say that Barry Skinner was a journalist was a bit of a stretch. Tracking him to his place of employment was as easy as following flies to a turd. The Weekly Titillator was exactly the kind of tabloid that revelled in the sort of innuendo and speculation that surrounded stories like Ruth Small's, suiting the cliché down to the ground.

Morrissey sat patiently waiting in one of the many grey, drab cells honeycombed throughout the Titillator's office 'hive'. Maybe it was the nature of his investigation, but he could almost imagine himself on some alien world populated by a variety of diverse creatures: some sentient and some, judging by the snippets of overheard conversations, not so much.

As a man approached the cubicle, Morrissey realised that Nurse Lorna's description of Skinner had been spot on. He was, indeed, an unnecessarily tall and angular fellow with eyes that throbbed and pulsed manically with each flash of his gap-toothed grin. The overall effect gave him a slightly warped quality, as if in God's genetic equation, The Almighty had forgotten to carry the '1'.

The man extended his hand, cold and slightly clammy. "Barry Skinner," he said, exhibiting just a bit too much enthusiasm. "Call me Barry. Or Baz. Your choice, really. And you are?"

"Morrissey. David Morrissey."

On a good day, Morrissey could claim to stand around 5' 10". This fellow stretched almost a foot beyond that. Morrissey half expected his knees to rise above the desktop as he sat, like some spindly stick insect perched on a leaf, but somehow the gangly reporter managed to fold himself into a practical enough package behind his desk.

"So. Mr. Morrissey. David. Dave! How can I help you?"

Before Morrissey could answer, the journalist lunged forward to retrieve a long coil of linked paperclips from a flimsy plastic tray. He unfurled the coil with an exaggerated flourish, his eyebrows dancing with mischief. "Get a load of this — my paperclip snake!"

"Yes," said Morrissey, "it's very...impressive."

"You know what they say about the size of a man's snake!"

Morrissey dreaded to think. "Look, Mr. Skinner — "

"— Barry, please. Or Baz. Your choice."

"Okay, Barry. I'm here about a woman."

"Aren't we all, mate! *Fworrr!*"

"Erm...actually, I'm here about a dead woman."

"Ah...awkward."

"Yes. Quite. In fact, it's about a dead woman you've apparently shown a great deal of interest in."

Barry winked. "Steady on, Dave. I do have some standards."

Morrissey's rubber band was beginning to tighten. "I'm talking about a woman called Ruth Small — died in a nursing home recently? I believe you went there to investigate her death."

The gormless smile dripped off Skinner's face like candle wax. "I might have." He leaned in closer. "I'm sorry, who are you again?"

"I'm here on behalf of the Ministry of Defence. Actually, I used to work with the M.O.D. in their UFO Hotline."

Barry's eyes widened past their bursting point. "You're *that* David Morrissey."

"You've heard of me? I guess you would have, being a publication of such..." he chose his words carefully, "...specific interests. I imagine some of my reports must have thrown a wet blanket over some of your more sensational stories."

39

Barry eyed him somewhat sceptically. "Yeah, something like that. Actually, I've only been here a couple of years, but I've heard your name in passing. So what can I do for you?"

"I suppose, Mr. Sk— Barry — that I'm wondering why the death of an old woman in a nursing home would be of any interest to The Weekly Titillator. Not exactly front-page news."

Barry laughed, a short sharp burst. "Let's not kid ourselves, Dave. We print crap. Quite often, we even make that crap up. But this old dear turned up on our radar as having some very curious connections of an extraterrestrial variety."

Morrissey kept his cards close to his chest. "What sort of connections?"

Barry looked surreptitiously from side to side. "Sorry, mate. That's highly classified."

"You're a tabloid newspaper; how classified could it be?"

Another blast of laughter. "You've got me there, Dave. Well, since we're on the same team, so to speak, I suppose I can tell you." He leaned in close, his bug eyes darting furtively. His version of Ruth Small's life turned out to be pretty much a carbon copy of what Morrissey had learned from the Red File. "Her campaign to uncover the truth of her extraterrestrial abduction became an obsession. She fetishised it to the point of conspiracy." His gaze was almost mesmerising. "Speculation is that she blew up that fertility clinic because she believed it to be a warehouse for alien DNA."

"Yikes. She certainly was committed."

"And that's not all." Barry hesitated, as if debating whether or not to finish his point. "There's another black hole of information in Ruth Small's life. Rumour has it that a number of years before she blew up the clinic, she had a second close encounter with an extraterrestrial. Very close."

Morrissey was almost afraid to ask. "What sort of encounter?"

Barry shrugged. "Who's to say, mate. Apparently, she tried to report it to the authorities, but they labelled her as some sort of crackpot. She eventually took her story to the press, but they all turned her down — except, this one."

"The Weekly Titillator?"

"Apparently. Allegedly she poured her heart and soul out in a tell-all article that claimed to expose all manner of alien conspiracies, including ties to a government coverup."

"How come I've never heard this story before? You'd think it would have made it across my desk at some point."

"The article never made it to the newsstands. I can't corroborate it because the story was squashed, all traces gone. As I said, *rumour.*"

"Who's got the power to silence the press?" Morrissey was well aware he was using the term press loosely, but his point stood.

"Did I mention the term 'government coverup'? Legend has it that the M.O.D. put the screws to the entire staff back in the day, threatened all manner of legal action if the paper didn't withdraw the story and all copies in print. All files regarding the case were either confiscated or destroyed. Or both."

A soft whistle steamed through Morrissey's teeth. "I don't suppose this M.O.D. legend has a name attached to it?"

"There was a name, but again it's only a rumour. Smythe. Archibald Smythe."

Archibald Bloody Smythe, you son of a bitch. Was there any aspect to this story he didn't have his fingerprints on. "You've got to be kidding me."

"You know him?"

"Let's just say his name keeps popping up." And his involvement keeps getting more suspect. At least it explained why the M.O.D. opened the file on her. "Anyway, this case is decades old. Why the interest now?"

"I thought that maybe her death had the potential for a major story. Thought it might tie up her conspiracies in one spectacular bow. But it turns out people are always dying in nursing homes. No one cares, mate." Barry's bug eyes squinted uncharacteristically. "Except you, that is. Which begs the question: why would this old woman be of interest to the M.O.D., specifically someone connected to the UFO Hotline? That department has been defunct for years now."

Maybe Barry Skinner wasn't as vacant as he first appeared to be. Morrissey decided to keep his response vague, to be on the safe side. "Just doing some housekeeping, tying up some loose ends. As you'd imagine, Ruth Small was also on an M.O.D. watchlist for many of the same reasons you've mentioned. The only problem is much of our information on her has been...lost. I'm trying to piece together what little I have into a cohesive narrative. I guess I was hoping you could fill in some of the gaps."

"All I've got is a story that paints Ruth Small as a poor unstable woman whose lifelong trauma drove her to commit unspeakable acts."

Morrissey surprised himself. "Is that what you really believe?"

"Look around you, Dave. I'm as partial to a good sensational story as the next crackpot, but believe it or not I'm more interested in the facts, no matter how weird they might seem. And this story seems just weird enough to warrant a deeper investigation."

Morrissey fished out the worn business card he'd retrieved from Ruth Small's doll and handed it to Barry. "Well it gets even weirder. Don't suppose you've come across this before?"

Barry studied the card carefully, as if it contained the names of every supermodel in the UK. "I think I have seen this before. Not the card, but the message." He grabbed a copy of the Titillator from his desk and flipped to the back pages. "There!" he said, triumphantly presenting Morrissey with a page of classified ads, highlighting one with the very same text from the business card. "Whoever this Alien Hunter is, they advertise in our paper."

"I suppose that makes some sort of twisted sense." Morrissey's stomach churned at the thought of getting answers. "Any way to tell who they are?"

"You bet your arse there is." Barry spun back to his computer and clicked away. "All I have to do is filter the marketing database and it's as simple...as...that! Your mystery Alien Hunter is a fellow called Fowler. Brian Fowler."

Morrissey's heart sank. "Are you certain?

"Why? Were you expecting someone else?"

"No. Not really." Lies. But the name meant nothing to Morrissey. In all his years at the UFO Hotline, such a character should have crossed his path; he was getting a little tired of discovering how much he didn't know about the shadows he'd spent his whole adult life chasing. "Don't suppose you have an address?"

"Oh, I can do a lot better than that." Barry continued tapping away. "It seems Brian Fowler's had a busy life: he's ex-army — medical discharge in 1981. Bit of a checkered past: several arrests, mostly for drunk and disorderly. One for Grievous Bodily Harm." Barry let out a long whistle. "Well I'll be...he's done some serious time, too — a twenty-stretch."

"For GBH?"

"No. Manslaughter. Looks like he was involved in the same fertility clinic bombing as our mysterious Ruth Small."

"Well, isn't that convenient. It certainly proves a link between them."

Barry continued reading from the file. "Apparently he was only released from prison a year ago."

"One day you're going to have to tell me how you come by all this information."

Barry winked a large bug-eye and tapped the side of his nose. "Now that is classified."

Morrissey shrugged. "Anyway, I guess that explains why he never showed up on my radar. But he didn't waste any time getting back to business, did he. The nurse at Meadowbrook said Ruth Small had two visitors within a week of her death. I don't know who the woman was, but I'd wager good money that the other one was this Fowler bloke. If you could just give me his address, I'll be on my way. I have a feeling that he has a very interesting story to tell."

"No problem, mate," said Barry, "but I'm coming with you. I've never met an honest to goodness Alien Hunter before."

"And I don't reckon you're going to now. He's probably just a disturbed old man with an extraterrestrial fixation." My specialty.

"And a history of violence."

"Remember the part about him being an old man?"

"Still, it might be wise to have some backup."

"I don't need backup."

Barry stared blankly at Morrissey. "You know I'll follow you anyway."

Morrissey sighed. Barry had been a great help so far but having a reporter tag along — especially one from a tabloid newspaper — was the last thing he needed. "Look, Barry. I fully respect that interviewing people is what you do for a living and I'm sure that you're really good at it when you put your mind to it, but I don't want to spook this guy. If you show up flexing your fancy reporter skills, he's liable to button up for good."

"I'll make you a deal. I come along, but I'll let you have your time alone with him first. Then, I get an exclusive."

"How much time?"

"Let's say an hour. I'll give you one hour on your own with him. I'll go for a coffee or wait in a pub — whatever. Then he's mine."

Morrissey chewed over his offer. In the end, it seemed better to have him along as an ally than as a complication. "Okay, Barry. You've got yourself a deal."

CHAPTER 5

Morrissey spun his scooter through the rush hour traffic like a fighter pilot evading a missile-lock — not an easy task for a four-stroke, liquid-cooled, single cylinder engine. Boasting 49 CCs of pure, unadulterated adequacy, it didn't exactly facilitate the luxury of a passenger — specifically this passenger.

The engine whined in protest as Barry perched precariously behind Morrissey like a giant praying mantis. Morrissey whined in protest at Barry's knobby knees as they poked and prodded in all the wrong places. He was almost sure he heard the scooter give a sigh of relief when Barry dismounted.

As far as alien-battling fortresses went, Brian Fowler's home was definitely absent a certain menace. There were no visible laser cannon batteries, particle beam weapons, atom scramblers, or defence shield thingamajigs. There may have been an intergalactic weapons cache in the back shed but from all outward appearances, the dingy, old end of terrace house didn't strike Morrissey as the hub of extraterrestrial combat.

"Not much of a lair, then," said Barry. "Still, I really don't think you should go in alone."

"You know, for an investigative reporter, you sound a lot like an old woman. Now be a good boy and go wait in the pub."

"Just remember, this bloke could be a nutter. Be on your guard."

"And you remember, one hour."

"And then I come in."

"But not before."

Barry faded into the dwindling twilight, ducking into the small pub on the corner. Morrissey almost wished he could join him. He switched off the scooter's headlamp, casting a blanket of gloom over Fowler's front step. The doorbell was soiled from the weather and probably lack of use; Morrissey pressed it tentatively, trying to avoid most of the grime. The sound shocked the still evening air, not so much a bell as a harsh, tinny rattle. He was just about to press the button again when he heard the dry squeal of metal against metal. A surprising number of locks and bolts unlatched before the door finally opened, bellowing out a rush of dank, musty air, thick with the sour pong of stale perspiration and cigarettes.

The man's gaunt face was etched by too much life and stained by too much nicotine, putting his age anywhere between fifty and eighty. "Yes? What is it?" His voice was much like the doorbell, tired and coarse from lack of use. "Who's there?"

"Mr. Fowler? My name is Morrissey." The old man's pale, watery eyes narrowed but he didn't answer. "You are Brian Fowler, aren't you?"

"What's this about?"

"It's probably something best discussed in private — as in, not in the street."

"Young man, I'm not in the habit of inviting strangers into my home. These days, you never know."

"It's about a woman called Ruth Small."

The old man's eyes widened slightly, gleaming in the dim streetlights. "What was your name again?"

"It's Morrissey. David Morrissey."

"Well, Mr. David Morrissey. I suppose you'd better come in."

Fowler shepherded him into the hallway, his grip stronger than Morrissey had anticipated. Only when he'd re-bolted the numerous locks did the old man seem to relax.

"About Ruth Small, Mr. Fowler. I just need — "

Fowler held up a bony hand. "Plenty of time for that. First, I'll make us some tea. Then we'll have a nice chat."

He led Morrissey into a small sitting room just off the front hallway before disappearing into the adjoining kitchen. The decor was a mishmash of pre-WWII appointments. Dark threadbare carpets struggled in vain to cover the peeling linoleum that led from one cheerless room to another. Bookshelves caked with dust ran the length of three of the four walls, upon which sat row after row of unknowable volumes. Interspersed amongst these were a selection of kitschy knick-knacks and scientific memorabilia. There was even a toy Dalek frozen in battle with a small ceramic poodle. Most jarring was a full-size autographed cardboard cut-out of William Shatner dressed in full Star Trek regalia; Morrissey imagined that every alien hunter needed to draw inspiration from somewhere.

True to the advertisement on his business card, Fowler returned from the kitchen with a tea tray laden with assorted nibbles. "Nothing aids civilised conversation more than a nice cup of tea, don't you think?"

Along with the tea, the tray contained a plate of sandwiches comprised of stale bread and fillings, which bore little resemblance to food. Also on the tray, for some unfathomable reason, was a bowl of plastic bananas. Morrissey declined the sandwiches — and the bananas. The tea, however, turned out to be pretty good, but time was ticking on his solo interview.

"Now about Ruth Small — "

"How do you know her?" said Fowler, catching Morrissey off guard.

"To be honest, I don't. But I was under the impression that you knew her — quite well, in fact."

"And where would you get that impression?"

Morrissey didn't have time to come at Fowler sideways. He plucked the crinkled Alien Hunter business card from his jacket pocket and tossed it onto the tea tray.

Fowler squinted at the card through heavily creased lids but didn't pick it up. His trembling lips pulled back into a grimace, cracking the crusted corners of his mouth. "It's clear you know who I am, then?"

"And about your brushes with the law — including your stint in prison for murder."

"Actually it was manslaughter. But what would any of that have to do with Ruth Small?"

"Let's not pretend we both don't know the answer to that."

"Very well," said Fowler, "but I had nothing to do with her death, if that's why you're here. It's the last thing I wanted."

"Then what did you want with her?"

The old man bought some time with a long, slow pull from his tea cup. He looked wistfully toward Cardboard William Shatner as if wordlessly soliciting his advice. "Are you familiar with the Rendlesham Incident, Mr. Morrissey?"

Morrissey's eyes narrowed, along with his patience. Any self-respecting UFO investigator knew of the events widely viewed as Britain's version of Roswell — as did every UFO conspiracy nut. In December of 1980 in a Suffolk forest, a series of mysterious lights were reported, along with the landing of a strange triangular craft in a nearby clearing. An M.O.D. investigation yielded no positive conclusions, and the mysterious craft was simply categorised as unknown. "Sure, I know it. But what does it have to do with any of this?"

Fowler stared off again into Cardboard Bill Shatner's flat, unfeeling eyes. "There was more to those lights than your precious Ministry of Defence cared to admit. I know…because I was there, stationed at one of the nearby RAF bases."

In all his years at the M.O.D., Morrissey had met more than a few people alleging to have definitive proof of a Rendlesham coverup. "Then why didn't your statement show up in the official records? I've never even heard of Brian Fowler before today."

Fowler leaned forward in his well-worn armchair, fuelled by a sudden agitation. "I was erased from the official records! We were coerced into signing documents, pressured to remain silent, even offered financial compensation in exchange for our cooperation. But I couldn't let the truth be stifled. I threatened to take the story to the press, to expose the incident for all the world to see. So, you know what your precious government did? They gave me a medical discharge. Psychological stresses, they cited. What press outlet would take me seriously with that stench following behind?"

"That's a pretty wild accusation — all a bit…cloak and dagger, don't you think?"

"I assure you that Agent Smythe was more than willing to take such measures to protect the government's secrets."

"Wait a minute — did you say Smythe?"

"Archibald Smythe. I'm not likely to forget the man pulling the strings of the investigation — and the coverup. A young, up-and-coming government stooge, eager to climb to the top of the executive ladder, no matter how many bodies he had to tread on to get there."

Jesus. Old Archie Smythe had certainly left a stain, first on the Ruth Small file and now on Fowler's. The more Morrissey pulled on the threads, the more this conspiracy unravelled. He viewed the so-called alien hunter in a somewhat different light; he decided he was going to have to pull on his threads with the utmost care. "I'm sorry, Mr. Fowler. I'm sure this has all been very distressing. I don't blame you for feeling resentment, but I still don't see how the possibility of a Rendlesham coverup connects to Ruth Small."

Fowler squinted, his thin lips bleeding into a cunning smile. "No. You really don't, do you?" The old man pushed himself up from his armchair and shuffled over to one of the bookshelves where he fished a rusted tin box from behind one of the stacks. He pulled a key from a cord around his neck and rattled the stubborn lock until it opened. He handed Morrissey the item within, glinting in the dim lighting.

He took the offering with some trepidation, turning it over in his hand. It was a small silver picture frame, a faded photo of a young woman within. His skin went cold and his stomach turned to lead. "This…this is a picture of my mother."

Fowler seemed amused by Morrissey's reaction. "Funny you should say that, Mr. Morrissey, because that is a picture of Ruth Small."

Morrissey tried in vain to reconcile the image in the frame with what Fowler was telling him. Facts crashed into reason; there were no survivors. He knew that picture; he'd seen it a thousand times as a child. "Look Fowler, I don't know what you're playing at but…" And then the world took a funny turn — literally. First to the right. And then a rather sharp bend to the left.

"What's the matter, Mr. Morrissey? You don't seem at all well."

He wasn't wrong. Perspective twisted into cruel shapes and his surroundings suddenly seemed a bit more spongy than they should. Morrissey could feel his blood boiling out of his skin as his hands began to tremble. Suddenly being in close proximity to a toilet seemed like a very wise idea. "I…I don't suppose I could…use your bathroom, could I?"

Fowler's lips appeared bound by elastic strings of saliva as his mouth moved soundlessly, like a fish gulping for air. Morrissey reached out to untangle them but couldn't coordinate his limbs. The old man began to shake so violently that Morrissey thought his teeth would fly from his mouth. But it wasn't Fowler doing the shaking, it was Morrissey's own eyes dancing in their sockets in perfect sync with the rhythmic thumping of his heart.

As he tried to steady himself, he came face to face with Cardboard Willian Shatner who chose that precise moment to swallow him whole. Morrissey's limbs dripped like treacle as he made a break for Fowler's toilet. The effort sapped him, and he suddenly realised he needed a bit of a lie down. As luck would have it, the floor was kind enough to come rushing up to meet him, albeit using rather excessive force.

The last thing Morrissey remembered before the lights went out was his mum whispering soothing words in his ear. He didn't think it at all odd that his mum bore a striking resemblance to William Shatner or that she was trying to insert a large plastic banana up his nose.

CHAPTER 6

Morrissey awoke to the smarmy grin of Cardboard William Shatner, snapping him back to a surreal reality he wanted no part of. He tried to stand but couldn't put theory into practice, realising he was bound to a rather solid chair by copious amounts of plastic cling film. He rocked his body to the left, then to the right, forward then backward, but could not break the bonds. He caught sight of his teacup, tipped on its side, the last drops trickling from its lip. You have got to be kidding me — Fowler drugged the tea? He should have known it tasted too good to be true.

"Ah, you're awake. About time, too." Fowler appeared from behind Morrissey, carrying a small worn leather suitcase. He placed it ceremoniously on the table and produced a wooden rolling pin wrapped in tinfoil from within. "Any longer and I'd have had to use The Probe," he said, waving it playfully, "but your people like that sort of thing, don't they."

There was so much wrong with those words that Morrissey didn't know where to start. He'd dealt with more than his fair share of passionate believers in his time but never before had one gone to the extremes of drugging him. "Look, Mr. Fowler, I'm not sure what

I've done to warrant...this, but I am sure we can talk about it rationally." Even though one of us is barking mad.

"My dear fellow, I've never been more rational in my entire life." Fowler dipped his head back into the suitcase and began mumbling to the contents. "Now where did I put those — there they are!" He smiled broadly as he snapped on a pair of rubber gloves and moved into Morrissey's blind spot. There was nothing more troubling than the promise of an attack from the rear.

A hollow rasp, followed by the rattle of metal on glass preceded the attack. Fowler's bony arm looped around Morrissey's neck, locking his jaw in its crook while his free hand slapped a thick coat of paste over Morrissey's mouth and nose, leaving him gagging. Fowler stood back to admire his handiwork.

Morrissey contorted his face. "Peanut butter? You spread peanut butter on me?"

"It's the only way to be sure."

"Sure of what? That you're a mental case?"

"I had to test, don't you see?"

"Test for what — to see how I taste on toast?"

Fowler shook his head slowly, suddenly weary. "The peanut, Mr. Morrissey. The story of the human race begins with a miracle of nature and ends with a simple peanut."

"What the Christ are you talking about?"

"For decades, now, we've been conditioned, each generation becoming weaker, more susceptible to outside pathogens. The children of today have to be carefully placed in bubble wrap so as not to fall victim to the simplest of challenges. You can barely swing a dead cat in a classroom without hitting a child who's allergic to it. Anaphylactic shock is only the thin edge of the wedge. When your people finally do arrive, they won't be attacking with starships and energy beams. All it will take to bring humanity to its knees is one carefully wielded peanut."

"Okay," said Morrissey, "that's it. I'm out. This has gone beyond a joke. What do you mean, *my people*?"

"Don't you see? If you'd had a reaction to the peanut butter it would have proven that you were human. But you did not react and that can only mean one thing."

"Not everyone is allergic to peanuts."

Fowler's eyes blazed. "Which only goes to show how rotten to the core this planet has become. And that is what I aim to prove.

Ruth Small was to have been my proof. She and I shared many of the same sensibilities — and the same burdens."

The mention of Ruth Small slapped Morrissey in the face with a fresh vengeance. "That picture, the one of my mum — where did you get it?"

"I got it from her room at Meadow Brook Estates. *Ruth Small's* room."

Nurse Lorna had said there was a picture missing, in a silver frame. But it couldn't be... "It can't be!"

"Your protestations notwithstanding, it can, and it is."

"Look, Fowler, sometimes people want to believe something so badly that they will cast out reason and rational thought in favour of hope. There's got to be another explanation."

"You are the one casting out reason, Mr. Morrissey. That picture is fact. I know it. And I think deep down, you know it, too. Ruth Small and Marion Morrissey are one and the same. She was to become my beacon of truth, my hope for vindication. But with her gone, it's now up to you. By coming here, you have saved me a trip to find you. For you will be my evidence. You will be my truth. Newspapers, television, the Internet — once I reveal you to the public, they will have no choice but to see how deep this insidious plot runs. They will have no choice but to believe me!"

Great, thought Morrissey. A grown man covered in peanut butter and wrapped in cling film. That'll show 'em. Not even The Weekly Titillator would buy that story. Of course — Barry! Morrissey couldn't see his watch through the layers of cling film, but he was willing to bet that his hour with Brian Fowler was almost at an end. With any luck, Barry would soon be calling for his promised exclusive. All Morrissey had to do was keep Fowler talking — and calm — until the cavalry arrived.

"Look, Mr. Fowler, I'm sorry for all you've been through — the way you were treated after Rendlesham, what Smythe turned you into. It can't have been easy." Morrissey actually felt sorry for the old man. "Let me go and I can help you find peace. I can help you get the counselling you need — the counselling you deserve. I can help you heal. Just let me go and I'll help you in any way I can." Come on, Barry.

Fowler's face lit up, fracturing into a thousand creases. "Oh, you're good. You're very good. You actually think I'd trust you of all people to bring peace to my life when you are the reason my life is in pieces?"

"I don't...I don't understand."

A dry cackle wheezed through Fowler's yellowed teeth. "No, you really don't, do you? No matter. You will in time. Now it is time for justice."

But justice would have to wait. The rusty old doorbell rattled through the house, jump-starting Morrissey's heart. He never imagined he would be so glad at the chance to see Barry's gap-toothed grin again, but elation quickly turned to dread. Fowler reached into the suitcase once more and produced a very real and very dangerous-looking pistol. It was an old Webley that probably hadn't seen use since Churchill was a lad. Fowler thumbed the barrel catch to check the load and then snapped it shut, ready for action. He tucked the pistol into the high waist of his trousers then, almost as an afterthought, he tied a grubby tea towel around Morrissey's mouth. "Can't have you causing any fuss, now, can we." Morrissey gagged, struggling to breathe through nostrils caked with peanut butter. Fowler placed a finger over his lips, making a shushing gesture. He patted the butt of his pistol for effect and then headed to the front door. Morrissey couldn't see the entrance, only the hallway leading to the door. He wanted to shout to Barry, to warn him, but all that came out were stifled sobs.

Multiple bolts and latches went about the business of unbolting and unlatching. Fowler's fragile voice was tinged with a sickly innocence as he opened the door. "Yes? Who is it?"

Apparently, it was chaos.

A high-pitched shriek of energy cut short the old man's scream. A series of dull wet thuds echoed in the hallway, followed by nothing but an ominous hum.

Morrissey's connection to current events had slowed to old-fashioned dial-up speed, the progress bar of the information download moving at a laboured stutter. An old song jangled through his brain, the one about the shoulder bone's connected to the back bone; the back bone's connected to the neck bone; the neck bone's connected to the head bone. The jumble of sizzling flesh, bloodied limbs, and scorched bones that used to be Brian Fowler were a case in point as to what happens when these simple laws of physiology were no longer observed.

A lone figure moved toward him through the sitting room doorway, carrying what looked like an industrial strength leaf-blower, the kind with the motor mounted on a backpack. A length of flexible tubing ran from the backpack behind the shoulder and connected to a long rigid shaft running under the forearm. His focus drifted from the weapon toward the face of the person wielding it, almost losing the *signal* in the process. The figure untied the soggy tea towel and plucked it from his mouth allowing the stream of events to finally complete its transfer.

"Kiki…what the —?" was all Morrissey could manage.

"You promised you'd call," said Kiki flatly, as she moved swiftly to tear away his plastic restraints.

No matter how hard he tried, Morrissey couldn't reconcile the woman he'd shared a bed with not twenty-four hours ago with the gun-wielding assassin that faced him now. It didn't help matters that there were lumps of barbecued old man arguing against her case. And if that wasn't enough, Barry chose that precise moment to pop his head around the doorframe.

"Jesus Christ, Dave. What the —?" It was all he could manage.

Kiki levelled her weapon toward him; Barry pushed away from the doorway, leaving a trail of profanities in his wake. Against Morrissey's protests, she fired. A stream of purple-white energy blistered the air, singeing the last few of Barry's expletives while chewing chunks of plaster and brick out of the wall and shredding the door into shrapnel. Morrissey fell against his old friend, Cardboard William Shatner, as Kiki pushed past him in pursuit of the retreating Barry. "Kiki, no — he's with me!" Kiki wheeled towards Morrissey, keeping her weapon trained down the hallway. She didn't speak but her eyes were fierce and decidedly less chocolatey than he remembered. She turned and raced toward the kitchen after Barry. Morrissey followed close behind, leaving the relative comfort of Shatner's cardboard embrace. Kiki raised her firing arm again. The muzzle flashed violently as Morrissey leapt toward her. Even with his intervention, the energy beam still blasted Barry in the back, sending him tumbling into the pantry.

Morrissey didn't have time to look on in horror. Kiki grabbed him roughly by the arm. "Come with me," she said calmly.

"I'm not going anywhere with you."

"Dave, I'm here to protect you."

"From what? You've already killed everyone in here." Morrissey's tone was cranked up to panic.

"I don't have time to explain — there may be others."

"Shouldn't we call someone? The police, maybe?"

"Do you want to explain this to the police?"

"No, but I've seen enough bad movies to know that nothing good ever comes from leaving a crime scene."

"I guarantee that nothing good is going to come if you remain at this 'crime scene'. Besides, you can always say that I threatened you."

Morrissey eyed her weapon, its muzzle still steaming from its recent workout. He decided that she might only be half joking.

"Now, give me your keys." Shock set Morrissey's feet in cement. "Keys, dammit!" He fumbled in his jacket pocket and handed her the keys to his scooter. As she pulled him from the house, he craned his neck for one last look at the damage but the smoke and confusion — both in the house and in his brain — obscured his view.

Kiki swung the power-pack of her weapon around to her front and leapt onto the scooter. Morrissey fastened his helmet and numbly climbed on behind her. As the engine hummed to life, he held on tightly — to Kiki and to whatever sanity he had left. She opened the throttle more than was healthy and the scooter pierced the evening calm with a new brand of mayhem.

Morrissey rode in silence, blind to everything but the destruction they'd left behind and the questions that were piling up on his conscience. Each potential answer yielded only more pieces to the puzzle that had become his life and Kiki seemed to be the only one with a grasp on his new reality.

When they reached The Crooked Crow, Kiki rode the scooter hard up onto the pavement and then dumped it amongst the bins. She quickly reoriented her weapon for action and charged it to life, fanning it across her field of view. A small group of revellers made their way down the street but paid them no undue attention. Once she was satisfied they posed no threat, she led Morrissey to the side entrance of his flat, backing toward the building, keeping him between her and his front door.

"Look, Kiki, you'd better tell me what the bloody hell is going on – "

"Get inside," she said, still scanning the streets.

Morrissey unlocked the door in a stupor and stumbled inside. Kiki quickly re-bolted the locks and pushed past him, charging up the stairs. Inside the flat, she stabbed at the shadows with the weapon as she checked each room for more phantoms. When she was satisfied that the flat was clear of intruders, she unslung her weapon and slipped it onto the bed — the same bed that she'd lain naked in, oh so long ago.

"Now can you tell me what the fuck is going on? What happened back there, why did you…" He could scarcely say the words without bile backing up in his throat. "Why did you kill those people?"

"Dave," said Kiki softly, apparently shifting from killer mode into woman-I-recently-had-sex-with mode. "I know this is a lot to take in and, on the surface, it looks pretty bad. But I promise you, it's all for your own good."

"My own good? I've just been dodging chunks of roasted pensioner, so don't you dare tell me that you killed those men for my own good."

"Okay. I won't. But I did. You really need to just take a breath and trust me."

"Trust you? I don't even know who you are right now. To think that you and I — that we — and now — it doesn't bear thinking about."

"Good. Then don't. Just shut up and do as I say."

"I'm not taking orders from a killer, thank you very much." As the words exited his mouth, he realised the folly of that statement.

"Dave, those men were out to harm you. Don't you understand the danger you're in?"

"You mean the kind of danger where your lover starts blasting people with a — what the hell is that thing, anyway?"

"You're hysterical, maybe in shock. Brian Fowler was an unstable man with a dangerous agenda. He had a history of violence and he was armed. You were not safe."

"He was unstable, yes, but he didn't want to kill me. He only wanted to show me off to the media as proof of — "

"Proof of what?"

"Well, I don't know exactly. You blew him apart before he could tell me. You didn't have to kill him, you know. Or Barry."

"He was a reporter."

"Well, reporter-ish."

"And that doesn't strike you as a coincidence? The man that holds you captive and wants to unleash you on the press is visited by — are you following closely — a man from the press." She spoke slowly, as if to a half-wit.

"Sure, when you put it like that, of course it sounds suspicious. But that's not how it..." Morrissey glazed over. Surely it couldn't be true. It didn't make sense that Barry and Fowler were working together. If they had the same agenda, there were easier ways to get him alone. "Wait a minute — how the hell do you know so much about these people? And me, for that matter? You and I only met last night. We *did* only meet last night, didn't we?" Morrissey suddenly felt like the thickest man on The Planet of the Thickies. "Just who the hell are you?"

"I'll explain everything. But first, you've got to get into the shower."

If this was a technique for dealing with people in shock, he wasn't aware of it. "I don't need a shower."

"Actually, we should both get into the shower."

On Morrissey's to-do list of sexual scenarios, 'The Shower Scene' ranked right up there with 'Strict-But-Sexy-Librarian' and 'The Naughty School Teacher', but bearing witness to human carnage didn't do his libido any favours. "I hardly think this is the time. Besides, after what you've done, I don't think that I can look at you in that way." Which wasn't exactly true.

"Can you possibly stop thinking about your penis for five minutes. We need to get into the shower now."

"I'm not — "

"For the love of God, Dave, just do as I say."

Something in her tone, mixed with the image of the powerful weapon lying on the bed told Morrissey that she was back in killer mode and that he should probably do as she said, no matter how bizarre the request. He began to remove his jacket while Kiki ran the water.

"You don't need to do that," she said.

"What — take my clothes off?"

"No. Not necessary."

"You want me to get into the shower with my clothes on?"

"It'll work better that way."

"This is crazy." Morrissey shook his head forlornly and stepped into the shower stall, fully clothed. "Jesus." The freezing water hardened his nipples almost instantly. His skin goose-pimpled and his genitals shrunk to raisins. So much for the Shower Scene Fantasy. Kiki stepped under the torrent and embraced him — out of affection, he very much doubted. Probably to share body warmth. In any case, he was grateful as it did help counter the chill. "Can we not have a bit of heat?" he said, as his saturated clothes weighed heavily on him and the numbing cold wrapped his body in ache.

She ignored him. She unzipped her jacket, revealing a small metallic disk affixed to her belt. She attached a similar disk to his belt and palmed it to life. Its surface lit up at her touch as she worked some sort of magic. When she was done, she pulled Morrissey even tighter toward her. He squeezed back, partly out of a selfish need for warmth and partly because despite the horrific absurdity of their situation, they had still shared a bond of intimacy that couldn't be severed so easily — no matter how much her recent actions made him cringe.

He looked into her eyes through the icy waterfall and could almost see beyond this surreal mess. Almost…if not for the sparks. Sparks? Crisp arcs of energy burst from Kiki's device, a few at first, only tingling and tickling. They blossomed quickly into a frenzy of tendrils lashing them both with wicked hot licks of blue fire until they were enshrouded in a storm of luminescent fibres. Morrissey had to shout over the sizzling. "What the hell is going on?"

"Don't worry. It'll be over soon."

Morrissey wished he had her confidence. He shuddered as the intense waves of energy needled his flesh, causing his muscles to spasm. His mouth agape in a rictus of protest, darkness cast its cloak over him. Kiki became more and more translucent until finally she disappeared completely. Then, in a spiral of chaos, the world dropped out from underneath him and he was both everywhere and nowhere at the same time.

CHAPTER 7

Morrissey awoke to the sharp tang of vomit and hoped very much that it was his own; he didn't fancy the alternative. Some of it was caked on his chin but some was fresh, oozing from the corners of his mouth. His heavy eyelids cried out in protest at the harsh light screaming from above. He pressed his trembling hands against his cold, damp forehead as his thoughts came in quick aggressive brushstrokes, forming a surreal canvas of events he couldn't quite shape into a cohesive picture. But as with most art, you sometimes had to take a step back to gain a better perspective.

Easier said than done. His bones burned as he rolled slowly away from the smell of sick and fear. The room simmered into focus. It was more of a cell really — stark, white, antiseptic. Besides the bed on which he sat, there was only a small metal table bolted to the floor with two plastic folding chairs leaning against it. Morrissey's skin prickled as he eyed the door he knew to be locked even before he tried it. He twisted the knob, pointlessly as he suspected. His body pulsed, drenched in sweat and tight with apprehension. They would be coming for him soon. He didn't know who *they* were, of course, but there had to be a they.

There was always a they.

As if on cue, he heard the rattle of keys and the snick-snick of the lock cycling open. He considered launching an assault with one of the plastic folding chairs but figured it wouldn't give them anything more damaging than a good laugh. So, he did what creatures have been doing since the dawn of time when backed into a corner — and that was to back into the corner.

The door swung open, revealing two men of mountainous proportions. They looked as if they'd both been chiselled from the same block of granite save for the fact that one of them sported a rather cheesy looking moustache. Both were dressed in plain white uniforms and wore matching expressions of strained patience. They made no overt moves of aggression, seeming only intent on blocking his escape. Finally, their wall of muscle parted; a tall, elderly fellow poured through the crack in their blockade, moving with an air of well-oiled authority. A warm, avuncular smile washed across his gaunt face as he motioned to the two white-coats.

"You may leave us. I don't think Mr. Morrissey is going to try to hurt me." Then he said to Morrissey, "You're not going to hurt me, are you?"

Morrissey eyed him warily. "I...I hadn't thought that far ahead."

The old man chuckled, the jocularity seeming a bit out of place. "There, you see. He doesn't want to hurt anyone." As the two white-coats turned to leave, the moustachioed version glared at Morrissey all the way out the door, which he wasted no time in locking behind him.

The man set down a tray with a bowl of soapy water and two steaming cups of what looked like tea. He took a seat on one of the chairs and gestured for Morrissey to do likewise. "Would you like to clean yourself up a bit?"

Morrissey placed the other chair as safe a distance from the old man as the small room would allow. As he scrubbed the worst of the sick from his face and clothes his gaze never left the curious eyes of his visitor. He thought about cracking a joke to defuse the tension but felt none of his usual levity forthcoming. "There are a million questions racing through my brain right now, but I'll settle for where the bloody hell am I?"

"Oh dear," said the old man. He pulled a small notebook from his jacket pocket and scribbled on a fresh page. "This is worse than I thought. Much worse." The man smiled weakly, as if embarrassed on Morrissey's behalf. "Perhaps you'd like some tea?" he said, gesturing to the tray.

Morrissey eyed the steaming cups with an inordinate amount of suspicion. A cold sweat bubbled up through his skin. "I — I don't think so. I don't think I...trust it."

The old man tut-tutted as he scribbled furiously in his notebook. "Well at least you're consistent. You've been saying that since you got here. No matter."

"You still haven't told me where *here* is."

"Rest assured, you are safe," said the old man. "I'm here to help."

"That doesn't really answer my question."

"My name is Dr. Cheevers, and I specialise in cases dealing with your...condition."

"I have a condition?"

"My dear fellow, I'm afraid you've suffered a rather...how should I put it...a rather nasty break from reality that has resulted in some fairly serious delusions."

Morrissey surveyed the bleak surroundings. "So, what — this is some sort of mental asylum?"

Dr. Cheevers chuckled. "Oh, nothing so barbaric. It is a place of healing, a place where you can feel safe."

Morrissey felt anything but. "You'll forgive me if I don't take your word for it." His memories dripped like treacle, like waking from a dream too incredible to be trusted but too real to be discounted. Fleeting glimpses of faces he couldn't quite place, names that didn't make sense, and all with an undercurrent of violence. "You mentioned delusions. What sort of delusions?"

"You seem to have developed a rather unhealthy fixation on things of an extraterrestrial nature." He flipped through the pages of his notebook. "UFOs. Alien abductions. Even laser blasters. Quite the fanciful imagination, don't you think?"

Morrissey scowled. "I'm not sure mockery is considered a proven psychological treatment."

Dr. Cheevers flushed. "In any case, we haven't been able to pinpoint a definitive trigger yet. But in each of your therapy sessions so far, one thing stands out —"

"Wait — what do you mean, sessions? Just how long have I been here, Doctor?"

Dr. Cheevers shifted awkwardly. "My dear boy, you've been here almost a week. But you mustn't focus on that, it will only add to your stress."

A week. And only a patchwork of memories to cover the gap.

"As I was saying," said Dr. Cheevers, "after each of your regression therapy sessions, you've reacted rather poorly, resulting in an almost complete mental reset and some rather aggressive physical manifestations." He gestured to Morrissey's vomit-stained clothing. "It's as if you're trying to block something from your past, something tragic? Possibly. Traumatic? Probably. When we last left off, you had recounted your mother's revelation that she had, herself, had an extraterrestrial experience."

Yes. His mum. The memories teased him, but it was like trying to grasp at smoke. "She never did tell me what the experience was, only that she'd tried to keep it in her past. She didn't want it to hurt me."

"And yet it did?"

Did it ever. "That day…it was the last time I ever saw her." His heart raced as he clutched at the chain around his neck, the place where her pinky ring hung as a constant reminder that she was once part of his life. Only when he felt the cool comfort of the talisman did he calm.

"I imagine that having your mother abandon you would certainly lay the groundwork for feelings of loneliness and alienation. Working your way through the foster care system is not an easy substitute for the indelible bond of blood ties."

"Is this supposed to make me feel better?"

Cheevers shrugged apologetically. "I'm merely trying to isolate a plausible trigger for your current trauma. The role your mother played is only part of the equation."

Something else was lurking in the shadows of his memory, something altogether unsettling. "Fowler," he whispered.

"Yes," said Dr. Cheevers, flipping through his notes. "You did mention a…Brian Fowler. Some sort of self-appointed alien hunter, as you described him."

Yes. Alien Hunter. "He tried to tell me that my mother and the woman who'd died in the nursing home, Ruth Small, were the same person. He even had a photo of her, claiming he took it from Ruth

Small's room. But there has to be another explanation, it doesn't make sense! It *can't* make sense. She can't have blown up that clinic and killed those people. It just wasn't in her nature. If only Fowler hadn't been killed, I could have — "

"Well, you see, there's the problem. We can't find any trace of this Brian Fowler. Dead or alive."

Morrissey stared at the old doctor as if he'd suddenly grown a third eye. "What are you talking about? I was there. He drugged me. Tied me to a chair. Covered me with — well, never mind that. I saw him blown to pieces. Along with a reporter, a...Skinner...Barry Skinner. That's it!"

"Do you see how irrational all this sounds?"

"Kiki. Ask Kiki Pashmina. She'll back me up. She was there, too. She — "

"I'm afraid, dear boy, that this Kiki person also does not exist. Except in your troubled imagination."

Morrissey felt his brain fogging up, pressure welling behind his eyes. "But...that can't be. It has to be true."

"I know you need it to be true to make sense of your current state of mind, but that does not make it so. All the more reason why we must identify a trigger for your trauma. We need to discover if there was something else from your past, something perhaps that your mother told you — about herself, about your birth father?"

"I never knew my birth father. He left us before I was born." Morrissey tried to clear the cobwebs. "But if there was something else, it must be pretty well-hidden. I'm beginning to learn my mother wasn't the woman I thought she was."

The doctor's gaze seemed to pierce Morrissey's soul. "And that is why we're here. If we are to determine the truth we must not go further into your past, but deeper into your mind, into your subconscious. It's what I'm here to help you with, Mr. Morrissey. All you have to do is trust me."

Morrissey tensed reflexively. He didn't trust himself at the moment, let alone this stranger. But despite his inner turmoil — or maybe because of it — it might be helpful to let someone else drive for a while, if only to make it easier to recognise the landmarks. He puffed out a sigh of resignation. "Okay, what do you need me to do?"

Dr. Cheevers produced a small vial of liquid from his jacket pocket. Morrissey thought it an odd place to keep such a thing. "You can start by taking your medication."

Something in the forefront of Morrissey's brain told him that the only way things were going to get better would be to give in to this doctor, but something else nagged him from the cold, frightened recesses of his mind that sent reason screaming for cover. "I...don't think so."

"Really, Mr. Morrissey, we go through this every time. You know we can't proceed without it. It will help you relax, help ease your anxiety."

"Sorry, Doc, but if I'm not going to drink the tea, I'm certainly not going to take that. End of."

"If you don't take your medicine, I'm going to have to call in the orderlies. And if I do, things are likely going to get a little...*messy*. You don't want things to get messy, do you? *Again*."

Morrissey chilled at the sudden shift in tone, the hardening of Dr. Cheevers' eyes, the darkening of his soul. "What happened to the friendly old man so concerned for my wellbeing?"

Dr. Cheevers sighed. "That time has passed, I'm afraid." He snapped his notebook closed and ceremoniously tucked it away in his jacket pocket. "My dear boy, why must you always do things the hard way?"

Unbidden, the massive moustachioed orderly entered the room, flexing a no-nonsense grimace. Dr. Cheevers waved him over. "Dose him. Wipe his engrams for this session. We'll start again." Moustache-Orderly produced a clear bulb of fluid from his waist pouch. The bulb had a decidedly angry needle jutting from its business end. "This will only hurt a lot," said Dr. Cheevers. "But don't worry, you won't remember any of it."

As Moustache-Orderly approached with the syringe at the ready, his clean-shaven counterpart burst into the room and spoke sinister whispers in Dr. Cheevers' ear.

"Are you certain?" Dr. Cheevers' eyes lit up. "Well, well, well. It seems we've been looking for answers in all the wrong places."

"What's that supposed to mean?"

"It means that we no longer have to rely on the vagaries of your subjective memory. The answers are far more tangible than that — and far easier to extract."

A voice barked over a loudspeaker, an unrecognisable warble, like a seal choking on a harmonica. Whatever it said unsettled Dr. Cheevers, a faint sheen of sweat glistening the old man's pale skin.

That was when the thunder came.

A sharp shudder ran from Morrissey's toes to his teeth. The single light fixture danced a jig on the ceiling as the room shifted ever so slightly, a momentary flicker within the blink of Morrissey's eye. A spider web of vibrant green pulsed from the ceiling light, sending snakes of energy charging around the room, leaving trails of translucent emptiness in their wake. The energy waves flared across the walls and floor and up the bodies of the two orderlies and Dr. Cheevers. In that brief glow, Morrissey could have sworn that their skins just...slipped away, revealing something altogether unrecognisable beneath. Then as quickly as the energy streams appeared, they dissipated, fizzing the room — and his captors — back to normal.

Morrissey blinked hard, willing away the illusion. Everyone exchanged awkward glances, each waiting for the other to give a sign that everything was okay. But nobody did. Because it wasn't. Not one little bit. The orderlies rushed Morrissey at Dr. Cheevers' command, the clean-shaven one securing him from behind while the other targeted his neck with the bloated syringe.

Confusion led to fear. Fear led to frustration. And frustration led to anger. It boiled through Morrissey like a fever, charging his limbs with an energy so raw, he felt his fists were set to explode. He kicked at Moustache-Orderly, toward the most vulnerable spot he could reach — square between his legs. Contact was direct and solid but instead of the soft package of genitals he expected, his foot hit something far too hard to be good news. Maybe the man was aroused by the violence; maybe he had a knob of steel. It made no difference. Morrissey's resolve was made of sterner stuff.

He snapped his head back into the rear orderly's chin, feeling as if he'd smacked cement. It weakened his captor's grip enough for him to wrench an arm free. His elbow pumped back like a piston, toward the man's face, but his balance was off and he only struck the side of the head. The man collapsed like a sack of potatoes, clutching at a disturbing green liquid pulsing from his ear.

Moustache-Orderly looked on in shock at his fallen colleague. The small victory charged Morrissey with a burst of adrenaline. He launched himself toward his attacker, striking him in the chest. As the orderly stumbled back, the syringe fell onto the bed. Morrissey slammed his fist hard into the man's face for good measure, feeling flesh and bone yield in unfamiliar ways.

Panic burned through him and he lunged toward the door. Dr. Cheevers, however, was more nimble than his years would suggest. The old man's hand struck Morrissey like a blade, hard in the throat. His leg hammered Morrissey full in the chest, pinwheeling him onto the bed.

"Jesus Christ!" His speech fought through mangled vocal cords.

Dr. Cheevers charged toward him while Moustache-Orderly circled from his flank. Morrissey felt the coldness of the syringe butt up against his leg. As Dr. Cheevers pulled him close by his shirt front, Morrissey seized the opportunity, jamming the syringe into Dr. Cheevers' neck, flushing the entire contents into the doctor's system. The old man tensed, his eyes bulging insanely. Moustache-Orderly rushed to steady him as he fell, then lowered him gently to the ground. Then he shifted his attention to Morrissey, throwing himself into a full-tilt tackle. His attack coincided with another bone-rattling tremor, sailing the orderly harmlessly over Morrissey's head and into the opposite wall where he bounced off and spun in mid-air.

Mid-air? What the...

Apparently, the laws of gravity were taking some much-needed time off. Morrissey felt himself lift off the bed; he grabbed the sheets as an anchor. The sensation was like floating in a swimming pool but without the heavy drag on his limbs. He could almost feel his organs sloshing about while his skin crawled off his bones.

An unconscious Dr. Cheevers drifted harmlessly nearby as did the clean-shaven orderly, pools of oozing green goo blobbing inches from his head. Moustache-Orderly was the only active threat, thrashing against the complete lack of resistance. He grasped the light fixture, pulling up toward the ceiling, then folded his body into a spring and launched himself like a missile.

Morrissey braced for the impact, unsure how to effect evasive manoeuvres in null gravity. Moustache-Orderly's aim was off but not by much. He caught Morrissey by the shoulder and the two spun around their fulcrum, careening off the cot and into the wall and then back up to the ceiling. Blows were struck on both sides, their cumulative momentum adding to the brutality. Eventually, Moustache-Orderly lost his grip and the two spun off on their respective trajectories, coming to rest at opposite ends of the room, Morrissey on the floor while the orderly remained wedged against the ceiling.

Before the orderly could launch another attack, the room went black. Even the sporadic energy tendrils had run silently into the shadows. Morrissey's skin tingled the way it does when you can feel someone's breath on your neck but can't, for the life of you, see anyone there. The orderly called out, his raspy tongue sounding even more ghoulish in the dark. Time was held firmly in place by bands of tension until the shriek of a siren pierced the black, jump-starting Morrissey's heart.

Vertical light nodes flared to life, scarring the walls with a garish phosphorescence. Morrissey found himself sitting on an unfamiliar, rough metal plating. The sudden return of gravity thumped the orderly hard to the ground; there was an angry thud followed by a sickening snap and a short, sharp squeal.

Morrissey scrambled to his feet, wondering what had happened to his cot. But it wasn't just the furniture that was gone. The whole room had morphed into a massive domed chamber, its entire surface dimpled with thousands of what looked like pot lights, peering with dead stares from their soulless craters.

Even more disturbing was the transformation of his captors. Earlier, when the rivulets of energy had snaked along their bodies, he'd caught fleeting glimpses of strange, unnatural beings beneath. Now, in the wake of the power interruption, he had no frame of reference against which to measure their true forms. He'd spent most of his adulthood in search of proof of extraterrestrial life and now it seemed that here it was, plain as day. All he could do was stare, gobsmacked.

The one who had called himself Dr. Cheevers now appeared as a grotesque stretch of peculiarity. He, or rather it, still had two arms and two legs and what could loosely be described as a head. But that's where the similarities to the old man ended. The arms were long and spindly twists of muscle, stretching awkwardly from broad, bony shoulder plates. Its legs looked as if they'd been stuck on backwards but turned out to be jointed much like a dog's. A smooth helmet of a head fused directly to its neck, forming a disturbingly phallic stub. Its rough, leathery skin was etched with deep grooves, twisting like melted plastic.

Whoever its Creator was, they'd been a bit stingy with the facial features. Where its mouth should have been was little more than a shrivelled ring of muscle, like an anus ridged with needle-sharp teeth. Directly above the mouth was an eye, a singular jet-black orb, staring blankly into the shadows. Its chest rose and fell slowly, puffing out laboured wisps of fetid breath. So not dead, then.

The two orderlies were of the same type — or species — or whatever — as one another but different from Cheevers. The creature formerly known as Moustache-Orderly lay still on the cold metal floor, his head twisted in a far too unnatural way. The other, the one that Morrissey had bashed in the head was conscious but only barely, struggling for each painful breath. It was taller than it had appeared in its human form and stouter around the middle, with a barrel chest. Two disproportionately wiry arms hung limply from its bulbous shoulders. Its pebbled skin, the colour of eggplant, glistened in the rude lighting while its blocky head sat uncomfortably on a tree stump of a neck. Its eyes, two large black eggs, twitched erratically in time with the being's uneven breaths. Where one might have expected to find ears were two gelatinous sacs, one of them reduced to a sagging membrane oozing with green goo.

Despite the circumstances, Morrissey felt no small amount of guilt at the damage he'd caused the creature, turning his fear into a curious sense of pity. He yelled above the shriek of alarms. "Look, I don't know if you can hear me — or even understand me — but I'm sorry…sorry for hurting you. But you did sort of have it coming. I was just trying to defend myself, what did you expect?" Morrissey found himself vacillating between outrage and empathy, finally giving in to the latter. "Are you okay?" Stupid question. "Is there anything I can do? Someone I can call?" An even stupider question.

A putrid foam sizzled from the creature's mouth while its head rolled forward, slowly and awkwardly, as if on a rusty hinge. It reached out, not toward Morrissey but toward the two plastic cups sitting in a pool of spilled tea.

"Is that what you want?" An odd time for a cup of tea.

Morrissey did his best to salvage some of the beverage and handed over the cup. To his surprise, the creature dumped the contents and instead, used the cup to scoop the spilled pools of green ooze. When the cup was half full, it pressed the container to the base of its deflated ear sac but couldn't maintain the pressure.

"Here," said Morrissey, figuring out the creature's plan, "let me." He gently poured the remaining contents into the pulpy mess at the side of the being's head. "Now what?"

An unintelligible wet gurgle percolated from its slack mouth. The creature waved a flaccid arm at the empty cup and then to the side of its head, forming a cover with its massive, sausage-fingered hand. Morrissey got the gist. He held the plastic cup against the deflated sac, forming a rudimentary seal. Slowly the wheezing began to abate, and the gasps lessened; the creature's breathing settled into a more comfortable rhythm.

On the other side of the domed chamber, the Dr. Cheevers-creature began to regain consciousness. Since a key part of Morrissey's escape plan involved being elsewhere when he did, he decided it was time to say his goodbyes. "Look mate, no hard feelings but I've got to go. Good luck with…you know…all that. Hope you've learned your lesson."

Morrissey left through a massive doorway that hadn't been there before. It led to an empty corridor, featureless except for the blisters of white light running its length. He picked a direction and charged blindly; common sense told him not to expect any giant EXIT signs, but it didn't stop him from hoping for one. He encountered no stairways or lifts, no windows — no obvious way out at all. On the bright side, he didn't encounter any resistance, either.

His thoughts turned to Kiki Pashmina — the woman he'd recently bedded, the woman who had killed to protect him, the woman who'd been the catalyst for this entire mess. If anyone knew a way out of this, he'd put money on it being her. If they'd been captured together, she was probably imprisoned somewhere in this facility. The problem would be finding exactly where.

He crossed several intersections but didn't deviate, finally coming to an abrupt halt at a very determined looking door. It featured a dim blue disk at its centre, about the size of a dinner plate which began to glow at his approach. He pressed it, gingerly at first, then with a firm fuck you. It pulsed a deeper blue and rotated a half-turn. Morrissey snapped his hand back as the door cleaved in two with a mechanical whine. Hope fed him ideas about it leading either to Kiki or to freedom. But as usual, hope was a dick.

Four figures of varying sizes and shapes blocked his path. Each wore a protective suit of some kind; one of them had too many limbs to make sense of while another looked to be no more than a child, barely three feet tall.

Within two thumping heartbeats, Morrissey spun and bolted, zigging at the first intersection he came to, zagging at the next. Left turn, right turn; it didn't matter. He fought only to put as much distance as he could between himself and the clattering of boots chasing behind. At each turn he imagined salvation, at each blank doorway, a sliver of hope. One more hallway, one more door. This one, maybe. And then...

Morrissey had seen countless photographs of Earth as viewed from space, taken by the few astronauts lucky enough to have had that exclusive adventure. He never thought in a million lifetimes that he'd be seeing the sight firsthand. She hung against the midnight velvet of space, surrounded by the billion pinprick lights of the universe. His home. Earth. No borders. No politics. No wars. It was the most beautiful, humbling and soul-chilling vision he'd ever seen. A line from a poem he'd once read as a teen snapped his life neatly into perspective: *And the world stretched its wonder around me, smothering me with insignificance.*

A cacophony of voices boiled over behind him. He barely noticed that none of them spoke any recognisable language, but he did notice that objects looking remarkably like weapons were trained in his direction. Slowly, the frenzied voices calmed and filtered down to one. It sounded female and, judging by the reaction of the others, was probably the leader. She spoke in a soft, relaxed manner that put Morrissey at ease despite the chaos. She lowered her weapon, motioning for the others to follow her lead. All of them complied, except for the child-like being.

The leader inched toward Morrissey, still speaking, still not being understood. Morrissey backed against the cold glass of the viewport and the leader stopped — stopped moving, stopped speaking. She nodded to the small figure, still with its weapon at the ready. And then the little bugger fired. Green light crackled as a web of energy splashed Morrissey, wrapping him in a body-numbing cocoon. He thumped to the ground, skin buzzing. Finally, his synapses gave in. No more. Enough. Morrissey had had enough.

PART TWO

CHAPTER 8

Curious sounds hummed through Morrissey's subconscious, floating just beyond his reach and reason. Occasionally one would ring true as a voice, the language unintelligible but a voice, nonetheless. Patterns and cadences soon followed, a smattering of English bubbling to the surface, eventually forming a patchwork of sentences with meaning and purpose.

"You're awake," claimed a voice. Morrissey had his doubts. The voice was female, soft and luxurious. Morrissey tried to shift his position for a better view but seemed unable to move. For one panicked moment, his memory flashed to his incarceration in Brian Fowler's lair; he did a quick visual check for plastic cling film but found none.

"The restraint field is for your own protection," said the Voice. "Apologies for any disorientation you may experience."

"Protection?" His own voice was little more than a croaky whisper. "So, I'm not a prisoner, then?"

"Why would you think this?"

"Oh, I don't know. I'm just sensing a theme." He remembered looking out from the viewport at the Earth, the distant image of his home splashed across the backdrop of empty space. He remembered the strangely outfitted creatures chasing him through Hell. He remembered green fire filling him with a numbing ache. "Or maybe it's because you shot me. It was you, wasn't it?"

"Not me, personally, though we do regret any discomfort you suffered. We did not have time for a more…leisurely extraction."

"Extraction? So, you were…rescuing me?"

"Rescue? Yes. This is correct. Now, if you are ready, I will disengage the restraint field."

"Oh, I'm ready." Except he wasn't. The bed whirred as it elevated him suddenly, spinning his insides in unpredictable ways. Momentum rather than conscious effort rolled him onto his side where he came face to face with the voice. "Jesus!"

Often you develop an impression of what a person looks like by the sound of their voice. Sometimes that voice fits the face perfectly, as with Scarlett Johansson or The Queen. But sometimes, the disparity can hit you in the face like a frying pan. This was one of those frying pans. The face hovered inches from him though it could only be loosely described as such. It was a slick, yellow jellied sphere, about the size of a bowling ball. A fringe of stiff bristles poked out from where a human's chin would be and a throbbing sphincter puckered and pulsed at its centre. Two flexible eyestalks, each about a foot in length, extended from the sides of the head. The end of each stalk was knobbed with golf ball-sized-orbs — eyeballs? — though they never blinked; they only stared deeply into his own bewildered gaze.

Its body was tubular, curved into a lazy 'S' shape, coloured in a sun splash of burnt oranges stippled with deep purples. The two-metre-long tube was segmented into dozens of chitinous plates, like the skin of a centipede. But unlike the centipede, this creature only had a dozen legs to deal with: six slender walking limbs extended from the belly of the 'S' while six more dextrous grasping limbs jutted from its upper segments.

"You must proceed with care," said the creature. "The tangler weapon we used to secure you had a considerable impact on your central nervous system. You have been recuperating in our Medical Pod since we brought you on board. It will take some time before you are fully recovered."

Morrissey wasn't up for moving much, anyway. He sank back into the padding of the bed. The Medical Pod contained four such beds that he could see, each outfitted with all manner of sophisticated gadgetry. "Does that mean you're a doctor?"

The creature cocked its head to one side, like a dog waiting for its master to give it a treat. "Doctor? In a manner of speaking. I am the med-tech of this vessel. I have been charged with your care. So it only seems fitting that I ask, how are you feeling?"

Morrissey pored over the odd features of the creature as its sphincter-mouth snapped with wet sucking sounds. "Just to recap: it seems I'm not dead, so that's a plus. And I'm not dreaming." He thumped the heavy gel pad of the bed cushion. "Or at least everything seems real enough. So, if I'm being honest, seeing you — talking to you, I feel...overwhelmed. You...you are speaking English, aren't you?"

"No. I am speaking Osian. You are hearing English."

"Okaaaaay. Well, I'm glad we cleared that up."

"Your cerebral cortex has been implanted with a bio-translation chip — a T-Chip, as we call it. The chip will feed off all aural and visual input, converting it into intelligible data."

"I don't suppose you could dumb it down a bit. I'm new to these parts. I mean, knowledge of the English language has to come from somewhere, doesn't it?"

"Knowledge of your language comes from you."

"Surely it has to be programmed?"

"The T-Chip uses your own brain to process the incoming data. It merely acts as a sophisticated filtering system. As I said, I speak Osian, you hear English. It is as simple as that."

Morrissey doubted very much whether it was that simple, but he let it be, for now. Though he did feel slightly violated at the thought of someone messing around in his brain. But at the same time, he marvelled at what the creature was telling him — that it could tell him at all. "So when I speak English, you hear, what was it — Ocean?"

"Osian. That is correct. The T-Chip is still in the process of synchronising with your brain patterns. You may experience some omissions in the language matrix for a while yet and there may be some colloquialisms that cannot be converted at all. But rest assured, you will find this a most necessary tool."

"In my head, I hear your voice as a female. Does that mean you are female?"

"You will find that gender nomenclature will vary greatly from planet to planet, race to race, species to species. The universe contains a broader spectrum of organisms than you may be used to. But the translator does attempt to contextually interpret linguistic patterns and cross-references them with how your brain perceives gender. It then selects an appropriate archetype suited to the respective species. So from your perspective and frame of reference, yes — I am a female."

Morrissey figured that it was like trying to imagine a female lobster. "What should I call you? Do you have a name?"

"I am called Lillum-Al-Ellum. You may call me Lillum."

"Very well, Lillum. My name is Morrissey. Dave Morrissey. You can call me Morrissey."

"Yes, this much we know of you."

"Hold on — my brain must really be fried. You said that I've been in this Med-Pod since you brought me on board — on board what, exactly?"

"Ah...unfortunately, this is a question for which I do not have authorization to answer."

"Well who does, then?"

"I do," said a new voice.

The door to the Medical Pod whooshed open and in loped an oddly striking specimen of both quiet grace and authoritative strength. It moved on only two legs which was refreshing after the shock of Lillum's multitude. It had two arms to match, long and willowy, sweeping with sinewy power. A slim, skeletal frame was tightly wound in a jumpsuit that seemed fashioned from strips of cobalt blue liquid metal. Its scalp was clean shaven, save for two amber braids which grew from the temples and laced at the nape of a long slender neck. Triangular flaps of skin fluttered softly above a thin gash of a mouth. Its pale, almost translucent flesh, was marbled with a faint network of veins. The being surveyed Morrissey with large, widely set eyes of the deepest violet.

"This is Sha'an, our commander," said Lillum. "She will take care of you from here."

Morrissey nodded to the newcomer. "Commander."

"You are a guest on our starship and not under my command. You may call me Sha'an."

If the translator chip — the T-Chip — was doing its job properly, this voice also registered as a female. "Very well, Sha'an it is. So we're travelling through space?" Sha'an nodded. "Like, right now — we're in space?"

Sha'an nodded again then turned to Lillum. "Is he alright?" Lillum did a pretty good imitation of a shrug for a being with no shoulders.

"It's just that...I've never been in space before," said Morrissey.

"When we found you, you were in space."

"Yes, but I didn't know that. What I mean is, all this is very new to me and I guess I have you to thank for my rescue. I don't suppose you could tell me what the hell you were rescuing me from?"

"With your help, this is what we hope to discover. What can you tell us of the being holding you captive?"

"There were three of them, actually. That I saw. The one running the show called himself Dr. Cheevers though I'm guessing he was about as much a doctor as he was a human being." Morrissey described the nightmare of Cheevers' true form. "How the hell did he pull off that trick, anyway?"

"He used a holo-chamber to simulate your native environment and the physical skins he and his crew wore."

"What about his human speech? I could understand everything he was saying but that was before I was implanted with this T-Chip thingy. How is that possible?"

"Such a facility would have a rudimentary linguistic matrix, though its range and capabilities would be limited."

"But how would the linguistic matrix even know English? It wasn't hooked up to my brain, was it? And the simulation in general — it was pretty convincing, right down to the institutional cups of tea."

Sha'an nodded. "The complexity of his ruse suggests access to a database of your homeworld."

"You're saying he had a file...on Earth?"

"Do you not study the myriad creatures of your own world in the interests of scientific discovery? Such things are always available for those willing to pay."

Morrissey felt violated on behalf of the entire human race. "Gives me the creeps."

"I do not understand — creeps? No matter. Tell me, did this Cheevers perform any physical examinations on you?"

"Not that I'm aware. Not while I was conscious, at least." Morrissey's skin crawled at the prospect of being probed by alien devices while he was unconscious. "He did question me quite a bit. He referred to them as therapy sessions but in retrospect I'd say they were more like interrogations."

Sha'an flicked a glance at Lillum, then burned her gaze back into Morrissey's eyes. "And what was it that he was hoping to learn through these...interrogations?"

"He said he was looking for the source of my delusions." Morrissey gestured to his alien surroundings. "But since they turned out not to be delusions, I can only surmise that there was something else of particular value on his shopping list. And he seemed certain that I knew what it was."

"Indeed. And what might that have been?"

Morrissey hesitated, eyeing them both warily. "Look, I'm not trying to be difficult, but I don't know you people. I'm still getting my head around the fact that you even exist. How do I know you're not working with this Dr. Cheevers, trying to lull me into a false sense of security to get the same information? How do I know he's not waiting on the other side of that door?"

Sha'an's eyes widened improbably. "Good! You do well to question our motives. Trust is a currency you are wise not to spend too freely — especially out here. Unfortunately, I cannot offer you a satisfactory answer. I cannot make you trust us."

It wasn't the answer Morrissey expected; that, in itself, bought her some credibility. "Maybe you could start by telling me exactly who you people are — are you military? Some sort of galactic police force?"

Sha'an peered at him through slitted eyelids, as if she were looking for just the right words for him to comprehend without sending him into shock. "We belong to an organisation called the Alien Liberation Front. At its root, the ALF is devoted to the search and rescue of sentient life forms being used for illegal experimentation."

Morrissey blanched. "What sort of experimentation?"

"It has long been acknowledged that a certain amount of biological testing is required to further develop the civilised worlds, to harness beneficial technologies, advance medical science."

"We do the same — with non-sentient lifeforms, that is," said Morrissey. "Some things just can't be replicated artificially."

"Just so. But there are strict rules governing these practices. However, some races operate on a more…flexible ethical scale, employing a specific brand of dark biology. They prey on those they judge to be lower lifeforms to use for their own scientific whims. They target civilisations in their technological infancy — like yours — and collect samples of these species against their will, treating them without mercy or compassion."

"So that's where you come in?"

"Just so. We attempt to bring the offending parties to justice, though this is not always achievable."

"Are you a government agency, part of some sort of interplanetary federation or something?"

"You are correct in surmising that the problems are widespread, across many star systems spanning many sectors of the known galaxy, but no one government is able to administer such laws. The bureaucracy would collapse under its own weight trying to achieve consensus on such matters. Alliances are sometimes formed, and they do what they can, but many governments turn a blind eye if it does not affect them directly. And sometimes, it is those very governments who are secretly funding the illegal research. We must tread very carefully."

"So you think Cheevers was running one of these illegal research facilities?"

"Possibly, but it does not fit the pattern. Interrogation is not usually part of the research protocol."

"Though he wasn't just asking questions. Right before you guys showed up, he said something about 'looking for answers in the wrong places'. I don't know what he meant but whatever it was, it didn't seem to be a result of my interrogations."

Sha'an looked to Lillum, their expressions unreadable. "That is most interesting. It is a shame we arrived when we did. Maybe we would have discovered his true objective."

"Are you kidding? I dread to think what they would have done to me next. By the way, how did you find me?"

"One of our agents reported that a sentient being was being held on that ship. We were bound by our code to act."

Morrissey's eyes lit up, a rush of hope burning through him like wildfire. "Do you mean Kiki? Is Kiki Pashmina working for you? Is she your agent?"

"I'm sorry, Morrissey," said Sha'an, "but we do not know this Kiki person."

"But if she isn't your agent, then who is she? And where is she?"

"We have as many questions about this situation as you do. Possibly more. But first, we must make you safe."

"You mean we're not safe here? I feel pretty safe. Can't you just take me home, then?"

"That is not advisable. Earth is not safe for you." Sha'an turned to Lillum. "Is he ready?"

Lillum checked her diagnostic readouts. "He is surprisingly resilient. Whether or not he is ready, that is not for knowing."

"Excuse me," said Morrissey, "I don't want to be a bother, but what do you mean, is he ready? Ready for what?"

"For transport."

"I thought you said I couldn't go home. Where are you taking me?"

"Whoever this Dr. Cheevers is, he seems most determined to analyse you. Two of his ships are on a direct intercept trajectory. Rescuing you was our first priority. Keeping you rescued must naturally follow. Lillum, tell Sakko to meet us in the launch bay with a full tactical kit."

Lillum's upper body shifted uneasily from side to side. "You're taking him yourself?" She looked toward a large rectangular tank throbbing in the corner of the Med-Pod. "I thought with Barrek in the recovery module, you'd want to stay with the ship."

"Syddyk can handle the ship while I'm gone. I must lead this mission myself." She placed a hand on one of Lillum's forearms. "Don't worry, we'll be fine."

Both Lillum's eyestalks drooped simultaneously.

Sha'an palmed open the door. "Come, Morrissey. We must go." She did not turn to see if he followed.

Lillum carved a strange, sideways zigzag in the air. "Do your people accept wishes of good fortune?"

"Why, am I going to need it?"

"I'm afraid you will. Very much."

Morrissey joined Sha'an in a clear, cylindrical lift; it dropped below decks with a swipe of her hand. "So…are we going anywhere nice?" he said, trying to force a smile into the sombre mood.

Sha'an's T-Chip obviously didn't deal well with sarcasm. "I do not understand. Nice? We are taking you to safety."

"Yes, I get that part, but I'm beginning to wonder why getting me to safety sounds like such a dangerous prospect. Where exactly is this safety zone?"

"Would it mean anything to you if I gave you a location? Your only point of reference is your homeworld."

She was right. It would be like picking a garden slug up from a tomato plant in Essex and telling him he was going to the Empire State Building. "Maybe there's no point in telling me where you're taking me, but you could tell me why it's safer than anywhere else. I can understand abstract concepts, you know."

"Very well. We are taking you to Xrrka."

"Is that a city? A planet?"

"Xrrka is the founder of the ALF and our prime benefactor. She will know the most prudent course of action to take. She will keep you safe until we can unravel your mystery. You must trust us, Morrissey. We are trying to do our best for you."

"I know and I'm sorry if I seem ungrateful. I just feel so…alienated." There was no other word for it.

"I understand but I will never lie to you. I fear it is going to get much worse before it gets better."

"Well, you could lie a little."

They exited the lift and headed through a massive doorway that led into a chamber of Morrissey's childhood wonders. Two hefty vessels were nested in giant conveyor racks on either side of the enormous shuttle hangar. If Earth's space shuttles were the Ford Transits of NASA's space program, these ships could only be compared to Ferraris: lean and muscular, sleek and sexy, with subtle delta curves and massive thrusters poised for business.

They climbed a gangway and entered the nearer of the two shuttles through its rear loading ramp. "We will travel to a nearby transit station, making several random hyperspace jumps to ensure we are not being followed. Once there, we will board a commercial transport, blending in with the masses. You will not draw undue attention.

Morrissey was agog. Hyperspace! At home, chemical rockets were still needed to struggle free of Earth's grip, and even then it would take three days to reach the moon. Interstellar travel was a distant wet dream for human aerospace engineers, yet it seemed these beings had cracked the superluminal code good and proper.

The shuttle was not designed for extended comfort. Its layout was pragmatic at best — functional yet compact, roomy enough to move around in but not lavish in its amenities. There were acceleration couches for four in the passenger cabin with two more in the cockpit for pilot and co-pilot.

Speaking of co-pilots, a large, densely packed creature bounded up the loading ramp toward them. It moved on two tree trunks that might have been legs, heavy sturdy steps clunking on the deck plating. A mound of flesh and bone, which turned out to be the creature's head, protruded from its V-shaped torso, reeling back into a chest cavity at the sight of Morrissey. It dumped the heavy tactical packs at his feet as it cranked its neck out toward him like a tortoise. Morrissey recoiled imperceptibly but dared not back down. He was, quite literally, playing with the big boys, now.

"This is Sakko," said Sha'an.

Morrissey tried to look the alien in the eye but found he had four from which to choose, each as black and still as the dead of space. Its face was roughly pitted with scar tissue and his breath smelt vaguely of sulphur. "I don't suppose you're the entertainment director?"

"I'm the muscle," said Sakko.

Morrissey wondered whether the translation was metaphorical in that Sakko was designed for strength of both body and spirit or whether it was a literal exclamation, as he surely was pure muscle.

"Sakko is a combat veteran from the Thetyl system. We may not have need of his skills where we're going, but it is better to have and not need than to need and not have."

Morrissey nodded absently. In all honesty, he'd rather not have and not need but he was literally out of his element.

"Come," she said. "We'd best get you situated."

As Morrissey eased into his acceleration chair, it whirred and whined, hugging him in all the right places. He'd been wondering how a ship built for such varied lifeforms would accommodate his human proportions. Customizable common elements only made sense.

A voice chimed through the comm system. "Sha'an, it's Syddyk. This is where we say our goodbyes."

"For now, Syddyk."

"For now. We're beginning the hangar depressurization sequence. You'll be ready to go in…one minute forty."

At his mark, a klaxon blared outside the shuttle and a mechanical voice droned on about clearing the deck of all personnel.

"Thank you, Syddyk. We're all locked up and strapping in. All systems are blue across the board. Hyperdrive is spun up and standing by. Take care of the ship while we're gone — and of one another."

"I will. But we'll see you soon."

Morrissey had only spent a short time with this crew, but he already sensed a tight bond between them, as if they'd all been through something epic and had come out the other side that much stronger for the experience.

Sha'an tugged on Morrissey's harness for one final safety check. "I must get to the cockpit. We will be disengaging soon." She moved quickly to her seat beside Sakko and belted in.

Metal cranked on metal as the conveyor track shifted the shuttle into launch position. There was a brief lurch as the thrusters fired, a warm idle at first, followed by a scream to action as the sleek vessel dropped from the belly of the mothership and cut a full burn into the dark of space. There was another flash from behind and then a steady crush of acceleration. Morrissey didn't get the visual sense of speed that years of movies and TV had conditioned him to expect. Except for the slight feeling of heaviness, he wouldn't have known he was moving at all.

Sha'an had explained that they needed to put distance between themselves and the mothership while they prepared for their solo hyperspace jump. It was critical that the jump-drive fields of the two vessels didn't overlap; apparently, that would be very bad for the health of all concerned.

After a few minutes of continuous acceleration, Morrissey felt the pressure ease. They coasted at this speed for another ten minutes before he heard Sha'an's voice over the comm. "Morrissey, we're about to make the first hyperspace jump. Brace yourself."

CHAPTER 9

A s the legendary space pirate, Han Solo, once said, "Travelin' through hyperspace ain't like dustin' crops." What he neglected to mention was that hyperspace was very much like being stretched across infinity as the empty void folded around you. He also failed to mention that it's like being blinded by a blowtorch as the stars sparked and twisted in a psychedelic tornado of searing fire. He failed to mention that it's like having your skin plugged into an electrical socket and your eyeballs peeled by a lemon zester. He never mentioned any of that...not once.

On the bright side, there were no inertial shears tearing your body atom from atom and no bone-crushing g-forces pancaking you into the bulkheads. In hyperspace, your brain was your own worst enemy, a fragile creature backed into a corner, grasping for logic to explain the spatial discord it perceived. Everyone reacted to hyperspace differently. Most got used to it — some went insane while trying. It was mind over matter, and it all depended on how strong your mind was.

At least, that's what Sha'an was trying to tell Morrissey as he lay rigid and white-knuckled in his acceleration chair, trying to breathe in through his nose and out through his mouth, just the way the manuals had always said.

She handed him a tube of clear fluid. "You should drink this. It will help you settle, fortify you for the next jump."

"You couldn't...have given me...that before?"

"You wouldn't have been able to keep it down."

Morrissey's muscles unlocked somewhat as he took a sip from the tube. It was cool and slightly sweet and went down like syrup. He handed the empty flask back to Sha'an and flexed blood into his starving extremities. "How long before the next jump?"

Sha'an checked her chrono. "Thirty-three minutes."

"Can't you drug me or put me to sleep or something? I don't need to be awake during this, do I?"

"When we rescued you from Cheevers' ship you were unconscious. You will acclimate much more easily if you are conscious now. One day your life may depend on it and you'll look back and thank me for the lesson. You will get used to it, I promise."

Sha'an's lips pinched upward. From Morrissey's perspective, it looked as if she'd just sucked a lemon but in the context of their conversation he took it as a smile. "Thank you, Sha'an."

"I will let you rest now."

"No. Wait. Don't go." Morrissey had so much to say, so much to ask, so much to process. "I will be able to go home soon, won't I?" She took too long to answer. "Sha'an?"

"We will do everything in our power to make it so."

"And what happens to me if you can't make it so? Will I end up like the other strays you rescue?"

"We do our best to repatriate them, or if we can't we find a suitable environment for them to live out a full and productive life. Some are beyond saving, so severe is the damage. Some cannot adjust to life outside of captivity, so devastating was the trauma they faced. But your situation is different. Cheevers had no other captives on his ship that we could find. This is not a common practice of specimen procurement. Such risks and expenses are highly unusual for one test subject. You seem to be...something else."

"I don't know whether to be flattered or frightened."

"Remember what I said: I will never lie to you. A certain amount of fear is usually wise. I find it helps with self-preservation."

"Not exactly the confidence builder I was hoping for."

"For the time being, you are safer with us than on your Earth."

Morrissey sunk back into his acceleration chair and thought wistfully of home. "You'd like it, you know, Earth. Sure people can be complete dicks to one another but at its core, it really is quite beautiful."

"I know," she said. "I've been there."

"You've been...to Earth?"

"A very long time ago."

"Was it an ALF mission?"

"It was long before I was recruited by Xrrka. It was a mission of a much more...personal nature." Sha'an flushed, betraying a subtle hint of words spoken out of turn. "A story for another time, I'm afraid."

Morrissey measured Sha'an's alien expression against his human sensibilities. He couldn't be sure if he saw regret or sorrow or...something else, but he chose not to press the matter. "What about the rest of the ALF team?"

"The ALF is largely comprised of volunteers, many of whom were liberated test subjects looking to repay their debt by helping others."

"Like Sakko?" Morrissey jerked his thumb toward the cockpit.

"Sakko was a prisoner of war when we found him. He was interned in a slave compound on a mining asteroid — one of the harshest, most brutal places I've ever encountered, a place where only the strongest of both body and mind could survive. It says a lot about him that he did. Naturally, he wanted to turn the death and despair he faced into a force for good."

"What about Xrrka, the being you're taking me to see? Was she a former test subject?"

"Not much is known about her history. Not much is asked. We are just grateful for her generosity and guidance."

"Well, it takes a special kind of courage to do what you all do. Don't think I'm not appreciative."

Sha'an flushed. "Not courage. Simply...duty."

Morrissey was beginning to gain a better understanding of what bound the ALF together. At least they would have some empathy for his plight and have his safety at the forefront of their motives. "Let's just hope Xrrka can figure out why I'm so special."

Sha'an pinched another smile and for the slimmest of moments, Morrissey felt a glimmer of hope — until Sakko's booming voice shattered the calm.

"Sha'an, we are three minutes from jump."

"Affirmative." She placed her hand on Morrissey's; it was warm and dry and slightly rubbery. "You need only relax. Focus on the now. The rest will work itself out. The jump should be smoother this time."

Right now, the next hyperspace jump was the last thing on Morrissey's mind.

CHAPTER 10

Morrissey gazed out from the main viewport in the passenger cabin and let the mind-bending dance of colour trip all his sensory alarms at once. It was his third hyperspace jump and not only had he grown accustomed to the swirling head and quivering stomach, he'd actually come to look forward to the mesmerising light show as well.

"I knew you would adjust," said Sha'an as she eased into the cabin behind him. Her voice was a refreshing breeze. "Some even become addicted to the experience."

"I don't doubt it. It really is something, isn't it. Hypnotic. I still can't seem to get my head around it. No matter how many times I try to step outside of myself, the fact that I'm travelling through space — through hyperspace — just blows my mind." Morrissey couldn't tell if his colloquialisms were making it through Sha'an's T-Chip in one piece. "It's not just the view that's amazing, it's everything. I've spent most of my adulthood in search of proof of extraterrestrial life. And here you are, standing right in front of me. Meeting you and the rest of the crew. I mean, how often do you get to meet a genuine alien?"

"Actually, there are quite a lot of us out here." She pinched a sly smile.

Morrissey had come to learn that Sha'an had a pretty good sense of humour. "You know what I mean, though. This kind of thing doesn't happen to me every day. Yet I feel...I don't know...at home. Does that make any sense?"

"Maybe you were always destined to roam amongst the stars."

Morrissey smiled to himself. Who would have thought it: Dave Morrissey, Intergalactic Adventurer!

But his daydreams would have to wait. Alarms rippled through the shuttle, charging Morrissey's heart with fresh dread. The ship groaned in protest, pitching and stretching before his eyes, sending him careening off the bulkheads. Sha'an, somewhat more surefooted, grabbed the handholds, pulling herself into the cockpit. Morrissey bounced in behind her on unsteady feet.

"Sakko! What the [untranslatable] is going on?" Sakko was furiously punching buttons and scanning the displays floating before him. Lights flared rudely across the consoles as the two aliens tried to establish exactly what was twisting the space around them. "Is it a planet? Did we pass too close to a star?"

"I don't know," said Sakko. "We're caught in the gravity well of...something. It's either going to pull us out of hyperspace or pull us apart." The ship shuddered violently as if it were making up its mind which it would be.

Sha'an made the decision for it. "Disengage the hyperdrive." Sakko fumbled with the controls, his stubby digits stuttering over the console. He wrenched back a lever and the cyclone of starlight slowed and snapped back into the pinpoint brilliance of normal space. The shuttle lurched as the conventional drive engines cut back in, fighting to stabilise their frenzied trajectory. "Give me a tactical display; I want to see what we're dealing with."

A three-dimensional representation of the surrounding space poured from a node in the cockpit ceiling, hanging like a cloud cubed into sectors, a blue pulse at the centre.

"I'm assuming that's us?" said Morrissey.

Sha'an nodded. An orange pulse throbbed slowly from above and behind, the distance between them growing shorter. "But what's that? Give me a visual. Set sensors to maximum." The main view screen lit up, showing nothing but the blackness of space. Or so Morrissey thought. "Magnify." The image shimmered. Sha'an muttered a string of unintelligible words, no doubt straining her T-Chip with profane excess. "It's not a planet. Or a star. It's a ship."

Morrissey strained to see out the viewports, trying to reconcile the tactical display with the real space around them. He thought it would be like the movies, where spaceships were lit up for dramatic effect. But this was no movie. He could barely make out the tiny, darkened hulk, a dim ghost smudged across the black, moving steadily — or not. He couldn't tell. "A ship? Is that so unusual? We are in space."

"Quite unusual," said Sha'an. "You may have heard that space is very, very big. The odds of two vessels coincidentally appearing in the same location in deep space are infinitesimal. Not to mention the fact that we are traversing an extremely remote sector of the galaxy."

"Is it possible that Cheevers found a way to follow us, after all?"

Sha'an checked her readouts. "I can't detect a transponder beacon, but the energy signature doesn't match Cheever's ship. That doesn't mean it's not one of his friends, though I still don't understand how they could have tracked us. We've made some very unpredictable course adjustments."

"Maybe the ship isn't following us," said Morrissey. "Maybe it was pulled out of hyperspace by the same thing that pulled us out?"

"It is a good guess, Morrissey, but there is nothing on the sensors big enough to have pulled us free."

"What would it take?"

"The hyperdrive of a starship can't properly function while under the influence of a gravity well of a significant stellar body — a star, a planet, even a large asteroid."

"So, another ship wouldn't have been able to destabilise us?"

Sha'an was fixated on the view screen. "No...a ship couldn't do that...unless..." This last was said to herself more than to Morrissey or Sakko.

"Unless what?"

"Unless it had an artificial gravity well generator on board. But that would be highly irregular — and highly illegal. Pirates have been known to use them to draw out their prey but they're generally not worth the expense – or the risk."

"But why would pirates be laying a trap in such a remote region of space?" said Morrissey. "Not exactly a great fishing spot. If someone were out to get us, they'd already have to know we were here."

"Just so," said Sha'an, "nothing good will come from this. Sakko, get us out of here." Silence. "Sakko! Evasive manoeuvres. Get us out — " Sha'an spun toward her co-pilot, coming face to muzzle with the business end of Sakko's pistol.

Morrissey backed away slowly.

Sakko strummed the flight console, then punched a control at his belt. Thunder rolled under the deck plating as warning lights strobed across the displays. "Sorry, Sha'an. We're not going anywhere. Not even a little. I've just disabled the Jump-Drive."

"You what? Why?"

Sakko's tortoise neck twisted in its socket. "I would have thought that was obvious. Financial gain is usually the best answer."

"But our mission, what about him?" Sha'an gestured to Morrissey. "We've got a responsibility to — "

"No. You've got a responsibility. I don't know him, and I certainly don't care about him."

"How could you? After all we've done to help you. We took you in, gave you a home. Think of your life in that prison — the brutality, the desperation."

"I am thinking of that life. I didn't struggle to survive for this. You liberated me, that much is true, but I'm not one of your wounded animals that you've patched up and patted on the head. I was desperate when I joined your crew, a former soldier with a fistful of skills and nowhere to ply them. I thought it would work out with the ALF but there's not a lot of money in philanthropy. Until now, that is." His grin dripped with menace.

"Surely your experiences taught you that those ways are not the path to inner peace?"

"My experiences taught me to look out for myself because no one else will."

You wouldn't be standing here if that were true. She didn't say the words but Morrissey saw them burning in her eyes. "And what about them?" Sha'an motioned toward the ship looming ever larger on the view screen. "Are they looking out for you?"

"I couldn't care less about them, either, only the feel of their currency. It seems they were very eager to reacquire this...*thing*. I couldn't resist the offer."

"But how...when?"

Sakko seemed amused. "After we rescued the human from Cheevers' ship, I sent them several coded transmissions hidden in our sensor sweeps. They've been following us every step of the way."

"I trusted you."

"As you can see, that is your problem, not mine."

Morrissey had been moving slowly around to Sakko's flank. If he could distract him, maybe jump him, then Sha'an could make a frontal attack. She was armed. If she could only —

Sakko, weapon still trained on Sha'an, was having none of it. "You just stay where you are, *Human*. I need you alive." He turned back to Sha'an. "You, on the other hand, I could go either way."

"You know I can't let you take him."

"I had a feeling you were going to say that." His pistol flashed, white hot. The blast took her hard in the chest, spinning her over the command chair and onto the deck.

Morrissey's stomach knotted as he leapt toward her slumped body. "Sha'an!"

"I said stay where you are, or money or no money I will end you!" Sakko dialled up the comm panel. "Hyperdrive is disabled. Engines are locked to my command. We're ready."

Morrissey didn't move. His eyes flicked nervously from the angry muzzle of Sakko's weapon to Sha'an's motionless body. The hole in her chest still crackled with energy, smoking her jumpsuit. The smell of burning flesh stung his nostrils. He'd only known her briefly, but the loss cut him surprisingly deeply, maybe because she was his only lifeline in this nightmare. It was now up to him and him alone.

If he could only get to Sha'an's weapon. Of course, then he'd still have to outshoot Sakko — a trained soldier — but at least he'd go down fighting. Maybe there was a better way. "Ready for what? When you spoke to that ship you said, 'we're ready'. Ready for what?"

Sakko looked about as dense as a black hole. "Ready to be picked up, is what. Ready to be paid. Ready to be rid of you."

"So, they want me? Alive?"

"More's the pity. If I had my way — "

"Ah, but you don't, do you. If it were up to you, you'd have me dead, wouldn't you?"

"You'd be a lot less bother, certainly. But unfortunately, a lot less valuable."

"You don't get it." Morrissey stared into as many of Sakko's vacant black eyes as he could manage. "My God, you're not very bright, are you. Don't they have schools in space?"

"That's enough!" Sakko waved his pistol with half-hearted menace. "What do you mean?"

"If I'm the valuable one, then what does that make you?"

"I'm the one they're going to reward."

Morrissey allowed himself a cheeky smirk. He shook his head slowly while moving ever-so-slightly closer to Sha'an. "No, no, no. If I'm of value to them, then I'm an asset. If they have to pay you, then where does that put you?" Sakko's features spasmed with confusion. "Come on, you can do it. Does the term liability translate? How about loose end? What about... *expendable*?"

"They need me."

"No. They *needed* you, sure. Sorry mate, but you fall squarely into the debit column. Once they have me, well, you can see how those books balance out."

Sakko ratcheted his tortoise-neck to full length. He gaped at the ship on the viewscreen, his dull eyes full of questions and doubts, his mouth moving without sound or sense. Morrissey jumped at the opportunity, bolting toward Sha'an's silent body and the weapon strapped to her hip. But Sakko wheeled, faster than Morrissey figured his bulk would permit, firing once. The splash of energy seared the bulkhead, missing him by mere inches.

Sakko cursed, holstered his weapon, and lunged across the short distance between them. He thrust his fist out toward Morrissey, a short, sharp blow to the back of his head. Morrissey tumbled out of the cockpit and crumpled into the passenger cabin. A double-fisted hammer smash from Sakko across his back forced much needed air from his lungs. A sharp slap of meaty hands came down around his skull, wrenching him to his feet, and then a club-arm swing spun him hard into the bulkhead. Morrissey's plan had seemed a lot less painful on the drawing board.

Sakko was relentless. A massive tree stump of a knee ploughed into Morrissey's groin, doubling him over. Morrissey could barely keep his insides, inside. The alien's powerful arm looped around his neck, tightening like a steel band. Pressure welled behind his eyes, his arms flailing as his energy ebbed.

And then he felt it — hard and irregular: the butt of Sakko's pistol. His fingers danced eagerly at its heel, but time and energy were running out. Morrissey focussed his remaining strength, counting on only one thing — that no matter how stout the tree, the smallest of its twigs could still be broken. He grappled with the alien's fingers until he found the smallest *twig*, wrenching it up, down and all around until it finally snapped with a sickening pop.

Sakko squealed like a stuck space-pig, and in that moment of pain his grip eased, just enough. Morrissey bit hard down on Sakko's wrist until it spurted blackness. He drove his elbow backward into the creature's sternum, which could have been his throat. Sakko staggered in a dazed mess, falling against a computer console, but not before Morrissey had lifted the alien's pistol from its holster.

"Alright! Now it's my turn." Morrissey gulped at the air, shaking with the rush of adrenaline. He fought to steady his aim with a two-handed firing stance. "Don't move. Actually, do move. You get those bloody engines back on line and get us the fuck out of here."

Sakko leered with a disquieting level of calm. "Well played, *Human*. I didn't think you had it in you. But I'm not going to do any such thing."

"You are, or so help me, I will shoot you so fucking hard."

"You won't shoot."

Morrissey fought to slow his racing pulse and ease his breaths. He summoned his calmest, coolest, most Clint Eastwoody voice. "Granted, I'm a little shaky so my aim might be slightly off. But rest assured, I will shoot if you don't get us moving. And at this distance, I don't imagine I'll miss, shaky or not."

Sakko laughed. He'd obviously never seen a Clint Eastwood movie before. "You won't shoot because — "

Morrissey fired. Click. Nothing happened. He pressed the firing stud again. Click. Still nothing. Once more with feeling. Click. Nothing. Shit.

"It's a biometric weapon, calibrated to my genetic signature only. So you are out of luck. That is, unless you have another weapon hidden away. You don't have another weapon, do you?"

Then, from Morrissey's periphery, light and energy scorched the air and struck Sakko in the stomach.

"No...but I do." The voice was weak, perched on the edge of oblivion. It was Sha'an. During Morrissey's struggle with Sakko, she'd managed to leverage herself into a serviceable firing position, aiming along the length of her body. Her pistol bucked again — once, twice — spinning Sakko backward. His massive body erupted in a fountain of charred bone and flesh, splattering the cabin with the grisly debris. He slumped heavily into an acceleration chair, his head dangling precariously by skin and muscle alone, seared ribbons of tissue sizzling like bacon. His body twitched for several seconds before finally falling still.

Morrissey shook involuntarily, revulsion turning to relief as he rushed to Sha'an's side. "Jesus. I thought you were dead."

"I am...or near enough to it. Quickly...we don't have much time..." She motioned to the viewscreen, the hulking ship moving steadily toward them like a predatory dinosaur.

Morrissey cradled her in his trembling arms, her chest wound still smouldering. Bubbles of dark blue blood soaked her tunic and frothed from her mouth. Sweat beaded her naked brow and her skin was as pale as frosted glass. "Tell me what to do. Is there a medical kit? Maybe I can patch you up."

"No time...have to leave."

"Yes, leave. That's a great idea. Can you get the engines working? Who's going to fly the ship? I hope you're able to fly the ship because I can't fly the ship." Morrissey was tap dancing dangerously close to panic.

"No...not ship. Escape pod."

Sure. Any starship worth its salt was bound to have an escape pod lying around. "Okay, we'll use the escape pod to get the hell out — "

"Not we...you."

It took a second or two for Sha'an's words to register. "Oh, no. I'm not going anywhere without you. We're both getting in that escape pod."

"Have to stay...have to stop...them." The enemy was all but upon them, now.

"No, Sha'an. We'll get out together. I'm not leaving you behind."

"Morrissey...please. I know this is a lot to ask...but there is no other way. I won't last...much longer."

He didn't know her internal physiology but there certainly did seem to be an awful lot of it on her jumpsuit.

"Please trust. This is...what we are. This is what we do."

"Okay. Okay." He tried to calm himself, for Sha'an's sake if not for his own. "What do I do?"

"The pod will get you as far as...the Hyraldi Sector. Close enough...to Phonsekka Station. There, you will board a commercial cargo vessel, as we planned. Deal only with...Nashek Freight and Transport. They are allies...Xrrka is on...JuHu Station in the Bandresek System."

Only a matter of hours ago, Morrissey had pleaded with Sha'an to tell him where they were going. Now he wished he'd kept his bloody mouth shut. "It's too much, Sha'an. I can't remember all that. I need you with me."

"You must memorise it, Morrissey. And you must not record...any of the plans for others to find. Your survival will depend on it."

Morrissey's head was spinning. He didn't know if he could keep all the names straight and he hoped the T-Chip wasn't adding an extra syllable or dotting an 'i' when it should have been crossing a 't'. He took a deep breath and repeated the unfamiliar words over and over until they set like jelly in his brain. "Okay. I think I've got it."

"Not *think*. You must *know*."

The words stumbled awkwardly out of Morrissey's mouth. "Hyraldi Sector to Phonsekka Station. Nashek Freight and Transport to Xrrka on JuHu Station, Bandresek System. Got it."

Sha'an seemed satisfied. "A distress beacon will transmit...once you exit hyperspace. You will be found...do not panic. Reveal as little...as possible. And remember...do not trust easily. This is a diverse enough hub...you won't stand out. Be wary of those...who question too deeply. The pod records...will show that it jettisoned...just prior to the destruction of this shuttle."

Morrissey's chest tightened, realising what she meant. Once he entered the escape pod, he knew he would never see Sha'an again. The thought filled him with a profound emptiness. She had been his safety net, but in a short time she had also become a trusted friend. He squeezed her bony hand; it was cold and sticky. He hoped the gesture conveyed some measure of comfort. Her lips pinched into the expression he'd decided was a smile. "Is there anyone I should contact, to tell them..." He couldn't finish the thought.

"The people who will grieve for me...will know of my fate soon enough. Your priority...is getting to Xrrka. She will know...what to do from there." Sha'an reached into a belt pouch and retrieved a small, flat rectangular tab. "This credit chip has enough currency…for any incidental expenses. Now…lift me to the control panel."

He hefted her slight frame to the pilot's console; she was lighter than he expected. Her fingers fumbled across the pad until she was satisfied. "It is done. The escape pod is programmed. All is ready."

Except me, thought Morrissey.

Sha'an pressed her forehead against his and held it. "We will not meet again, David Morrissey. But knowing you…this short time…has brightened my passage through this universe…and will help light the way…into the next."

He didn't know what to say. "I'm not a praying man, Sha'an. And even if I were, none of it would mean anything to you."

"It is enough that you are here…at my end."

A lump caught him unexpectedly in the throat. It was a good thing he had no words left to speak.

"Make this count," she said.

An elliptical panel in the bulkhead slid aside, revealing a narrow chute. Sha'an motioned for Morrissey to enter. He squeezed her hand one more time before reluctantly climbing into the opening and sliding into the waiting pod. The door hissed shut the minute he thudded onto a padded acceleration couch.

Restraints wound around his shoulders and waist automatically, securing him in place. The entire space was little more than a coffin: eight feet long, four feet wide, and three feet high. He could sit up, but only just. Display screens lined the sides of the enclosure, all facing him with dead stares. A control panel hummed to life directly in front of his face; from his prone perspective, it appeared on the ceiling of the pod. Sha'an had said that all the pod functions would be automated so he touched nothing.

An image burst to life on the display screen, that of the large ship manoeuvring into position above the small shuttle so that its belly angled toward its prey, the heavy doors yawning wide to swallow them whole. If Sha'an was going to eject the pod before that happened, she was cutting it awfully close. For one brief, sick moment, he feared she may already be dead. Then a small panel lit up beneath the main viewer; strange symbols flashed orange across its face, accompanied by a mechanical alien voice.

"Malak sood... Malak sevet... Malak akt… Sookh…"

The language was unintelligible — at first. But as his T-Chip worked its subtle magic on his brain, the symbols slowly morphed into recognisable forms, the mechanical voice shifting into familiar English.

"...Elet... Neenh... Selet... Five... Four..."

The numbers flared from orange to blue and cycled through their final sequence. "...Three... Two... One..."

The pod shuddered with the heavy clank of metal on metal; the laboured whine of hydraulics echoed through the small space as the shuttle released its clamps. Boosters fired and the small craft surged from the launch tube, sliding into the black. The image on the screen switched to rear-view, showing the predator engulfing Sha'an's shuttle in one gulp, the heavy doors sealing around it. In only seconds, Sha'an was gone, to what fate, he could only guess.

If they'd spotted him, then her sacrifice was for nothing. They would certainly pursue him — or worse. But there was no time for them to act. In the space of a blink, the large ship coughed violently and buckled at its middle, right where Sha'an's shuttle had entered. It haemorrhaged fire briefly before the vacuum of space choked the life from it. Sha'an's plan had worked. The chain reaction was inevitably fatal as the ship — both ships — splintered into a billion shards before his eyes and the waves of dying energy gently buffeted his pod.

Hoping against hope, he half expected to see Sha'an rocketing toward the escape pod on a jetpack in a glorious flight of victory. But the reality was bleak, and isolation was his only companion. The viewscreen cycled back to forward view, the observation panels displaying only emptiness around him. And right on schedule, space warped and stars stretched into long threads of light, spinning a kaleidoscopic tapestry of colour as the small pod lurched warily into hyperspace. Morrissey took a deep, long, lonely breath. It was going to be a bumpy ride.

CHAPTER 11

True to Sha'an's plan, the escape pod was picked up by a long-range patrol shortly after emerging from hyperspace. The last thing Morrissey remembered was the pod being torn open like a can of sardines and him being gassed into unconsciousness. He awoke in a small booth facing a blank wall that suddenly flashed with a pale sheen. A voice spoke in a heavy mechanical thrum.

"File open. Case number 137-229HP-00213N. Species: Unknown. Origin: Unknown. Gender: Unknown. Status...Pending."

Morrissey took some minor offence at the 'unknown gender' reference but more troubling was that his status was 'pending'. Pending what was the question. As if in answer, the glowing wall panel shifted from opaque to transparent, revealing a metal drum about a metre in height. The lower half of the stout cylinder was studded with glowing lights while the upper tier consisted of a series of stacked rings, rotating independently of one another. An array of sockets pitted the metallic skin, all bare except for two, which sported long, articulated appendages of roughly human proportions. Atop the rings was a spherical node the size of a human head, embedded with two ocular disks, a nose-like knob, and a gleaming silver grille where a person's mouth would be.

The robot's voice had a canned synthetic quality, carefully measured in the pseudo rhythms of humanoid speech. "You have reached the Nogarra Refugee Processing Centre. This avatar has been chosen to emulate your physiological attributes in order to help you acclimate to your new surroundings." There was a long pause, then, "You are welcome. Your file will be processed with all the expediency our laws allow."

"Hang on a minute," said Morrissey, "I'm not a refugee. My ship blew up, is all. I escaped — hence the escape pod."

The robot ignored him. "If you require legal assistance, a list of representatives will be provided at your expense. In the interim, you will be held in a security housing centre suited to your biological requirements pending your hearing."

"Erm…just how long is this going to take?"

"The backlog places your file priority at…4.3 years."

Morrissey stared dead-faced at the robot. "4.3 years. Years? Look mate, I think my T-Chip must be broken. I don't suppose you meant hours? Or even days? I'll settle for days."

"We cannot be held responsible for T-Chip malfunctions. All belongings, including biological enhancements, remain the sole responsibility of the claimant."

"That's not what I meant. I just want to confirm that you actually meant years."

"Due to the high volume of open cases, your file will be processed in approximately 4.3 years. Plus or minus."

Morrissey wanted to collapse into a fetal ball. He tried to reason as much as one can with a robot. "If you could check the logs of my escape pod, you'll see that I'm not a refugee. My ship blowing up wasn't exactly planned."

"You will be given an opportunity to present your evidence at the time of your hearing in — "

"— I know, in 4.3 years."

"Correction, 4.45 years. The backlog has grown since this interview began. This is a very popular planet."

Morrissey bit his tongue and flexed his patience. "Look, I'm not trying to jump the queue, but doesn't it make more sense to take a few minutes to check the escape logs now rather than have to provide me with room and board for almost five years?"

"Such a course of action would fall outside normal operating protocols." The robot whirred quietly to itself as if baffled by the logical conundrum. "There would, however, be an administration fee."

Now we're getting somewhere. "How much?"

"10,000 credits," said the robot without missing a beat.

The sum sounded painful, but Morrissey reminded himself that on Earth, 10,000 rupees was only about 100 pounds. Sha'an had said there might be incidental costs. He fumbled in his jacket pocket for the credit chip she'd given him. His stomach knotted until he felt the slim tab of plastic turn over in his fingers. "Here, take it out of this."

The transparent shielding separating them rose into the ceiling as a panel opened in the robot's torso. "Place the tab in the reader slot."

Morrissey inserted the chip into the slot opening. Lighted digits rose from the display, indicating a balance of 15,000 credits. He winced as the figures began rolling back with sickening speed, not stopping until the balance read 2,000. 2000? "Erm, I thought you said the fee was 10,000. You deducted 13,000."

"The figure has been amended to reflect additional fees."

"Such as?"

"Administration tax, processing tax, handling charges, handling charge tax, landing fees — "

"Landing fees? I didn't exactly have a choice."

The robot ignored him. "Landing fee tax. Legal fees. And a conversion rate fee."

As the mechanical cash register finally came to the end of its seemingly endless list of charges, Morrissey could have sworn he heard it run out of breath; he wanted to kick it right in the gearbox. "I don't suppose there's any point in launching an appeal?"

"Wait time for a hearing with The Appellate Panel is — "

"Never mind."

"Press your right thumb against the pad to initiate the transaction."

Morrissey did as the robot directed and watched his lifeline melt away. The panel pulsed blue, indicating the transaction was complete. "So how long before you can check my escape pod's logs?"

"Accessing." The robot whirred quietly to itself for a period bordering on too long.

"Is anything the matter? The logs back up my story, no?"

Suddenly the robot jolted back to life, its voice almost cheery — in a phoney, telemarketer sort of way. "Please forgive the delay; the investigation is complete."

"That was…quick?"

"All relevant logs have been retrieved, catalogued, and filed with the central hub. Your refugee claim has been reclassified and processed."

"See? That didn't hurt, did it?" said Morrissey, apparently to himself.

A thin metal tube extended from the robot's nether regions. It latched onto Morrissey's forearm and held him firmly while it tattooed him with an intricate swirl of fluorescent yellow ink. "This is your visitor visa. It is valid for precisely five days, after which your profile will be transmitted to local authorities, and you will be tagged as a fugitive and arrested on sight."

A tongue of transparent plastic oozed from a dispensary slot in the robot's belly. On it were some vague images of items resembling food. "Please accept this restaurant voucher as a welcome gift and enjoy with our compliments. It is valid at almost three dining establishments in the district. Welcome to Phonsekka Prime."

"Thanks. I think. Wait — did you say Phonsekka Prime?"

"That is correct."

"Does that mean I'm close to Phonsekka Station?"

"The station orbits Phonsekka Prime. There are regular shuttles leaving from the spaceport daily."

"I don't suppose we're close to the spaceport?" Morrissey knew his luck wouldn't be that good.

"For your convenience there is a public transit terminal located to the west of the facility. You may obtain transit to the port from there. Follow the blue line toward the exit and have a nice day."

Morrissey decided that he would not have a nice day, partly because it would be next to impossible and partly just to spite the robot. Ahead, a wall panel retracted to reveal the aforementioned glowing blue strip, illuminating Morrissey's way to freedom. Well, sort of.

Morrissey's first true taste of an alien world was bitter and metallic, much like his experience with the Refugee Robot. The air was cool and damp as it pumped its way into his lungs and did God knows what to his circulatory system. The gravity of Phonsekka Prime seemed similar to Earth's, but he was sure he felt an extra spring in his step that wasn't reflected in his spirits.

He'd been popped out onto a busy thoroughfare teeming with a vast array of alien life: bipeds, quadrupeds, milli-peds — even undulating, gelatinous no-peds. Port cities on Earth were often a result of varied cultures rubbing up against one another in unique and exotic ways; if the myriad alien races on display were any indication, Phonsekka Prime seemed to be no different.

On the bright side, none of the passersby gave him a second glance, let alone a first. This relative anonymity calmed him somewhat as Sha'an's overriding piece of advice was for him to keep a low profile on his journey to find Xrrka. But first he had to get to the spaceport and book passage to Phonsekka Station. One step at a time.

His first step, however, was almost his last. A giant metallic hamster-ball of a vehicle rumbled past him — almost over him. It stopped several metres away where one of the aforementioned blobby no-peds poured out of a side hatch and began hurling curses at him that were only half-translatable. Apparently, he was standing in the alien's parking spot — or violating its mother's sitting hole...or something. Morrissey held his hands up in what he hoped was the universal display of apology and then quickly moved away from the brewing trouble.

In the distance, ships' contrails scarred the pale grey-green of the early evening sky; he could just about make out the spark of a vessel's thrusters lifting it out of the atmosphere. Seemed like a sensible place to keep a spaceport.

A quick scan of the bustling concourse revealed the public transit terminal the Refugee Robot had referenced. Street signs blurred as his T-Chip filtered the information, feeding sense to his human brain. The bad news was that there seemed to be a transit strike; no mass ground transports were running. Shit.

Plan B lay with a string of taxis stretched across the far side of the depot, fifty metres away. He tapped on the window of one of the parked vehicles. Inside was a lanky, ruddy-faced being, a bit more naked than Morrissey would have liked. Four of his limbs rested casually on his steering pad while two more fanned over an info tablet showing what might have been alien pornography. The creature eyed Morrissey up and down, seemingly without the benefit of eyes. He raised two of his left limbs, gesturing vaguely toward the front of the vehicle queue, before sinking back into his tablet. Morrissey was glad to leave him to it.

At the first taxi in line, the door hissed open before Morrissey could speak.

"Destination?" said the frog-faced driver.

"Erm…the spaceport, please."

"Enter, citizen."

Morrissey didn't need to be told twice. "Before we go, I just want to be sure that I can get a shuttle to Phonsekka Station from there, right?"

"Yes, citizen. Most definite."

"Then by all means, drive on."

The air-taxi did not, in fact, drive on. "Payment?"

"Ah, yes, sorry. I'm new here. How...?"

"Cash is preference. Credit is easy to counterfeit."

"I'm afraid all I have is credit."

The driver hummed to himself. "Tab? Chip? Digi-Sensor? Opti-Cash?"

Morrissey showed the driver his credit tab, looking awkward yet hopeful. "How's this?"

"Digi-Sensor — is good. Hard to clone. Insert there."

A plate in the back of the driver's seat slid up, revealing a series of grimy slots. Morrissey found one that matched the dimensions of his credit tab and slid the plastic wafer in. The slot chirped as it accepted the tab and a readout appeared in the plate and on a heads-up display for the driver. A muffled voice buzzed from the small speaker. "Authenticate." Morrissey pressed his thumb against the plate as he'd done in the Refugee Centre. The screen flashed from orange to blue. Once the driver was satisfied, he lifted the vehicle a half dozen metres and sped over the ground traffic toward the spaceport. The gleaming towers that had twisted gracefully toward the heavens like spun crystal, gave way to lower, more modest structures. It made sense to keep the flight paths clear for traffic.

Morrissey felt some of his tension ease as the taxi skated over the sprawling cityscape and he began to relax — physically and emotionally. *Ping*. He'd averted a serious incarceration at the hands of the local authorities, and he'd done it using his own ingenuity. *Ping.* The accomplishment filled him with a suitable sense of pride, boosting his confidence and elevating his hopes. *Ping.* If he could navigate the bureaucracy of an alien world, well, the galaxy was the limit! *Ping.* All he had to do was book a shuttle to Phonsekka Station and find his way to Nashek Freight and Transport. Piece of cake. *Ping.* He just hoped that they were as friendly to the ALF's cause as Sha'an had intimated.

Buzz! Buzz! Buzz! Buzz! Buzz! His stomach knotted as the air-taxi dropped like a stone. "What is it? What's wrong? Is something wrong with the taxi? Are we going to crash?" Morrissey gripped the handrails on either side of his seat, as if the action would prevent him from being squashed like a grape if they did hit dirt.

But they didn't. Instead, the driver descended to street level where he skimmed smoothly into the nearest parking bay. He turned to Morrissey as the door hissed open. "End of journey."

Morrissey scanned the surroundings. "This is the spaceport?"

"Not."

"Then I don't understand. I paid to get to the spaceport."

"Not. Insufficient funds. End of journey."

"But I did pay. You saw me put my credit tab in the slot. Surely there was enough credit to get me to the spaceport."

"Surge Pricing in effect due to transit strike. Rates higher."

"You couldn't have told me that before we left, before dropping me here...in the middle of nowhere?"

"Not responsible."

"Are you bloody kidding me?" And then it dawned on him. The steady Ping that had kept rhythm throughout the short trip had, in fact, been the countdown of his funds burning through the credit meter as the distance piled up. Morrissey tried to force himself to a simmer. "Okay...how far to the spaceport from here?"

"Six, maybe eight kilometres. Maybe."

Morrissey had lost his bearings and could no longer see any evidence of aerial traffic in the darkening sky. "Which direction?"

The driver shrugged vaguely ahead.

Morrissey stewed. "I don't suppose you know when the last shuttle leaves?"

"Not. No more shuttles today."

Prick. "But why didn't you say — oh, forget it. Morrissey took his credit tab from the reader, empty or not. "Thank you so much for all your help." He wondered whether sarcasm made it through the driver's T-Chip and then realised he didn't care — it made him feel better. The air-taxi door almost scissored him in half as he exited the vehicle, the vehicle's repellers kicking up dirt and gravel, adding injury to insult.

Getting to Phonsekka Station was proving more difficult than Sha'an had made it seem. He'd have to wait until tomorrow to find a way onto a shuttle and then wheedle his way onto a Nashek transport. Piece of cake.

But first he'd have to find somewhere to spend the night. Judging by the seedy surroundings, he didn't fancy his chances. In some ways, this part of Phonsekka Prime resembled some of the more questionable sections of east London, both in foreboding mood and oppressive atmosphere. The fetid street stretched before him in a vulgar splash of red and green neon. Endless rows of garish establishments were stitched together by marquees even his T-Chip struggled to decipher. Dirt and grime of dubious origins smothered the prefab structures like a plague. Rusted doors and cracked plastic windows leaked noises that could have been songs of merriment or shrieks of mayhem. If the sense of smell was the doorway to memory, the pungent aromas steaming from the blackened air vents struck no familiar chords, but they did remind him that it had been forever since he'd had something to eat.

He fished around his pockets for the food voucher gifted to him by the Refugee Robot. He hadn't given it much thought at the time but now he treasured it like pure gold. The images on the voucher were generic at best; he only hoped he could find a restaurant that would honour it.

Before he could try his luck at the first establishment, a voice poked at him from behind. Three figures oozed from the depths of the shadows. Morrissey didn't like to judge on appearances alone but these three were pushing it. If they were up to no good, they certainly looked the part.

The first being was taller than Morrissey and bipedal. Though his frame was slim, there was something about the jagged protuberances poking through his tunic that suggested a certain menace. In the psychedelic street lighting, its slick skin glistened like gasoline and water swirling in the moonlight. As it drew closer, facial features sharpened into focus and Morrissey kind of wished they hadn't. Its conical skull was interspersed with a forest of vacillating tendrils. At the tip of each tendril was a puff of white fibres, like the feathery seeds of a dandelion. With no visible eyes, Morrissey figured these to be its sensory organs. Most disturbing was the being's mouth — a vertical gash that split its face, peeling back rhythmically, revealing double rows of needle-sharp teeth.

The creature's two comrades began a slow flanking manoeuvre, almost predatory. The one on the left had a powerful, squat body. Club fists, each the size of Morrissey's head, throbbed at the end of massive arms. The rough purple bark of its skull was studded with bony grey knobs while large ochre eyes looked impassively from under heavy lids. The third being looked as if it had woken in a hurry and put its skin on inside-out, sinews and arteries pulsing in a grisly network of chaos. Its head resembled a coconut with a prehensile snout drooping from the lower half.

The trio pushed in tighter, slowly herding him toward a nearby alley. Dandelion-Head leaned in too close for Morrissey's liking, its tendrils weaving in a curious dance.

"Nice night for walk, yes?"

It was disconcerting watching the sounds come from a mouth that was, for all intents and purposes, stuck on sideways. Morrissey nodded noncommittally. "I suppose it is."

"Maybe you like some company, yes?"

Okay. Harmless. Forthright. A little weird, perhaps. Morrissey chose his next words carefully. "Hey, thanks. That's really…no…I'm great. No problems here." Apparently, he didn't choose his words carefully at all.

"Maybe you pay us for some company, then," said Dandelion-Head, nudging him ever closer to the alley opening.

Morrissey suddenly had the disturbing thought that these aliens might be the local street prostitutes. His genitals initiated a sharp retreat and every orifice he owned went into sphincter-lock. "Erm…really…that's quite alright. No offence, fellas," *if you are fellas*, "but I've had a rough day — a rough few days, actually, and I'd really rather just be alone. I'm sure you understand."

The three aliens didn't seem to understand at all, pushing him hard against the alley wall.

"Alright, lads. Steady on. That's a bit unnecessary."

"Maybe you pay us to leave, then. Yes. You pay us, we go." Dandelion-Head waved half his tendrils toward his sidekicks who rippled in agreement.

"Look, I'm sorry but I don't have any money to give you. I just spent my last credits on an air-taxi to nowhere. Honest. Do you think I would have chosen to be dropped off here? Erm...no offence."

Dandelion-Head's tendrils stiffened, and his words puffed out in rancid gusts. "Most of the beings we threaten are not honest. Most say things that do not mean the truths. So we must believe that you are likewise. This can only equal the fact that you do have monies. For this reason, plus the fact that we enjoy, we must now hurt you. Yes?"

The creature's hand splayed across Morrissey's chest, its scabby nails biting into his flesh, the pressure slowly squeezing the life from his lungs. "Actually, I'd really rather you didn't, if it's all the same to you. I'm not lying. All I have is this food voucher. You can have it if you want — I'm really not very hungry." Anymore. Morrissey held the thin tab of plastic out before him.

Dandelion-Head snatched it from his grip and stuffed it into his face-gash, his razor-like teeth scissoring it to pulp. He spat it back into Morrissey's face. "I not much like your food *wowtcha*."

Morrissey swiped at the sticky strings of saliva. "That's not exactly how it's supposed to work."

"This is joke? I not much like your joke, either." The short, sharp blow to the throat choked Morrissey's words from his mouth before he could protest. "I don't recognise your species, but you resemble stupid. I tell you that I hurt you, yet you do not reveal the truths. You repeat the talking that is not truths. Why is that? It cannot make good for your health. It is simplest just to present your money. So...where is *my* money?"

Morrissey fought to recapture his breath. "Look, mate...you're not going to like this...but I can't give you what I don't — "

Another blow to the midsection ended his thought. Dandelion-Head's two sidekicks pinned him to the wall, keeping him from collapsing. "Then what is this?" said Dandelion-Head, ripping the credit tab from Morrissey's pocket.

"It's empty. I told you, I just spent all my credits on an air-cab."

"We will see," he said as he stuffed the tab into his tunic. "What else are you hiding? You look like you have much places in your body for hiding — we will begin our search in those places, yes?" A splash of light caught the shine of Morrissey's mum's ring dangling from his neck; a tantalising prize to be sure. "Ah! This is my money, yes?"

"No," said Morrissey, defiance creeping unsteadily back into his tone. "No it bloody isn't." It was his only tangible tie to his past, and right now it was the only thing tethering him to home; a link to his mother — at least the memory of the mother that loved him as a child. He gripped the ring as if his life depended on it, because it just might.

The creature threatened to put Morrissey's convictions to the test, wrenching Morrissey's wrist until it snapped, crushing his hand for good measure. "This is not the easy way, yes? You should do this the easy way."

Morrissey's brain lit up with all the colours of pain at once. Tears streamed unbidden down his cheeks as he tried in vain to support the bones hanging loosely in a glove of skin. He bit down hard on his tongue to avoid fainting, not giving the alien thug the satisfaction of a scream.

Dandelion-Head tore the chain from Morrissey's neck, eying the ring curiously before stuffing it into his tunic stash. "Hmmm. Not so hard after all. Now, we will find the rest of your money. Yes?"

"Oh no you bloody don't!" Morrissey had never needed to be much of a fighter; innate affability was sort of his superpower — on Earth. But on this world, he couldn't trust those same sensibilities. He was going to have to make a stand, for better or worse. He clenched his unbroken hand into a fist and swung. Unfortunately, his blow simply ended up glancing off Dandelion-head's razor dental work.

The creature hissed through a spray of saliva. "Do not fight it. It will only make things worse. Much worse." His double row of nostrils flared, erupting in a fine mist. The acrid vapour stung Morrissey's eyes and burned his throat. One of Dandelion-Head's sidekicks — Knob-Head — drew a long tube from a thigh holster and jabbed him in the ribs. Morrissey convulsed in a shower of sparks. He fought to both fend off his attacker and steady himself, managing neither with any success.

Coconut-Head decided to join the fray, braying as he hoisted Morrissey to his feet with two sets of arms. Another jab from Knob-Head's weapon twisted Morrissey in a blaze of agony. He fought the urge to vomit, quite unsuccessfully, spewing the last remnants of his stomach in violent, heaving waves. Garbled chants from his assailants sizzled through Morrissey's T-Chip. Scattered words filtered through the chaos, none of them forming a sentence he wanted to be a part of.

Another electric blow from a tube-weapon crumpled him into a trembling heap. Through a haze of fire, he saw his opportunity. As Dandelion-Head shambled ever closer, Morrissey chose his target — the bulbous masses at the midpoint of the alien's legs. Maybe they were his knees, maybe they were his genitals. That they were a target was all that mattered. He primed his leg for one last, possibly futile, assault. And when Dandelion-Head stepped within his striking radius, he let loose his spring-loaded limb and fired, heel first, directly into the mass of bone and muscle.

Dandelion-Head fell hard to the ground. Knob-Head and Coconut-Head stood dumbfounded, indecision stretched across their gormless faces. They looked to one another. Then at Morrissey. Then to Dandelion-Head. Then back to Morrissey. Then one final knowing glance to one another before raising their stun tubes — and plunging them into Dandelion-Head. It seemed that even on this alien world, wild animals would prey on the weak in order to claim a higher standing in the food chain.

They were relentless, thrusting their weapons into any tender bit that offered itself up for a target. Dandelion-Head crackled and sizzled, squealing with fear and rage and probably confused panic. It was all Morrissey could do to not root for the two alien thugs to finish what he could not. When they were done, Dandelion-Head's cries had simmered down to a mix of wet gurgles and low, guttural moans while he oozed bodily fluids from most of his visible orifices.

Morrissey's grim satisfaction was short-lived; Knob-Head and Coconut-Head turned their attention back to him. Breathing heavily but far from exhausted, Knob-Head positioned himself for attack. "Do not worry," he said, his voice sounding like a bag of marbles being flushed down the toilet, "we did not forget about you." His first jab struck Morrissey in the kidney, sending stabs of fire raging through his entire body. The second jab came from Coconut-Head, almost blowing his heart through his chest. The third jab never came.

Knob-Head's arm exploded from the shoulder, splattering charred flesh and black goo across the alley wall. Coconut-Head turned to see his friend's limp body tumble hard to the grimy street.

His attack was too late; the second energy blast caught him in the upper torso, spinning him in purple flame before he fell into a smoking heap on the ground.

Through the dense clouds of searing pain, Morrissey could make out a figure in the hazy glow of the streetlights. He…she…it…prodded each of the fallen assailants with the muzzle of what looked like a very angry leaf blower. When none of them stirred, the figure moved forward. If it spoke to him, Morrissey was oblivious. If it were here to save him, he was unable to offer thanks. If it was going to kill him, he was past caring.

Morrissey's breath burned through his lungs in raw, rapid bursts. Consciousness became a luxury too dear to possess, finally giving way to the darkness that eagerly awaited. And for that, he was truly grateful.

CHAPTER 12

Morrissey couldn't swim. Or, more to the point, he couldn't float. As a boy, he'd never made it past the minnow level of his primary school swimming class. That is, he could hold his breath underwater for at least thirty-seconds and he could front crawl his way across the width of the local community pool — in the shallow end. That was it. As for treading water, forget it. "No natural buoyancy," he was told, whatever that meant. The minute solid ground was beyond the reach of his longest toe, panic set in.

So when he opened his eyes to find himself floating in a dense, greenish, viscous soup, panic was the first thing on his To-Do list. His body spasmed in rebellion, involuntary breath-holding naturally followed. Intellectually, he knew that panic would only burn more of the precious oxygen from his bloodstream, but panic had nothing to do with intellect.

His lungs already felt heavy with the pressure of fluid as he gulped at the nonexistent air. A muffled drone fought through the thumping fear in his brain. Somehow it registered as language; the possible source, fuzzy and distant. An insect-like creature floated several metres away — no, not floating. It was perched on a different plane, outside of his own liquid environment. Its chiselled head craned sharply back and forth, its mouthparts waving in time to the speech that filtered through Morrissey's T-Chip.

"Do not resist," it said. "Simply breathe. In. Out. Let it flow naturally. Do not fight it."

A week ago, this impossible sight would have qualified Morrissey for a spot on the Olympic Hallucination Team. But after the things he'd seen recently, the impossible seemed to be the rule rather than the exception. He took the creature's advice at face value and tried to calm himself. It was difficult to unlearn a lifetime of basic instincts but after several minutes, he was able to fight the dull weight of suffocation and force his diaphragm to synchronise with his brain. Finally, his breathing — if you could call it that — settled into a comfortable enough rhythm. The bug obviously didn't want him dead.

With his heartbeat back at subcritical levels, he took stock of his surroundings. The soupy suspension was actually contained within a giant blob several metres in diameter. The blob, itself, was floating in a much larger tank. The insect creature was crawling on the outside of that tank. Similar jellied blobs floated nearby; occasionally one would bump up against Morrissey's blob, causing it to tumble away languidly. The sensation was oddly soothing, and he soon found himself drifting off into...

Morrissey had no proof that he'd slept, yet he felt oddly rejuvenated and more at peace than he'd been in quite a while. There was no way to tell how long he'd been playing this life-sized game of slow-motion pinball but when a chime sounded, he somehow knew that playtime was over.

The blob rippled, sinking to the bottom of the tank. Morrissey felt a tightening around his head as the jelly contracted and undulated around him, squeezing him through its insides until his feet nudged the outer membranes. A large sphincter puckered, nibbling at him piece by piece until he was sucked into the swollen opening and through a translucent, body-hugging tube. A circular doorway irised open and, with a robust whoosh, he was excreted from the blob like a giant turd. He dropped to the padded floor of a cubic cell with a wet, sucking smack while the blob rose serenely into the misty heights above.

Thick, pasty slime clung to his naked flesh like afterbirth. With each breath of real air, he was finally able to cough the remaining sludge from his body in several violent barks, his lungs re-inflating in raw, burning pops. Warm jets of water blasted him from all sides; he welcomed the shower, rubbing the jelly from cracks and crevices he never knew he had. When the last of the residue had been chased down the cube's drainage pores, heated air from unseen vents blew him dry, leaving him as pink and clean as a newborn. What would come next? Lather, rinse, repeat? Perhaps a dousing of baby powder? A full body massage? Nothing would surprise him at the moment. So when his freshly laundered clothes dropped from a chute in the wall, he didn't even flinch.

Morrissey slipped on his gear, drawing solace from the action and comfort from the tangible ties to his humanity. When he was dressed, a human-sized section of the wall shimmered and slid aside. Morrissey accepted the invitation, finding himself in a tunnel of iridescent spun glass. He followed it to a chamber decorated in deep reds with splashes of yellow and orange thrown in for garish measure. Odd-shaped lumps were placed about the room; Morrissey assumed them to be furniture and took a seat on the least uncomfortable-looking of the bunch.

Whoever was behind this setup had likely played a part in his rescue from the thugs in the alley and his subsequent recuperation. Logic suggested they meant him no harm. Of course, the same inference might be made by the Christmas goose being fattened up before the slaughter. He would have to tread carefully.

A smaller section of the wall shimmered and slid aside, admitting a cobalt blue insectoid creature similar to the one outside the jelly-blob tank. Or maybe it was the very same one, allowing for the colour distortion of the jelly-blob suspension.

The creature had six legs like Earth insects: four for locomotion and two upper forelimbs for doing all sorts of pokey alien things. Its eyes were not the usual compound eyes you'd expect from an insect; they were simple eyes, instead, each as big as a human fist. Its body was covered in a flexible material which stretched and sagged as it moved, suggesting an endoskeleton covered with skin rather than the chitinous exoskeleton of an insect. The head resembled a praying mantis' triangular wedge but instead of mandibles, a series of supple tendrils vacillated at the being's mouth. Maybe this creature had evolved from an insect ancestor or maybe it was something else entirely.

It clattered across the chamber, settling itself on a low, saddle-shaped stool. It said nothing, just stared, scrutinising Morrissey with an obvious curiosity. But he refused to be baited. He didn't have the energy to fence with the alien or speculate on its intentions. If they'd wanted to shove a probe up his arse, they'd probably already done it. He was perfectly happy to sit in silence, if only for the peace and quiet.

Finally, it spoke, the voice a soft feminine melodic trill. "What are you?"

The implications were endless. The question that had challenged humankind since Australopithecus Afarensis first saw its reflection in the watering hole, was now being posed by a creature for which Morrissey had absolutely no frame of reference. Best to answer in the broadest sense. "I'm human."

"Where are you from…human?"

"I'm from a city called London, if that means anything, but I have a feeling that's not quite what you were getting at."

"I refer to your homeworld — your planet of origin."

"Earth. It's called Earth. Well, I call it Earth. I have no idea what you'd call it." Morrissey was feeling a bit prickly.

"And where is this…Earth? What sector of space?"

"Well, you've got me there. I've never had to give directions to a planet before. I could mention some of our constellations but I'm guessing those names wouldn't mean much to you, either. But hey, I've got an idea: why don't you tell me who you are."

The alien cocked its head to one side, mouth tendrils oscillating slowly. "Perhaps the name you are called by, then?"

Morrissey sighed. That was a tricky one. Sha'an had warned him to play his cards close to his chest. But by this point, there was little reason to lie. "It's Morrissey. Dave Morrissey."

"Now tell me, Morrissey-Dave-Morrissey, what is it you're doing here?"

"You tell me. I don't even know where *here* is."

The alien looked absently past Morrissey, deep into the shadows beyond before answering. "You are on JuHu Station, in the Bandresek System."

"JuHu? Really?" If his memory served him correctly, this was exactly where Sha'an wanted him to end up.

"This means something to you?

Morrissey caught himself and held his cards just a little bit closer. "It's just that the last thing I remember was getting a shit-kicking on a planet called Phonsekka Prime."

"I do not know this…shit-kicking you speak of, but I do know Phonsekka Prime."

"It's a figure of speech where I come from. It means I was being beaten to within an inch of my life."

"What was your reason for being on Phonsekka Prime — aside from this shit-kicking?"

Morrissey couldn't tell if the creature was making a joke. Nonetheless, he didn't know how to start — or even if he should start. He didn't know if he could trust this alien. And if he did trust it, he didn't know how much he could actually explain in a way that didn't sound crazy. He decided to follow Sha'an's advice and keep it simple. Truthful but simple. "The ship I was travelling on malfunctioned, and I had to escape in a life pod. I was rescued and taken to Phonsekka Prime." This much they could verify and probably already had.

"Where were you heading when your ship malfunctioned?"

Now things were really getting tricky; Morrissey would have to box clever. "Well, coincidentally, I was trying to get here, to JuHu Station. Just how did I get here, anyway?"

"What is on JuHu Station for Morrissey-Dave-Morrissey?"

He thought quickly, aiming for the generic. "Employment. I thought it might be a good place to find work. I hear it's quite the hub of activity."

"And your plan was to wander the station until this work presented itself?"

"I'd heard of an entertainment complex here that's quite popular, run by someone called Xrrka. Do you know it?"

"Everyone who comes to JuHu Station eventually knows it. I dare say everyone in the quadrant knows it. But what sort of skills can you offer Xrrka?"

"Well, I know how to pull a pint — how to serve drinks. I know how to run a service business, how to handle employees. I'm pretty good with people. Usually. I'm sure I could — look, I don't mean to be rude, but I'm not entirely sure what business this is of yours."

The alien remained silent, as if considering Morrissey's answers. "Look, am I in some sort of trouble? Are you the Space Police, or something? Do I need a lawyer? Because I'll be honest, I am fresh out of giving a fuck. I'm tired of being pushed around and — "

The alien was looking off into the shadows, again.

"Sorry, am I boring you? Maybe you could give me some answers. You could start by telling me exactly where I am and what the bloody hell I'm doing here?"

"You are in a place of healing — a medical facility, if you will. You were in dire need of repair after your…shit-kicking."

The memory slapped him with a painful reality; a body, battered, bruised and electrocuted; a hand, shattered, nothing but a sack of loose bones. He flexed it tentatively, then with enthusiasm — good as new, not a loose nut or bolt in sight. "So, you're a doctor, then?"

The being's mouth tendrils vacillated wildly, its voice vibrating in a high-pitched chirp. "No, not a doctor."

Morrissey gestured out the viewport toward the large tank housing the jelly-blobs. "I don't suppose they're doctors?"

"Not doctors in your sense of the word, but the Kelpin did facilitate your recovery. They absorb the injured into their mass, feasting on the dead tissue, rejuvenating the affected areas whilst secreting enzymes and proteins to accelerate the healing process. Respiration in a liquid environment is less stressful to your cardiopulmonary system and aids in the infusion of natural medications."

"I suppose I owe you — and them — my thanks, at least."

"You owe me the truth, the truth about why you were headed to JuHu Station."

"I already told you the truth, I was looking for work. Anything beyond that is between me and Xrrka. So, if you know their whereabouts, I'd appreciate the directions. Otherwise, I think I'll be on my way."

"Very well, yes."

"Yes, what?"

"Yes, I can direct you to Xrrka — because I am Xrrka."

Morrissey didn't know exactly what he'd been expecting Xrrka to look like, but he was pretty certain this wasn't it. He was still coming to terms with his new expanded universe where sentience didn't always equate with humanoids. "If you really are Xrrka, then you already know why I'm here."

"I do."

"Then why all the games? The cryptic interrogation? Why not just put me out of my misery?"

"Perhaps because of the fact that you were sent on a mission to find me with two ALF agents as your escort, yet you have arrived here without either one of them. You will understand this gives us great cause for speculation, much of which does not weigh in your favour."

She was right. A lot had happened to him since he'd set out to find her. "I get it and I get why you would have questions, but you have to understand that I didn't exactly sign up for being chased halfway across the galaxy. I'd much rather be tucked up at home, but apparently that's not an option."

"How do we know you have not been compromised? You were held captive by the being called Cheevers for long enough. How do we know he has not manipulated you? And you still haven't told me what happened to my two agents."

No. He hadn't. And he didn't quite know how to, either. "There's no easy way to say this, Xrrka, but I'm afraid they're both dead."

Xrrka's mouth tendrils stiffened. "Did they die at your hands?"

"What? No. Of course not. How could you even think — look, I don't know what you think of humans, but we aren't all murderous barbarians."

"How then, did they die?"

Morrissey told Xrrka of Sakko's betrayal and Sha'an's fatal wounds. "I tried to get her to come with me but…she sacrificed her life to save mine. I'm so sorry."

Xrrka nodded solemnly. "The rest we know. That will be all for now."

"But I still don't know what I'm doing here."

She made her way through a portal in the wall. "Someone will be along shortly to help you understand — someone you can trust."

Wouldn't that be a neat trick. The list of people in the galaxy out to make his life a living hell was growing exponentially. Finding someone who was actually on his side would be a miracle, indeed.

As if on cue, a patch of wall behind him thrummed and shimmered. A thin, gangly figure stepped out of the shadows, taller than Morrissey by a good foot and a half. Its skin glistened with a deep teal and rich purple, likely vestigial camouflage from a distant psychedelic jungle. Large, flat, burnt orange eyes blinked slowly, giving the vaguely lightbulb-shaped face an expression of sleepy surprise. The figure extended a reedy, four-fingered hand. "I'm the one who saved your arse on Phonsekka Prime. My name is Barrek." He flashed Morrissey an oddly familiar gap-toothed grin. "But you can call me Barry. Or Baz. Your choice."

CHAPTER 13

The question wasn't whether there was life on other planets, it was whether there was a nightlife. According to the brochures, there was always a nightlife at Xrrka's Place. Occupying a sizeable chunk of JuHu Station, Xrrka's was a sharp splash of colour in the stark black of space. Far from the single, cosy drinking establishment the name implied, it was more of an intergalactic nexus of sensory pleasures, comprising a variety of venues geared toward eating, drinking, gaming, sleeping, and of course the universal constant, *sexing*. With such a wide range of amusements, it drew traffic from all the major hyperspace lanes, making it one of the most profitable endeavours in the quadrant.

Each establishment was hermetically separated from the others for the safety and comfort of the respective patrons, which ranged from oxygen-breathers, methane-breathers, ammonia-breathers, helium-breathers, and even zero-g floaters. There was even a club designed for underwater dwellers, though how you served them drinks was a mystery. The bottom line was all were welcome and all left satisfied.

Morrissey occupied a small table in an O2 bar called Club Nebula. The alien called Barrek — formerly the human tabloid journalist called Barry — had chosen it because he claimed it most resembled the drinking establishments of Earth. He was right, but only in the most general sense. Certainly, it had tables and chairs and served drinks, but beyond that it was unlike any pub Morrissey had ever visited.

Nests of transparent pods blistered the ceiling, each featuring a menagerie of gyrating, undulating, and possibly fornicating dancers writhing to the thrum of unfamiliar rhythms. The locals might have deemed them erotic but to Morrissey, they may as well have been gutting fish.

The clientele comprised a simmering stew of heaving bodies of all shapes, sizes and smells. Several foot-long beetle-like creatures brushed up against Morrissey's feet, causing the hairs on the back of his neck to jump to attention. He almost kicked them away, instinctively, until he realised they were just another group of drunken patrons trying to find a table in the crowded space.

In the darkened pods, some talked, some ate, some smoked — and some did things Morrissey dared not speculate on. Yet despite the surface weirdness, it was clear that even on the fringes of space, creatures still needed a place to congregate at the end of a long day to swap stories, celebrate their victories, or drown their sorrows. Maybe Barry had a point, after all.

A caterpillar-like being sidled up to Morrissey. It was a fleshy pale yellow, looking like it had been dredged in pancake batter and rolled in pubic hair. Half of its three metre length was reared upright, oscillating aggressively toward him. Eight stubby limbs flapped frantically at its sides while a sucker-like opening at its head snapped and popped inches from Morrissey's face. He tensed, fearing another close encounter of the violent kind.

Thankfully, Barrek-Barry chose that moment to return with the drinks, forcing his way between Morrissey and his new friend. He leaned in close to the sucker-faced worm, having to yell above the din. Even so, Morrissey's T-Chip couldn't filter out the noise enough to make sense of it. The worm stopped undulating and peered awkwardly around Barrek-Barry at Morrissey. It did what could only be described as a double-take before slowly slinking off to another corner of the throbbing bar.

"Thanks," said Morrissey. "I thought I was going to get my arse kicked again."

Barrek-Barry switched back to Human-English. "He fancied a dance with you, is all. I told him you were with me." The odd alien winked a large saucer-eye and flashed his gap-toothed grin.

Morrissey smiled uneasily. Life amongst the stars was certainly going to take some getting used to.

Barrek-Barry set down two highball glasses filled with a frothy, deep crimson liquid. "Here, get that down your neck."

Morrissey marvelled at the alien's casual use of the English language, finding it an odd juxtaposition hearing Barry's strong London accent coming from Barrek's alien body. Though he'd have to adjust his thinking on what constituted an alien; as far as he could tell in the diverse bar, he was just as alien.

"What should we drink to?" said Barrek-Barry.

"How about saving my life, for starters," said Morrissey.

Dimpled patches at the alien's temples flushed a deep purple. "It was nothing, mate. Literally all in a day's work."

"Hardly. If you hadn't shown up when you did…well, I owe you one, is all. Cheers." Morrissey took a tentative sip of the strange brew. It tingled as it went down, sizzling his mouth and throat in a tangy, malty, almost spicy swirl. "Not bad. Not bad at all."

"You also might like this." He handed Morrissey a small velvet bag cinched at the top by a short, braided cord.

Morrissey untied the cord and dumped the contents into his hand; a lump caught him in the throat unexpectedly. He never thought he'd see his mum's ring ever again. "Where did you…"

"I took it off the goon in the alley. He wasn't using it anymore. I had to replace the chain, but it should do the trick."

Morrissey looped the chain around his neck, feeling the comfortable weight of the ring at his chest. Funny how the smallest of gestures can choke the most surprising emotions from you when you least expect it. "I…I don't know what to say. Thank you…again, it seems." He took a self-conscious pull on his drink, awkwardly shifting the focus to his surroundings. "This is quite the place. Really changes your perspective on life out there — I mean, out here."

"Must be quite jarring for you, all these strange faces, learning that you're not alone in the universe."

"It's more than a bit surreal, for sure. I've spent much of my existence looking for proof of extraterrestrial life and now, here I am having a drink with it. But I am surprised to see so many humanoids. Back home, scientists are always going on about how life on other planets may not even be recognisable as life as we know it. And yet..." Morrissey made a sweeping gesture around the bar.

"The universe is full of alien species you couldn't even begin to imagine — or recognise. But as with all living creatures, similar organisms tend to hang around together. Take Earth, for instance. You've got a billion different species sharing one planet, but you wouldn't expect to see an octopus going for a drink with a chimpanzee, would you? It basically comes down to practicality. Similar environments, similar species. Right now, on some distant world, on the edge of some volcano, two patches of sentient lichen are having this exact same conversation over a pint of their local brew. But if it's strange faces you want, you've got a front row seat at Xrrka's."

Morrissey smiled and took another sip of his drink. "Speaking of strange faces, I think you've got some explaining to do. So, you are obviously one, then — an alien?"

"That depends on your perspective, doesn't it."

"Fair enough. But it's safe to say that you're not human."

"Nope. Not human. At all. I'm Fahri."

"You're a fairy?"

"Not *fairy*. Fahri."

"And your name is Barrek?"

"Yep. But you may as well stick with Barry if that'll help you adjust, it's close enough. Besides, the name has kind of grown on me."

"Barry it is, then. But — the change...how did you manage it? It wasn't like the holographic set up that Cheevers used, was it?"

"That's only good for short term, minimal contact situations. For deep cover, you need a full genetic modification."

"You mean you were actually transformed into a human? You can do that?"

"Pretty much. It's not easy and it costs. The core genetic matrix stays intact along with some fixed biological imperatives but it can stand up to some pretty rigorous scrutiny. Had you convinced, didn't it?"

"And you can change back, just like that?"

"Takes a bit of time. And you've got to make sure to archive a pure copy of your genome. Even then, the longer you remain in your foreign form, the more chance of side effects."

"What sort of side effects?"

Barry smiled widely, a full set of human teeth fighting for space in his Fahri mouth. "I got off lucky. A mate of mine was once undercover for five years. When they tried to restore his true form, his family barely recognised him. They kept him as a pet in the end."

Morrissey couldn't tell if Barry was joking. "So that was you, recuperating in the ALF Med-Pod?"

Barry nodded. "Thanks to your nutter of a girlfriend. You really know how to pick 'em."

"Kiki, yeah. Sorry about that. I really thought she'd killed you. And she isn't exactly my girlfriend, we only met the night before."

"Awfully protective for a one-night stand."

"You're telling me — she certainly seemed to know a lot about me. She said there were people after me, trying to hurt me. She almost had me convinced that you and Fowler had the whole plot cooked up from the beginning."

"Still, I wish I knew who she was working for," said Barry. "The only trace she left behind was her weapon. Seemed a shame to let it go to waste."

"And you're sure she wasn't on Cheevers' ship?"

"Not sure at all. Sha'an didn't report any other captives, but she was sort of in a hurry to get you out of there. Besides, I wouldn't worry about her. Your girlfriend-not-girlfriend strikes me as someone who can take care of herself."

Morrissey's stomach twisted. Sha'an. "Barry, I'm sorry. I never thought — you and Sha'an must have been close."

Barry's expression took on a more solemn look than one might expect from a goggle-eyed alien. "I owe her my life a dozen times over."

"I wish I could have done more. She gave her life to save mine."

"Yeah, that sounds like her. I'm glad you saw her at her best."

Morrissey raised his glass. "To Sha'an."

Barry echoed his toast as they took a long drink to her memory.

"You said you were under deep cover on Earth," said Morrissey.

It was Barry's turn to lose himself in his drink. "Sha'an told you what the ALF does?"

Morrissey nodded. "She said you rescue alien test subjects from illegal research labs. Or something."

"Or something. And Earth has provided a prime pool of test subjects for centuries. You're the perfect farm. As a race, you're technologically underdeveloped, you're self-absorbed, and let's face it, you're painfully naive about the true nature of the universe. Humans are easy pickings."

"Don't hold back, Barry. Tell me what you really think."

"It's not your fault. You're not the only species to be abused like this and I'm afraid you won't be the last. The Vemen are extremely resourceful."

"Vemen?"

"They're the race mostly behind the research farms. Very handy with genetic manipulation, shall we say."

"So, you were sent to Earth to act as what, a watchdog?"

"In a manner of speaking. I was assigned to Earth to monitor any unusual extraterrestrial activity."

"Like the Ruth Small case?"

"Well, that was before the ALF officially existed. We've only had agents stationed on Earth for the last several years, but yes, that's why our database is so comprehensive. Even so, piecing together her life story was no easy feat as you can imagine."

"I still don't understand where I figure into all of this."

"Then drink up and let's go and see Xrrka. She's got some news for you." As they stood, a sea of beings behind them parted to let the distinctive blue insectoid through. "Xrrka, we were just coming to see you."

"Then I have saved you some trouble. It is good that we meet here as we may be in need of a drink — or several. But we must talk in private."

Morrissey wondered where in the swollen club they'd find some privacy, but Xrrka was already leading them to a booth on the far side of the bar. As busy as the place was, the booth remained empty; Morrissey felt like a VIP being ushered past the velvet rope as he drew some curious stares from the other patrons.

When they were seated, a silvery-skinned arachnoid brought them a tray of drinks — two more of the ruby brews for Morrissey and Barry and a pitcher of an amber concoction for Xrrka. As the server scuttled away, Xrrka waved one of her forelimbs across a lighted panel at the edge of the table, sealing the booth in an opaque envelope. "We are alone," she said. "They cannot hear or see us."

Nor could Morrissey see the throbbing mass of patrons through the digital fog nor hear the cacophony of alien tongues or thumping beat of music. They waited for Xrrka to break the deafening silence. She poured herself a glass of her brew, leaning into it, allowing the ring of mouth tendrils to hold it in place as she took a long, satisfying pull, draining half its contents. Finally, she spoke. "I know your time was brief with her, but how well did you get to know Sha'an?"

Morrissey was surprised by the question — and surprised by the knot in his stomach. "Not nearly well enough, but I'd like to think I got a good measure of her character. She gave her life for mine and I won't soon forget it."

"Did she tell you that she'd been to your homeworld before — to Earth?"

"She did. But she was decidedly vague; I got the impression there was a much larger story attached."

Xrrka took another sip of her drink. "There was. I think it's probably best if I show you." She waved a forelimb across a panel, sinking the booth into darkness. With a pulse of light, Morrissey was back on Earth, or so it seemed; the room shifted, filling with sights both foreign and familiar at the same time. The images were seen from the first-person view of a figure flanked by two others, armoured soldiers by the looks of them. The holographic representation was grainy, but the fidelity was surprisingly true to life.

"What exactly am I looking at, Xrrka?"

"This is the visual feed from Sha'an's tactical display during her mission to your home of Earth."

Morrissey nodded absently, disoriented by the content but thoroughly absorbed by the immersive VR experience. He followed as the trio moved down the hallway of a building and arrived at a door where they placed rectangular plates around the frame. Within seconds the door blew inwards and they moved quickly through. A man jumped up from the bed, shielding himself from the debris. He leapt over a woman, understandably startled by the events, then pulled her up in front of him. The three soldiers now had their weapons trained on the man as he held the woman hostage with a corkscrew to her neck.

"Who's the couple? Should I know them?"

Xrrka paused the video feed, leaving them suspended within the three-dimensional tableau. "Sha'an had been tracking a brutal genetic terrorist called Chendra Vaziil who eventually made his way to Earth. He had taken great measures to disguise his true self, manipulating his DNA in order to hide amongst your kind." She gestured to Barry as an example. "Unfortunately, this procedure can be used for evil as well as for good."

"And the woman? Who is — " Before Xrrka could answer, a stab of cold reality knifed him in the gut. "It's…my mother, isn't it?"

"Just so. This is the woman you knew as your mother, indeed. But it is also the woman we have known as Ruth Small.

Morrissey's skin went cold as his reason dropped off the face of the Earth. She looked younger than he remembered but there was no mistaking that the image before him was of his mum. "So, it's true, then. Fowler wasn't lying."

"Afraid not, mate," said Barry. "We ran tests on DNA samples retrieved from Ruth Small's nursing home. The results confirm she's your mum."

Morrissey tried to tie all the implications of what he was watching into a neat bow but all he ended up with was a stomach tied in knots. The only real mother he'd known and loved was, indeed, the sad, old Ruth Small, her days as Marion Morrissey, apparently a vain attempt to escape a tortured past. He'd always held out hope that he might, one day, see her again, feel her loving embrace. But now he had to mourn the loss of a mother he never really knew at all.

Yet even as he watched the ghostly tableaux before him, he felt the urge to reach out to her, to warn her, to save her. Then he reminded himself that this story had played itself out decades ago, the consequences long since cemented in time. Nothing he could do would save her from the tortured life she would lead and the tragically lonely end she would face.

Xrrka restarted the video feed. A lot of the techno-speak went over Morrissey's head but the gist of it was that Sha'an and her team had continued the standoff with the terrorist, but he had somehow gained the upper hand by threatening to destroy the Earth. And just as it seemed that this Vaziil was going to escape, Morrissey's mum spoke, only a single word. Shoot, she said. An interminable silence filled the seconds before Sha'an fired a blast into her quarry. In the process, Marion Morrissey suffered a neck wound — the cause of the scar that Morrissey had come to know so well.

The scene ended in a blaze of electric haze and the disappearance of the terrorist. Xrrka stopped the feed and raised the lights in the booth. "The footage ends there. Sha'an and her team tended your mother's wound as best they could, but had to leave before the local authorities arrived."

Time moved through quicksand as Morrissey fought to process what he'd just witnessed. "So, my mother was willing to risk her own life to help capture this Vaziil character? Why would she do that? She seemed so calm about it. So composed. So resolved."

"She wasn't just an innocent bystander," said Barry. "She'd spent months getting close to Vaziil, gaining his trust, building a rapport with him. Little did she know that the man was an intergalactic mass murderer."

Morrissey shook his head in puzzlement. "How do you know all this?"

"Fowler. Or his notes, anyway. The team grabbed what evidence they could from his house when they came to retrieve me. He logged all his interactions with your mum — or the woman he knew as Ruth Small; seems she reverted to her true identity after she left you. Made for some very interesting reading."

"Okay, so what was her plan? What did she plan on doing with Vaziil?"

"Getting proof, I would imagine. Turns out your mum was abducted by extraterrestrials at a very early age. She needed to justify the pain that had grown within her. Somehow, she'd twigged that Vaziil was not all he claimed to be and figured the best way to uncover the truth was from within. She had guts, I'll give her that, and when Sha'an arrived to apprehend him, she knew she'd been vindicated. Her command to shoot was probably a way for her to gain closure."

"What your mother did not know was how vile and vicious a being Vaziil was," said Xrrka. "He has a history of genocide, and we believe him to be responsible for much of the illegal experiments we seek to stop — genetic butchery, in point of fact. He was responsible for the deaths of tens of thousands of Sha'an's people, an entire colony obliterated. But his brutality didn't begin there. Nor did it end there." She reminded Morrissey of Vaziil's threat to destroy the Earth to gain his freedom.

"But that flash of light at the end of the video, that was Vaziil escaping?"

Xrrka nodded. "I am afraid so. He has not been seen since."

Morrissey knocked back the rest of his drink in one gulp. His entire world had literally and figuratively been turned on its head. Humans, so wrapped up in their own petty grievances, had no idea how close to annihilation they'd come. He thought about how close his own mother had been to the nexus of that destruction. "So Ruth Small's death — my mother's death — is somehow linked to this Vaziil character?"

"This is our belief," said Xrrka.

"Then I'm assuming that the hunt for him continues?"

"Just so," said Xrrka. "His capture and punishment have become our top priority."

Morrissey shifted awkwardly in his seat, unsure if he should broach the question that had been needling him since he'd first learned of the ALF. "What is your involvement in all this, Xrrka? Did Vaziil harm your people as well?"

Barry's eyes bugged as he motioned to shush Morrissey. "You can't ask her that!"

"I'm sorry. I think I've got a right. I just want to know who I'm dealing with. Sha'an mentioned that not much is known about your history and yet you seem decidedly obsessed with capturing this creature."

Xrrka motioned to Barry, as if to calm his fears. "It's alright, Barrek. It is only fair that David know my stake in this matter."

Morrissey wondered if he was going to regret opening this can of worms.

CHAPTER 14

Xrrka sucked back half her drink in one gulp. Her eyes drifted to the shadowy mass of pub patrons shifting silently outside their protective bubble, perhaps finding solace in the rhythmic energy. "My species is called Fai-Lok. On my world, I was a respected scientist — a biologist, to be precise. I had always held a powerful fascination for the intricacies of physiology and our interaction with our ecosystem. My quest for knowledge drove me toward avenues of inquiry other specialists would never have contemplated. It propelled me to levels of achievement in my field that I never thought possible.

"As our peoples began to reach out toward the stars, so did my passions. My dreams of studying organisms not of our world were soon realised and I became the leading expert in exobiology, exalted among my peers. I tell you this not to bolster my own image in your eyes, but to help you fully understand how tightly I was bound to the events that followed." Xrrka drained her glass and reached for a top-up, swallowing another significant gulp before continuing. "These dreams, however, soon turned dark as nightmares. Our forays into the depths of space had attracted the attention of a host of other civilisations, not all of them benign. The point of my case, the Holrathon — Chendra Vaziil's race. They arrived at the edge of our system in small numbers at first. Subjugation through brute force was their goal, and the devastation they inflicted was vast. They burned our skies and scorched our lands. We fought bravely but our weapons were no match for their technologies. We perished by the millions. And this was only the first wave, the vanguard for a much larger force.

"So, we fought back in the only way we knew how — with our minds. A scientific task force was assembled, of which I was an integral part. We were charged with finding a biological weakness in the Holrathon, something that could be used against them. We studied their wounded, their fallen soldiers, every aspect of their physiology and chemistry until finally, we found their weakness. It was a poisonous gland, once used to fend off predatory threats, now just a vestigial appendage from millennia past. Primitive Holrathon were able to contract the gland at will, causing a cellular disruption that would kill both the attacker and themselves — their version of a suicide bomb. It was crude but effective — and open to manipulation. Our team was able to replicate the chemical trigger and modify it in a way to activate the gland remotely, without the need to initiate a local threat. This method of delivery could be achieved on a wide scale with relative ease. Any moral quandaries were outweighed by our survival instincts. We were at war, on the verge of extinction."

"I'm not judging," said Morrissey. "I get it — in order to stop being bullied, you've got to put the bully down once and for all. And I guess it worked or you wouldn't be here."

"It worked…only too well."

Barry sensed her agitation. "How many casualties, Xrrka?"

Xrrka stared intently into her glass. "Numbers too large to count, I'm afraid. The entire invasion fleet, along with all colonies in range of our trigger — and much of the Holrathon homeworld — wiped out. We could not predict the scope of the Holrathon hive mind. The trigger was relayed to all members of their species within the sector. We estimated hundreds of millions dead, probably more."

A stunned silence sizzled the air. "I knew that the Holrathon had suffered great casualties in their conflicts," said Barry, "but I had no idea the cause…"

Morrissey whistled through his teeth. "You couldn't have known, Xrrka. You did what you had to do."

"Perhaps," she said, softly. "This was the justification our politicians employed, but our moral position was not so easily salved. I took some solace that my actions helped save my people and gave them a future where they would have had none, but those of us behind the development and use of the weapon felt a heavy burden.

"The Holrathon were decimated, their society broken. We appealed to their government, offered them reparations, tried to help them rebuild their devastated world. In time, they did cease their warring ways, turning themselves inward, becoming more insular. But for some, the poison had already set in, twisting their pain and suffering into a bitter vengeance. A small but powerful resistance simmered, fuelled by one of their most accomplished geneticists — Vaziil. He corrected the genetic flaw that had caused the downfall of his race, but his vision did not stop there. He began experimenting on every alien species he could lay his hands on, exploring and exploiting their weaknesses. He began slowly, with the lower species of primitive worlds, but his lust for biological destruction could not be sated and soon he was alone on his journey of revenge, leaving his own people to lick their wounds while he pursued his twisted version of justice.

"It was only when he coerced the Vemen to do his bidding that he was able to make use of their vast extraterrestrial libraries to weaponise his technology. That is when his reign of terror truly began to spread across the galaxy: the wanton slaughter of untold sentient species." She cast her gaze directly at Morrissey, large, wet eyes rimmed with sadness and regret. "Chendra Vaziil may be a monster but he's a monster I helped create. I shall live with that mark on my soul, always."

"I'm so sorry, Xrrka. That is a heavy load to carry — I shouldn't have said anything."

"No, it is good that we all know where we stand. One thing you must learn, David, is that the universe is neither black nor white. You simply have to come to terms with living in the grey."

Morrissey pushed past the awkward silence, trying desperately to steer the conversation back to something constructive. "The weapon that Vaziil threatened Earth with, what happened to it?"

"Sha'an never did find any trace of it, but Vaziil's reputation does not include idle threats. This is why we began stationing agents on Earth, to monitor any activity that might indicate the presence of such a device."

"And you, my little pink friend," said Barry, "seem to be the focal point of all that activity."

Xrrka took another long pull from her drink; Morrissey was beginning to read this as a bad sign.

"Barrek tells me that where you come from, it is a tradition to share both good news and bad. First, I will share the good news. Based on the intelligence you provided, we have identified the being that held you captive — the one you knew as Dr. Cheevers — as a Bendekkon arms dealer called eNdeen — a sort of terrorist for hire, if you will, stirring up trouble in whatever way will award him the greatest profit."

"You've certainly got a strange definition of good news."

"Just so," said Xrrka. "The bad news is that we suspect eNdeen believes you hold the key to some significant technology. Your mother's connection to Vaziil and his unique abilities suggests that this key is related to weapons technology, possibly the very weapon Vaziil levelled at your planet."

"What knowledge could I have of an alien weapon that may or may not have existed before I was even born? My mum didn't even tell me of her alien abduction, she certainly didn't read me any bedtime stories about a planet destroying weapon."

Xrrka wobbled her head in a way that suggested a negative. "The secrets eNdeen thought were hidden in your memories were actually hidden in your DNA. We've run our own tests and have detected a genetic marker of non-human origin hidden deep within your genome in a string of non-coding DNA."

"You might know it as junk DNA," offered Barry.

"I might," said Morrissey, feeling very much like he should have paid a bit more attention in his biology lectures, "or I might not, but I'm more interested in the non-human part of the equation— you mean alien? Are you saying I've got an alien tag inside me, like a wild animal? What is it, some sort of intergalactic GPS?"

"Not a tracking device," said Xrrka. "Not a transmitter — at least, not any type we're familiar with. It's a densely packed, intricately coded genetic string."

"How the bloody hell would an alien string of DNA get into my genes in the first place? Somebody must have put it there."

Xrrka and Barry exchanged an awkward glance that transcended their alienness. "Speculation is dangerous at this point. It is a question that will require further investigation, I'm afraid. The foreign sequence is encoded with a very sophisticated level of encryption, one that we have yet to breach. The DNA sample we took from you reveals the encrypted marker but the marker itself is rendered inert upon extraction and cannot be accurately analysed. The plasmid containing the alien code must remain with the host to ensure its viability."

"I'm going to pretend I understood most of what you just said and guess that I'm the host in this equation?"

"Just so. But again, the good news is that if we cannot decrypt it, neither can eNdeen — certainly not without a live sample of your genome to play with. There is a small portion of the genetic sequence that's been damaged, most likely while he was analysing you. Whether or not he gleaned any data from it, we cannot be certain, but we can be certain that he will stop at nothing to recapture you, to obtain the rest of that information. We must break the encryption before that happens."

"Why can't I just hide from him? People keep telling me that space is really big — surely it's big enough to hide one human?"

"Not if you ever want to go home, mate," said Barry. "You know he'll just keep coming for you. And it won't just be you in danger."

Morrissey winced. Sha'an's death still weighed heavily on his soul; he didn't want any more death on his conscience. "And I guess somewhere at the end of this, you're hoping this eNdeen bloke will lead you to Vaziil."

Xrrka's mouthparts stiffened. "One step at a time, David."

"Okay. What do you need me to do?"

"I'm afraid you have another journey ahead of you to meet with a specialist in this type of DNA analysis."

"Wouldn't it be easier if this specialist were to come here? And by easier, I mean not life-threatening to me."

"It would. But he will not. He cannot. He is in what you would call exile. Once he has analysed your live DNA and interpreted the marker, we will better know how to proceed."

Morrissey's brain ached. The things he'd encountered had challenged his reality beyond reason and he was beyond questioning the chain of events. "Okay," he said, slowly shaking his head, "I'm in. Just tell me one thing — is it going to hurt?"

PART THREE

CHAPTER 15

Morrissey felt like a little boy on his first day of school being seen off by his mum. He waited with Xrrka at the entrance to one of the station's docking tubes, knees wobbly with anticipation. Nictating membranes fluttered over Xrrka's fist-sized eyeballs as she cocked her head toward him. He half expected her to wet a hanky with her saliva and wipe his face clean before sending him on his way with a packed lunch.

"The universe is not always a safe place, David."

"I've sort of noticed," said Morrissey.

"You must, therefore, accept my gratitude for your undertaking."

"Seems like the right thing to do. Though I'm not completely altruistic. The selfish part of me just wants my life back to normal. And to be honest, I'm tired of playing the victim."

"This is good to hear. You cannot keep subjecting your soft human form to such physical stresses."

"It hasn't exactly been by choice."

"Learn what you can from Barrek and his crew. They will do their best to look after you, but you must learn to look after yourself."

"Yes, Mum."

Xrrka cocked her head like a curious dog. "I do not understand — *mum?*"

"It's a term of endearment. Affection. And one of respect."

"Then I gladly accept the appellation with honour."

Morrissey had first viewed Xrrka with a healthy amount of cynicism, but as he learned who she was and what she was fighting for, he'd come to realise that her maternal influence stretched not just over him, but over the whole ALF organisation. "Actually, I kind of wish you were coming with us. I find your presence…reassuring."

"I will be with you in spirit, but my body will be of more use here." Xrrka's mouth tendrils curled into what might have been a smile as she gestured down the docking tube. "Unfortunately, our time together is at an end — for now."

A transit pod hummed toward them before coming to a spongy stop. The canopy retracted, revealing a grinning Barry in the driver's seat. He'd gone on ahead to run his pre-flight checks and brief the crew on their new mission, and had now returned to pick up his passenger.

"All aboard," said Barry.

Morrissey cast a final glance toward Xrrka and smiled weakly. The last time he'd left an ALF friend behind, he never saw her again. He hoped fate wouldn't repeat the same cruel trick. The canopy slipped back into place as he climbed into the passenger seat. With nothing more than a whisper and a hum, the small car rotated 180 degrees and cruised smoothly away on its magnetic cushion down the shaft of the tube.

Morrissey caught his first glimpse of the ALF ship flashing between the struts of the docking tube's skeleton as the pod raced forward. The overall impression was that of a giant insect. The nose of the ship was a bulbous wedge, like the head of a wasp. A stubby neck led to a streamlined ovoid about three times the size of the head, which, in turn, led to a massive thorax ringed by three muscular thrusters throbbing with the promise of unimaginable power.

"It's called the *T'Taro Briiga,*" said Barry.

"What does it mean? My T-Chip isn't translating."

"*The Souls of Briiga*. Briiga was the Thon Pahl colony decimated in one of Vaziil's terror attacks. Sha'an named it in honour of her fallen people — this was her ship."

They rode in a solemn silence until the pod came to rest at the centre of the T'Taro Briiga. Barry popped out like a loose spring; Morrissey exited somewhat more cautiously. As he entered the airlock, he felt a slight resistance, as if tethered by some unseen restraint. A fizz of energy buzzed through him, tickling his flesh like a spiderweb.

Barry answered his unasked question. "Don't worry. It's just the point where the artificial gravities of the space station and the ship rub up against one another. Perfectly normal."

Morrissey nodded absently, adjusting his perception of normal. "If you say so." The outer hatch sealed behind them with a metallic thunk. A disk on the bulkhead shifted from glowing orange to glowing blue and the inner hatch hissed open to reveal a small welcoming committee. It was a committee of just one but the one was, indeed, small. At no more than three feet tall, its hairless skin was speckled with yellow and green, its round face staring with large, wet eyes the colour of honey. The fact that it wore a pistol at his side did not escape Morrissey's attention.

The being extended its child-like hand. "So, you're our lone monkey?"

"The who's-it-what-now?" said Morrissey.

"I think he means solitary human," said Barry. "Sometimes the T-Chip can be a bit too literal. This is Kheni, by the way — our engineer. Kheni, this is Morrissey."

"Apologies," said Kheni. "No offence meant."

"No problem. Lone monkey? I kind of like that. Just about sums up how I feel, too."

A high-pitched squeal pierced the room; if Morrissey hadn't known better, he would have feared for his life at the being galloping toward him. It was Lillum, the arthropod-like medic who had treated him when he'd first arrived aboard, oh so long ago.

"Morrissey, you have returned safely!"

"Believe me, I had my doubts I ever would."

"I am only sorry Sha'an is not with you." Lillum's jellied orb of a head swayed slowly from side to side, her eyestalks drooping in symmetry.

"I'm sorry, too. I could tell you two were close. But it's good to see you again."

Lillum turned to Barry. "Shall I show him to his quarters, Captain?"

"It's okay. I'll take him." His temples flushed a deep violet. "And I told you not to call me that."

"Somebody has to take over from Sha'an," said Kheni, "and Xrrka did put you in charge of the mission."

"Maybe. But there's no need to make a fuss about it. By the way, where's Syd? I wanted him to meet Morrissey."

"He's still prepping for departure."

"Syddyk is Kheni's brother," said Barry. "He's our astrogator, amongst other things."

"How many in the crew?"

"We were six, including me. Now we're down two, so you may have to take a turn in the pilot's chair."

Morrissey stared blankly at the gangly alien. "You're kidding, of course?"

"Of course." Barry gave a sly wink. "Pilot training can wait — a few days. Again, kidding! But we are stretched pretty thin so we might have to find something for you to do to earn your keep."

Barry gave Morrissey a brief rundown of the layout of the ship as he led him to his cabin. The crew quarters stretched along the upper deck of the thorax, leaving the Med-Pod and Engineering to the aft, or the abdomen. Below the main deck was the cargo hold and the two shuttle bays, only one of which was still occupied.

They passed through a small recreational lounge and a mess hall before coming to the eight crew cabins. Each was customised with the necessary amenities to suit the respective species of its occupant. Morrissey was given one of the vacant berths since Sha'an's still contained all her belongings and Sakko's still smelt heavily of betrayal.

The room was small, yet functional, containing a toilet/shower wet room, a small desk console, and a sleep tube situated above the desk. The elliptical entrance to the tube could be completely sealed off for a peaceful night's sleep or, in more dire circumstances, to convert into a self-contained living environment. In the most extreme cases, it would also function as an escape pod. There was also a small closet, though his only clothes were literally those on his back. When he checked inside, he found a couple of gunmetal grey jumpsuits that were roughly his size.

"I hope they fit," said Barry. "Lillum tried her best to calculate your size. She also left some toiletries that should do you. I gave her the rundown on human hygiene, and she improvised from there."

"That's very thoughtful. I'm sure it will be just like home." Except for the fact that it wasn't.

"Why don't you get acquainted with the room — freshen up, whatever. We should be ready to go in about an hour. The door lock is biometric if you want some privacy, you can key it to your palm print."

Like Sakko's gun. "Sounds good to me." The sooner this mission was over, the sooner he could go home. In theory…

Top priority was making sure the toilet accommodated his human excretions. It wouldn't do to leave that sort of thing to chance. Once it was cleared for use, he lay on his bunk — a comfortable enough gel-pad — and tried to shut out the swirling nightmare that had become his life. Just as he was about to find his happy place, tucked up in his own bed above The Crooked Crow, the cabin door chimed.

It was Barry. "Hope I'm not disturbing anything important."

"Just engaging in some pretty intense wallowing."

"I wouldn't blame you, mate. We are in some pretty intense shit, but you might want to take a break and join us on the bridge. We're prepped and loaded and cleared for departure. You could probably use the distraction."

Morrissey doubted it — the best part about feeling sorry for yourself was that you didn't need any help doing it. Nonetheless, he followed Barry half-heartedly. As the door to the bridge hummed open, Morrissey stood slack-jawed. The room was domed, like the inside of a planetarium, perhaps four metres in diameter. Several control stations ringed the circumference while a command cluster was nested at the centre. Barry took his position in a chair that screamed authority, casting him in an altogether different light than when they'd first met.

"Don't take this the wrong way," said Morrissey, "but I never would have pegged you as the command type. When I met you on Earth, you just seemed like a — "

"— like a lover not a fighter?"

"Actually, like a bit of a knob."

"Ha! Yes, well, part of that was my cover."

"You had me fooled."

Despite the dome's size, Morrissey felt closed in and realised it was because there was only a single viewscreen at the head of the bridge. "Hey, how come there aren't any windows?"

"Who needs windows when you can do this!" Barry's fingers swiped gracefully across an armrest console. The blue-grey curves of the bulkheads instantly faded to black, and Morrissey's field of view exploded into a panoramic, up down wraparound view of the emptiness of space. A wave of vertigo gripped him as he seemingly floated in the nothingness. The effect was both mind-bogglingly exhilarating and pants-wettingly disorienting. He grabbed a nearby handhold to steady himself.

"How cool is that? You can expand the view as much, or as little as you like," said Barry as he dialled the view back down to the original three metre panel set into the central bulkhead. "It displays true-view, tactical, thermal, infrared — pretty much anything you need."

"He's just showing off," said Kheni, who sat ensconced in a honeycomb of thrumming consoles and 3D monitors. Only it wasn't Kheni. The being had the same diminutive build, the same skin colouring. Only this fellow sported a sharp shock of orange hair sprouting from the crown of his head, tied tight with black bands, and his eyes were crystal blue rather than Kheni's distinctive amber.

"You must be Syddyk."

"Good to meet you, Morrissey. And by the way, the bridge does have several real viewports, but they are fully shielded during general operations. We like to keep our command and control well-protected. If you want an unobstructed view of the real outside, there's an observation blister in the recreational lounge."

"I'll keep that in mind, thanks."

Barry's command chair rose dramatically on a hydraulic arm and angled him toward the forward view screen.

Syddyk gestured to a pair of jump-seats located to the rear of the command sphere and helped Morrissey secure himself in place.

"Alright, kids," said Barry, "hold onto your hats. Syd, manoeuvring thrusters at your control. Standby to disengage from the station."

There was a grinding clunk of metal on metal and then an ominous silence. "We're clear of all moorings and free to navigate," said Syddyk.

JuHu Station clung peacefully at their side. It was Morrissey's first view of the exterior of the massive structure. From what he could see, it was far from the sleek, symmetrical gem of engineering its reputation suggested. Instead, it was a swollen, misshapen cluster of mis-matched modules, borne of generations of galactic industrial growth, stitched together by a burgeoning hyperspace trade. It wasn't pretty but it stood out as a beacon of prosperity and abundance in the isolation of cold space.

Barry reactivated the full-screen wraparound view in time for Morrissey to see JuHu Station drop from sight beneath them as The Briiga rolled away. In an aeroplane, you would have the horizon line as a point of orientation but in three-dimensional zero-g, there was no such luxury — or restriction. In space, there was no up, no down. No left, no right. Only millions of possible trajectories to chase. This sense of freedom appealed to Morrissey but also made him feel very, very small.

"Course set and locked in," said Syddyk.

A voice burst through the comm. It was Kheni. "Engines at optimal, Barrek. All systems blue across the board."

"Drive thrusters at zero-point-one-zero," said Barry. "Initiate."

Morrissey felt the ship surge forward as JuHu Station shrunk rapidly behind them. Barry's command chair swooped dramatically around to face him. "Well, we're on our way!"

Morrissey's rush of euphoria was tempered by the grim reality of the mission that lay ahead. "Tell me more about this genetic specialist we're meeting."

Barry shrugged. "We don't really know that much about him. We know he's a Thuwom and he's called Bryndevaan. His last known whereabouts was a planet called Chyll. But beyond that, he's a bit of an enigma."

"You never did say why he's in exile."

"All a bit classified, I'm afraid. Need-to-know sort of thing."

"And I don't need to know?"

"Actually, I don't even know. I'm sure Xrrka has her reasons."

"How long before we get to this...Chyll?"

"Syd, what's our timeline?"

Syddyk checked the navigation network. "We've got about six hours before we make our first hyperspace jump. Then two days of evasive jumps, just to be safe. Then another half day of normal space on the other side. Call it three days."

"You should probably get some rest. There's no night and day in space but we try to keep a regular sleep cycle. We're on a thirty-hour day — that's pretty much the average of what we're all used to — and we're nearing the end of our pseudo-day. Tomorrow we'll set you up with some training. If you're going to function as part of the crew, you've got to know the basics."

Morrissey resisted the thought, still in the mindset that his stay on the ship would be all too temporary, but then he remembered Xrrka's parting advice about the need to soak up all he could learn. The knowledge might just save his life — or someone else's.

CHAPTER 16

Morrissey awoke refreshed and hungry. Sleep had come easily to him, at least it did once he'd gotten used to the rhythmic moan and groan of the ship's drive engines. After a quick shower, he dressed in one of the jumpsuits Lillum had provided. Overall, it was a good fit and made him feel like he was actually part of the team. Now he just had to earn it.

In the galley, Kheni, Syddyk, and Lillum were in the middle of breakfast, though none of the dishes looked familiar. Kheni and Syddyk were each eating a dish of purplish noodles, which might have been at home in some remote Asian village on Earth — except that the noodles were wriggling out of their bowls. Lillum was heartily slurping from a dish of grey-green porridge. At Morrissey's approach, she bounded over to him like a playful puppy, porridge still oozing from her mouth-hole.

"Come in! Come in! Sit down. You must eat!"

Morrissey took another look at the meals on offer. "Must I?" he said, weakly. "Don't suppose there's any chance of a fry up?"

"I do not know 'fry up' but based on your biological assessment and some input from Barrek, I have programmed your nutritional requirements into the food dispenser. For now, I've kept the flavour profiles quite neutral, but we can fine tune them as your tolerances become more apparent. You may choose anything from the Blue or Green menus but stay away from the Red Menu. You won't enjoy the Red."

"Thanks, Lillum. Very kind of you to take such an interest." After showing him how the dispenser worked, he selected one item from each recommended menu. Best to start off slow. She wasn't kidding about the neutral flavours; if not for the texture — which was dubious at best — he wouldn't have known he was eating at all.

He tried to wash it down with something that was identified as water. This was something else he'd have to get used to, the fact that his drinking water and his waste output were pretty much one and the same, separated only by a few hours in the multi-filtration system. He was assured that it was 100% potable and besides tasting a bit metallic, it seemed just as cool, clear, and watery as that on Earth.

Unlike the bridge, the galley did have exposed viewports. He could tell by the frenetic cyclone swirling around the ship that they'd already jumped into hyperspace sometime during the night.

"Right on schedule," said Syddyk.

"I guess I must have slept through it."

Kheni gave Morrissey a playful slap on the back. "Then you're already getting your space legs!"

Morrissey smiled, a small sense of pride welling within him. Sha'an's coaching had certainly paid off. As he tucked back into the breakfast of the bland, a comm unit chimed and a small hologram of Barry's face burst from a display node.

"Morning, Dave. Hope you slept well. We've got an exciting day planned for you."

"Not too exciting, I hope?"

"Don't worry, we'll ease you in slowly. Trust me."

Over the next three days, Morrissey received a crash course in life and death aboard a starship, starting in Engineering. He'd never been very mechanically inclined; he knew enough to check the fluids in his scooter and fill it up with petrol. If the situation required it, he could push-start it in a pinch. Beyond that, he was more than happy to place his trust in the skills of a trained professional. On the T'Taro Briiga, that trusted professional was Kheni. Morrissey wasn't expected to be able to recalibrate the Inertial Compensator or balance the output of the Hyperdrive Unit or maximise the levels of the radiation shielding.

"I just want you to have a healthy understanding of what makes the ship tick," said Kheni. And on a starship like The Briiga, that was the fusion reactor. On Earth, nuclear fusion technology was still a distant practical reality. But out here, it powered everything from the artificial gravity generator to the weapons systems, from the jump-drive to life support. Basically, anything that kept you alive on a starship was the bailiwick of the Engineering Section. The crucial take-home point was that the systems were very delicate — so don't fiddle with them. If anything appeared to be out of the norm, Morrissey was to run and tell a grownup immediately.

After a lunch chosen from the Green Menu — which included, much to Morrissey's surprise, a rather satisfying facsimile of a cup of tea — he headed to the bridge where he was to learn the basics — the very basics — of ship navigation and hyperdrive dynamics from Barry. The physics sent his brain into a mind-numbing tailspin, but the theory left him mesmerised. In essence, the Hyperdrive Unit, or Jump-Drive, allowed a starship to pass into an adjacent dimension called, unsurprisingly, hyperspace. In this dimension, a ship could cover unimaginable distances in a fraction of the time it would take in normal space.

"Hyperspace is an incredibly complex network of interstellar conduits — or hyperspace lanes — but you still have to travel in normal space to get to the conduits. It's like taking the side streets to get to the motorway. The Jump-Drive's nav-computer does most of the heavy lifting, detecting the hyperspace conduits and calculating the optimum insertion vector."

Needless to say, hyperspace travel wasn't without its risks. Objects in normal space cast an equivalent shadow in hyperspace and posed severe dangers if not factored into jump routes. Computer safeguards were in place to detect such obstacles but an astrogator worth their paycheque could tweak the numbers to manoeuvre around the stellar threats in the first place, saving travel time and possibly even lives.

Exiting hyperspace posed the same threats, so calculations for a safe exit point were paramount. Morrissey shivered as he recalled the harrowing experience of being wrenched from hyperspace by Sakko's conspirators. And you'd better pray to your space god that your Hyperdrive Unit didn't crap out after a jump, or you could be blown out of hyperspace in a million different pieces or be cast adrift inside of it for all eternity. The thought was enough to make Morrissey want to open a window.

Morrissey's favourite lesson by far was Syddyk's instruction on weapons. "It's not that I want to put you in the line of fire," said Barry, "but if you're going to be part of this team, you should probably know how to defend yourself — or your crew mates. And Syd is the best we've got."

Syddyk began in broad strokes, which included a lot of technobabble about sensor clusters, communication arrays, and ship's armaments, which included two plasma cannons, a point defence network, and a respectable missile battery. "There's all kinds of unfriendly out here in the black," he warned. "You've got to be prepared." But he quickly moved to a tutorial on small arms training.

He had sectioned off a narrow channel in the cargo bay for use as a makeshift firing range. He presented Morrissey with an assortment of personal weaponry from what he called The Human Collection, leftovers from Barry's undercover mission on Earth. It was from this collection that Morrissey was to assemble his personal arsenal.

None of the weapons available to him had the biometric safeguard that Sakko The Traitor had employed; Syddyk felt them too prone to technical glitches and misfires — or worse, no-fires. Not to mention the fact that rigging one for use with an atmospheric suit required far too much faffing about.

After careful consideration, Syddyk set Morrissey up with a charged particle beam emitter — basically an energy blaster — which fired an accelerated pulse of charged particles at its target. For training purposes, the weapon would be set to fire only low-yield bursts at a series of hovering disks. Baby steps.

Morrissey had grown up watching Clint Eastwood's Spaghetti Westerns and had practised his quick draw technique endlessly in front of the mirror with his toy six-shooter. But Syddyk made it clear that this new weapon was no toy, ensuring that Morrissey felt comfortable with both the physical and mental weight the weapon carried with it before allowing him to load a live power pack into the chamber.

Syddyk queued up the first wave of targets as he and Barry watched from the sidelines. Morrissey thumbed the status toggle to blue and took a two-handed firing stance, giving himself a stern, silent reminder not to make pew-pew noises with his mouth when he fired.

As the targets began their slow dance, he held his breath as instructed, steadily building pressure on the firing stud. And...*whizzz!* The weapon crackled, kicking back with a subtle recoil. Morrissey blinked, startled by the discharge. He fired again. And again. After twenty shots, a chime sounded, and the sequence ended. Morrissey made his weapon safe, thumbing the status toggle back to orange.

"You realise you're supposed to hit the targets," said Barry, chuckling.

"In all fairness, he didn't do too badly," said Syddyk, "for a first attempt. I think you may have even frightened one or two of them."

Morrissey shrugged sheepishly. "Let's do it again."

"That's my cue," said Barry. "I'm due on the bridge."

"By the time I'm done with him, he'll be able to shoot better than you."

"I'm counting on it." Barry left the cargo bay.

"Now, Morrissey, this time, try not to blink when you fire. And remember, spatial awareness is key — don't aim where the target is, but where you anticipate it to be headed. Lead the target."

The sequence restarted, the targets cycling into view. This time he did better, making solid contact with three targets and a glancing blow on another.

"Better, but you're still blinking."

"It's the muzzle flash. Blinking is unconscious."

"Hold on, I have something that might help." Syddyk palmed open a storage locker and began rummaging around inside, almost tumbling headfirst into the compartment. He emerged with a look of victory. "Here, try these."

He handed Morrissey a pair of goggles, two clear, bulbous teardrops held together by a thick, black strap. Morrissey looked dubious but snapped them over his eyes anyway. The band tightened, automatically conforming to his human head.

"There is a node at the left temple. Dial it all the way upward."

Morrissey found the nubbin and dialled it as far as it would go. Instantly, his world sunk into a dull, green soup.

"That setting should help filter out the glare. Now let's try it again."

Morrissey tried the firing cycle again, this time with his fancy new flash-suppressing goggles on full whack. His results were much better, managing to hit seven targets within the timed sequence.

"Very good! Now, with each target cycle, you can dial down the register of the lenses. Eventually, you won't need them at all. You can keep the goggles. Not all of the settings are functional, but you may find further use for them."

Morrissey enjoyed his time on the target range; it reminded him of his youth, plinking at tin cans with his pellet gun. By midday, he'd grown quite adept at target hunting and was able to hit ten targets with ten shots almost every time, albeit on the slowest speed. He cast a glance at his diminutive tutor. "Let's see how a pro does it, Syd."

"I am practised enough."

"Come on, show me how it's done."

"Very well, Morrissey, but only to humour you."

Syddyk unholstered his pistol — a child-sized version of Morrissey's. He checked the charge as a matter of course and thumbed it to *active*. The targets began their hypnotic dance, though this time their speed was dizzying. In one fluid motion, Syddyk whipped up his pistol and locked into a firing stance. The weapon flashed, fast and steady. And then it was over. All the targets were down; Morrissey was almost certain that Syddyk had hit two of them with one shot.

"That was…amazing!"

"Not amazing. Just training."

"Where do you get that kind of training? Were you in the military?"

"I did not shoot before the ALF."

If it were possible for Syddyk's eyes to look sadder, Morrissey couldn't imagine it. "It's none of my business, Syd. I shouldn't have asked. I've only had a small taste of what it's like being dragged away from your home. I can't begin to understand what you and Kheni went through."

"We were not taken from our home."

"I don't understand. I thought — "

"Kheni and I were not abducted. We were propagated in captivity."

Morrissey winced as the implications settled into an uncomfortable truth. He realised that animals on Earth were bred in zoos but he couldn't imagine the same bleak prospects for a sentient being. "I — I don't know what to say."

"You do not need to say anything. We were bred as part of an experimental cloning program."

"You're clones? But you aren't identical, are you?"

"Each of the test subjects in our batch started from the same DNA source. From there, certain…alterations were made to our genetic sequences. We were tested for all manner of tolerances: extremes of temperature, atmospheric conditions, resistance to disease, and toxins — whatever permutation the Vemen could devise to further their studies. Usually, the aim was to either enhance a trait to measure the result or strip it entirely to evaluate the absence. I was certain that sometimes they just did it for sport."

"It sounds barbaric. How did you survive?"

"We almost did not. Three hundred and seventy of my race were created for this program. At the time of our liberation, there were only twenty-five of us left. When the ALF boarded the station, our captors tried to destroy all evidence of their treachery — Kheni and I were the only ones who survived."

"Syd, I'm so sorry." His words felt hollow.

"Sha'an always blamed herself for our severe casualties, but if it weren't for her team's intervention we would all have perished eventually. At least now, Kheni and I have the chance to right some serious wrongs."

"Is that why you stayed with the ALF?"

"Xrrka and her people tried to repatriate us but what little data there was of our origin was destroyed in the melee. We know our race — Mo-Ahn — but not much more. Imagine if you were found on some random station with no information about your home — would you know how to find your way? Yet Xrrka has never tired in her quest to find ours."

Morrissey felt no small amount of shame for whinging about not being able to return to Earth. He couldn't imagine what it would be like not to have known it at all; perhaps in some twisted way, it was better not to know the life you were missing but he dared not suggest that to Syddyk.

"The only thing that keeps me going is Kheni. We bonded as brothers during our incarceration and drew solace from one another as our numbers dwindled. We had no family until Xrrka and the ALF took us in and gave us a home…and a purpose. They are our family now. They are our home."

Morrissey wanted to hug the little fella but didn't know how the gesture would be received. Thankfully, Barry returned to break the melancholy.

"How's our student doing?"

"I would be most proud to have him fighting by my side," said Syddyk.

"That's good to hear but fighting isn't exactly what I had in mind. I just want him to be able to defend himself."

Morrissey wasn't in any particular rush to jump into battle. "Don't worry, I get it."

"And I want you to wear your sidearm at all times, day and night — at least during waking hours. It might feel a bit odd at first, but by the time we hit the surface of Chyll I want it to feel like a natural extension of yourself."

"Isn't that a bit…you know…wild-westy? I mean, wouldn't I just be inviting trouble?"

"Trouble doesn't need an invitation. The trick is to be ready when it knocks on the door."

As Sha'an would have said, better to have and not need than to need and not have. "I noticed that Lillum is the only one of the crew who isn't armed."

"Lillum is a healer — it goes against her vows."

"What if push came to shove — would she be able to push back?"

"Let's hope we never have to find out."

CHAPTER 17

The T'Taro Briiga spun out of hyperspace just before lunch, the particular shade of black looking very much the same as the one they'd left three days earlier. Morrissey had joined Barry, Kheni, and Lillum in the galley; he'd spent much of the morning honing his shooting skills with a variety of energy weapons and had worked up quite an appetite. Unfortunately, all that was waiting for him was a sublimely bland selection from the Green Menu, which tasted very much like baked cardboard glazed with mucous. He was only too happy for the distraction of Syddyk's holo-image bursting from a comm node.

"The Briiga has a shadow," said Syddyk.

Morrissey looked to Barry for clarification, but Barry just shrugged. "Erm…what do you mean, it has a shadow?"

"A shadow. A twin. Just at the edge of our sensor range. The signal is weak but it's definitely on a parallel trajectory."

"Any chance it's an asteroid?" said Kheni.

Holo-Syddyk shook his head. *"Not unless it's a really clever asteroid that graduated from The Asteroid Course-Changing School for Gifted Asteroids. I've made several deliberate course changes over the last twenty minutes, and it's matched every one."*

"That doesn't sound good," said Morrissey. "Sha'an said that the chances of two ships appearing in the same area of space at the same time were very, very slim."

"We're pretty far off the major shipping lanes," said Barry, "and there are no inhabited planets in this sector. Could it be a ghost image, maybe our own ship reflecting back on our sensors?"

"It's possible," said Syddyk, *"but considering what's at stake, we can't afford to take any chances."*

"Agreed. If it is another ship, it could still be a coincidence. No one could have known we were taking this route. Can you boost our sensors at all?"

"I've already got the array pushed to the max, but I can send out a few probes to create a relay network. That should extend the range by about a third."

"Good. Do it. And if it deviates, I want to know immediately."

Holo-Syddyk fizzed back into the comm node with a short salute.

"If it is another ship," said Morrissey, "how would they have known where to find us? I thought you couldn't track a ship in hyperspace?"

"You can't. In theory. They would have to have very specific information about our itinerary. Or…Kheni, I need you to run another scan on The Briiga, nose to tail. Look for any kind of signal that doesn't belong. And send a coded message to Xrrka, updating her on our status." Kheni was up with a stern nod. "Lillum, prep the Med-Pod. I'm hoping we won't need it but…well, you know. Just in case."

"Is there anything I should be doing?" said Morrissey.

"You can help me prep the shuttle. If we have to bug out in a hurry, I want to be sure we're ready."

Morrissey was helping Barry secure the shuttle for manoeuvres — actually he was pretty much just shuffling cargo containers around in an attempt to feel useful — when Kheni buzzed through on Barry's wrist comm. *"I've completed a full ship-wide sweep, Barrek — twice. We're clean. If we are being tracked, it's being done by powers I can't fathom."*

"Okay, thanks. Did you contact Xrrka?"

"Done. She's working on it from her end."

"Good lad. You'd better begin your landing prep. We'll be in range of Chyll, soon."

"Will do." Kheni disconnected.

"Shit," said Barry.

"That's good news, no?" said Morrissey. "If we're not being tracked, then whoever that ship is — if it is even a ship — is just there by accident, a coincidence, right?"

"That's one theory."

"And it's a theory I'm growing quite fond of."

"Another theory is that it is a ship that has a very sneaky way of tracking us. And I don't like sneaky."

"I thought I was the paranoid one."

"I guess you're rubbing off on me."

Barry's wrist comm chimed again. This time it was Syddyk. "It's gone."

"What? The ship?"

"The ship. Gone. Vanished. Off the sensor grid."

Morrissey tried his best to match Barry's long strides as he raced to the bridge. "So what does that mean?"

Barry did not look impressed. "It means that either we are no longer in danger...or," he said, jumping the steps three at a time, "...it means that we are in a great deal of danger."

"My vote is for the first one."

"Couldn't agree more, mate." Barry burst into the Command Sphere. "Status report."

"I'd just finished syncing the probes," said Syddyk. "The moment I fired up the relay, pfffft. Gone."

"Maybe there was a sensor glitch in the first place and the probe relay fixed it," said Morrissey hopefully.

"Or maybe," said Barry, "our ghost ship knew he'd been rumbled and buggered off into hyperspace."

"It was no sensor error, Barrek. Definitely a ship. I can be sure of that now. The probes were able to relay a small data packet just before the vessel jumped." He flashed an image on the main viewer. Faint and grainy as the image was, it was definitely manmade — or some sort of being-made.

"That's no asteroid," said Morrissey.

"Not even a bit," said Syddyk. "It's armed, though. Look. There…and there." He highlighted two threatening protuberances. "Pirates, maybe?"

"Maybe," said Barry. "There could be a base hidden out here — it's certainly isolated enough. But probably too isolated to make a good feeding ground for pirates. And if they were pirates, why would they jump away? Why not attack?"

"Spies," said Morrissey quietly.

"Why are you whispering?" said Barry.

"I don't know…shouldn't we keep quiet or something?"

"You know sound can't travel in space, right?"

"Erm…yes. Right. Rookie mistake."

"In any case," said Barry, "if that was a spy ship, then we have to assume it's reported our position — and figured out where we're headed."

"Can't we just lay low for a bit and then come back later?" said Morrissey.

"There isn't any later. We've got to get to Chyll before they return — probably with friends. We should make Chyll's orbit in about four hours. We've got a pretty good head start but it'll be close. Syd, you'd better fire up the plasma cannons. We might be having company."

CHAPTER 18

Chyll technically wasn't Morrissey's first alien world, but it was the first one he'd been able to see coming. The planet swelled ahead like a giant marble smeared with lush greeny-blues, scabs of harsh ruddy browns, and a tangle of white cotton woven throughout. According to the scant records on file, it was a primitive world devoid of sentient indigenous life, with a history as bleak and barren as its terrain. It was so far off the galactic superhighway that it lacked any strategic importance whatsoever. In fact, if you were to find the arsehole of the universe, Chyll would be the haemorrhoid that dangled from it. It was, therefore, the perfect place for the Thuwom called Bryndevaan to live out its life in exile. No one would notice him — no one would care if they did. And no one would ever think to look for him here. Until now.

Barry pushed the ship steadily toward its orbit while Kheni fed the crew updates from engineering. Syddyk had taken up a position in the dorsal plasma cannon blister, giving him a three hundred and sixty degree perspective to complement the targeting array. The ventral cannon remained slaved to the bridge under Barry's control. There had been no further sightings of the ghost ship, but Barry wasn't taking any chances. He'd considered taking the shuttle down to the surface but decided he couldn't afford to thin out the crew any further. Besides, The Briiga had more firepower than the shuttle should the need arise.

The Briiga slowed to orbital velocity, skipping nimbly across the upper atmosphere and allowing Morrissey a stunning view of the crisp turquoise shell hugging the gentle curve of the planet's surface. Barry adjusted the shield focus, causing a burning shimmer on the ventral display panels; Morrissey felt as if he were going to catch fire. As the ship sliced down toward the planet it shuddered violently as frictional shears raked across the hull, plasma flares searing its underbelly. Morrissey's thoughts turned to a distant memory of the Space Shuttle Columbia as it disintegrated upon re-entry and wondered if this was how those astronauts felt before fate took them. But Barry sat, calm as you like, stroking the flight controls as if it were business as usual. Finally, the ship broke atmosphere and settled into a graceful descent while Chyll's gravity began to take hold.

The full wraparound panoramic display was active, which only heightened Morrissey's sense that he was going to slam face first into the planet surface. Fierce, jagged mountain peaks stabbed angrily at the ship as it descended while silver snakes of shimmering water twisted through the valleys in the cold, pale morning sunlight. Their target was a temperate region just north of the equator in the eastern hemisphere, currently experiencing its version of autumn.

They skimmed over miles of flat, grey, crusty earth, baked by sun and time, until finally setting down at the foot of an imposing mountain range. Manoeuvring thrusters kicked up an ashen storm of dust and debris as the landing gear grappled with the uneven planet surface. Only when all stations reported secure did Morrissey unbuckle from his seat.

"Nice landing," he said, relieved to be on solid ground once again.

Barry smiled a human-toothed grin. "Piece of cake. Now comes the tricky part."

The Briiga had done all it could to get the crew as close as possible to their final destination. The tricky part involved a twenty-kilometre road trip — minus the road — along a dried-out riverbed that snaked its way into the heart of the valley ahead and deep into the belly of the black mountains.

The crew had assembled in the shuttle bay where they systematically moved through their debarking protocols. Morrissey outfitted himself with the necessary equipment for the mission, ticking off the list of items he was told he'd need and asking for help with the ones he was unsure of. Chyll had a gravity less than half that of Earth's, but its atmosphere was still breathable. There would be no need for pressure suits on this trip though all personnel were required to carry rebreathers just in case.

Morrissey also carried the goggles Syddyk had given him to help with his target practice. So far, he'd only been able to figure out the polarising and zoom settings, so if he needed a pair of magnifying sunglasses, he was all set to go. There were infrared and thermal imaging settings, but he hadn't had time to fine tune them to any purpose. He snapped them on, feeling like a bit of a bug-eyed knob, but no one seemed to notice — or care.

Each team member, excluding Lillum, was to carry a long gun to complement their sidearm. Morrissey had only just gotten used to the feel of a pistol strapped to his thigh but did as ordered. He chose a stubby, plasma carbine, capable of long-range, single shot action as well as semi-auto and full-on auto-fire. The weapon pressure-clipped to a quick-release chest rig, leaving both his hands free.

When the team was ready, they piled into an all-terrain ground transport vehicle, the name of which loosely translated to The Nomad. The seats were mostly designed to accommodate the bipedal contingent but there was a special saddle which accounted for Lillum's serpentine body.

The vehicle's engines fired to life, pulsing an electric thrum through the deck plate, charging Morrissey with a fresh buzz of trepidation. The massive bay doors cleaved before them and The Nomad poured out onto Chyll's bleak surface, its treads biting heartily into the baked ground, cracking and popping the brittle rock as it rumbled onto the wasteland. Morrissey cast a wistful look back as the T'Taro Briiga sealed up behind them, a lonely sentinel in the stark surroundings.

Without the comforting embrace of the ship's artificial gravity, Morrissey was already feeling the lighter pull of Chyll's forces. Each dip and bump lifted him gently off his seat; had he not been tethered by his safety harness, he would have bounced through the roof.

"It'll take some getting used to," said Barry. "Wait until you start walking — you're going to feel like you can fly, but you can't. So don't try, is my point. You may feel as light as a feather but your body still has the same mass. If you fall, it's gonna hurt." Morrissey nodded absently as Barry addressed the whole crew. "Remember, people, if you do have to use your weapons, check your fire. Your aim is liable to be a bit wilder in this gravity."

Heavy metal shutters hummed open, exposing panoramic plexi-shields. Morrissey suddenly felt more vulnerable than ever. His eyes darted into every nook and crevice on the landscape, searching for imminent doom.

"Relax," said Syddyk. "We're running constant sensor sweeps for any activity and so far, there's only been a scattering of life signs."

"Yeah, but what kind of life?" said Morrissey. "I know you guys have been on a ton of planets, but this is still new to me."

"Don't worry," said Barry. "Syd's right, we're completely safe in here."

Morrissey cracked a thin smile, not wholly convinced.

As they rolled deeper into the narrowing valley, their progress slowed on the uneven terrain. The sensor blips that had been few began to multiply and congregate, morphing into a single blob of heat signatures. Morrissey scanned the rock face for a real-world corroboration.

"I can't see anything," he said. "How big are they supposed to be?" Remembering his goggles, he cycled through each of the settings. Infrared verified The Nomad's readouts, revealing a solid orange glow blanketing the sunward side of the mountain. The thermal image was able to isolate individual organisms that formed the cluster. "I see them, just sitting there, plain as day."

"I've got them," said Syddyk, pointing to his sensor display.

There were hundreds of them, spanning dozens of metres across the rock face. "You don't think they're dangerous, do you?"

Lillum's head bobbed casually. "I think they're absorbing the heat from the sun."

"You mean...sunbathing?"

"Not for pleasure. It might be how they feed. See the canopies on their backs."

Morrissey zoomed in for a closer look at one of the creatures. Its body was a translucent tube about a metre in length — a sausage, really — supported by a multitude of thin leg filaments. Sprouting from the back of each sausage was a delicate oval membrane that fanned out atop the tube like a parasol — or a solar collector. The herd did seem to be soaking up the energy of Chyll's weak sunlight, maintaining a fairly rigid pattern within the sun's blanket.

One of the smaller sun-grazers began to stray into the shadows, toward a three-metre gash in the rock. The crevice was rimmed with gentle mounds of purplish moss, perhaps another food source for the creatures. As the sun-grazer made contact with the moss, a balloon of swollen flesh suddenly billowed from the gash with lightning speed, latching onto the unsuspecting creature. The sun-grazer kicked frantically against the distended skin of the balloon-predator for only seconds before the swollen sac deflated as quickly as it had appeared, sucking its meal deep into the black hole of the rock.

"Did you see that?" said Morrissey. "Something in the rock face — some sort of balloon creature...Jesus...it just grabbed one of those things and...one second it was there, the next...gone."

"Circle of life, mate," said Barry. "Just nature taking its course."

"I don't want to be one of nature's courses."

Barry thumped the bulkhead of The Nomad. "Don't worry, Dave. As long as we're in here, we're as safe as — "

The Nomad lurched to a sudden stop as it rounded a bend. Kheni swore softly in some untranslatable slang. "Looks like we're going the rest of the way on foot."

Morrissey glared daggers at Barry. "You have got to be kidding me. After what we just saw out there — I ain't going anywhere on foot."

"I don't think we have a choice." Barry pointed out the front view port; a barrier stretched across their path from one side of the narrow choke point to the other, rising twenty metres into the air. It was a ragged, crystalline latticework of honeycombed cells, each roughly two metres in diameter and a metre deep.

"Is it part of the mountain?" said Morrissey.

"No, it's not natural," said Lillum, reading from her scanners. "It's composed of an organic resin. Extremely dense molecular structure."

"Organic? As in, something actually made that?"

"It would seem so."

"Alright," said Barry, "let's go. Up and out."

Morrissey's nerves were being peeled like an onion. "Look guys, I'm no exobiologist, but I'm guessing that whatever made that thing isn't something you can squash with your foot."

"Nevertheless, we can't drive any further. How far, Kheni?"

"Two klicks, give or take."

"You heard the man," said Barry. "Time to be brave little soldiers."

Hydraulics groaned as The Nomad's exit ramp hit the sunburned ground with a resigned thud. Morrissey's last sterile breath was stolen by a crisp slap of alien air. A soft, cool breeze whistled over the cliffs, a single cloud hovered on the horizon, and the weathered landscape looked serene enough, but he wasn't fooled for a minute.

Kheni and Barry were first down the ramp, fanning their weapons in tight arcs across the horizon. Syddyk bounced out next, taking point around the front of the vehicle. Lillum nudged Morrissey with a prickly forelimb. "We are next." She scuttled down the ramp, handling the reduced gravity with ease. Morrissey finally unlocked his muscles and moved warily behind her. Each tentative step pushed him twice as far and twice as high; his momentum sent him barreling into Lillum's stubby tail section. It was going to take some serious coordination to move without launching himself into space.

As Barry sealed up The Nomad, Morrissey heard the squeal of his hopes dying with the high-pitched whine of the mag-lock. Syddyk stood guard, his carbine in one hand and a portable scanner in the other, shaking his head slowly.

"What is it?" said Barry.

He gestured to the barrier. Each cell of the crystalline lattice was ringed with a multitude of translucent, barbed spines, about a metre long. Desiccated husks of long-dead fauna clung eerily to many of the spines, offering a grim testament to their purpose.

"We'll have to go over," said Kheni. "Up the mountain and over the barrier."

Morrissey threw him a dubious glare.

Thankfully, Barry had other plans. He tapped tentatively at one of the razored spears with the butt of his rifle. It trilled in the crisp air like a tuning fork. He slammed a bit harder. Then harder, still. Finally, the spear snapped, leaving a jagged stump singing in the breeze. "The barrier may be as hard as rock but these tines are relatively brittle. Give me a hand."

The group bashed at the giant teeth until they'd chipped a wide enough gap for them all to slink through. One by one, they twisted through the cavity. As the smallest, Syddyk and Kheni went through first, taking defensive positions on the other side. Morrissey was next, followed by Lillum. As the biggest of the bunch, she was at the greatest risk but her chitinous shell afforded her the greatest defence. Barry went last, contorting his gangly frame as best he could.

"Can you tag this cell, Syd? These spikes are hard to see. If we need to make a hasty retreat, I don't want any mishaps."

Syddyk marked the opening with a laser tagger on his scanner and then set his sights on the cliffs ahead. "We've got about nineteen hundred metres to go."

"And we've got some time to make up," said Barry. "We'd better get our collective fingers out."

They moved out in formation, Syddyk maintaining point while Kheni brought up the rear. Barry and Lillum flanked Morrissey, which was a bit embarrassing considering Lillum wasn't even armed. By the time they'd gone five hundred metres, he could hop with enough confidence that he was no longer holding them back. As their pace quickened, so did his enjoyment, so much so that a slight giddiness soon enveloped him. Giddy...and lightheaded. Shit. "I think something's wrong. I don't feel so good."

Lillum moved quickly to his side, waving a med-scanner over his chest. "His breathing is shallow and laboured. Heartbeat is elevated. And I don't think blue is a good colour for a human. David, you're suffering from the early stages of hypoxia. Do you understand me?" Morrissey nodded. "You must use your rebreather." She placed the facemask over his nose and mouth, making sure it formed a proper seal. "Take normal breaths, slow and steady."

"Is everyone else okay?" said Barry. They all nodded. "No shame, Dave. You're still new at this. We all process oxygen in slightly different ways. You're doing quite well...considering."

"Considering...I'm a human?"

"Nobody's perfect." Barry winked a saucer eye. "Take your time. It's just a quiet stroll in the country. No pressure. We'll move on whenever you're ready."

Except there was pressure; time was ticking. Morrissey breathed in the concentrated oxygen as directed; nausea faded and the ache in his head eased. There were still some traces of giddiness but that could have been genuine euphoria. The sun was shining and only a single cloud in the sky, a beautiful day on an alien world.

Lillum finally deemed him fit to continue under the proviso that he keep his rebreather on. They were making good time when Syddyk signalled to stop, directing his scanner up toward one of the mountain ridges. Darkness swelled from the craggy gash — a cave opening? "Up there," he said. "One hundred metres up that face — that's where we are to go."

Morrissey was reminded of the balloon predator swallowing the sun-grazer on a similar mountain face. "The Thuwom lives in there?"

Barry chuckled. "You didn't think he lived in a three-bedroom bungalow with lake views, did you?"

"No, but it doesn't hurt to hope."

"We're almost there," said Kheni. "Let's not waste — "

"Wait," said Lillum. "Do you hear that?"

It started softly, like pebbles on a rooftop, building to the heavy clatter of a rockslide. From behind them, the sound grew louder, nearer. Morrissey could have sworn that the earth was on the move, a sea of rubble flowing toward them. He flipped the setting on his goggles to thermal in time to see that what was thundering toward them was not rubble at all. It was most definitely alive.

He didn't recognise them at first, not with their solar canopies retracted, but as the frantic horde drew closer, there was no mistaking the sun-grazers they'd seen earlier. The creatures that had been so docile, languidly lapping up the energy from Chyll's sun, were now a skittering stampede. Their bodies, once camouflaged by the black mountain rock, now more clearly revealed their shape and number against the bleached valley bed.

Running would do no good at this distance; the team held their ground, bracing for the attack. "Erm...ready your weapons," said Barry. "Wait for my signal."

Barry, Syddyk, and Kheni already had their weapons drawn and charged to life. Morrissey was a bit slower springing his carbine free from its bracket. He thumbed it to *active*, waving it vaguely toward the creatures. Adrenaline flushed his system and pounded his legs to jelly. These weren't floating targets on a firing range. He only hoped he could pull the trigger when the time came. And the time was coming.

Fifty metres...

Morrissey could feel tension burn through the team, though he was sure none of them showed it but him.

Forty metres…

The subtle vibration of the stampede rattled the ground and jangled his nerves.

Thirty metres…

His finger twitched over the firing stud of his rifle.

Twenty metres…

Barry would certainly give the order to fire…any…time…now…

And then at ten metres, without breaking stride, the river of sun-grazers parted like The Red Sea, coursing around the group with barely a how-do-you-do. The team kept their weapons primed and ready for the attack that never came. "Well," said Barry, as the last of the creatures left them in a fog of dust. "That was interesting."

"It's as if they're afraid," said Lillum.

"Afraid of what?" said Morrissey.

"Of that." Kheni turned their attention to the sky. The single cloud that had kept a distant vigil over them was now much, much closer. The core of its mass was still a good distance away, but the leading edge was almost upon them. The first particles struck, delicate white fibrous puffs, each no bigger than a peppercorn.

Then the biting began. First Kheni. Then Syddyk. Barry's cries soon followed. "The little fuckers!"

Even Lillum wasn't immune. The puffs stung like pinpricks through the gaps in her crispy coating and into her soft tissues. Only Morrissey was spared. Whatever these things were, they apparently didn't like the taste of human. They swiped and swatted at the tiny pests, leaving smears of their own blood on their exposed flesh. Finally, the wave of Floaters ebbed, leaving the group tending their annoying wounds.

"What the bloody hell was that all about?" said Barry.

"And what in the name of [untranslatable] is that?" Lillum motioned to a creature galloping toward them. What it looked like was a low, squat sheep, zigging and zagging toward them at an erratic pace. What it sounded like, however, had no earthly equivalent, an ear-shattering shriek echoing through the valley.

The team targeted the new threat instinctively. Its movement slowed as it dragged its body closer, bucking and twitching until it fell into a spasming heap. Its bleating finally ceased, along with its motion. Up close, they could see it was not a sheep-like creature at all. It was another of the sun-grazers, its body covered with dozens of the fluffy white Floaters, only bigger than before, some the size of golf balls. Each throbbing, pulsing orb was tethered to the sun-grazer by hundreds of filaments as fine as angel hair, sucking hard at the creature's precious life juices.

Kheni swung at the deadly Floaters with the butt of his plasma rifle, but they clung as ferociously as they fed. Not that it would do any good — the sun-grazer was long past dead. When the Floaters had sufficiently gorged themselves, they rolled away from their feast, leaving only a soggy carcass. Syddyk kicked hard at one of them, sending it bouncing across the gravel like a dazed water balloon.

Morrissey was unable to turn away from the grisly scene. Barry snapped him out of it. "We've got to get out of here," he said, gesturing to the new wave of rapidly approaching Floaters, this time the size of baseballs. "Everyone to the cave — now!"

They bounded as fast and hard as they could, finding renewed strength through the fear. Barry brought up the rear, firing systematically into the cloud; the Floaters burst by the dozens, exploding with sizzling pops, but it wasn't enough. He barely made a dent in their numbers.

Lillum stumbled at the foot of the rise. Morrissey, only slightly ahead of her, grabbed her awkwardly, trying to adjust his centre of gravity so he could lift her. At Kheni and Syddyk's arrival, they got her hopping again.

"Syd," said Barry, "get Morrissey to the cave. I'll take care of Lillum." Kheni shifted into the rear fire position.

Syddyk and Morrissey reached the edge of the ridge below the cave entrance with Barry and Lillum close behind. Morrissey stretched an arm down while Barry pushed from below and together, they hoisted Lillum up to relative safety. That was when they heard the cries.

Kheni lay crumpled on the rocks below as more and more of the Floaters latched onto his flesh and bit through his jumpsuit. He fired his weapon as fast as he could until agony forced it from his grip. Thrashing with all his remaining might, he crushed as many of the pulsing masses as he could, but it was far from enough. When one disengaged, two more attached.

The ALF crew looked on in horror, too far to be of use. Their weapons were ready, but their will was not, for fear of hitting their crew mate, their friend, their brother. Brother. Syddyk's eyes were swollen as he began his scramble down the ridge.

Barry grabbed his arm. "No! It's too dangerous."

"But he's dying! He's my only…I can't…"

"You can't go down there — you'll be killed, too."

"I can," said Morrissey. "They didn't attack me. I'll get him."

"Oh no you bloody won't," said Barry. "We can't take the risk they won't go for you now."

"But we can't just leave him to those…things."

"No, we can't." Syddyk's voice was calm and resolute. Kneeling at the edge of the ridge, he slowly and methodically shouldered his plasma rifle. Carefully adjusting the sights, he drew in a single breath. Kheni raised his head one last time. Syddyk fired, only once. The blast struck his brother in the forehead, a short, wet pop. And he was gone. "They won't take him from me." Syddyk spoke quietly but they all heard him. And they all felt him.

CHAPTER 19

A week ago, Morrissey had never had occasion to fear for his life. Now it seemed like standard operating procedure. He knew the mission was dangerous, that any one of them could be injured or killed at any time, but he never actually thought that fate would call their bluff.

He flicked a cautious glance toward Syddyk, unable to meet his eyes. Obviously, he hadn't known Kheni nearly as well as the others so he could barely imagine their sense of loss, let alone how Syddyk must feel, being the one who pulled the trigger on his only family — his only blood. The words I'm sorry seemed insultingly trite but he didn't know what else to say.

Syddyk beat him to it. "You did not kill him."

There was something in Syddyk's eyes that betrayed his words. Sadness, obviously. Anger? Possibly. A veiled accusation? Morrissey wouldn't blame him. Unwitting pawn or not, he was now responsible for two ALF deaths and the debt weighed heavily on him. "Still, it wouldn't have happened if it weren't for me and my situation."

166

Syddyk's lips twisted into a bitter smile. "Kheni knew the risks — we all do — but we've got to continue with the mission so that he did not die in vain." It was more of a plea than a statement.

"Only when you're ready, Syd," said Barry. "I need your focus, now more than ever."

"And you have it. My brother is gone, there is no changing that. There will be time enough to mourn when we are off this rock."

"If you're sure. I need you to set up a comm-link. When we find this Thuwom, we're going to need to confer with Xrrka and I want a clean signal to The *Briiga*'s ansible beacon."

Syddyk retrieved an elongated egg-shaped object from his pack. He inserted his thumb into a divot near its base and slammed the pod into the gravel near the cave opening. The egg split into eight leaves as a soft energy pulsed from within. A few minor configurations later he said, "Link established. Signal is solid."

"Then I guess we're going in," said Barry. "Take it slow and steady — no bouncing around. We don't know how cramped it's going to get in there."

"David, you might want to conserve your O2," said Lillum. "You should be okay without your rebreather for a while." Morrissey reluctantly removed his face mask and stowed it in his belt pouch, a naked vulnerability washing over him.

Inside the cave, the dying shadows sparked his imagination with enough creeps to make the skin crawl right off his bones. Darkness soon swallowed the team as the path took them downward and they charged their personal beacons to compensate. Morrissey thought he could do one better and flipped on his goggles. He dialled up the thermal setting but that only revealed the ghostly white glow of his comrades moving against the cold slate grey backdrop, so he switched back to his beacon.

The air cooled significantly as they sunk deeper into the cave, the vague sting of sulphur and rotting fish assaulting his sense of smell. Up ahead, Barry gave the signal to stop; they all froze, primed for attack or defence, whichever came first. Their beams knotted together, coming to rest on the object of his concern. It towered above them, a rack of jagged limbs stretching toward a bulbous, translucent torso. Spiny barbs jutted from what could have been a mouth.

Barry quietly ordered the team to extinguish their beacons; Morrissey complied reluctantly. If I can't see it, it doesn't exist, right? Wrong. Knowing it was still there, lurking in the oppressive dark, waiting to strike, did little to staunch the flow of terror. He switched his goggles back onto the thermal setting but saw no heat signature other than from his friends. Maybe the creature could mask its body temperature. He flipped the goggles off again, allowing his eyes to adjust to the threat naturally.

They edged slowly backward in the pervasive gloom, all but Syddyk who moved inch by inch toward the creature. Morrissey wanted to scream out, to yank him back from his folly. Maybe Syddyk had a plan. Maybe he had a death wish. When he was close enough, he reached out to the grotesque figure, extending his rifle toward one of its massive limbs. As he pushed tentatively with the muzzle of his weapon, Morrissey could almost feel their collective heartbeats stop.

"I think it's dead," said Syddyk.

"How can you be sure?" whispered Barry.

Syddyk gave it another shove with his rifle. "I am sure."

"How sure?"

"Enough to stake my life on, apparently."

"And ours, thanks very much." Barry exhaled slowly. "Next time, a little warning."

Lillum didn't seem convinced. "It could be in hibernation."

Barry inched forward, scanner at the ready. "No, Syd's right. It's not registering any life signs."

"I'm with Lillum," said Morrissey. "It might just be playing dead."

Dead or not, it didn't seem interested in immediate attack. "If it's not dead, it's certainly a lazy bugger," said Barry. He gave it one last shove, then signalled them to reactivate their beacons. The harsh lights pored over the creature's spindly frame. Morrissey counted twelve angry limbs, each about five metres long, with knobby joints along the way. Its torso was a disturbing amalgam of head and body rolled into one unsightly blob roughly the size of a Smart Car, the grey-green of its carapace bristling with crystalline cilia. On Earth, a creature of such proportions would be crushed by its own weight, but with Chyll's relatively weak gravity it could flourish. "I don't suppose this is our Thuwom friend?"

"Thankfully, no," said Barry.

Lillum tapped busily at the creature's skin with a variety of medical instruments. "It's just a husk, an empty shell. All the living tissue has long since decomposed."

"Seems an odd place to leave a corpse," said Syddyk. "It's as if it's been staged for some effect."

"Like a scarecrow," said Morrissey.

"Ska-arkroooow?" Syddyk mouthed the word awkwardly. "What is this?"

"On Earth, farmers use them to frighten away pests, birds — any unwanted animal that might damage their crops."

"I wonder what this is designed to scare away," said Lillum.

"Well...me, for a start," said Morrissey.

"Or maybe the Floaters. They didn't seem interested in following us into the cave — something must be keeping them out."

Morrissey poked at it gingerly. It felt like death, cold and chalky. "I think the better question is what is it protecting?"

"That would be me." The voice was an eerie trill echoing from the depths of the shadows. A figure sidled out from a crevice behind them. Their beacons splashed across what could only be described as a giant purple tongue. It stood erect at almost two metres though to say it stood would be implying it had legs, which it did not. The tip of the tongue frayed into a fibrous fringe that oscillated steadily back and forth. An assortment of fleshy tubes, each as long and thick as a human forearm, punched through its skin at random intervals, then retracted back into its slick body. There were no eyes or mouth in the traditional sense, though when it spoke a foot long vertical gash split open at its middle, revealing a series of taut chords thrumming in sync with its words.

"Remain still," it said. "Especially after placing down your weapons." One of the tubular appendages was ringed with a donut-shaped cuff that could have been a weapon. Or it could have been a donut. "You asked who has placed this creature here and I offer myself as your answer. The fact that I have killed such a beast would make you wise to follow my directions. So, as I say, place down your weapons, immediately."

Barry started the ball rolling. He calmly unslung his rifle and laid it on the rock floor. Then he unbuckled his pistol belt and placed it beside. Syddyk followed his lead without hesitation so Morrissey did likewise; ironically, he suddenly felt naked without his pistol at his side.

"Now, tell me who you are and why I shouldn't shoot you where you stand."

Barry moved toward the creature, hands still raised. "Because we've come a long way to find you."

Morrissey looked on in wonder as the object of their mission revealed itself.

The creature's head-fringe pulled back as if blown by a stiff wind. "That is not possible for exactly two reasons. One, no one knows that I am here. And two, no one knows who I am."

"You and I both know that's not true," said Barry. "You are Bryndevaan the Thuwom."

Its head-fringe bristled aggressively. "How is this knowledge inside you?"

"We were sent here to find you, Bryndevaan. We need your help."

"I have no help to give. You will, therefore, leave now."

"Xrrka said you might be a little less than forthcoming."

The Thuwom went silent, his appendages locked in protest. "How is it you know the Xrrka name?"

"She's the one who sent us. How else would we find you? We are members of the ALF — I know you know the organisation."

"It is Xrrka's organisation, true enough, but I do not know you…" Bryndevaan's head-fringe fanned across them all, "…any of you. Much of what you say could be falsehoods."

Barry's large saucer eyes pulsed with a sense of urgency. "Xrrka wouldn't divulge your whereabouts unless it was an extreme emergency."

Bryndevaan looked about as irritated as any man-sized tongue could possibly look. "Your logic is circular. You and I both know that there would be many ways to extract information from Xrrka, all of them, I imagine, against her will."

"This is getting us nowhere. If you don't believe me, then maybe you'll believe her." With the toe of his boot, Barry tipped a control on his weapons belt at his feet. A spray of coloured light ignited from a node on the belt and shimmered into a life-sized hologram of Xrrka. The reception was poor in the cave and the image was grainy, but Morrissey felt comforted at the sight, nonetheless.

"Greetings, Bryndevaan," said the hologram.

"Xrrka. It is, indeed, you."

"I don't blame you for doubting. It has been many years."

"And yet your presence changes nothing. What I have told your errand-runner is fact — I cannot help you."

"We are not asking for much, only that you utilise your considerable skills to analyse the DNA of this human specimen." Holo-Xrrka gestured to Morrissey, who was impressed by the technology allowing such interactive communication at such a great distance.

"Did you forget that it was the use of those considerable skills that have made my exile necessary?"

"I did not forget, nor have I told my colleagues the reason for your current situation. I have honoured the conditions of your exile and respected your privacy, but I would not ask if the situation were not grave."

"Gravity notwithstanding, my resolution is unmovable."

The spin of the conversation was dizzying. Morrissey had literally crossed the stars to unravel his genetic mystery and he'd be damned if it was all for nothing. "Excuse me. I know I'm the new guy in the galaxy so maybe I should just let the grownups talk, but seeing as I'm also the guy about to get probed, maybe I could toss an idea or two into the ring — if I may, Xrrka?" He didn't give her time to object. "Bryndevaan — may I call you Bryndevaan?" If the creature had shoulders, it would have shrugged. "Bryndevaan, you and I are very much alike."

The Thuwom's head-fringe rippled. "I see no physical pleasantness comparable to my own."

Morrissey suppressed a smile. "What I mean is that we share something in common. You see, I don't want to be here. And you don't want me to be here. Yet here we both are." He motioned to his team. "And we have fought long and hard to get here. We've even lost friends along the way." He caught Syddyk's eye, holding his wistful gaze for a moment of reassurance. "These people are good people, honourable people, but they're not just going to walk away empty handed — not after all they've sacrificed to find you."

"Threats will not work. I still — "

"Who said anything about threats? I'm talking about *reason*. Compassion. That's what's going to get us through this."

For the first time since they'd found him, the Thuwom's stubborn will seemed to weaken. "I...I do not understand." Neither, it seemed, did the rest of the crew.

"Our mission seems to be causing you a great deal of anxiety and it seems to stem from your reason for being here. Maybe if you told us why you're in exile we could get past the stress triggers and actually do something productive."

Xrrka interrupted. *"David, I'm not sure this is such a wise idea."*

"Please, Xrrka, we've got nothing to lose." She gave him a conditional nod. "What about it, Bryndevaan — why are you here? Why are you in exile?"

The wait was interminable. Morrissey was beginning to wonder if he'd opened the wrong can of worms. The Thuwom's head-fringe sagged, as if all the life had suddenly drained from him. Finally, he spoke. "Thuwom aren't social creatures, not by conventional standards. Our communal bonds are formed over vast interstellar distances. Using our sensory glands, we are able to detect members of our species across the expanse of space. It is how we interact, how we communicate, how we attract a mate, and ultimately breed. This innate ability can also be used to analyse biological matter at the molecular level through minimal contact. Once the object DNA is sampled, it is imprinted in the Thuwom biological matrix for analysis. Under normal circumstances, it is a thoroughly benign aspect of our being.

"During my time as a captive on a Vemen research facility, I was probed, scanned, tested beyond torture. I was virtually torn apart and pieced back together. The Vemen are clinically brutal in their studies and their methods are not without purpose. When they discovered my special ability, the same ability you seek to exploit, they attempted many times to emulate its genetic complexity — to graft it onto other species. When this failed, they tried to magnify my own ability and control it. They applied it to many of their experiments, but all were met with tragic results. The one obstacle in their way was my strength of will. They could not break me down — until they found my weakness. My mate.

"They kept us separated, subjecting us to the same tortures to gauge our individual reactions and resolve, measuring the influence on one another in a variety of environments. Ultimately, they used our bond as a weapon against us, offering amnesty for my mate in exchange for my unwavering cooperation. I would have done anything to keep them safe, so I had no choice but to accept their terms. Who amongst you would have not done the same.

"To my shame, I collaborated with them, aided them in their experiments, helped them commit atrocities against my fellow captives allowing them to expand their horrific genetic advancements. The only thing that kept me going and salved my conscience was the knowledge that my mate was safe. Until I learned they weren't. When our connection was severed, I realised they'd coerced them the same as me, fed them the same lies they fed me. The silence between us could only mean that one way or another, my mate had succumbed to their brutality.

"When the Vemen facility was finally liberated, I was without hope and near death, a scrap of shrivelled tissue, tattered of mind and body. My betrayals were uncovered and I was put on trial as an enemy collaborator. In some way, it was a relief for my soul, and I welcomed the punishment for my sins. Imprisonment or execution, it made no difference. My will to live had perished with my mate."

The group was speechless, firing only horrified glances at Xrrka. She offered them no answers. Morrissey blanched at the Thuwom's words. "That is a tragic tale, Bryndevaan."

"Tragedy barely scorches the surface. The price had to be paid, but Xrrka had another method in mind for settling the debt. In her kindness and wisdom and forward thinking, she acknowledged the mitigating factors that led to my transgressions and pleaded with the magistrates to exercise clemency. In the end, the sentence of exile was imposed — a more fitting punishment, to be sure. Instead of dying with my shame and dishonour, I am cursed to live with it."

Morrissey looked around the dim cave. He knew that each member of the ALF had suffered their own personal holocaust at the hands of the Vemen; their feelings about Bryndevaan's declaration were etched into each of their faces. It was no wonder Xrrka had kept the Thuwom's truth from them. "Well, this is awkward. Look, Bryndevaan, I guess there are a few ways this could go. I'm sure some of my friends wouldn't mind throttling you to death right about now." Lillum gasped; Holo-Xrrka matched her horror. Morrissey gave her a subtle hand wave that he hoped she understood. Trust me. I know what I'm doing…I think. "But at least your story is now out in the open and we can all take a deep breath before moving beyond it. You did what you thought you had to do to keep your loved one safe. You can't fix it, you can't travel back in time to change the past." He flicked a questioning glance at Barry. "You can't, can you?" Barry shook his head. "Just checking.

Anyway, it probably wasn't the most honourable life choice you could have made but you can make a better choice for the future. You can help others survive the horrors that you had to endure. It's within you to make amends — and to finally pay your debt in full."

After an agonising silence, Bryndevaan finally lowered his donut-weapon, his appendage drooping like a flaccid penis. The Thuwom undulated toward Morrissey on a fleshy skirt that squelched as he moved. "What is your name, Pink One?"

"It's Morrissey."

"*Moorishheeee*. You speak with great persuasion."

"Let's just say that I want my life back almost as much as you want yours."

"Very well. I will help you. I will taste your DNA, as you request. Then you and all your people will leave me to be as I was."

"That's all we can ask."

"*I was becoming worried about your tactics, David,*" said Xrrka, "*but you have a natural compassion that serves you well — serves us all well.*"

"I'm just trying to see both sides of the coin. I know this won't be easy for you guys. You don't have to like him, just work with him. Let him do whatever it is he has to do, then we can be on our way. Barry, what do you say?"

"We really don't have a choice. The mission comes first. And it's not like you're going to marry him."

"I agree," said Lillum. "I cannot judge another's history."

"What about you, Syd? You're pretty quiet. I know this might be hardest for you in light of…well, you know." He couldn't bring himself to say the words. "Are you going to be okay working with him?"

Syddyk seemed as if in a trance, his large wet eyes looking through to the ends of the universe. "As Barrek says, the mission comes first. After that, we cannot know what will happen."

It would have to do.

"*Good,*" said Holo-Xrrka. "*Then we must waste no more time.*"

As they strapped on their weapons, Morrissey leaned in close to Barry. "Are you sure he's going to be okay?"

"Syd? He's a trouper. The mission will keep him focussed. He may very well fall apart when all this is over but we'll be there for him if he does. Don't worry."

Morrissey was dubious but let it go. "By the way, Xrrka, that bit about Bryndevaan tasting my DNA — that was just a figure of speech, right? Or a translation glitch?"

"Ah," she said. It was the first time he'd seen her lost for words. "Not exactly."

CHAPTER 20

Thuwom didn't need much in the way of creature comforts: a few rocks for furniture, a pit lined with a dense, scratchy moss to sleep in, and a steady supply of the local arthropods for food. The remnants of the latter lay scattered in a dank corner of the cave and were the source of the foul smell they'd encountered on the way in.

"Forgive my waste area," said Bryndevaan. "I was not expecting company."

"So that's your…toilet?" said Morrissey.

"No. My waste is filtered through my digestive system until there is nothing remaining but a mucous discharge. I smear it liberally around the entrance to my cave as it is quite effective as a pest repellent."

In the centre of the cave was a metre-high mound covered by a dried leathery mat. Bryndevaan pulled the mat from the mound, revealing a stockpile of fist-sized boulders containing the same concentrated luminescent material that scarred the walls. Their cumulative glow filled the space with a cool radiance — an ominous setting for the task ahead.

"So how does this work?" said Morrissey.

"Firstly, I will absorb a selection of your DNA in order to analyse."

Morrissey looked hopelessly around the sparse cave. "Surely you need some sort of equipment?"

"Perhaps *analyse* is not the best translation. More so, I interpret. Your chromosomes will sing their song through my body, each in concert with the next, resulting in a comprehensive recital of your genetic matrix. Any anomalies will strike a harsh discord with the rest of your melody. The results will resonate in peaks and crescendos through my being as clear and vibrant as if you, yourself, were reading them off a data-slim."

"You make it sound almost…pleasant."

"Of course, I will first need to access a body cavity."

Or maybe not. "Erm…which cavity did you have in mind?"

"Any will suffice — a nasal port, a mouth opening. Even a waste orifice."

"Let's go with the mouth, shall we? Better for all concerned, I think."

"As you wish."

"Okay, then. I'm ready whenever you are." Except he wasn't. The ALF team circled Morrissey as if offering him up for sacrifice, but there was nothing they needed to do; all that would follow was up to Morrissey and Bryndevaan, alone.

The Thuwom undulated toward him; Morrissey recoiled slightly. "Shouldn't you at least, I don't know, maybe wash your hands — or wash…*something*?" He looked helplessly at his friends. "Lillum — couldn't you lend this guy a swab or something?"

"There is almost no cause for concern. My appendages are self-sterilising."

Morrissey's stomach knotted. It wasn't every day you were probed by a two-metre tongue. Most of Bryndevaan's arm-tubes had retracted into his body except for three. Two of them wrapped around Morrissey's chest while the third appeared level with his mouth.

"Wide opening," said Bryndevaan.

Morrissey closed his eyes and thought of England. He stretched his mouth as wide as it would go, fighting the urge to block the passage with his tongue. The arm-tube pushed slowly into the opening like a slab of raw liver, reminding him of his first awkward adventures French kissing Jenny Plunkett, but it only got worse from there. The appendage stiffened, as if a thousand suction cups had taken root and were breathing him in from the inside out. He gagged reflexively as the arm-tube formed to the shape of his mouth. For a time bordering on way too long, his entire head locked tightly around the limb; he felt like he was going to suffocate and vomit all at once. Breath struggled to find a passage; his lungs burned from the effort. A flood of tears blurred his vision and just when he thought his head would burst from the pressure welling within, it was over. He sputtered as the tube retracted, leaving him in a heaving mess. Lillum offered him her flask of water, which he sucked back greedily to wash the sourness from his mouth.

Bryndevaan stood locked in a shuddering trance. A dozen of his appendages jutted out at random angles, making him look like some sort of modern art coat rack. His head-fringe fanned rhythmically while his mouth-gash stood agape, the vocal cords strumming a cacophonous jangle.

The crew looked on with no small measure of anxiety, unsure how long the impromptu choral recital would last. Finally, the Thuwom collapsed to the gravel in a wobbling heap of flesh and muscle. Lillum bobbed from side to side, her medical knowledge finding no use. Morrissey thought the creature might be dead, that somehow, his DNA had sent the poor fellow into anaphylactic shock. Then as quickly as he fell, Bryndevaan popped up like an inflatable toy clown, the kind that just won't stay down. A fist-sized orifice yawned open near the base of his fleshy skirt, spewing a stew of gelatinous chunks onto the cave floor. The Thuwom heaved and wheezed and sobbed and then...

"It is done."

Lillum rushed to his side. "Are you alright?"

"What did you find?" said Holo-Xrrka, getting straight to the point.

The creature's skin glistened with a sickly sheen. "Your song began as a light breeze...a lilting melody — at first. But it quickly became angry...bitter...melancholic...a chorus of rage-filled venom...a searing dirge..."

"Okay, okay. I get it," said Morrissey, "it wasn't exactly a Top 40 hit. Fine. But did you happen to learn anything that doesn't involve its musical merits?"

Bryndevaan turned to Holo-Xrrka. "Why…why did you not tell me?" Xrrka didn't answer. "I recognised this human's song…all too well."

"What does that mean?" said Morrissey. "Why would he recognise it? Is that a good thing?"

"No," said Bryndevaan. "It is most certainly not good."

"Am I going to die? Do I have a disease? Is it cancer?" Morrissey was working himself into a lather.

"What I have found is far more foul."

"What's worse than cancer?"

Bryndevaan seemed to sag, as if he'd been drained of all fluids, leaving only a wrinkly bag of skin. "If I would have known what this thing was, I never would have agreed to taste him."

"Steady on, mate," said Morrissey. "You didn't exactly taste like sunshine and lollipops, yourself."

"Tell us what you found," said Holo-Xrrka, sounding very much as if she already knew the answer.

"You did not tell me that this…human…carries the song…the genetic code…of the one called Vaziil." They all froze, as if their worst nightmare were being stitched together into one horrific tapestry. Bryndevaan began to ripple. "That is why you sent this human to me, of all beings."

Holo-Xrrka's head bobbed slowly. *"I didn't know for certain. Genetically, he presented as human. I'm sorry, Bryndevaan, but we had to be sure."*

Morrissey was beginning to get a feel for Xrrka's facial expressions and what he saw wasn't reassuring. At all. "Vaziil? Wait — what? The genetic terrorist you're all after — that guy? You said eNdeen wanted me because he thought I had something to do with Vaziil's weapons technology, not his bloody DNA!"

Xrrka turned to Morrissey. *"I'm sorry, David, but Bryndevaan is correct. I did not divulge our speculations about Vaziil's connection to your hidden genetic marker until we could be sure, but they have now proven true. Sha'an knew of my suspicions — that's why I assigned her to your case."*

"Okay, I get it. This Vaziil character is a very bad guy. But none of this explains why I have his DNA inside me."

Barry shifted awkwardly. "Yeah…it sort of does. Remember how your mother got close to Vaziil, suspecting he was an extraterrestrial? Well, suffice it to say that she got *really* close to him."

It took a moment for the penny to drop, and when it did, Morrissey didn't know whether to laugh or cry or curl up on the cave floor. "Nope. Not buying it. How the hell is that supposed to have happened? I mean, come on — now I know you're having a laugh. So you're saying that my dear mum went undercover — literally — to root out an alien infiltrator, that she was so obsessed with discovering the truth about aliens on Earth that she slept with a man she suspected of being one of them, and who just happened to be a galactic terrorist? And to cap it all off, I'm their lovechild? You have got to be shitting me!"

"To be fair," said Barry said, "she didn't know he was a terrorist."

Morrissey glared daggers at him. "That's not helping!"

Holo-Xrrka reached out across the digital space between them. *"I know it is difficult, David, but what Barrek says is true."*

"How could it be? Vaziil is an alien — surely you can't breed two different species? There'd be more chance of my dad being a chimp, right?" It was more of a plea than a question.

Holo-Xrrka shook her head slowly. *"Under normal circumstances, yes, but you forget that Vaziil had transformed his genetic matrix to appear human — he virtually was human. We suspect that this is what made the interspecies fertilisation possible."*

"I doubt even Vaziil could have predicted that outcome," said Lillum.

"But do not fret, David," said Holo-Xrrka, *"for all intents and purposes, you are human. The foreign matter in your genome lies dormant."*

"Great. And what if it suddenly wakes up? What am I supposed to do, sit around and wait for my tentacles to drop? Am I going to suddenly have some creature bursting out of my chest?"

Barry stared blankly at Morrissey. "Am I going to have to slap you? Am I?"

Morrissey breathed deeply until his blood settled. "Okay." He wasn't quite finished sulking but he realised it served no purpose. "So we've uncovered my family tree, now what? I suppose you'll want to use me as bait to catch this…Vaziil? Was that your plan all along? Put the poor human on the hook and see what bites?"

Xrrka curled her mouthparts into a smile as if to ease his pain. *"No David. Not bait. But we...appreciate...help..."* And then she was gone. Her image swirled and faded, fizzing back into the node at Barry's belt.

Barry thumbed the projector controls. "We've lost her signal. The transmitter seems fine. It must be the link to the ansible."

Syddyk checked his scanner. "We've got company. I'll go take a look." He scooped up his rifle and headed toward the mouth of the cave. He didn't get very far before the first blast echoed in the distance. They all instinctively shouldered their weapons, including Morrissey.

Barry doused the light from the boulders with the mat, casting the group into a protective twilight. "Bryndevaan, is there another way out of here?"

"There is only one of me. I need only one entrance."

"Great. Syd, you're with me. Dave, you stay here with Lillum and Bryndevaan. Put him to use. Both of you take firing positions, there...and there." He indicated the two choke points.

"I confess," said Bryndevaan, "that my weapon is not entirely functional."

"How not functional?"

"Not at all, in fact. The power pack ran dry a year after I arrived on this world."

Barry sighed. "Okay, Dave. It's up to you. If anyone but us comes back, you start shooting."

"What if they're friendlies?"

"If they get past us, they won't be."

Syddyk scanned ahead into the darkness as he and Barry moved toward the commotion. When they reached Bryndevaan's scarecrow, all hell broke loose. Bursts of fire sizzled the air, cracking backwards and forwards in a storm of electric chaos, strobing the cave like a disco. The noise and flash subsided as quickly as it began, sinking the cave into an interminable silence.

Morrissey saw the dim silhouette of the giant arachnoid scarecrow lean precariously to one side, then crumple in a heap of limbs, smoke, and debris. He tensed in the semidarkness, cycling his goggles through all the settings. Then he saw them, two figures in stark relief, moving toward their position. Their weapons flared in his thermal imager, burning with the heat of combat. He hoped against hope that it was Barry and Syddyk, returning in victory, but these beings were far too broad and angular to fit their profiles. A prickle of tension twisted his insides as he realised that Lillum and Bryndevaan's fates were now in his cold sweaty hands, alone.

Surprise would have to be his ally. Surprise and darkness. Surprise, darkness, and guile. That should do it. He'd wait for the creatures to come within firing range and then attack them from the shadows. He'd catch them with their stinking alien pants down and —

"You may as well come out, human. We can see where you're hiding."

Bugger. There went the element of surprise. Okay, Plan B. What the hell was Plan B? Morrissey forced calm through his fraying nerves. "Okay, so we can see one another, but you should know that I'm armed and I'm not afraid to shoot." The last part was a bit of a stretch; just about every patch of skin that could sweat was soaked with fear.

A noise emanated from the direction of his attackers that could have been gravel pouring down a drainpipe but was probably their laughter. "You won't shoot. You're not a killer. You don't have the instinct."

"You obviously don't know humans very well. Give a human an olive branch and he'll likely beat you to death with it. We're hardwired to kill if someone so much as takes our parking space. Someone even looks at us the wrong way and they're dead meat. And I have a strong feeling that I'm not going to like the way you look at me."

He doubted very much whether his attackers could decipher the threats hidden within his bravado, but it made him feel a little better. It did little, however, to slow their advance. One circled from the right, blipping in and out of Morrissey's thermal imager as he passed through the cave's natural outcroppings. The other bounded directly toward him, bold as you like with his weapon raised for action.

A tight spiral of electric blue cut a swathe inches wide of his location. Maybe it was a warning shot, or maybe he'd just been taken off eNdeen's Christmas list. He couldn't wait around to find out which. He shouldered his carbine and jerked back on the firing stud, stitching a ragged line of energy pulses a laughable distance off target.

The approaching being hesitated only long enough to assess Morrissey's lack of skill and focus his aim for another attack. Morrissey took a deep breath and let Syddyk's weapons training take control of his actions. He cycled the firing mode to semi-auto and flipped the sniper scope to blue, tabbing the zoom once, twice, then as far as it would go.

Time dripped like treacle as his breath held steady. Slowly, he eased it out as pressure increased on the trigger stud. With the reaction of the weapon measured and accounted for, he barely noticed the precise nanosecond when the firing mechanism completed its circuit.

The blast hit its mark, striking the alien dead in the chest, spinning him backward like a rag doll. Morrissey staggered on trembling legs toward his fallen target, weapon still outstretched. The being twitched, body armour melted, a melon-sized crater sizzling its upper torso. Then…it twitched no more. From his periphery, reality snapped Morrissey back — a faint snick, almost imperceptible against the thumping of his heart. A shouted warning: something told him it was Lillum.

He turned numbly to face the second attacker who'd been creeping up on his flank. He was just in time to see its head pop sideways in a shower of sparks and charred bone. Morrissey's face was a pale sheet of disbelief. The adrenaline rush took its toll and he felt the sour burn of vomit surge up his gullet and spray across his victim's still form.

Hands patted his back and held him steady. It was only when someone tried to take his rifle from his limp grasp that he realised the someone was Barry. "It's okay, mate. I'm just going to hold onto this for a minute. You're in a bit of a state. Probably best if you're not waving it around."

Syddyk bent over the smouldering corpse. "Straaken. Bunch of filthy mercenaries. He had it coming."

Morrissey gazed blankly at his victim. "Straaken? Is that his race? How could a whole alien race have one job? They can't all be mercenaries. Are there no doctors? No lawyers? What about teachers? Who picks up the garbage? Someone has to work in the shops. And what about telemarketers? Surely some of them must be telemarketers?"

"Alright," said Barry, "point taken, not all of them are mercenaries. But these two, definitely nasty pieces of work." Then he said to Lillum. "Is he going to be alright?"

"He could be suffering from some sort of mental trauma. Shock, perhaps. I can't be sure with humans."

Morrissey's brain waded through quicksand as the weight of his actions plucked a sour tune on his conscience. "Not in shock, just coming to terms, is all." He climbed slowly out of his stupor. "You said they were mercenaries?"

"But not your average point and shoot variety," said Barry. "Straaken are more like a highly disciplined paramilitary group than a bunch of blasters for hire."

"But I thought eNdeen wanted me alive. I don't think these two got the memo."

"I don't think these two work for eNdeen. From your description of eNdeen's henchmen, it sounds like he's using Gyrth mercs, not Straaken."

Barry was right; these were different aliens. A mane of coarse white hair raged back along a sloping skull; a ridged brow draped heavily over its dead eyes. Its rebreather mask had fallen away, revealing a ghoulish death-grimace of long angular teeth buried deep within sunken cheeks. All the while, the gamey stench of its charred, grey flesh stung Morrissey's eyes. "Great. So I've got two sets of aliens after me." Morrissey poked at the dead Straaken. "If they're not eNdeen's, then who hired them?"

"Isn't that a question," said Barry. "Anything, Syd?"

Syddyk had been rifling through the mercenaries' pouches for any usable intel. "Nothing. Doesn't surprise me, though. Very professional."

"Whoever they're working for, we'd better get moving before any more of them show up. That includes you, Bryndevaan."

Bryndevaan oozed out from the niche he'd wedged himself into during the firefight. "I see no reason why I should leave."

"Are you kidding me?" said Morrissey. "I'd have thought the dead aliens decorating your living room would be reason enough."

"Chyll is where I must live out my exile. It is my punishment. I will not leave."

"Oh yes you bloody will," said Barry. "This is no longer your home. It's a battlefield."

The Thuwom's head-fringed fluttered from one corpse to another. "This is not my battle. You and your pet human have brought this fight here. I feel certain that the trouble will leave when you do."

"You may have noticed that this human is quite popular at the moment and there are some very nasty beings willing to do some very nasty things to obtain him." He cast a dubious eye at the fallen mercenary. "Or eliminate him. They wouldn't think twice about lobbing a nuke in here just to tie up loose ends."

"You speak in speculations with no basis in fact. I will remain and take whatever comes." Bryndevaan set his body into a rigid stump.

"Let him stay," said Syddyk. "Let him die. He's done his job — he's nothing to us, now."

"You can't mean that?" Lillum's eyes wobbled over him.

With all Syddyk had been through, with all he'd lost, Morrissey wouldn't blame him if he did mean it, but Syddyk shrugged. "No," he said, thoughtfully, "but he's lucky we answer to a higher moral code than these scum. We could just as easily fry him right here and now and be on our way."

"I do not know your code," said Bryndevaan. "Perhaps you intend on delivering me to Vaziil so he may continue his experiments. I do not know what you people are capable of."

"That's enough!" All eyes — and head-fringes — turned to Morrissey. "Enough self-pity. Enough moaning. Yes, you've done some bad things, things you never thought yourself capable of. We all have. I've just killed another living being and I never thought I'd be capable of that but here we are. If we wanted to deliver you to Vaziil we could have tranquilised you and carried you to the ship easier than this. There certainly would have been a lot less whinging. Yes, it's our mess and I'm sorry we've gotten you involved, but we're trying to get you out in the safest way possible. So for the love of whatever god you might worship, will you please stop your bellyaching and gather what you need for travel because you're leaving with us whether you like it or not."

Bryndevaan's body went mushy in the middle. "You speak persuasively, Pink One. Very well — I will come with you."

Morrissey let out an exhausted sigh. "Hallelujah."

"Alright, then," said Barry. "Let's move, people." Then he said to Morrissey, "You've really got a way with him, Dave."

"I don't want a way with him. I just want away."
"All in good time, mate. All in good time."

CHAPTER 21

At the mouth of the cave, they found the portable comm-link relay reduced to a charred shell, smoke pouring from its access nodes. Barry and Syddyk scoured the valley for signs of more Straaken mercenaries while Lillum and Morrissey scoured the skies for signs of the floating puff-ball killers that had sucked Kheni dry.

"Getting back to the Nomad without being attacked is going to be a problem," said Barry.

"What about him?" said Syddyk, gesturing to the Thuwom. "He's lived here for years without being eaten."

"Yeah, Bryndevaan." Barry leaned in close to his head-fringe. "What's your secret?"

"I have seen the creatures you speak of, yes. I have seen them feed, mostly at midday when the sun is warming the mountain. They have never perceived me as appetising. I do not know why."

"You said your excrement acts as a repellent," said Lillum. "Perhaps this is what keeps them at bay?"

"Not excrement as such. It is a mucous discharge. And no, I do not cover myself in my own waste."

Barry's eyes spun with the beginning of a plan. "But maybe we should."

"Maybe we should *what*?" said Morrissey, dreading the answer.

"Maybe we should cover ourselves in Bryndevaan's discharge. If it does keep those things away from his cave, it might just work for us."

"Uh-uh. No way. I am not rubbing his snot all over my body. End of."

"It might be the only way to keep those Floaters off our backs."

"I don't care. It was bad enough having one of his arms shoved down my throat — if it even was an arm. I've got to draw the line somewhere. Besides, we don't even know if it'll work. He said they're not interested in him with or without the discharge."

"It would be a small price to pay, Dave."

"And it would be a pointless price to pay," said Bryndevaan. "You would most likely be exchanging one flavour of death for another. My waste discharge contains a powerful toxin that would be most harmful to your central nervous systems."

Lillum waggled her head. "I don't have the time or the means to test it, Barrek. We cannot take the risk."

"They didn't attack Morrissey, either," said Syddyk. Morrissey couldn't tell if his tone was accusatory or not.

"That's right," said Barry. "So what do you and our Thuwom friend have in common? Any thoughts, Lil?"

"There could be any one of a million physiological parallels, though it would be hard to imagine one upon first glance."

Morrissey had been running the same problem over and over in his head ever since Kheni's death, mostly out of a sense of guilt. A connection to Earth tickled a past memory. And then it struck him. "Mosquitoes."

"Excuse me?" said Barry.

"What is...moz-kee-toz?" said Lillum.

"They're insects, from Earth — my homeworld." The group looked on with a dubious mix of interest, bewilderment, and impatience. "These goggles you gave me, Syd, they hold the key. When we first entered Bryndevaan's cave, I cycled through the settings to test them out in the darkness. One of them seemed to be some sort of gas analysis function, revealing emissions from each one of you — from your mouths and nasal openings, mostly. I thought it fairly useless at the time but now I'm not so sure. When the Straaken showed up, I tried it again, but it displayed no such emissions from them. The significance didn't hit me until now."

Barry was finally riding Morrissey's wavelength. "You think those Floaters are attracted to our gas emissions?"

"Most people think the female mosquito is attracted to the blood of her food source, but she's actually drawn to the carbon dioxide her victims exhale."

"And you were wearing your rebreather when the creatures swarmed us," said Lillum. "Your CO2 emissions were trapped in the collectors. To the Floaters, you were invisible."

"As were the Straaken."

"And Bryndevaan?" said Syddyk. "Surely he exhales?"

"What about it, Bryndevaan?" said Barry. "You said you process and recycle most of your waste — does that include respiration?"

"Well, my waste gases are recycled as a matter of efficiency. It's a very complex system with a rather interesting —"

"Is the carbon dioxide recycled or not, yes or no?" said Barry, his impatience growing.

"Of course. It is used for internal food production."

"Lil, you're the medical expert. Does it make enough sense to risk our lives on?"

Lillum cocked her head to one side. "I think it might. But then again, we don't have much choice. We cannot remain here."

"Hang on," said Morrissey. "What if I'm wrong? I don't want any more deaths on my conscience."

"But if you're right, we're home free," said Barry.

Morrissey realised the implications of the discovery. If he'd only figured out the puzzle sooner, Kheni might still be alive.

"You couldn't have known," said Syddyk, as if reading his thoughts. "But we know now — at least we have a fighting chance."

At Barry's instruction they all strapped on their rebreathers, checking the seals and settings before allowing them the luxury of confidence. With the all-clear given, they stepped into the harsh, midday sunlight, the sudden glare stabbing at Morrissey's eyes like hot needles; his goggles polarised automatically to compensate.

As they bounced down the mountain, Morrissey's heart plugged his throat when he spotted the swarm of Floaters — a gauzy cloud, hundreds of metres above, drifting innocently in the light breeze. The team froze at the sight, hoping for the best but expecting the worst. So far, Morrissey's theory was holding up.

At the foot of the mountain, they came across the unavoidable. Kheni's shrivelled corpse lay face down in the chalky dust, barely recognisable save for his blood-soaked jumpsuit. Morrissey wanted to pull Syddyk away, to shield him from the grisly image, but Syddyk didn't shy away from the horror.

"We'll take him with us, but not now." The small alien reached into his backpack for a thermal blanket and gently wrapped it around his fallen brother, carefully tucking in the sides as if putting him to bed. "First we secure the area and our transport. Then I will return for him." Nobody argued his logic, and in a further show of pragmatism, Syddyk retrieved Kheni's weapons and supply packs, distributing the load amongst the team before they continued.

At the crystalline lattice, Morrissey could just about make out the welcome outline of The Nomad through the barbed cells. He wanted to rush the vehicle, to kiss the tires it rolled on, dangers be damned, but Barry's signal to halt caught him off guard. Syddyk acknowledged Barry's further unspoken gesture and scuttled up the cliffside. From a concealed position, he scanned ahead with his binoculars while the rest of the team braced for his report. Finally, he skidded back down to join them.

"Well, the good news is that The Nomad seems to be in one piece."

"And the bad news?" said Morrissey. These days there was always bad news.

"The bad news is that it's surrounded by Straaken soldiers. Four of them that I can see. There may be more, is my point."

"Any sign they know we're here?" said Barry.

"They don't seem to be on alert status."

"I guess they figured their two friends in the cave would have handled us with ease. Arrogant pricks."

"Surely we show up on their scanners," said Morrissey.

"Unless the lattice is confounding their readings," said Lillum.

"Then let's use that to our advantage," said Barry. "Syd, check for snipers. If these mercs are half as good as their reputation suggests, it's a good bet they've got cover up in the mountains."

Syddyk scanned the terrain. "If they're up there, they're well hidden. Or maybe our scanners are buggered, too."

"I think I should return to my cave," said Bryndevaan.

Barry wagged his finger. "No one is returning to any cave. Syd, do you think you could take them out from here?"

"What, all of them?" Syddyk looked dubious. "I could splash one, maybe two of them, before they found cover."

"Too bad we can't persuade those Floaters to pay them a visit," said Morrissey.

"Maybe we can." Syddyk's brow knotted as his teeth clenched. "It looks like they're all wearing rebreathers. They must be or they'd have already been attacked by them?" He thumbed up to the 'cloud' in the sky. "They're fairly standard devices. If I can shoot the CO_2 canisters, then the escaping gas should draw those floating killers right to them."

"No, wait," said Morrissey. "I wasn't serious, I was just thinking out loud."

"And it was a good thought."

"But isn't it a little...I don't know...cold-blooded?"

"They should have thought of that before," said Syddyk.

Morrissey chilled at Syddyk's tone. "Can't we stun them, or something?"

"The two in the cave were wearing Scatter Armour — they're probably all similarly equipped. A stun shot would easily be deflected. Barrek, we don't have time to debate this. It's either them or us."

Barry nodded numbly. "Alright, Syd. Do it."

They inched awkwardly toward The Nomad, careful not to bounce into view of the mercenaries. Syddyk found a craggy outcrop and settled himself into a makeshift sniper's nest, using the light distortion of the crystalline lattice to his advantage.

Barry acted as a spotter, combing the area with the binoculars. "There are five, now."

"I need only one," said Syddyk, "and I have him in my sights. The stores from his CO_2 collector should be enough to cloud the whole lot of them."

Syddyk was an artist with his weapon; he forced calm through his body, slowing his breathing to almost nothing. Morrissey found he was unconsciously doing the same. The small alien fine-tuned the rifle settings — Syddyk mentioning the need to focus a lower yield blast.

The weapon coughed, a single, high-pitched whoosh. The targeted Straaken rocked with the impact and stumbled, checking his body for wounds that weren't there. His cohorts dropped into crouching positions, fanning their weapons in defensive arcs.

Syddyk fired once more, puncturing a second soldier's collector for good measure before the mercenaries took cover behind the sharp angles of The Nomad. They fired blindly into the mountains while pressing themselves into one appetising lump.

Morrissey cycled to the gas analysis setting on his goggles, confirming the mercenaries were now enveloped in a cloud of CO_2. He checked the skies, but so far the Floaters weren't taking the bait. Then, just as he was beginning to doubt his mosquito theory, the assault began. Like iron filings to a magnet, the floating killers swirled from their position and zeroed in on the tight knot of mercenaries. By the time they hit, it was already too late. The enemy weapons-fire burned in earnest but fizzled out in futility.

Morrissey took no pleasure as the agonised cries began. Lillum's eyestalks bobbed downward, unable to bear witness to the slaughter. Even Bryndevaan reacted in a sombre song of chilling tones that rippled through his trembling flesh. Only Syddyk and Barry remained focussed, ready to dispatch any errant soldier. There were none.

Once the Floaters had sated themselves, their engorged bodies bounced slowly through the valley and away. When the last of the cries had fallen silent and Morrissey had deemed the area CO_2-free, the team cautiously moved in. But they didn't get very far before a bolt of plasma blistered past them, missing Morrissey by mere inches. Bryndevaan wasn't so lucky. The blast seared through his flesh at human shoulder level. The Thuwom wobbled, screaming a symphony of panic. A blur of movement up in the rocks caught Morrissey's eye as the sniper fought to reacquire his target.

Barry pushed Bryndevaan hard to the ground. By the second shot, the team had split into two. Barry had dragged Bryndevaan into a small outcropping that Syddyk had found for them to hide under, while Morrissey and Lillum pressed themselves flat against the same side of the valley as the sniper.

Bryndevaan's short, sharp squeals echoed across the narrow gap that divided the two groups. Lillum bobbed anxiously, unable to lend aid. Barry poked his head out from his cover only to be met by a fresh stream of energy.

Morrissey's wrist-comm chirped. *"Dave, are you guys okay?"*

"Define okay. We're not injured, if that's what you mean. What about you?"

"The sniper has us pinned. Are you in the clear?"

"I don't think he's got a line of sight on us, but we can't exactly move."

"How's Bryndevaan?" said Lillum, linking into the comm. "He does not sound good."

"Hard to tell. There's certainly a lot of ooze. I've slapped a field dressing on him, so let's hope the nano-meds can figure their way through Thuwom physiology until you can take a look at him. Which may be a while — I think the sniper is going to wait us out, maybe until reinforcements arrive." Barry made another foray above the firing line, almost getting his head seared off for his efforts. *"It's no good. Syd and I are buttoned up, good. Is there anything you can do on your end?"*

Morrissey had neither the desire nor the experience to play the hero but no matter how many times he did the math, he kept coming out as the single common denominator. "Erm…look, Barry, since the sniper can't see me, why don't I try to creep up on him and take him by surprise?"

"Sounds like a good plan."

"Oh," said Morrissey, "I was kind of hoping you'd think it sounded like an insanely bad plan even though I was a jolly good sport for suggesting it."

"Under normal circumstances, I might, but we can't wait around for more mercs to arrive. Just be careful."

"Oh, hey, I hadn't thought of that, but sure. Careful." Great.

The average human heart will beat over two billion times in its lifespan. Morrissey was certain he'd used up half of those beats in only the last few seconds. Adrenaline pumped hard through his trembling body, pulsing thunder through his ears. His breath was like a steam locomotive, puffing out in frantic gusts and fogging his rebreather mask. He took one more carefully measured gulp of air before slowly scraping his body along the mountain face toward the sniper. Lillum mewled softly as he crab-crawled as far as he could go. When he'd reached the point of exposure, he sprung his carbine free from its cradle. The catch release sounded like a hammer against his fragile nerves, but the sniper did not react.

He rose in slow, measured increments until finally, with unsteady hands, he trained his weapon dead at the Straaken's torso. But he didn't fire. Not quite yet. The lie he told himself was that the mercenary might be more valuable to them alive than dead. The truth was that he wanted to avoid any more unnecessary bloodshed, especially at his own hands. He felt he should at least offer the fellow a chance to surrender.

"Don't move," he said, simple yet forceful. And also, stupid. Of course he was going to move.

Sure enough, the alien turned toward him, his stare cold and impassive. Even through the Straaken's rebreather, Morrissey could see its cunning smile, teeth bared in a grisly taunt. His eyes burned dry from his still gaze and he blinked to clear his view. In that instant, the Straaken seemed to shimmer briefly before shifting back to normal. "I said don't move. Now put your weapon on the ground — slowly." The Straaken stared blankly at him, unmoving, unflinching, unafraid. "Look, I may be new at this whole close encounters thing, but I'm not afraid to shoot you dead if I have to. Just ask your friends back in the cave — the extra crispy ones." Morrissey quivered at the memory of his first kill. The Straaken chuckled, a low guttural rumble, as his rifle moved ever so subtly in Morrissey's direction. "Don't," said Morrissey. "Do *not* do that. It doesn't have to end that way. Just play nice and we can all go on with our lives. All you have to do is put your weapon down and we can have a nice chat about why you and your friends are trying to kill me."

Barry chirped over Morrissey's wrist-comm. *"Just shoot him!"*

Morrissey mentally waved away the advice. "You know, this is really awkward. My boss is watching and he's very hard to please. He'd really like to see this wrapped up as soon as possible and I'm trying to make a good impression. So, what do you say? Don't let your arrogance get you killed." Morrissey found he was pleading for both their sakes. Just play nice.

The Straaken had other plans. His rifle jerked upward, leaving Morrissey no choice. He fired three rapid bursts in response, directly into the soldier's chest. Or at least, he thought he did. The Straaken flinched but did not fall. Instead, the blasts splashed harmlessly against an invisible shield of energy, which explained the previous shimmer effect.

The creature took advantage of Morrissey's overconfidence, returning a deadly spray of energy. Barry and Syddyk provided a salvo of cover fire, allowing Morrissey to pour himself back down the rock face to safety.

"Are you alright?" said Lillum.

"Nothing hurt but my pride." But he'd lost the element of surprise. Undaunted, he scoured the valley for an advantage but saw none — at first. It may have been nothing. It might be everything. Just beyond the sniper's position was a three-metre vertical gash in the rock face, similar to the one that had been home to the balloon predator that had plucked the sun-grazer from the mountain earlier that morning. There was no guarantee it housed one of those creatures, but it was ringed with the same purplish moss. His speculation was that the predator reacted to vibrations around the opening, much the same way a spider reacts to tremors along its web. All he had to do was to knock on the door.

He scooped up a handful of loose pebbles, choosing to employ the shotgun method as there would be no second chances. He whispered into his wrist-comm. "Barry, I need you to stick your head up from the rocks on my signal."

There was a long static-filled pause before Barry responded. *"Say again, Dave. It sounded like you wanted me to get my head blown off."*

"Well, it doesn't have to be your head. Anything will do. I just need a distraction."

"Okaaaaay. What have you got up your sleeve?"

"Let's just say that I'm trying to encourage the circle of life."

Another long pause. *"Okay. If you say so, I guess I'm ready. Just give me the signal."*

"On my mark…and…now!"

Right on cue, a knot of fabric tied to the butt of Barry's rifle bobbed above the parapet of his hideout, and right on cue, it was met with a swift blast from the Straaken's weapon. In that split second of divided attention, Morrissey ejected himself from cover using Chyll's reduced gravity to give him some much-needed lift. The fistful of rock-shot arced toward the crevice behind the sniper and clattered to the side of the opening. Morrissey thumped to the ground, crumpling to one knee. The Straaken caught the movement and spun toward him with his weapon raised. Time froze like a snapshot as their eyes locked in a dead black stare. Whether it was confidence or fear that rooted Morrissey in place, it didn't matter; the Straaken took a hair more than too long to react.

A bubble of flesh exploded from the cavity, plastering its swollen sac against the flailing Straaken. For what seemed like an eternity, the mercenary hung in midair, raw shock splattered across his face.

Finally, the cold stab of mortality morphed into pale resignation as the balloon-predator sucked quickly back into the crevice, taking its fresh meal with it. A moment of regret was all Morrissey allowed himself before relief washed it away in heaving waves.

Lillum wasted no time in galloping toward Bryndevaan's side. His whimper strummed softly as he lay flaccid on the rocky ground, looking very much like a giant flank steak that had been tenderised just a bit too much. The field dressing that Barry had applied had slowed the flow of Thuwom blood but not managed much else From her med-pouch, Lillum produced a thumb-sized canister and flipped a stud at its base. A fine mist hissed over the alien's seared flesh. She fired up a slim silver tube, a blue arc of fire pulsing at its tapered nozzle. "Do not worry. This is only going to hurt a bit. Or a lot. I cannot be sure. The point is, you have no choice so prepare yourself." Bryndevaan's whine stretched into high pitch as she brought the instrument close.

"How much time do you need?" said Barry.

"Twenty minutes. At least."

"You've got ten. At most. I'm not entirely convinced we're out of the shit quite yet. Syd, give her cover while she operates. Dave, you're with me."

At the crystalline lattice, a couple of unlucky mercenaries hung impaled on several spiny barbs like sides of beef in a butcher shop. Barry scanned for their tagged safe cell and led them through. "I want to send Xrrka an update as soon as possible."

They approached The Nomad with weapons ready. The sight was grisly, to say the least; a pulpy soup of half-eaten Straaken soldiers stained the ground, only marginally recognisable as the lifeforms they once were. Barry poked at the carcasses, searching for any usable tech. "Waste not, want not."

It sounded callous but Morrissey couldn't argue the pragmatism; any advantage that could be taken, should be, but Morrissey held onto his humanity with both hands as he fought to pry a weapon from one Straaken's particularly stubborn death grip. The rifle finally snapped away, taking much of the being's arm with it. "Jesus…that is just not cool. At all." He picked delicately at the sticky remains, tossing the weapon into the pile with the rest of the booty.

"Why don't you go fire up The Nomad," said Barry. "Get it nice and warm for us."

Morrissey appreciated the show of empathy. "If you think that's best."

"You remember how to start it, don't you?"

He managed a wry smile. "Sure I do. Big green button, says GO."

CHAPTER 22

Morrissey placed his palm against the entrance sensor-lock of The Nomad. The panel pulsed from orange to blue and the door hissed open. A belch of stale air washed over him, as comforting as freshly baked bread. He sealed the door behind him and secured his carbine in the weapons hold before heading to the cockpit.

Servos whirred as the driver's seat conformed to his human proportions. He stared blankly at the command console, waiting for something familiar to jump out from the jumble of controls. Finally, he found the pressure pad that would reawaken the sleeping beast and thumbed it to active. Systems hummed to life all around him, the vibration of energy feeding him with relief. Everything seemed as if it was going to be alright.

Except that it wasn't.

A slight shift in air pressure. A foul, greasy odour. A blur of movement. Morrissey leapt to his feet and instinctively drew his pistol, stabbing at the threat with a quivering mix of dread and menace.

The hulking figure rose slowly from the shadows. "You really should invest in a better security system." Its voice was like rolling thunder.

Morrissey stood face to chest with yet another in an annoying line of Straaken mercenaries. Like the others, this one was also forged from cables of steel-wrapped muscle and sinew. He eyed Morrissey with a wicked gleam — eye being the operative word. A ragged scar tore across his sloping forehead, cleaving his right eye socket in two. Morrissey couldn't decide if this made him less dangerous or more.

"Who the fuck are you?" said Morrissey. The Straaken's weapon rested against the console a metre away yet he made no overt moves toward it. "If you're looking for a ride, I'm afraid we don't take hitchhikers. Maybe you could catch a lift with your friends — oh, wait, you don't have any left."

"Yes, that was a good trick, getting that cloud of floating killers to do what you could not."

"And I've got a million tricks up my sleeve so you might want to be careful what you say next." Morrissey was surprised by his own defiance. "The last of your kind who bet against me was swallowed by a very hungry balloon, so you've got exactly one chance to tell me why you and your friends are trying to kill me."

The Straaken barked a laugh, deep and throaty. "I'd have thought that was obvious, even to a human. You've got quite the price on your head, for anyone bold enough to chance it. Turns out there are all manner of beings who view you as some sort of threat to their existence." The Straaken eyed him up and down. "Personally, I don't see it."

"Price? You mean a...a bounty? As in, I'm a wanted man?"

The Straaken nodded. "More like a dead man."

"But...why? How?"

"Bounty hunter trick of the trade. We keep a thorough network of contacts throughout the quadrant who feed us information on...beings of interest, shall we say. You were tagged at the refugee centre on Phonsekka Prime."

Morrissey thought back to the Visitor Visa stamp that the refugee robot had tattooed him with. Shit. He knew he hated that robot for a reason. "Okay, if I've got a death warrant out on me, then why aren't I dead already? You could have shot me as I walked through that door."

"Because sitting here, waiting for you, I began to wonder if you're worth so much dead, how much would you be worth alive?"

"Well I appreciate the change of heart but either way, your plan has failed. So I'm going to give you a similar chance to get the fuck off this bus with your life and off this planet. Otherwise, someone's going to get hurt and my money is on you."

"I'm afraid I can't do that."

"Don't underestimate yourself. I'm sure you can do anything you put your mind to. Besides, I'm the one with the gun, or hadn't you noticed." He pumped his pistol toward the Straaken for good measure. "Speaking of which, no sudden moves. Turns out I'm pretty good with this thing."

"I'm sure that you are, but you won't use it."

The Straaken's confidence unnerved him; it was time to call for reinforcements. He tabbed his wrist-comm. "Hey, Barry, it's Morrissey. We've got a little situation here. Bit of an intruder alert, you might say. No need to panic but if you'd like to…you know…lend a hand, I wouldn't say no." Silence. "Barry? Do you read? Syddyk? Lillum? Can anyone hear me?"

"I'm afraid they can't." The Straaken's meaty slab of a hand motioned to one of the display consoles. "If you don't mind?"

Morrissey's confidence spiralled into a black hole as he took the soldier's meaning. "Okay. Slowly. No tricks."

"I wouldn't dream of it." The mercenary stroked the panel to life, the display revealing an exterior view of the valley. Syddyk lay crumpled on the ground, clutching desperately at a leg wound. Lillum stood protectively over him while trying to shield the prone Bryndevaan. Barry stood with arms outstretched, his weapons lying uselessly on the ground. Two Straaken mercenaries controlled the scene — one with his rifle aimed at Barry's head while the other covered the rest from the rear.

"You see," said the Straaken, "no need for tricks."

The mercenary's comm buzzed, a gravelly voice crackling to life. *"Muurn? Report. Is the target neutralised?"*

"Not quite yet, Lorkaan. He's holding me at gunpoint. Looks like he wants to do things the hard way."

"Tell him that we'll spare his friends if he surrenders his life."

"If that's your boss," said Morrissey, "tell him that it's only the hard way if you make it hard. This could all be so very easy if you just let all of us go on our way."

The mercenary shook his bony head. "I already told you that's not going to happen."

Morrissey's stomach knotted as he stared helplessly at the monitors. These people were his friends; he'd fought beside them, even watched them die — for him. "Okay, then. *Muurn*, is it? Let's do it the hard way." He spun his finger slowly. "Turn around and move toward the exit." Muurn did so wordlessly. "Hands up, open palms." Morrissey grasped the Straaken by the collar-ring of his combat suit and pressed the muzzle of his pistol firmly into the hard muscle of his neck, prodding him toward the exit. "Open it." Muurn hesitated. "You obviously found your way in so you can bloody well find your way out. Now open it, smart arse."

The breached door yielded to the Straaken's palm print. "Do you mind?" said Muurn, gesturing to his rebreather. "Don't want to attract any unwanted attention."

Morrissey acquiesced, and then snapped on his own rebreather as he pushed against his captive, jerking him down the ramp. "If you so much as tiptoe in the wrong direction, I will shoot you dead. Understand?" Muurn gave his best impression of a shrug.

Outside, Morrissey took a strategic position out of the line of fire of each of the Straaken, using the towering Muurn for cover.

Barry flashed a weak smile. "Sorry, mate. They caught us by surprise."

"Silence!" The Straaken mercenary guarding Barry smashed him between the shoulders with the butt of his rifle, crumpling him to his knees.

"Don't worry, Barry. I've got this." Morrissey peeked out from the cover of his Straaken shield. "Whoever is in command, now's the chance to walk away with your lives."

The Straaken covering Barry spoke. "Is this a human sense of humour?"

"You must be Lorkaan," said Morrissey. "Well, Lorkaan. I've tried to reason with your friend here, but he's a stubborn bugger. Maybe you've got more sense."

Lorkaan ignored him. "Muurn, why is this thing not dead?"

"Think about it, Lorkaan. Dead, he yields payment only once. Alive, who knows how much he would be worth. There are those that would pay handsomely for him. This could set us up for life!"

"We signed on for his death warrant, nothing more."

"It's so hard to get good help these days, isn't it?" said Morrissey. "Now, last chance, fellas. Just let me and my friends go and we can all go our separate ways. Maybe we'll even look back on this day as the time we all learned a valuable lesson about being swell to one another. It's simple. Just walk away."

Lorkaan's eyes burned with the blackness of hell. "We are not walking away from anything. You're worth too much." He turned his weapon to Barry's head. "Now I will give you one last chance. One way or another, there will be bloodshed."

Well, he was right about that.

A blue pulse blasted through Lorkaan's forehead. Two more blasts took out the second mercenary guarding Lillum and Syddyk. Morrissey held onto his hostage for dear life. Barry tightened his defensive position to a crouch.

From behind Morrissey, two figures approached, weapons outstretched. They were large, stout-chested beings with squarish heads set upon stumpy necks — the same aliens he'd seen back on eNdeen's ship. Gyrth? They were kitted out in full combat armour but weren't wearing rebreathers; Gyrth didn't need them, in theory, filtering their respiration through the gelatinous sacs at the sides of their heads.

From the opposite side of the valley, three more figures approached: two more Gyrth, flanking a third smaller figure that moved with deadly authority. Behind its crimson cowl, Morrissey felt unseen eyes pierce his soul. He peered tenuously around the bulk of his hostage as the being pulled the cover from its face, leaving Morrissey's sense of reason scattering for cover.

Kiki Pashmina, the woman who'd shared his bed and his body only a few days earlier and untold light years away, now stood before him on an alien world, acting as if the only thing that had changed was the scenery. "Sorry we're late," she said. "I thought it best to use the element of surprise. So…*surprise!*"

Kiki had gone from lover to protector to God knows what in three disturbing moves. A million thoughts raced through Morrissey's mind, not the least of which was, "Kiki? What the…what the Christ are you doing here? I thought…" In truth, he had no idea what he thought. "I thought you'd been captured by eNdeen. Do you know how guilty I felt for leaving you behind?"

"That's very sweet, Dave, but as you can see, I'm quite capable of taking care of myself."

Morrissey could see, but he couldn't understand. After rescuing him from Fowler, she'd claimed to be helping him. But now, here she was with some of the very beings who'd turned his life into a living Hell. "Don't get me wrong, Kiki. I'm glad you're okay but I can't for the life of me fathom what you're doing here with them." He motioned to the two Gyrth sidekicks.

"All will be explained in good time. Now honestly, that gun. It just doesn't suit you. Don't you think you should put it down before you hurt someone?"

Morrissey was numb. "What? The gun…yes. I mean, no! I mean, don't move." That told her.

"But I'm not moving, Dave."

"Good. Then let's keep it that way. Now I'll ask you again, what are you doing here?"

"Dave," she said, taking mock offence, "I've come for you, silly."

"Kiki, the last time I saw you, you said you were trying to protect me and I ended up at the sharp end of the universe. You'll forgive me if I don't fall helplessly into your arms."

"Well, I was right, wasn't I?" She gestured to the fallen Straaken mercenaries. "There were people out to harm you. There still are. That's two you owe me."

"I…owe you? That's rich. I'm not sure you fully understand the concept of the frying pan and the fire."

"Look, Dave, I'd love to hang about and talk over old times but we're on a bit of a tight schedule. So if you'll just come with me —
"

"Uh-uh. Not this time. I'm not going anywhere with you."

She folded back her cape, exposing her holstered sidearm. "Awww, isn't that cute. You actually think you have a choice."

"How's this for choice: I'll offer you the same deal I offered the Straaken. You and your friends put your weapons down and let me and mine go. Or I start shooting."

"Well, now. Aren't you the grown up. What's next, long trousers? Who would have thought you'd graduated to threats of violence."

"Threats. Stern warnings. Even insults. I'm multifaceted. Just ask Muurn, here. I've killed once today and I'll do it again if I have to."

The Straaken addressed Kiki, trying to make the best of a bad situation. "I do not know who you are or who you work for but

203

between you and me, the human may have killed but he's not a killer. Too soft."

Morrissey gave him a good shake. "Shut up or you're next."

"You see, all talk. I think he's embarrassed that I'm the reason he's still alive. My partners had no vision. But I want a better life, I plan on rising above the drek. So, if you cut me in on your deal, I can guarantee this human's cooperation."

Kiki cocked her head to one side. "You know, Straaken, that's a really generous offer. I'll be sure to take it under advisement." In one cool motion, she whipped up her pistol and shot Muurn dead in his chest. Then she put one more plasma bolt straight through his good eye, knocking him backward. Morrissey let the lifeless body thud to the ground before it crushed him. "Oops," she said. "Now what, Dave? No more shield. There are five of us and I doubt your new-found killer instinct has made you that good of a shot. You'll never get us all before we shoot at least one of your friends. But which one to start with? So many to choose from." She cycled her aim playfully over each of his ALF friends while keeping her acid glare firmly on him. "Your call, Big Man."

Bitch. Morrissey flashed a look from one mercenary to the other and then back to Kiki. In open combat, he didn't stand a chance; he didn't even have eyes on the two he knew were behind him. But he did have one more card to play. "Okay. I'll come with you." His friends let out a collective gasp. "On one condition."

"And what might that be, as if I couldn't guess?"

"My friends go free." He chose his words carefully so as not to leave any loophole for last minute betrayals. "They're free to leave, unhindered. No tricks. No treachery. No sabotage. No reprisals."

"And why would I grant this condition when I could just kill them all and take you anyway?"

Morrissey peeled off his rebreather and sucked in a lungful of crisp Chyll air. He breathed out slowly as if enjoying an expensive cigar. "Because if you don't let them go, in a matter of minutes, I'm going to be swarmed by a horde of ravenous, puffball killers that will suck the life juices from my body and leave nothing but a sack of soggy skin and bones. And if I've been following along correctly, that'll sort of make me useless to you." For the first time since this intergalactic nightmare began, Morrissey finally felt like he had some control over his life. Granted, his life might not last much longer, but at least he'd go out on his own terms.

Kiki eyed him curiously for the longest breath Morrissey had ever held. "You'd actually sacrifice yourself for...these?" She motioned to his wounded comrades. "I admire your conviction, Dave, but I didn't figure you for such a sentimentalist."

"That's why it never would have worked between us. That, and the fact that you're a coldblooded killer." He checked the skies for the floating puff balls — so far so good. "So what'll it be?"

"You know, you're almost more trouble than you're worth. Almost." Kiki rolled her eyes. "Fine. Never let it be said that I don't have a heart. They can leave — as long as they stay out of my business."

"I'm not officially your business until they have left so the ball is in your court."

Kiki waved the Gyrth mercenaries back, allowing the ALF team to make their exit. They were a sad sight, indeed, as they hobbled toward The Nomad. Barry leaned in toward Morrissey as he passed.

"You don't have to do this," he whispered. "We'll find another way."

"There is no other way," said Morrissey, forcing a smile.

"But you can't trust her."

"I'm not. I'm trusting this." Morrissey gave a subtle nod toward the visitor visa tattoo he'd received from the refugee centre on Phonsekka Prime. "Those Straaken bounty hunters tracked me using this. I'm pretty sure that Kiki did, too. I'm trusting that you can do the same." He gave a cunning wink. Barry smiled, somewhat more reservedly.

"Quickly," said Kiki. "I'm not getting any younger."

Barry joined the rest of the ALF team as the ramp lifted them into the belly of The Nomad. After a few agonising minutes, the engines revved, and the vehicle slowly crunched across the blistered terrain. As Morrissey watched his friends melt into the horizon, something whimpered softly, and he realised it was him.

"Very touching, Dave."

Morrissey ignored her. Only when The Nomad had disappeared from view did he refasten his rebreather, drawing comfort from its security. Kiki walked casually toward him and struck him in the throat with the heel of her hand. Morrissey staggered, sucking hard at the recycled air. It wasn't exactly the loving embrace he'd envisioned. She grabbed his wrist and twisted it backward, wrenching the pistol from his grip. Eyeing the refugee tattoo emblazoned on his arm, she nodded to one of the Gyrth. "I want this deactivated. Take the arm if you have to. I don't want his friends, or any more bounty hunters, showing up unannounced. I don't trust those ALF do-gooders."

"No, wait!" said Morrissey as the Gyrth pinned his arms.

"Don't be so glum, lover. I thought you'd be glad to have a little alone time with me."

One of the Gyrth mercenaries gave Morrissey a short, sharp slap with his knobby hand. "Jesus! Was that really necessary?"

The mercenary looked to Kiki who shrugged her ambivalence. Apparently, it was necessary. Another sharp slap from the Gyrth and Morrissey poured messily across the dry rock bed. At least he wouldn't be awake for the ride.

PART FOUR

CHAPTER 23

Morrissey pawed at the wet stickiness oozing from the back of his head. Somewhere in the lonely corner of his brain that dealt with such things, it registered as blood, but its significance eluded him. His forearm burned; a quick scan revealed a raw, blackened patch where the refugee tattoo tracker used to be. Shit. So much for his plans of rescue. He was well and truly alone and at the mercy of Kiki and her merry band of mercenaries.

The blank walls of his empty grey cell weren't much help; a quick search revealed no consoles with fantastically helpful buttons or satisfying levers to fiddle with. There wasn't even a door, just a hard, silicone rubber slab — ostensibly a bed — moulded to the wall. Even the grim lighting seeped from the bulkheads with a conspicuous reluctance.

An odd sensation tickled his skin; subtle tremors underfoot, along with the simmering hum all around him, suggested he was on a starship. His sense of survival told him to be ready for anything, but his common sense told him that he was ready for absolutely nothing.

"Hello?" he ventured softly. "I know you people are watching me." Job one would be drawing them out. Before he could devise a cunning plan, a section of the far wall glowed blue and settled into a soft, semi-opacity. Through the haze of energy, he could make out the considerable bulk of two Gyrth soldiers. They were barely distinguishable from one another save for a noticeable height difference and the fact that the taller of the two had a thick braid of wiry hair spiralled atop his blocky head, settling into a turd-like bun. Very fetching.

"Step back from the doorway," the shorter of the two said. Both had weapons drawn so there was little incentive to argue the matter. Shorty depressed a button on his belt and the door's energy shield vanished with a fizz. A figure drove a wedge between their hulking forms; it was Kiki, all slinky jump-suit and low-slung plasma pistol.

"Give me a minute with him." It wasn't a question, but they looked to one another for confirmation before stepping back.

Morrissey had once thought her the most beautiful woman in his world but now he could barely bring himself to look at her. "I was just thinking about you."

"Nothing too erotic, I hope."

"Not exactly. I was just wondering what kind of person could do the things you've done and still be able to look themselves in the mirror."

"Really, Dave. Don't be so melodramatic. It wasn't anything personal, just business."

"I'd say it was bloody personal. The things we did." He cast a sideways glance at the silent Gyrth sentinels, but they showed no overt interest. "How was that not personal? And what kind of business involves abduction?"

"It's called being a bounty hunter, Dave. Look it up — it's in the job description."

"Bounty hunter? You're no better than them." He jerked his thumb at the mercenaries, addressing them with mock deference. "No offence."

"I'm *waaaaay* better than them," said Kiki. "Light years. I was hired specifically because I'm better than them."

Morrissey felt ill. He'd hoped that Kiki had been something else, something…more. He'd hoped that maybe she'd been coerced into her brutality. He'd hoped that somehow, hidden in her motives, was something slightly more noble. He didn't know what it would take to mitigate her actions but even a misguided vendetta would be better than this. "So it's all about money? You're betraying your species for money?"

"Betraying my — my god! I knew humans weren't the brightest stars in the galaxy but really. Haven't you gotten it yet?" Morrissey stared at her blankly, realising that he had not, in fact, gotten it. "I'll say it slowly for your simple monkey brain to comprehend: I...am...not...human."

Morrissey grappled with her words as if she'd just asked him to split an atom with a butter knife. "What do you mean, not human?"

"Exactly what it says on the packet. Not human. Alien. Extraterrestrial. Not from your world. I mean, that I've been genetically altered to wear your skin so I could walk amongst you, infiltrate your species, consort with your kind." Kiki shuddered. "And believe me, it wasn't easy."

Morrissey felt like the stupidest stupid person who had ever attended a convention of unimaginably stupid people but had been kicked out for being too stupid. Even with Barry's detailed explanation of how such things were possible along with the revelation that he was the by-product of human-alien rumpy-pumpy, it had never occurred to him that Kiki was anything but human. "But that can't be." He played their night of sexual acrobatics over in his head, the realisation causing a full-on genital retreat. "So, when we...you know...did it, was I...was I even in the right...place?"

Kiki shook her head slowly. "Not even close."

A thought chilled his gut. "Jesus, Kiki, you're not one of them, are you?" he said, nodding to the two soldiers towering beside her."

"Boggles the mind, doesn't it." A wicked smile cracked her beauty as she let him sweat before answering. "No. I'm not Gyrth."

Thankful for small mercies, Morrissey looked up at the vacuous black-egg eyes of Turd Head and shrugged. "Seriously, mate, no offence. I'm sure you're a very handsome bloke where you come from." Then he said to Kiki, "What are you, then?"

"Does it matter?"

He didn't suppose it did. "Well, I guess you weren't lying the night we met when you said you had a fascination with all things extraterrestrial. I bet your name isn't even Kiki, is it?"

"Actually, it's QiQi."

"Isn't that what I said?"

"It's spelled differently."

"Whatever. I'm still trying to figure out why you'd partner with these thugs." He gave Turd Head the stink eye. "Okay, that time I meant offence."

"The Gyrth aren't my partners. They're more like…accessories."

"But you *are* working for eNdeen, aren't you? It's him that's paying the bills, isn't it??

Kiki — rather, QiQi — squinted through her lovely chocolate almond eyes. "What do you know of eNdeen?"

"Aside from the fact that he's an interplanetary terrorist for hire, selling war and death to the highest bidder, I don't know nearly enough."

"One being's war is another's commerce. Who am I to judge."

"So you have no moral problem with this? There's no ethical quandary that keeps you up at night?"

"Listen, lover, I go where the work is. They don't give details and I don't ask. All that matters is that I get paid."

"And you don't care who gets hurt in the process? Or gets killed? Tell me, are you responsible for my mother's death? I'm guessing it was you who visited her the day she died. That's right, the woman you visited in the nursing home — Ruth Small — was my mother, Marion Morrissey." Morrissey felt a wave of nausea, a stab of empathy for the mother he never really knew at all.

"Of course I knew she was your mother, you simpleton, but I didn't kill her, not intentionally. Marion Morrissey, or Ruth Small, or whatever you want to call her, was a means to an end — my only lead to eNdeen's big prize. But she was a frail and weak old woman, even by human standards. In the end, her body couldn't stand up to my tactics. Couldn't be helped. Her mind, however, was surprisingly resilient. She resisted my probes admirably. It took a lot before she gave up your name, but in the end, she just couldn't resist talking about her little Davey."

"Jesus. You are one cold heart." But there was one piece of the puzzle that didn't quite fit. "How did you find her? She'd changed her name after she disappeared. Vaziil wouldn't have known her Ruth Small identity."

"That's where your old boss came in. He was very well-known to us."

"You…you talked to Smythe, too?"

QiQi snorted mockingly. "Now he was a bit more durable. Took a lot more effort. Very cooperative in the end, though. Led me right to dear old mum."

"Are you trying to tell me that he knew about my connection to Vaziil all along? Recruited me for the M.O.D. UFO Hotline for what reason — to monitor me?"

"You do the math, sunshine."

And then it sunk in. Jesus. The Red File. Morrissey dreaded to think what lurid details were contained in the original, un-redacted version. Maybe Smythe had been grooming him all along so he could keep him close, keep him under a watchful eye, like a bug under glass. "So what, you killed him?"

"I couldn't very well leave him lying around for just anyone to talk to." She tapped the side of her head. "Sonic disruptor to the brain, indistinguishable from an aneurysm."

"You are unbelievable. Don't you have a conscience?" He didn't expect an answer. "And now that you've got me, what are you going to do with me? Am I next on your hit list?"

"My instructions were simply to deliver you to eNdeen, unharmed. End of. To be honest, I thought it would be an easy contract. I didn't expect you to be quite so...feisty. You've got guts, I'll give you that."

"And what's eNdeen going to do with me? Liquify my brain with a Magimix? Play marbles with my eyeballs?"

"Relax, Dave. If he wanted you dead, you'd be dead already. Believe me, sentimental he is not. Apparently, you have some very serious technological value. That's all I know."

"Enough!" It was Turd Head. "You wished to speak with the human and you have done so. You've already said too much."

QiQi seemed annoyed but didn't protest. "Well, I guess that's me told."

Morrissey found her dynamic with the Gyrth curiously disturbing. Up until now, he'd believed her to be in control of the mercenaries. He'd hoped to capitalise on her domination as a way to bargain for his life. But judging by the exchange, he just might have it backward. He needed a new strategy. "It's not too late. If money is all you're interested in, I'm sure the ALF would pay you for your trouble."

"The ALF? They couldn't afford me. Besides, changing teams midway through a contract is bad for business. For what it's worth,

Dave, being with you wasn't all bad. You're pretty good...down there. For a human."

Morrissey couldn't tell whether she was rubbing salt into his wound or offering some pale comfort to a condemned man. "Thanks. I'll try to remember that when eNdeen has my knob stuffed and mounted on his wall."

Both Gyrth jostled past QiQi. "We are done, here," said Turd Head as he aimed a sleek tube toward Morrissey. Its muzzle flashed bright orange, then a cool blossom of numbness lifted him off the ground and enveloped him in a zero-g bubble of energy. Morrissey's muscles ratcheted in toward his body, locking him into a fetal position as Turd Head yanked him by the energy leash.

The cocoon bobbed and spun as it bounced down the corridor, not so gently careening off the hard edges of the bulkheads, spinning Morrissey in a twist of nausea.

"We have arrived," said Turd Head, flatly. He deactivated the restraining bubble; Morrissey thumped to the deck.

Morrissey rubbed the feeling back into his limbs. "What do you mean, arrived? Arrived where?"

"Arrived at our destination. Arrived at *your* destination — your *final* destination."

"Look mate, I'll give you an 'A' for melodrama but I'm afraid I'm going to have to give you an 'F' for sense-making." The viewport spun with a psychedelic chaos. "We're still in hyperspace. How could we have arrived if we're still in hyperspace?" As unsettling as it was, the question answered itself. Fact — they were still in hyperspace, but they had also reached their destination. Well, a destination of sorts.

They had come to a stop at the entrance to a docking tube. Compared to the massive, multilevel construct he'd seen on JuHu Station, this one was primitive — a sinewy ten-metre framework of metal struts, cables and conduit, binding the ship in a fragile embrace with an object of unfathomable origins.

It was about ten times the size of the ship they were travelling on, a bleak grey blob, vaguely potato shaped. At first glance, it appeared to be an asteroid or a small moon. Sheathed in a series of interlocking plates, like the scales of a fish, it reflected little light except at the point where the docking tube made its seal. Random craters of varying sizes pockmarked its surface, as if the structure had been subjected to massive bombardment over time. Whatever the place was, it didn't seem fit for human habitation.

As they reached the opposite airlock, the heavy door cycled open revealing two more Gyrth soldiers. Between them was a figure that Morrissey didn't recognise — at first. The last time he'd seen the creature, he'd been splayed in an unconscious heap across the deck of an alien ship masquerading as a mental hospital. "Dr. Cheevers, I presume. Or perhaps you prefer eNdeen?"

"Mr. Morrissey," said eNdeen, the tight sphincter of his mouth puckering like the arsehole he was. "You have led us on a merry chase, haven't you."

"Just wanted you to get your money's worth."

eNdeen let loose a raucous laugh, the sound like knives sparking off a grindstone. "Is that sarcasm? Perhaps resentment? You can't blame me — I'm a simple businessman, after all."

"In my world, you're a prick."

"*Prrr-ickkk-k-k-k?*" eNdeen turned the word awkwardly in his sphincter-mouth. "An interesting term. I suspect, however, that I wouldn't like its meaning."

"That's okay. It was more for my peace of mind, anyway."

"As long as we're all happy." eNdeen nodded his phallic helmet head to the Gyrth soldiers. "Bring him."

Before they could move, QiQi pushed herself through the wall of mercenaries. "Not so fast, eNdeen. We're not all happy."

"Ah, QiQi. I didn't see you there. How good of you to see me off." eNdeen's voice oozed with a sickly oil.

"It's the least I can do — considering I've not been paid."

"Payment? Yes. But we do not yet know if the human will yield results, do we?"

"No. We don't. But then again, *we* don't care. You contracted me to secure and deliver the package and I have done so — at great personal risk. I've been locked in this form longer than we bargained. On top of the fee we agreed on, I'm adding the cost of shedding this skin. The least you can do is pay for any side effects I might incur."

The smooth contours of eNdeen's phallic head betrayed no intent or disposition. A guttural croak belched from deep within him. "Yes, you did deliver the...package, but at what cost? You were supposed to be discreet but instead, you've attracted the vulgar attentions of every bounty hunter in the quadrant."

"Hey, it's not my fault he escaped from your ship. That was down to your hired help." She jerked a derisive thumb toward the Gyrth mercenaries. "You get what you pay for."

"How very true," said eNdeen. His single eye surveyed her with an almost contemptuous interest. "Very well." He nodded to his two Gyrth escorts. "My associates will see to your compensation."

QiQi smiled. "I'd like to say it was nice doing business with you but we needn't push it. On the other hand, if you should ever require my services again, you can reach me through the usual channels."

"No, QiQi. I will have no need of you again. Ever, as it happens."

QiQi's look of smug satisfaction quickly tightened into apprehension as she realised eNdeen balanced his books in an entirely fatal way. She grabbed for her pistol but was a hair too slow. Shorty disarmed her handily while Turd Head enveloped her in his steel grip.

Morrissey had never seen her look so vulnerable in all the — well, in the short time he'd known her. It was the last image he had of her before he was wrenched away by eNdeen's Gyrth guards and jostled down the narrow docking tube. Despite the misery she'd caused him, he couldn't deny the sharp stab of pity he felt for her; alien or not, they had shared an intimacy that had left a residue.

Inside the strange alien structure, the hatch cycled shut and the docking tube slowly retracted. Morrissey turned to catch one fleeting glimpse out the viewport: a lone, distant figure, pinwheeling from the other ship's airlock in a blur of spinning limbs. The body spun quickly out of sight, forcing him to conjure the unimaginable horrors of QiQi's last moments.

"Explosive decompression isn't a very pleasant way to die," said eNdeen, "just in case you were wondering." Morrissey wasn't. He knew the vacuum of space showed no kindness to organic tissue; he didn't imagine that hyperspace would be any more forgiving. eNdeen revelled in his discomfort. "The term suggests that the body will literally explode but what actually happens is far, far worse. Her body will swell horribly. Any exposed fluids will vaporise — boil away, if you will. The instinct to hold one's breath would be futile. It's more than likely her lungs would rupture. She might live for a couple of minutes, but she will wish that she had not. If she's lucky, she will pass out long before she feels the torture. Not a pretty sight, however you look at it."

Morrissey fought back nausea. "I really think you should look up the word prick. It suits you to a T. When you're done with me, I suppose you'll dispose of me, too?"

"Oh how I do enjoy the human sense of humour. My dear Mr. Morrissey, when we're done with you, there will likely be very little to dispose of."

CHAPTER 24

Ndeen sealed the airlock as the Gyrth jostled Morrissey into the main chamber. An earthy hum seared his nostrils and his skin tingled with an energy he couldn't quite account for. The airlock seemed rudely out of place in the new decor, a baffling mix of high-tech and no-tech. Whatever fixtures and fittings there were had been added as an afterthought rather than integrated into the natural design, as if blocks of Lego had been crudely wedged into a watermelon.

Lighted nodes studded the rough curves of the walls, casting the large chamber in a sullen glow. The inner surfaces lacked the scaly plating that encased the exterior, instead appearing almost organic — dense and fibrous in some places, porous and delicate in others. It was as if he'd taken up residence inside a giant sponge.

Several apertures of varying diameters yawned at him from awkward angles and heights. Turd Head nudged him toward one of the lower orifices. Morrissey peered into the cavity, the cold light from within beckoning to him half-heartedly. "You expect me to go in there?" He shook his head slowly. "Sorry, mate. I don't think so." He'd always had a fear of tight spaces. Even watching footage of

216

spelunkers squeezing themselves through impossibly constricting cave passages was enough to send him into a tizzy. "Not gonna happen."

"I'm afraid it is," said eNdeen. Turd Head and Shorty left him no choice, shoving him roughly into the entrance. It seemed big enough at its opening, but the conduit tapered as it twisted inward. Where it went from there was anybody's guess. But on the bright side, if eNdeen and his merry band of Gyrth were coming with him, it stood to reason there would be room for them all, no?

The passage meandered without sense or purpose, twisting and turning, rising and sinking in unpredictable and impractical directions, but it never narrowed to less than shoulder width. Morrissey stumbled on the uneven ground, but his escorts fared little better. At several points along the route, the tunnel splintered off into multiple feeder passages and Turd Head had to consult his scanner before proceeding.

Finally, they reached another aftermarket doorway. Shorty swiped his meaty palm across a panel in the wall and the heavy slab groaned and parted. Clusters of machinery welcomed them, whirring and humming in a symphony of misery.

eNdeen spread his arms wide around him, looking every bit like the proud father. "Do you like it?"

"It's just creepy enough to suit you."

"It may not be much to look at but as you humans say, it's all about location, location, location."

Ain't that the truth. Morrissey expected a villain of eNdeen's calibre to have a secret lair — it went with the membership. The fact that his lair was hidden in the thick of hyperspace did not bode well for his rescue prospects. "Where are we? I mean, is this a ship?"

"It does challenge the mind, doesn't it. We shouldn't even be able to maintain a stationary position in hyperspace, certainly not without a hyperspace generator, yet here we are. Everything about this construct runs contrary to the laws of physics as we understand. Fortunately, the Frayd operated under somewhat more flexible laws."

"Could you be any more cryptic? Who the hell are the Frayd?"

"Were. The operative word is were. The Frayd are long since extinct. Not much is known about them, to be honest. Only whispers of whispers passed down along the millennia. They once numbered in the billions when most sentient species were still splashing about in their respective primordial pools. And now…nothing."

"What happened to them?"

"We did, of course. Not we, specifically — I can't take credit for that one. But as the civilisations of the galaxy pushed out toward the stars, the very technology that gave them the freedom to do so also soured The Frayd's native environment — hyperspace. The results were inevitably fatal. The Frayd perished — an entire race, extinct."

Morrissey's stomach knotted. "So this…" he said, gesturing to the cold dank walls around him, "this station is all that's left of them?"

"Oh no, Mr. Morrissey. This station isn't a station. This station is a Frayd."

The hairs on the back of Morrissey's neck not only stood at attention, they also threatened to walk off the job entirely. "Are you saying that we're standing inside…a dead alien?"

eNdeen's single eye pulsed with excitement. "The universe is a wondrous place, is it not? The breadth of knowledge that died with these beings is enough to bring a tear to my eye."

It was starting to make sense: the random configuration of the tunnels, the ill-fitting hardware, the pervasive pall of death. "Doesn't it bother you, using one of their bodies as a…as a base camp?"

"Galactic expansion was inevitable. The Frayd were simply victims of progress. I certainly can't be held responsible for their inability to adapt to change."

"You could at least show a little compassion."

"Compassion is best left to priests and politicians. I'm a pragmatist."

"You're a terrorist."

"My dear human, the universe is rarely so black and white. To be a terrorist, you must believe in a cause. My only cause is profit."

"I can't believe I've travelled halfway around the galaxy and people still screw each other over for money. The universe sucks."

"It is precisely that universal constant that drives me. There is nothing more lucrative than war — the desire to conquer, the desire to control, the desire to destroy. I simply take advantage of the very weaknesses that permeate all of creation."

"Whatever. What you do is who you are. Whatever you do to me, wherever you go after this, you've killed people by the thousands —

directly or indirectly, it doesn't matter. You'll always be a mass murderer. No matter where you hide or what disguise you wear —" And then it hit him. The word terrorist had been ringing such sour notes in his head for so long that he couldn't quite put a tune to it. Until now. "My god. It's you, isn't it?"

eNdeen's singular eye flared curiously. "What is me?"

"All this time we've been trying to figure out what you want from me and it's been staring me in the DNA all along."

"My dear human, I'm afraid you have me at a loss."

"I'm not stupid, eNdeen. You people seem to change your appearance as often as I change my underwear. What's to say that years ago, you didn't take the genetic form of a human — on Earth. Ring any bells?"

eNdeen's mouth-sphincter twisted into a cruel smile. "You can't possibly think — you do! How delicious. You poor fool." His tone clicked into one of unmistakable mockery. "Luke...I am your father!" eNdeen's laughter grated. "Don't be surprised: I am quite familiar with your popular culture references, but it doesn't make your theory any less absurd."

"Are you saying that you're not Chendra Vaziil? Not my biological father?" Morrissey could barely get the words out of his mouth without choking on them.

"No, human, I am afraid not."

"And why should I believe you?"

eNdeen gestured to a panel on the wall and stroked it to life. From the dark recesses of the ceiling, a hydraulic arm lowered with a strained whine, releasing a metallic pod to the ground with a heavy thunk.

"Because this, Mr. Morrissey, is Chendra Vaziil." Of all the words that eNdeen could have uttered, these made the least sense.

The pod split like a clamshell, twisting Morrissey's curiosity into horror. Sound came first — a stifled wheeze, a bubbling rasp. Not quite the 'hello, son' Morrissey was expecting. The visuals were a chaotic fusion of countless alien genomes rolled into one amorphous blob. Even its blobs had blobs, shimmering and wobbling in the dim light; there was a lot of wobbling. Some areas of its ruddy skin were dry, almost scaly, while others glistened with a gelatinous glaze. Random patches were thatched with bristles of coarse hair while a ragged stripe of quills fanned along its midsection with each laboured breath.

The only hint of a face was a nest of bulging orbs twitching furtively in Morrissey's direction. Below the eyes was the being's mouth — or it's beak. Or snout. Whatever it was, a sickly grey mucous oozed lazily from its crusty edges before being sucked quickly back through a puckering orifice near its tip. Limbs jutted awkwardly from parts unexpected. Something that may have been a hand beckoned with tentacles rather than fingers in a repulsively hypnotic gesture.

"You have got to be kidding me," said Morrissey.

"The family resemblance is staggering, no?" eNdeen belched a stream of laughter.

"What the hell makes you think that I'm related to...to *this*?"

"Not *think*. The genetic markers are irrefutable, I have it on very good authority." eNdeen led Morrissey across the chamber to a figure seated behind a bank of consoles. It was a hairless grey humanoid, no more than four feet tall. Its head was bulbously out of proportion to its slight frame. Delicate limbs flowed over the consoles, nimble fingers dancing furiously over the controls. Large, coal black teardrop eyes surveyed Morrissey impassively.

"I know him," said Morrissey. "Not him, specifically; I know his kind."

"The Vemen?"

"That's a Vemen?" Barry had mentioned that Earth had been targeted by the Vemen for centuries for the purpose of genetic experimentation. He should have figured that the perpetrators of such heinous acts were the clichés of the universe. For decades, images of little grey aliens had haunted the nightmares of UFO abductees. The creatures were iconic, their influence permeating the public consciousness to the point of parody. And now he was staring one dead in the face. He felt like a child who'd been assured all his life that there is no reason to fear the dark, only to find that the bogeyman is alive and well and living under his bed. How he would love to parade the bug-eyed little shit through the halls of the Ministry of Defence for a little slice of fried I-told-you-so.

"Is this thing supposed to prove something?"

"The Vemen are extremely accomplished in the field of xenobiology and the...manipulation, shall we say, of alien genomes. They're obsessively meticulous in what they do. The absence of a moral compass tends to liberate one's perception of brutality.

Apparently, they find humans to be particularly malleable. They were the ones who confirmed your rather unique ancestry.

"My initial intel only provided enough information to point in your direction as the source of some powerful weapons technology, the form of which remained a mystery. Upon our first meeting, I was able to decrypt only a portion of the hidden data within your DNA — a series of coordinates that led me to this Frayd, nested deep within the chaotic corridors of hyperspace. On board the Frayd corpse, there was a team of Vemen exobiologists working on something far beyond my comprehension — all to do with this pathetic creature." eNdeen gestured to Vaziil's swollen form twitching in its pod. "Even so, it was obvious even to me that his DNA contained a rather intriguing amalgam, holding much promise. As you can imagine, I couldn't get much sense from this jumble of genes and had to resort to some rather more inventive measures. It took more than a little torture to draw the truth from the Vemen as to its identity. You'd be surprised how motivated they can be when they see their colleagues being peeled alive." The sole Vemen technician remained focussed on his console. "Hruuvun, here, was quite cooperative — in the end. Isn't that right, Hruuvun?" The Vemen's egg-head bobbled slowly from side to side. "He confirmed that this being is, in fact, the infamous galactic terrorist, Chendra Vaziil. He'd been hiding from authorities for years, adopting a multitude of genetic profiles to cover his tracks, resulting in some rather unfortunate side effects, the culmination of which you see before you.

"Hruuvun also confessed that many years ago, Vaziil had been on your home planet developing a weapon — a very powerful weapon that could… how did you put it, Hruuvun — a weapon that could untie the universe. Very poetic for a scientist but very evocative, don't you think?"

Morrissey gave only a vague nod but inside, his stomach turned to ice, his head churning with a desperate mix of disbelief, revulsion, and sheer panic. "And where am I supposed to fit into this equation?"

eNdeen clicked his scabby claws with excitement. "As you can see, Vaziil's DNA is barely holding his skin together at the moment; I have been assured that if I help restore his genome to its full integrity, I will be granted access to this weapon — how could I resist such an opportunity. That's where you come in. As his offspring, the encrypted data packet hidden within your own DNA contains an archive of Vaziil's genome. And it just so happens that our Vemen friend, here, has the necessary skill set to extract and decrypt it — in exchange for his continued existence, of course." eNdeen glared at the Vemen, his sphincter mouth cracking what might have been a grin.

Morrissey chuckled drily. "So, you need my DNA? Well why didn't you say so. Apparently, I'm giving out free samples to anyone who asks. Didn't you hear? How much do you need?"

"I'm not the geneticist but I would imagine we'd need quite a bit of it. Well, the good bits, at least. What do you say, Hruuvun? The good bits?" More head-bobbling from the Vemen.

"Not to sound selfish, but once you've got your weapon, what happens to me?"

"Not only do I not know, I don't particularly care. I need you alive only until the requisite sequence has been extracted, decrypted, and verified. After that, who knows. Hruuvun, any thoughts on the matter?" A non-committal head bobble from the Vemen. "I'm afraid Hruuvun doesn't fancy your chances."

Morrissey had run out of optimism. Rescue was now a far distant fantasy. He backed away from his fate, stumbling directly into the chest armour of Turd Head who glared down at him in an I-don't-have-the-patience-for-this sort of way.

eNdeen inched closer, his fetid breath stinging Morrissey's eyes. "You must have realised by now that resistance is futile." He nodded to the Gyrth. "Prepare him. We have no more time to waste."

CHAPTER 25

Morrissey's tongue tore like Velcro from the roof of his mouth as he sucked at the stale air. He'd awoken to find himself half submerged in a vat of suspension gel, a spiderweb of translucent cables crisscrossing his exposed flesh, feeding directly into the porous walls of the Frayd.

Across from him stood the pod of his biological father, Chendra Vaziil, connected to the Frayd carcass by a similar network of cables. His father's appearance had certainly improved since Morrissey had first laid eyes on him. His body was leaner, less blobby; the boils and pustules had smoothed and deflated. His skin had taken on a more homogeneous finish, as if it were bound in leather rather than smothered in pudding. Much of the hair had moulted and the spiny quills lining his midsection had fallen away, leaving only brittle stubs. Hand-tentacles had been replaced by flesh and bone and his formerly mushy head had set into a sturdy plated skull. His eyes had pretty much decided they'd work best as a pair, the superfluous ones looking like nothing more than dried scabs. As far as limbs went, there were now only four — two spindly arms draping from broad, powerful shoulders and two sturdy legs stretching towards a pair of stumpy feet.

Two Gyrth soldiers stood guard at the entrance to the chamber, brandishing their blasters in an unnecessarily aggressive manner; it wasn't as if Morrissey could make a run for it. The bobble-headed Vemen called Hruuvun sat at a computer console nearby, tapping at keypads and fiddling with levers in ways that suggested no good purpose. eNdeen supervised over his shoulder, his single eye throbbing with a palpable hunger. "Is he awake yet?"

Hruuvun nodded meekly, gesturing to Vaziil's pod as eNdeen pushed past him.

Surprisingly, Vaziil spoke, his voice a vast improvement over the desperate wet gurgles he'd only been able to manage before the transfusion had begun. "Is the process...complete?"

eNdeen thumped solidly on Morrissey's pod. "Don't worry. Everything is going according to plan. The Vemen has been able to download the archive of your DNA stored within the human and as you can see, your genetic health is improving nicely. You'll soon be restored to the handsome devil you once were."

"Then why halt...the transfusion?"

"Well that's a really interesting question, isn't it, and one I have a feeling that only you can answer." eNdeen tapped his claw heavily against Vaziil's hardened skull plate. "You see, I was promised a very powerful weapon in exchange for restoring you to your full health and I expect to be paid."

"I don't know what deal...you struck with these...creatures...but it is no deal of mine."

"Hmmm. I thought you might say something like that. But there's one thing you should know about me, Vaziil — I'm very good at what I do. And to remain successful in my field, you have to know how to read a being. It can not only mean the difference between profit and loss, but also between life and death. What I see when I look at you is someone of considerable talent, yes, but also someone who is very cautious. It would only make sense that a being of such accomplishments would keep records of their work and those records would need to be protected. It wouldn't do to store such treasures on a clumsy info pad, nor would you trust your life's work to the common security of a public vault. Someone of your stature would want to keep your intellectual property close at hand, always within reach. And what better storage medium would there be than your own DNA — your entire career in genetic terror neatly contained within your festering bulk. So close...and yet, so far. The ultimate irony — years of cellular abuse has corrupted that data beyond use to anyone. Until now." eNdeen gestured to Morrissey's pod. "I have surmised that the human's hidden data packet will not only restore the archive of your genome, but also has the potential to rebuild the stored archive of your life's work, including the promised weapons technology. Just think, the entire breadth of your twisted knowledge combined with my ambition would be deliciously lucrative, to say the least.

"The only problem is that Hruuvun, here, is having a hell of a time decrypting anything beyond your genome. He's trying his best — or at least he says he is — but so far it seems beyond him." The Vemen looked at Vaziil and shrugged his small shoulders. "So I think it would be really...beneficial to all concerned if you would give up whatever protocols we need to access this data so that we can all take advantage of the wonderful opportunities presented to us."

Vaziil twitched. "You may be...correct, eNdeen, but I cannot...give you access to that data."

"My dear Vaziil, you don't have a choice. Without me you'd be nothing more than a stain on the furniture."

Morrissey felt sick. And dirty. And violated. He felt Vaziil's DNA coursing through his body as if it were a plague, leaving nothing but rot and decay in its wake. "Okay, fellas. I only understood about half of all that but what's clear to me is that my role in all this is at an end. So if you'll kindly just unplug me from this...hell, I'll be on my way. Decrypt the data. Don't decrypt it. I don't give a shit. You guys sort it out amongst yourselves. I'm out."

"Oh no, Mr. Morrissey," said eNdeen, "you're not going anywhere just yet. You're still very much a key to my plans. If things don't work out with your father, my new friend Hruuvun is going to unravel every strand of your DNA until I get what I want."

A low rumble slowly erupted from Vaziil's flaccid mouth. "You are indeed...a clever being, eNdeen, but in all your machinations...there is one thing that you did not account for."

"And what is that?"

"Vemen loyalty is not...as flexible as you might imagine."

If eNdeen had a brow, it would have knotted. "What do you mean?"

"You see…your new friend Hruuvun…is actually my old friend Hruuvun. He's been working for me all along."

eNdeen snapped a look at the Vemen who bobbled his head ambiguously. "That's impossible! We had to torture the Vemen technicians for the information about you. Hruuvun, himself, suffered terribly."

"A necessary sacrifice…and a testament to his loyalty. I know the power of greed. I know it needs to be fed. You needed to be…incentivised. Do you really think it was chance…that led you to the human…that brought you to this Frayd? Hruuvun fed you just enough to keep you searching…to keep you hunting…to keep you wanting. Your quest for power was…predictable. And fortunately…inevitable."

eNdeen was paralysed by confusion. "It…can't be."

"It can. And it is. You see, I never go anywhere…without an exit strategy."

A klaxon punctuated Vaziil's declaration, bursting through the chamber and almost through Morrissey's heart.

"Apologies, Sir." A frazzled voice pumped through the main comm station.

"What is it?"

"A ship has docked at one of the auxiliary hangars."

"A ship? Docked? How — what ship?"

"Unknown, Khyr eNdeen. We didn't detect its approach or its transponder beacon. There must be some interference with our sensors."

"That's beside the point — no ship could track us in hyperspace. Unless…" For a being with only one eye and a suck-hole for a mouth, eNdeen certainly looked pissed. "This is you, isn't it, Vaziil? Your exit strategy, I presume? Well, we'll see about that." He barked into the comm. "Send a squad to intercept — no, belay that. Send a squad here to protect our package. Station all remaining troops at the main docking bay. I want The Krassus ready for departure when I get there."

"Yes, Khyr eNdeen."

"Ready to turn…and run," said Vaziil.

"I didn't survive this long in the business without being prepared for any eventuality." eNdeen signalled to the two Gyrth soldiers. "Guard Vaziil and the human as if your lives depended on it — because they do." He motioned to the Vemen traitor. "And secure him. I don't want him touching anything. Reinforcements are on the way." The Gyrth grunted their acknowledgement as eNdeen clattered from the chamber.

Morrissey shifted awkwardly in his pod, trying to raise himself from the suspension gel and untangle the nest of tubes and wires. Things were about to get ugly and he didn't plan on being helpless when they did. He stared into the creepy little Vemen's blank face. "Hey you. Hruuvun, is it? How would you like to earn yourself a pardon? All you have to do is get me out of here and I'll forget I ever saw you." *If it were only that easy.*

"I'd keep my mouth shut if I were you." One of the Gyrth jabbed the business end of his rifle toward the Vemen. "You're not that far from a termination order."

Hruuvun bobbled his head and did as he was told. Morrissey cursed the whole lot of them. Escape was looking pretty grim. Even at his best, he wouldn't have been able to overpower the two hefty soldiers. And if by some magic he did, he had no idea where he would go on a station teeming with mercenaries. Whatever his plan was, he'd have to act before eNdeen's reinforcements arrived.

Too late. A chime sounded. One of the Gyrth palmed the door, weapon loosely at the ready. The other stood guard over the Vemen. The door parted; sound and light filled the chamber. Two sharp cracks of energy burst through the mercenary's chest. He staggered backward, clutching hopelessly at his smoking wounds. Two more bursts found their mark, spinning the second soldier off his feet.

The hulking shooter moved smoothly yet warily into the chamber, scanning for further threats. It was Gyrth, surprisingly. If he was one of eNdeen's promised reinforcements, he was certainly going about it the wrong way. The soldier secured the door behind him, then pressed the steaming muzzle of his rifle into the Vemen's cold, grey face. His voice was full of gravel and menace. "It would be very wise of you to begin detaching the human from this contraption. Do it quickly and do it carefully or you will be harmed. I will only tell you once."

The Vemen bobbled his head in agreement then reached into the pod, sinking his wiry hands deep into the suspension gel. One by one, he began unplugging the tubes and contacts from Morrissey's skin. Morrissey fought the urge to snap the little grey weasel's neck — retribution for centuries of mass human violations. He turned, instead, to the Gyrth.

227

"If you're here to abduct me, you're going to have to wait in line."

The alien leaned in close, his black egg-like eyes rolling carefully over Morrissey's face. "You don't remember me, do you?"

"Should I?" said Morrissey.

"Perhaps not. When we last met, it was under some rather…chaotic circumstances."

"You're going to have to refresh my memory, mate. As you can see from my current accommodations, my life has been one continuous string of chaos lately."

"I thought you might remember your first. Alien, that is."

"My…first? Look, I don't have time for games. I've seen a lot of aliens in the last couple of weeks and most of them weren't doing me any favours. You don't seriously expect me to remember —

"And then he did. He had seen many aliens recently — many Gyrth, in fact — but this one was different. This one had a metallic patch at the side of his head, covering the area where one of his breathing sacs would be…like a bandage over a wound. "It's…you. From Dr. Cheevers' ship — I mean, eNdeen. You were one of his holographic orderlies."

"True and correct on both counts, to my shame."

It seemed so long ago, now. Back on eNdeen's shipboard holographic psychiatric hospital, Morrissey had grappled with this Gyrth and had inadvertently done some considerable damage to his breathing sac. "You survived then, obviously?"

"Thanks to you."

"You almost died because of me."

"You were only defending yourself. I should not have been on active duty during my moulting phase."

"What are you doing here?"

"I am here for you. You risked your life for mine when you could have just ensured your own escape. You saved my life. Now I am bound by my honour to save yours."

Awkward. "No offence, mate, but I didn't think you lot were much for honour."

"You cannot judge us all by their standards." He thumbed toward his lifeless colleagues. "I only took the job because the advert promised limitless opportunities to see the galaxy. What a load of bunk. Besides, eNdeen is a kraptuk."

"I'm not exactly sure what that means but I have a feeling I'd agree."

The Gyrth held out his massive hand, smothering Morrissey's own in his grip. "I am called Vintzan-Thanagram Esh, but you may call me Vintz."

"Alright, Vintz, what's the plan?"

"Priority is to get you free of this equipment."

Morrissey glared down at the Vemen. "And how's that going?"

Hruuvun bobbled his head vigorously. Despite his expressionless face, he looked quite sheepish as he pulled the last of the tubes from Morrissey's tingling flesh.

"Do you feel strong enough for travel?" said Vintz.

"I'll bloody well have to be. eNdeen has dispatched reinforcements to this location and is massing the rest of his troops at the main docking bay. There's also a mystery ship docked, probably to rescue him." Morrissey thumbed derisively at Vaziil. "It's going to get awfully crowded in here soon with people out to kill us."

"Right — we'll need a ship. Aside from eNdeen's, there are two troop transports docked with the station. We'll take one of them, although it's likely we'll have to fight for it."

"Anything to get off this rock." Morrissey climbed from the cocoon and stood on legs that felt like they belonged to someone else. The damp chill on his skin reminded him he was naked. "I suppose some clothes might be in order."

Hruuvun spoke up, his voice little more than a brittle mumble. "Your coverings are in this storage locker. Accept them with my compliments." He even managed a thin smile.

Morrissey wanted to punch him in the throat but gave him a civil grunt instead. "What do we do with the Vemen? You can't shoot him in cold blood...can you?"

Vintz hefted his weapon thoughtfully. "I suppose not, but we can't let him go."

"Oh yes," said Hruuvun, "you can leave me here, with most certainty. I will not betray your plans."

"I have a feeling your allegiance changes with the wind," said Morrissey. He turned to Vintz. "At the end of the day, I think he'll stay loyal to Vaziil but who knows who he'll sidle up to along the way."

Vintz motioned to Morrissey's empty transfusion pod. "Get in there, Vemen."

Hruuvun hesitated only long enough for Vintz to raise his weapon in a half-threat and then hopped into the cocoon. Vintz forced the lid shut then stripped a tab of metallic tape from his utility pouch, slapping it onto the latch. It flared vigorously, sealing the Vemen securely inside the metal egg. Karma, baby.

There was still the question of what to do with the elephant in the room. Morrissey shrugged. "What about Vaziil? We can't very well leave the most wanted terrorist in the galaxy lying around for eNdeen to play with."

"Him, I can shoot in cold blood."

"But you can't. At least, I don't think you should. Shouldn't he stand trial or something?"

"These are questions not for me."

They weren't questions for Morrissey, either. If only Sha'an were here, she'd know what to do, but she was long gone now. He tried to imagine what would happen to such a criminal on Earth. When SEAL Team Six caught up with Osama Bin Laden, they executed him on the spot. No muss. No fuss. But he didn't know if his conscience could take the weight of a cold-blooded execution. However, if Vaziil somehow escaped and he could have done something to stop him from wreaking havoc again, Morrissey didn't know if he could live with that on his conscience, either.

"I can't believe I'm saying this, Vintz, but I think you should...you know...shoot him."

Vintz casually unholstered his sidearm, thumbing the weapon to *active*. Without hesitation, he aimed directly into Vaziil's face.

Morrissey tensed, waiting for the shot. Then... "Wait!"

Vintz bristled. "Now what?"

"Maybe I should be the one...to do it."

"You? Why?"

"He is my father. On some level, that must make it my responsibility."

"You don't have to."

"Yeah, I kinda do."

Morrissey numbly took the pistol from Vintz. He had killed, and very recently, but this felt very different. An execution, cold and simple. No, far from simple. Slowly he raised the weapon and pointed it toward the being he'd only recently learned was his biological father. "Look, I know we're supposed to be related and all, but...well...you've apparently done some really bad things that have hurt a great number of people. I'd like to say it was good to meet you but I really could have done without any of this. I would have been happier believing that my dad was dead. And now, I guess you will be."

"We all have our place...in history."

"And I suppose this is mine. So...no hard feelings, then?"

"There is no blame."

No. Just guilt. "I guess that's as close to a father-son moment as we're likely to have." And then it clicked. "No," he said, lowering the pistol to his side. "I can't. I won't kill you." If this terrorist was truly Morrissey's father, he wanted to be nothing like him. There were countless beings who'd suffered at Vaziil's hands who were far better suited to decide his fate. "We need to take him with us."

Vintz shrugged. "If you say so. But it won't be easy."

"I find doing the right thing rarely is."

Vaziil let out a stifled wheeze, as if he'd been holding onto what may well have been his last breath. "Thank you," he said.

"I'm not doing this for you," said Morrissey. "If I'm not very much mistaken, you'll be facing a far darker fate than I would have dealt you.

"Still, you might want to...to..."

"To what?"

"To...duck."

Too late. The room flashed white hot as the chamber doors buckled inward. Air and space compressed, blowing Morrissey and Vintz across the floor. Thunder rolled through his head and chaos ruled his thoughts. Somewhere, far away, a phone was ringing and he wished desperately for someone to answer it. Unfortunately, the ringing was in his teeth.

A squad of Gyrth soldiers poured through the doorway, the barrage of blaster fire announcing their intentions in no uncertain terms. A meaty hand tugged Morrissey sharply across the pitted ground, dumping him behind the transfusion pod containing Hruuvun. "Stay down," said Vintz. Energy bolts seared the air, blistering the pod with angry welts. From inside came the muffled squeals of the traitorous Vemen. Too bad. Should have thought of that before you hitched your star to a wanted criminal.

Using the wheeled pod for cover, Vintz manoeuvred them away from their attackers until they butted up against the far wall of the chamber. He returned fire in short bursts. Morrissey felt helpless until he realised he'd somehow managed to hold onto Vintz's pistol through the mayhem. Taking up a firing position alongside his new ally, he employed his weapons training and took calm, measured shots.

Vintz quickly dispatched two of the Gyrth mercenaries, leaving eight to contend with. Two of the remainder were focused solely on preparing Vaziil for transit while two more were providing cover fire. The remaining four were creeping their way along the curve of the chamber, using the computer stations as cover.

"Watch your flank," said Vintz.

"I see them." Morrissey peppered their path with a few blasts from his pistol. Several more volleys yielded little in the way of results. "Their priority seems to be retrieving Vaziil. What if we focus our fire on the central soldiers, the one's giving cover to his pod? They'll have to fill in the gaps."

Vintz smiled broadly. "Who's a clever human, then!"

At Vintz's direction, Morrissey targeted Vaziil's protection detail while Vintz continued to defend their flank. Nothing like life and death pressure to sharpen one's aim. Morrissey got down low, finding a firing solution between the struts of the transfusion pod. He fired. Once. A miss. Twice. A hit. The soldier took the blast in the leg and fell forward. Morrissey fired once more to keep him down. Almost immediately, one of the flanking troops fell back to fill the void.

They kept up the pattern, taking down two more soldiers, the pod sustaining considerable damage in the process. Morrissey wasn't sure how much more of a beating it could bear. Judging by the panicked wailing coming from within, Hruuvun was wondering the same thing. Two more soldiers fell — one at Morrissey's hand and one at Vintz's.

"Only three left," said Morrissey. "It's pretty much a stalemate."

"We cannot remain here indefinitely. Your value to them seems to have expired. Once they've removed Vaziil's pod, there will be nothing to stop them from bombarding us with grenades. I suggest we not be here when that happens."

"Where do you suggest we go? Those soldiers are blocking the only exit."

"What about up there?" Vintz pointed to an access port three metres off the ground. Morrissey didn't remember seeing it before, but with all the chaos that wasn't saying much. "Where does it lead?"

"Anywhere but here."

A storm of enemy fire crisscrossed their path. The port was four metres away. Even under the protection of the pod, they would be exposed.

"I will draw their fire while you run for the opening. It's the only way."

"The only way to get you killed," said Morrissey. "I don't think your Gyrth pals are going to welcome you back to the team with open arms. Either we both go or we both stay."

"Your concern is appreciated but we really have no other choice."

"I can't leave you behind, not after you saved my life. Besides, even if I can find one of those troop shuttles, it's not as if I can fly it."

Vintz gave Morrissey a lumpy smile. "Very well, but we'll need a diversion, and quickly." The Gyrth mercenaries were unplugging the last of the cables tethering Vaziil's pod to the Frayd carcass.

"How much of that stuff do you have with you, the stuff you used to seal the Vemen into the pod?"

"A fair amount, but it's not an explosive." A cunning grin stretched across Vintz's broad face. "But it doesn't have to be. If I can rig it to blow, it might cause enough of a light show to blind those soldiers for a minute or two. I'll need a detonator, some sort of energy source."

Morrissey waved his pistol. "How about this? Maybe use its power cell?"

Another hearty smile. "I like the way you think, human. Here, take my rifle and give me some cover."

Morrissey unleashed a respectable amount of fire while Vintz jerry-rigged his makeshift flash-bomb.

"I'm ready," said Vintz.

"Okay, then. On three."

"On three, what?"

"A three-count. It's how we do these sorts of things on Earth. At least in movies and TV shows. I count down and then we go. Simple as. Ready?"

"Ready."

"Three…"

And then Vintz threw the package; he had a lot to learn about Earthbound entertainment. The flash-bomb blew instantly, strobing the chamber with a blinding phosphorescence. This time, Morrissey didn't look — he couldn't. He just fired wildly and ran as if the devil were chasing him. When they reached the opening, Vintz heaved him up into the cavity like a sack of potatoes. The lip of the entrance was spongy and coated with a thin layer of mucous. He had to use the hard edges of the rifle to pull himself into the hole while Vintz shoved from below.

Ahead lay blackness with only the faintest suggestion of light in the distance. Down in the chamber, the searing flare from the flash-bomb was already fading, indicating their window of escape had almost closed.

"You might want to hurry, Vintz. Hurrying would be good."

Vintz jumped, grabbing the slick edge of the orifice with his knobby fingers. Morrissey tried his best to pull the Gyrth up into the tunnel but it was like wrestling with concrete. "Jesus, Vintz! You weigh a ton!"

Thank God for the alien's upper body strength; within seconds, he'd managed to hoist himself up into the tight space, narrowly dodging several energy blasts as he pulled his legs in. There wasn't much room to manoeuvre; Morrissey pushed all thoughts of his claustrophobia to the parts of his brain that weren't fighting for their lives. He slung the rifle across his back and began a low army crawl into the darkness ahead until the tunnel widened to the point where he could manage a respectable crouch.

Vintz, on the other hand, was having no such luck. One of the Gyrth mercenaries had forced his way into the opening, half inside, half out, firing wildly at his quarry. Vintz dodged the enemy fire as best he could, pressing his considerable bulk into the tight curve running from the narrow entrance. Morrissey tried to fire back but didn't have a clear line of sight around Vintz. He tossed the rifle down toward him, but it fell far short of its mark. His new Gyrth ally was pinned down and unarmed; it was only a matter of time before one of the enemy blasts found its target.

As Morrissey prepared himself for the inevitable, the opening of the tunnel suddenly snapped closed like the shutter of a camera. The halo of light surrounding the enemy Gyrth pinched to blackness; one more panicked energy blast seared the air, followed by a heavy wet thud. Then silence.

Vintz fumbled in his utility belt and squeezed a beam emitter to life. In the cool eerie light, they saw it — the mercenary, or what was left of him. The tunnel opening had scissored him in two, just below the shoulders, leaving nothing but an awkwardly shaped hump of bloodied meat.

"Jesus," said Morrissey quietly.

Vintz muttered something comparable before prying the soldier's weapon from his twitching grip. "Here, take this."

Morrissey took the rifle absently. "Did you see that? It cut him in half...the tunnel...just squeezed shut and...gone. I don't want to get squeezed like that, Vintz."

"Then we'd best move quickly." Vintz handed Morrissey the beam emitter.

Morrissey waddled away, the emitter carving a desperate path along the dark tunnel, which dipped and rose without the courtesy of a warning. After what seemed like hours but was probably only a few minutes, they reached an opening. Morrissey stopped suddenly and stared into the growing light. "What if it closes on us as we're climbing out?"

"We cannot stay in the tunnel."

"I know. But I don't want to end up like that guy." He thumbed back toward the half-soldier. "What if there's an automatic trigger?"

"There's only one way to find out."

"Easy for you to say." Unfortunately Morrissey was first in line and the tapered exit was too narrow for them to jockey positions. He inched toward the rim and gingerly peered over the edge. There was no nest of angry Gyrth lurking below, so he braced himself for a smooth exit.

"Come on, then," said Vintz.

"Alright, alright. I'm going." Morrissey took a deep breath before heaving his body through the gap in one go. He hit the ground with a thud and bounced into a forward roll. Vintz thumped down behind him — just as the tunnel mouth puckered shut.

"See! I told you!" said Morrissey, fixated on the newly sealed exit. He finally shook his brain loose and stood on legs of jelly. Only it wasn't his legs that were wobbly. "Do you feel that?"

Vintz was up and alert, fanning his rifle across the empty chamber. "Feel what?"

"The ground. It's...different." He'd half expected to crack his head open on impact, but his landing had been more like diving into a memory foam mattress, only with a slightly more gamey aroma.

"Perhaps this section of the Frayd is composed of a different type of tissue, like bone is different from cartilage."

"Maybe. But didn't you find the tunnel a bit...wetter than expected? And then there's that." He gestured to the upper arcs of the chamber which glistened with a vibrant blue goo. "I don't remember seeing any of that before. Seems a bit out of place in a desiccated carcass."

Vintz's granite jaw cracked a smirk. "As long as it's not shooting at us, I'm happy to put up with a bit of slime. Now I suggest we focus on extracting ourselves from this carcass."

The chamber was a storage hold of some sort. Equipment of all sizes was piled against the sloping walls, some of it still wrapped in its packaging. Vintz attacked it like a child on Christmas morning. He tossed Morrissey a couple of spare energy packs for his rifle as well as a chunky little pistol. Morrissey checked the charge and action as Syddyk had trained him to do and then holstered it, missing the feel of his own ALF-issued weapon.

"Aha!" said Vintz. "This is what I was looking for." He hefted a small data screen, studded with Gyrth-sized tactile pads. As he tabbed it to life, a three-dimensional display pulsed from a node at the base. Vintz studied the graphic, hissing something wholly untranslatable. "This is not good," he said, shaking his massive block head.

"Then be a good chap and turn it off, and we'll pretend we didn't see it."

"I'm detecting a peculiar buildup of energy."

"I told you to turn it off," said Morrissey, more to himself than to Vintz. "Building up where?"

Vintz stared with black-egg eyes. "Everywhere, but the focal point seems to be at the core of the station."

"Dare I ask what's at the core of the station?"

"A small nuclear reactor, that's all. It provides power to the entire facility but these readings...I've never seen readings like this before — electromagnetic radiation in wavelengths that are...unrecognisable. They seem to be shifting their patterns at an incredible rate, building to very unhealthy levels."

"Unhealthy as in, 'hey, too many doughnuts will make you fat' or 'hey, probably best not to poke that gorilla in the arse with a sharp stick'?"

Vintz stumbled over Morrissey's analogy but seemed to get the gist. "I think the second one. The point is, the energy is building to critical levels."

"Doesn't that seem fishy to you?"

"Fish-ee?"

"I mean, too convenient to be mere coincidence. You think it could be sabotage? eNdeen's plan has gone tits up, Vaziil's double-crossed him. Blowing up the Frayd is a pretty effective way to deal with Vaziil's rescue team."

"And with us," said Vintz.

"Then we'd better get to that troop transport and get the hell out of here."

Vintz shook his head grimly. "I can't guarantee we'll make it in time before this place is vaporised. We'll have to try and shut down the reactor."

Of course we do. "How long do we have?

"Difficult to say. Perhaps fifty-five minutes."

"Will that be enough?"

"We'll know in fifty-six minutes."

Morrissey didn't know if this passed for Gyrth humour, but he wasn't entirely amused.

CHAPTER 26

Vintz eased out into the corridor with his weapon at the ready. Morrissey followed close behind and suddenly felt like he'd stepped into a disco, flashes of light and colour arcing across his path. The floor bucked and swayed wildly while cavities in the walls irised open in a blink and then puckered shut just as quickly. He collapsed to his knees, his stomach in free-fall and his nerves on fire.

"Are you alright?" said Vintz.

"I...I think so. I just...maybe it's motion sickness," which Morrissey doubted, "or possibly the stench in here. What the fuck is going on?" he said, motioning to the frantic light show.

"I'm getting the impression that this station — this Frayd — is not as dead as we were led to believe."

"You think. So, what then?"

"Hibernation would be my guess," said Vintz.

"Why would it wake up now?"

"I'm guessing it's got something to do with the power buildup. Wouldn't you find it hard to sleep with a nuclear reactor plugged into your central nervous system?"

The two ran as fast as the unstable Frayd would allow, springing off the surfaces like children in a bouncy castle. At each new chamber, Vintz flashed the scanner to check for enemy threats, but the Frayd's energy fluctuations were playing havoc with the readouts. The closer they got to the core, the more violent and unpredictable the creature's convulsions became. Their footfalls squelched into the spongy ground, now slick with the same bluish gel they'd seen oozing from the walls. At the entrance to the reactor chamber, the heavy doors cleaved with a stubborn resignation, belching a raw, chemical stench that burned Morrissey's eyes. "Alright," he said, as his breath tore in rasps through his aching lungs. "Now what the bloody hell does a nuclear reactor look like?"

Vintz gestured to a massive column of Frayd tissue running from floor to ceiling, a violent energy pulsing from within. "I'm almost certain it's not supposed to look like that. It seems the Frayd creature has swallowed it." He ran his scanner up and down the column, shaking his heavy head at the results. "Strange. Those erratic energy readings I was detecting before — this creature seems to be feeding off them, devouring them, even thriving."

"Is that good or bad?"

"Difficult to say. It might siphon enough of the excess energy to stop the reactor from overloading altogether or…"

"Or what?" said Morrissey.

"Or it might decide it's had enough and blast our atoms across hyperspace."

"So, is there an off switch?"

Before Vintz could answer, a chime sounded from his scanner. He swore at the device as he directed it at the door on the opposite side of the chamber. "Soldiers approaching. Two of them, if these readings can be trusted." Vintz directed Morrissey to a defensive position while he stationed himself on the other side of the entrance. The heavy door groaned open revealing two beings silhouetted in the doorway, both armed. But they were not Gyrth, not by any stretch of the imagination.

Time melted into a sticky mess. Vintz aimed his weapon for a kill-shot; Morrissey called for him to stop but his voice was smothered by the thrum of the reactor. His only remaining option was to fire — not at the approaching aliens, but at Vintz. Not to hit him. Just close enough to disrupt his aim. The bolt seared across his line of sight, blistering a computer panel mounted beyond his head. He turned to Morrissey, his weapon jerking in confusion.

"Everyone just hold your bloody fire! Nobody shoot. They're friendlies — very friendly." Morrissey bounded toward the newcomers who were just as relieved to see him as he was them. "Barry! Syd! I can't believe it. You actually found me." Morrissey hugged his shipmates. "I didn't think there was a chance. When they burned off my tracker tattoo, I kind of lost all hope."

"You've got Bryndevaan to thank for that," said Barry. "Turns out his innate ability to sense genetic patterns across vast distances came in quite handy. You were the last DNA that he tasted. The poor bugger almost roasted his nut homing in on you. Plugged himself into our nav-system and pretty much flew us here. He lost the scent at one point, went into one of his trances. We thought we'd lost him completely but then he seemed more focused than ever, babbling on and on that he must find them, whatever that meant. Got us here in the end, though."

"I'll thank him when I see him — which will be soon, yes?"

"That depends — where's eNdeen?"

"He was heading to the main hangar after your ship docked — which he thought was here to rescue Vaziil."

"Vaziil is here?"

"Oh, I guess I should have mentioned that off the top. eNdeen is using Vaziil for some sort of weapons technology locked in his DNA — apparently, I'm the key to restoring it. Well done, me. But it turns out Vaziil has been using eNdeen all along, just to get his genes back together."

"Maybe it was Vaziil's DNA the Thuwom was tracking," said Syddyk. "He did seem awfully triggered by it when he analysed you."

"I doubt it. Vaziil's genetic signature was little more than the scribble of a madman when I last saw him."

"Where's Vaziil now?" said Barry.

"Last we saw," said Morrissey, "he was being packed up by a squad of Gyrth mercenaries. eNdeen is doing a runner and taking his prize with him."

"Speaking of Gyrth mercenaries," said Syddyk, "who's your new friend?"

"This is Vintz. He's okay, he saved my life."

"Isn't that convenient." Syddyk's weapon didn't stray from Vintz's torso.

"It's okay, Syd," said Morrissey. "He genuinely wants to help."

"Help save his own skin, maybe."

"Look, fellas, I wouldn't have made it this far without him."

"Syd's right," said Barry, "he *is* a mercenary. Looking after one's own interests is sort of their stock in trade. How do we know we can trust him?"

Morrissey gently redirected the muzzle of Syddyk's blaster toward the ground. "Because *I* trust him."

"I understand your concerns," said Vintz, "but could we possibly have this discussion at a more suitable time and place? We don't have a lot left — time, that is."

"He's right," Morrissey said, gesturing to the column of throbbing Frayd tissue. "The reactor core is overloading and we might all soon be space dust. And if the reactor doesn't kill us, this atmosphere will." The air felt like sandpaper in his lungs.

Barry eyed the structure with wonder. "That's a reactor core? We picked up the strange readings but couldn't tell the source. It caused a helluva lot of interference. How much time do we have?"

Vintz did a time-check. "Thirty-eight minutes. Give or take."

Morrissey nodded aggressively. "We've got thirty-eight minutes to take the reactor offline or Vintz's loyalties are going to be the least of our problems."

"Then I would suggest," said Syddyk, "that our best course of action is to get off this station and hope that the detonation takes care of eNdeen and Vaziil — two birds with one reactor."

"And normally I'd be right there behind you," said Morrissey, "except for one thing — this station isn't a station. It's a lifeform. A sentient life form called a Frayd."

It took a second for the term to register. "But the Frayd died out millennia ago," said Barry.

"That's what eNdeen thought. He assumed it was just a corpse, a dead husk, but he was wrong — this one is still alive. You may have noticed its song and dance routine on the way in. For all we know, it might be the last of its kind. We can't just let it die without trying to save it. Isn't this exactly the kind of stuff the ALF is duty bound to fight for?"

Barry sighed heavily. "What do you say, Syd, think you can shut it down?"

Syddyk cycled his scanner over the Frayd tissue until it whined from the effort. "Not so you'd notice. Maybe if Lillum were here, and if we had a week to play with it. I've never seen anything like it — the reactor seems to have completely melded with the organic matter." His already impossibly large eyes seemed even wider as his face paled. "But these energy readings are what's really troubling me, they're off the scale. The damage caused by such a detonation within hyperspace would be unpredictable at best. At worst…catastrophic."

"What does that mean?" said Morrissey. "How bad could it be — " Before he could finish his thought, Morrissey collapsed again, his nerves burning with a raw energy, tying his limbs into rigid knots.

Barry gently unravelled him and lifted him to his feet. "Dave, what is it? Is it the air? I didn't bring a rebreather."

"No…it's not that. It's the Frayd. It's…dying. The reactor energy — it's killing it."

Syddyk ran another series of scans. "He's not lying. The creature is absorbing the energy at an alarming rate. Its cells are decaying — like it's being eaten alive." He turned to Morrissey. "But how did you know?"

"I…I just…felt it. It's like I'm…connected to it."

"That's impossible," said Barry.

"Take a look around you. This whole situation…is impossible. When I underwent the DNA transfusion with Vaziil, we were filtered through the Frayd. Maybe somehow, we…bonded?"

Syddyk flashed his scanner around the chamber. "And I don't think he's the only one," he said, gesturing to a patch of Frayd tissue about two metres from the floor. Embedded within was a translucent cell roughly three metres by two. The object inside was barely visible through the semi-opaque casing but oddly familiar all the same.

"That looks like…like Bryndevaan," said Morrissey.

"Or his mate," said Barry. "His mate! That's how he tracked you. He must have picked up on her — or him. Or them. Their genetic signature. So they've been alive all this time, all these years, held captive in this dying Frayd."

"But why?"

"I suppose I should answer that." The voice chilled as the being entered the chamber, looking much stronger and healthier than when Morrissey had last seen him. It was Vaziil, a squad of Gyrth mercenaries in a protective orbit around him, displaying a disturbing example of their flexible allegiance. His loyal Vemen technician, Hruuvun, trailed close behind. "But first, if you wouldn't mind placing your weapons down. There is no way for you to win this fight."

Despite the array of angry looking blasters trained on them, Morrissey's defiance led the charge. "We'll give it a damn good try. We're dead anyway if we stay here."

"I can see you don't get your brains from my side of the genetic equation," said Vaziil dismissively. "Only a fool doesn't see when he's free. I have no further interest in you, or your comrades. I have what I need." He stroked the leathery skin of his restored flesh. A ring of barbs around his mouth spread into a prickly smile. "I'm feeling much more myself, thanks to you, *Son*."

That last word hit like a punch in the pants. Morrissey wasn't sure if it was because of his role in his father's restoration or the fact that Vaziil felt absolutely no emotional connection to him. "Believe me, *Dad*, if I'd have known what you wanted my genes for, I would have jumped out the nearest airlock a long time ago, but we're here now so I'll do everything within my power to stop you."

"But that's exactly my point — you don't have any power. None of any consequence, at least," said Vazill, drawing attention to his soldiers. "I've come this far, waited this long — I don't intend to be stopped now."

Barry held up a finger. "Erm...stopped from doing what, exactly?"

"Ahhh, well that's where this noble creature comes into play." Vaziil gestured around the reactor chamber like a circus barker presenting the greatest show on Earth. "eNdeen wanted a weapon. I give you the Frayd. For millennia, these creatures have lain dormant, taking refuge in the remote regions of hyperspace, free from the toxic fallout of intergalactic travellers. This solar system — your home solar system, human — was their ideal resting ground."

"You mean, we're close to Earth?" said Morrissey, both elated and petrified at the same time.

"That can't be," said Syddyk. "It took us half a day to reach Morrissey's homeworld from the nearest hyperspace conduit."

"And that's the beauty of The Frayd," said Vaziil. "Their intimate connection to the secret twists and turns of the hyperspace corridors is exactly what makes them the perfect tool — and the perfect weapon, being able to strike where it's least expected."

"You're weaponizing a living creature?" said Barry. "By juicing it with radiation?"

"Overloading the nuclear reactor was merely the catalyst to awaken and feed this beast. The data packet hidden within the human has restored my DNA and unlocked the coded sequence needed to complete its activation." He motioned to Bryndevaan's mate encased in the Frayd's wall. "The sensory organs of the Thuwom incorporated into the Frayd's tissue will act as a navigation system — a targeting array if you will — allowing me to direct this weapon toward any genetic profile I select from my restored database."

Syddyk nodded silently to Barry, his scanner readouts confirming Vaziil's words. Morrissey paled as the true nature of Vaziil's horror finally sank in, all the threads of his depraved scheme intertwining into one inescapable noose; the threat he'd levelled against Earth so many years ago when confronted by Sha'an had finally come to fruition. "But why strike at Earth?" said Morrissey. "What have humans ever done to you to deserve this?"

"Calm yourself, ape. Your precious Earth isn't my target — not yet at least. This is merely a staging area."

"Then what is your target?" said Syddyk nervously.

Vaziil's features twisted. "Perhaps you should ask your benefactor. Xrrka and I have a long and savage history."

"The perspective of a madman," said Barry. "She told us what you did to her planet — and what she had to do to fight back. Funny how the losing side always has a skewed view of history."

Vaziil shrugged. "Ah, but only time will tell which is the losing side. Soon there will only be one version of events left to be told. Xrrka's home base, JuHu Station, is the perfect testing ground for the Frayd weapon — a nexus of hyperspace corridors linking traffic from all sectors of the quadrant. Its detonation will tear those local hyperspace lanes to shreds, devouring all adjacent matter in its blast wave. The devastation will be exquisite, the isolation, absolute. And one by one, star systems will fall."

Morrissey choked on his bile. "How can you be so callous about the death of billions? And for what — kicks? Sport? Entertainment?"

Vaziil seemed to take offence. "My dear imbecilic child, I understand you've seen little outside your own backward planet, but even you should acknowledge that all sentient species fear what is different — fear the Other. When diverse cultures encounter one another, destruction is inevitable." Vaziil glowered from beneath the bony ridges of his skull plating. "I've travelled from one end of this galaxy to the other and the only constant is that the universe is a cesspool of violence. The best way to avoid such violence is to prevent species interaction in the first place. A segregated galaxy is a peaceful galaxy — I am merely keeping the peace."

"That's rich," said Morrissey. "Everyone keeps telling me that you're one of the greatest genocidal maniacs the galaxy has ever known."

Vaziil raised his hands in a show of contrition. "Then you should pay heed to my words. It's true, my people's thirst for conquest ultimately led to their undoing. That's why I want to burn out the cancer of galactic expansion and cauterise the wounds. I simply want to put the galaxy back together, with all the pieces in their rightful places."

"So, when it comes down to it, you're just a cranky old racist yelling at the neighbourhood kids to get off his lawn."

Vaziil gestured to Barry. "As your friend here says, it's all a matter of perspective, and this Frayd creature is only the beginning. There are many of its kind lying dormant throughout the galaxy and in time, all will fulfil their purpose in my new destiny: to help restore the natural order of the universe."

"By committing genocide on a galactic scale?"

"Untying the universe is the only way to save the universe."

"You can't untie centuries of galactic trade and expansion," said Barry. "Aside from the physical devastation you will wreak, hundreds of worlds, thousands of sentient species rely on those hyperspace conduits for their very survival. Without them they'll wither and die. Tearing these worlds apart is just as much of a death sentence as blasting them to atoms. You're condemning us all to a new dark age."

"I believe humans have an expression: you cannot make an...omelette, I think is the word...without breaking some eggs. Besides, there is peace in darkness."

"You are off your nut," said Morrissey, "but you're right about people fearing what they don't know or don't understand. Earth is a

microcosmic case in point. How do you think I felt being fired off
into space where a dozen different alien races seemed intent on
skinning me alive at every turn? If anyone has a reason to fear the
other, it's me. But don't you see, it's only by exposure to those other
elements that we can ever hope to learn acceptance and embrace our
differences. I'm sure we can expand our limited horizons
peacefully."

Syddyk aimed his weapon at Vaziil's head. "Why are we even
bothering trying to reason with him? Let's just fry him and put an
end to this."

The Gyrth soldiers countered with their own show of strength,
but Vaziil held them off with a wave of his hand. "You see, your
comrade is just illustrating my point — such violent natures will
never be tamed. They can only be isolated — or eliminated. I don't
particularly care which. Now, as you are all keenly aware, time is of
the essence." Vaziil turned his attention to his Vemen technician
who had been prepping a series of cables attached to the Frayd
bulkhead. "Is everything set, Hruuvun?" As the Vemen nodded,
Vaziil caught sight of Vintz, who had been silently moving around
to flank him. "I thought I'd made myself clear — I don't have time
for any more nonsense. Besides, I imagine your Gyrth brethren are
going to want to have a stiff word or two with you before we're
done."

It was just enough of a distraction. Morrissey didn't know where
he summoned the courage from or exactly what he planned to do
with it, but he chose that time to lunge at Vaziil through the wall of
soldiers. One of the Gyrth mercenaries shifted his aim and fired
directly into Morrissey's centre mass. As if anticipating the attack,
Vintz hurled himself between the two, taking the full force of the
energy blast in his body armour. As one might expect, chaos ensued.
Barry ducked behind the Frayd reactor column, splashing two of the
mercenaries in rapid succession. Syddyk dove into a side roll and
took out two more with equal efficiency. Vintz ignored the sizzling
hole burning through his armoured plating and fired his weapon on
full auto into his former workmates.

Morrissey continued his play for Vaziil, tackling him with as
much success as a rabbit might attack a wolf. The two grappled,
twisting through the blaster fire, while soldiers fell around them.
Morrissey drove his fists as hard as he could into anything that felt
soft enough to do damage. Vaziil fought valiantly and probably

would have broken every bone in Morrissey's body if he'd been at full strength — and if the Frayd hadn't been undulating up a storm. It was Morrissey's only advantage and much to his surprise, ended with him pressing Vaziil into the softening flesh of the reactor chamber while holding his pistol hard against his father's chest.

When the blaster fire ceased, Vaziil's squad of mercenaries lay smouldering on the ground, some clinging tenuously to life, some not so much. Like the self-serving coward he was, Hruuvun seemed to have escaped the chamber altogether during the fray. Barry, Syddyk, and Vintz secured the area before joining Morrissey as he restrained Vaziil.

"Okay," said Morrissey, his breath tearing through his aching lungs, "now you're going to shut that bloody reactor down…deactivate your monstrosity of a weapon…and spare the Frayd's life…or I'm going to bloody well end yours." Morrissey's tone scared even himself, but he was running out of time and patience.

Vaziil seemed awfully calm for someone with a gun to their chest. "You don't understand, do you? None of this matters."

"It matters if you want to live."

"Listen to your son, Vaziil," said Barry. "We can end this quietly, peacefully." He surveyed the carnage around the chamber. "Well, relatively peacefully. Yes, you'll stand trial for your crimes and perhaps you'll eventually be sentenced to death. Or you can die right here, right now. It all depends on you shutting down this weapon."

"I'd take his deal, *Dad*." Morrissey spat this last word. "There is no escape from this."

"Haven't you figured it out yet? I am the last piece of the puzzle, the final circuit in the weapon. The very gland that Xrrka manipulated so long ago to devastate my species will be the trigger that sets this creature off on one gloriously cataclysmic mission of destruction." Vaziil smiled in that chilling way that aliens seemed to have the patent on. "Escape is not my plan."

And with that, he stopped resisting, letting his body sink into the Frayd's flesh as if easing into a hot bath. Morrissey fought to regain his grip as the Frayd enveloped him but Barry yanked him back.

"No, Dave! It'll take you, too."

Morrissey collapsed, not because the loss of his biological father was too much to bear but from a physical weakening of his limbs coupled with an overriding urge to vomit. He didn't know whether it was a reaction to the adrenaline pumping through his veins or due to the communal trauma he seemed to be sharing with the Frayd. "I'm okay," he said as Barry and Vintz lifted him to his feet. "But what do we do now?"

"Nothing's changed," said Barry. "We still have to shut this thing down."

"But how? Our only chance just got eaten."

"Did he? Vaziil didn't seem particularly troubled by the turn of events, so let's assume that somehow he's still alive in there." He pointed to the pulsating wall of Frayd. "And let's also assume that this has been part of his cunning plan all along. That means that whatever genetic trickery he's concocted with the Frayd necessitated him joining with it. I don't know if that means he can control the Frayd from within or trigger the detonation or what, but it's clear that he thinks his plan is still in motion."

Morrissey thought carefully. Vaziil did tell eNdeen that he always had an exit strategy — the same thing he'd said to Sha'an all those years ago on Earth. "So, if the next step was for him to transport the Frayd weapon to JuHu Station and trigger it there — using the Thuwom for navigation," he said, gesturing to Bryndevaan's mate encased in the Frayd's bulkhead, "then we've got to stop him."

"Right," said Barry. "So, if we can't shut down the reactor…"

"…we disable the navigation," said Morrissey. "But how —"

Before they could devise a strategy, Syddyk fanned his rifle in rough arcs around the Thuwom's tomb, carving deep incisions into the walls — there was no time for finesse. The Frayd bucked and roiled, but eventually the casing erupted and the Thuwom poured out, falling flaccid on the ground. Syddyk finished the job, firing into the crater, severing whatever tubes and connections were keeping them tethered. He scanned the fallen Thuwom for life signs.

"They're still with us, barely, but at least it's no longer hooked into the Frayd."

"Okay," said Barry. "Well, I guess that's Vaziil's navigation system out of commission."

They all seemed to sag with relief, taking time for a much-needed breath. All except Morrissey. "Erm…I hate to be the wet blanket, but this thing is still going to blow, right? And if it's not going anywhere then it's going to blow right on Earth's doorstep? So…still a problem?"

"Shit! Yeah, no time to lollygag." Barry chewed his lip like it was gum. "Okay. Okay." He turned to Vintz. "Look, you've shown us you're loyal to Morrissey by putting yourself between him and a blaster bolt, and that's not nothing. But if you really want to prove your loyalty, you'll show your new best friends, here, the fastest route back to our ship. I'm guessing you know the layout of this place?" Vintz nodded, tapping the scanner at his belt. "You can carry the Thuwom. If you give any trouble, Syddyk still might shoot you, despite your good deeds. Your choice."

Vintz nodded meekly and Barry continued. "Syd, I need you to get back to The Briiga and prep for dust-off." He held up his hands at Syddyk's unspoken protest. "Now listen to me carefully: I want you to arm a couple of EMP nukes and target these coordinates. If we hit it before the power builds to critical levels, then the EMPs should short out the reactor which, in theory, should stop the Frayd from overloading. Hopefully it will just…go back to sleep and Morrissey's homeworld will be safe." Morrissey took some solace from Barry's confidence, but he wasn't sure it would be enough.

"You know you can't be here when the EMP hits, don't you," said Syddyk. "Best case scenario: your plan works, all power shuts down — that includes life support. You won't be able to launch any escape shuttles, and we won't even be able to dock to pick you up if there's no power to the station. Not to mention the fact that the energy burst will probably fry your central nervous system. Worst case scenario…" Syddyk mimicked an expansive explosion with his tiny hands.

"Well, it's not exactly Plan A," said Barry.

"What's Plan A?"

"eNdeen?" said Morrissey.

Barry nodded. "I'm going to see if I can persuade him to take the reactor offline the easy way, maybe show us the off switch."

"By yourself. Uh-uh. This place is crawling with Gyrth mercenaries. Syd's right: you need backup. I'm coming with you."

"No, Dave. Absolutely not. You need to get to the ship. I can't guarantee this will work and like Syd said, you don't want to be here if it doesn't."

"It's my world, my responsibility. Besides, I may as well try to be of use where I can. I've had a bit of experience with eNdeen, and

I think I can get into his head." Barry looked dubious but Morrissey wasn't taking no for an answer. "Come on, mate, we're wasting time."

Finally, Barry gave in. "Alright, then. Let's get going. Syd, give us thirty minutes. If you don't hear from us by then, you won't be. Send in the nukes and bug the hell out of here."

Syddyk nodded grimly. There were no tearful farewells, no emotional speeches. Just duty. Respect. And friendship. Morrissey hoped it would be enough.

CHAPTER 27

Getting to the main hangar wasn't exactly a walk in the park. Morrissey and Barry went their separate ways, each along a tortuous trek through the twisted guts of the awakening Frayd. It was a risky gambit, especially without a reliable comm signal, but Barry promised Morrissey they would be reunited on opposite sides of the docking bay. From there they could launch their two-pronged attack.

Morrissey arrived at a passageway, dimly lit and fitted with a series of monitoring stations at regular intervals, their housings hanging limply in the softening walls. The tunnel exit to the hangar lay beyond, down an awkward thirty-degree slope. He peered over the edge at the deck below, spinning him in a wave of vertigo. As he steadied himself at the tunnel mouth, he gulped at the relatively fresh air while he waited for Barry to get into position across the hangar.

The scene looked like a members' meeting of the Thugs-R-Us club as a cluster of heavily armed Gyrth mercenaries milled about, waiting to be told what to shoot at. At the centre of the knot of troops stood eNdeen, barking orders in an attempt to maintain his control.

Finally, Barry's tinny voice crackled faintly over the comm. "Dave, I'm in place. What's your status?"

"Just got here." Morrissey could see his friend perched at the opposite opening and gave a vague wave, feeling a bit foolish under the circumstances. "I've done a quick headcount and I don't fancy our odds."

"When has that ever stopped us. Besides, we've got the element of surprise on our side."

"Funny. Every time I think we've got the element of surprise on our side, we end up getting fisted."

"Well, it's now or never, mate. We've got to stop eNdeen from getting on that ship. Choose your targets carefully — we need him alive. Ready?"

"As I'll ever be." Morrissey tried to breathe deeply but his nerves were having none of it. A sizzling crack shattered his fragile calm. He spun to face the unseen threat behind him, levelling his weapon down the gaping tunnel, but all he saw was the flicker of lights and the spark of exploding electronics. Darkness rippled toward him as, one by one, the fixtures popped and fittings shattered. The tunnel coiled like an angry serpent, vital air constricting as the walls clenched. Morrissey's stomach turned to lead at the memory of the Gyrth mercenary who'd been cleaved in two in a similar tunnel. He flipped on his comm to warn Barry, but his friend's expletive laden voice was already ripping the radio waves.

"Dave! Get the hell out of there!"

Morrissey didn't need to be told twice. He launched himself from the opening just as the orifice sucked shut behind him. He hit the meaty ground with a wet thud. Folds of Frayd tissue tangled him like bedsheets as he fought to regain his footing. Barry fared little better, his gangly frame splatting down across the other side of the hangar.

On the bright side, the odds were even; eNdeen and the Gyrth mercenaries were dancing to the same frenetic tune. When the spasms calmed, the chamber fell into a stunned silence, the disparate congregation preparing for an uncertain combat. Barry set the tone, diving into a forward roll and coming up with his blaster ablaze.

The first Gyrth spun backward and stayed down. A second took two hits from Morrissey as he ran for cover, but his body armour absorbed most of the energy. The remaining mercenaries wasted no time in taking defensive positions behind cargo pods and along the protective curves of the chamber.

Blaster fire seared the acrid air in a crisscross of chaos. Several Gyrth mercenaries went down and stayed down. Much to Morrissey's dismay, several more kept firing, each barrage scorching the walls of the Frayd, burning away valuable cover. Morrissey's vision swam in a wave of nausea and disorientation as he steadied himself against a cargo pod.

"Dave! Are you hit?" said Barry.

It took a moment before Morrissey's tongue could move. "No…not me. The Frayd. I can feel every blast like it's searing into my own skin." He climbed slowly to his feet, leaning on his friend for support. Barry covered his retreat with a salvo of his own but it wasn't enough. They were both pinned down as eNdeen's Gyrth troopers closed in for the kill. But they were a hair too slow.

The Frayd chose that moment to give the hangar a fresh toss. The cavity swelled, heaving them all into the air like rag dolls, juggling the cargo pods like dice. Bodies caromed off walls and thumped off containers. Pockets of Frayd flesh blistered the slick surfaces of the chamber, absorbing several of the cowering mercenaries into the pulsating membranes. Morrissey arched away from a fleshy blossom just in time to avoid being swallowed.

By the time the tantrum had abated, the trembling cavity was littered with mashed and mangled victims, half-absorbed limbs protruding from the Frayd tissue like gnarled tree roots. Morrissey did a quick inventory of his most prized body parts, relieved to find he was still in one piece. Barry, however, lay motionless on the soggy ground, seemingly intact but Morrissey couldn't tell if he was alive or dead.

eNdeen was quick to his feet, along with his last surviving mercenary, though both were unarmed.

Morrissey thrust his carbine in their direction. "Okay, that's enough — nobody move!"

The Gyrth soldier, apparently trying for employee of the month, insisted on making a play for a nearby blaster rifle. "Seriously," said Morrissey, "you're actually going to try it?" The soldier backed away slowly, his arms raised.

"Well," said eNdeen, "it seems you have us at a disadvantage. But I doubt you would kill — how do you humans put it — in cold blood?"

"I'll make an exception in your case."

"Then why waste the opportunity? Because you can't, can you? I imagine I could walk through that docking tube and onto my ship, and there is nothing you would do to stop me."

"Believe me, if it's a choice between letting you escape and shooting you dead, I'll take option two every time. Luckily for you, there's a third option."

This time the mercenary didn't waver and made a grab for the weapon. Morrissey blasted as many energy bolts into his chest as it took to pierce his armour; the soldier crumpled into a sizzling lump.

eNdeen shrivelled slightly. "So, the human has grown quite the spine since we last talked. Very well, I'm intrigued. What is this third option?"

"Take a look around you, eNdeen. This Frayd isn't dead after all, is it. And that's because there's a nuclear reactor shoved up its arse. Vaziil's plan — Vaziil's weapon — it is the Frayd. He's set it to overload, and when it does it's going to tear apart hyperspace like tissue paper. And us along with it."

eNdeen's eye widened as he surveyed the creature in a new light. "This is my weapon?"

"You're missing the point. You don't have a weapon. Vaziil has double-crossed you. He needed you to get all the parts in place so he could complete his plans — you don't factor in beyond that."

"Then I'm sorry my soft-brained friend but you have me at a loss. While I acknowledge that this Frayd creature is not as dead as I was led to believe, I'm not sure what you expect me to do about its sudden revival."

"I expect you to tell us how to shut down the reactor before it blows or we're all going to be seeing the galaxy from a whole new perspective — including you."

eNdeen held up a scabby claw in protest. "You forget, I have a ship." He motioned to the docking tube leading to his starship. "A ship, I might add, that is manned by a rather large contingent of mercenaries."

"And you seem to forget that I have a gun. Do you really think you can summon them before I put a bolt through your eye?"

"Perhaps not. But if what you say is true, then I'm sure you'll want to get to your ship just as much as I want to get to mine. Then we can both avoid the fallout."

"Except the fallout involves the death of over seven billion lives on my home planet. But of course, you don't care about life, do you. Unless it's your own." Morrissey settled his aim on eNdeen's single eye; he could have sworn he saw him flinch. "It's all about profit and loss for you. Well, there is no profit in death, eNdeen, and brother, your debt is due."

Before Morrissey had decided if he was actually going to pull the trigger, the hangar door groaned open, a cadre of Gyrth troops erupting through the entrance.

eNdeen inflated with renewed arrogance. "Ah, my little pink friend. It seems the tables have turned. It would probably be best for your health if you dropped your weapon. We don't want any complications at this point, do we — considering the dire circumstances you so eloquently detailed."

The mercenaries moved quickly and calmly through the hangar, almost ignoring Morrissey and eNdeen save for the fact that they kept their weapons trained on them both as they passed. At the centre of the cluster of troops was none other than Hruuvun. Somehow he'd made his way unscathed and now seemed to be directing the mercenaries toward the docking tube. As they moved through and onto eNdeen's ship, Hruuvun turned and gave one last fuck-you-I'm-outta-here bobble-headed nod before sealing the outer airlock.

eNdeen wrenched himself from his shock and raced toward the docking tube. "NO! Wait!"

"Oh no you bloody don't!" Morrissey lunged, grabbing eNdeen's leg. Twisting him to the ground was like wrestling with an alligator. eNdeen pumped his free leg like a piston, battering Morrissey's head like a piñata. Morrissey held on as if all their lives depended on it, slowly climbing through the pain and up eNdeen's prone frame. Pummelling his phallic head was like punching a cast iron frying pan, blow after blow until his fists were bloody. But eNdeen was too strong and too fast. He continued to batter Morrissey's head with his gnarled fists, snapping him into darkness and then was up like a rocket. A lunge here. A slice there. Morrissey didn't have a chance, collapsing into a wheezing heap against a crushed cargo pod.

eNdeen finally launched himself into the docking tube, his last chance at the freedom of his waiting ship only an airlock away. Only his ship was no longer waiting. The groaning clunk of the docking clamps echoed through the tube as they released their grip. eNdeen beat his scabby claws against the airlock doors; Morrissey could have sworn he heard the alien whimper as the ship rolled away from the Frayd. Then with little more than a shrinking flash, it dropped from sight — catapulting through hyperspace and out of sight.

Morrissey rushed to the airlock controls, cycling the inner doors shut, trapping eNdeen like a spider under glass. He tapped on the comm mic. "So I guess you've made your choice, and I guess I've got no more use for you." He moved his hand to the outer airlock release.

eNdeen recovered quickly. "Wait! Don't you see? We're on the same side, you and I. We've both been betrayed by Vaziil — imagine, your own father. Don't you humans have a saying — the enemy of my enemy is my friend?"

"Sometimes, eNdeen, the enemy of my enemy is just another effing enemy. And I have had enough enemies to last a lifetime." Morrissey began the purge sequence.

"I'll do anything. Take me as your prisoner. You have a ship — we can leave in that. Please. Just don't — don't let me die this way. Not this way."

eNdeen's balance sheet was extensive, written in the blood of thousands. Morrissey thought of QiQi and the cold fate he'd dealt her. He thought of his friend Sha'an, who'd been crushed in the wheels of his schemes. Vengeance wasn't always the best answer, but sometimes it was a bonus. He looked deep into eNdeen's black soul and couldn't think of a better suited fate. "Actually, eNdeen, it should be exactly this way."

As he moved to cycle the purge disk, a hand clamped over his. It was Barry, his grip shaky yet reassuring. "You don't want to carry that sort of darkness in your soul. You're better than that."

Morrissey wasn't sure he was, but he slowly relinquished his hold on the controls, feeling the weight of the universe slip from his shoulders.

eNdeen seemed to sag with relief. "You won't regret this. I'm sure we can be of great help to one another."

Barry turned to the alien and shrugged. "He may be better than that," he said, nodding to Morrissey, "but I'm not."

And with a steady twist of the controls, the purge sequence initiated. eNdeen clattered hopelessly against the plexi-shield walls of the tube, proving no match for the pull of vacuum. His body tumbled backward, bouncing off the carbon fibre bulkheads and out into the psychedelic storm of hyperspace where he was no doubt shredded across the light years.

"For Sha'an," said Barry as he stared out after him.

"Thanks, mate. I would've done it but I'm glad I didn't have to."

"Any time."

"You look awful by the way."

Barry's shoulder was a scorched mess of bone and flesh and melted body armour. "I'll live. I'm guessing eNdeen didn't tell us where the off switch was?"

"Not so much."

Barry punched his comm. "Syd, do you read? Status report."

"I'm here, Barrek. The Briiga is prepped for a fast burn — if we have to, and the EMPs are armed and ready to go. Any luck with eNdeen?"

Barry cast another glance out the viewport. "Erm...that's a negative, my friend. How much time before the Frayd blows?"

"Lillum's been running a diagnostic scan. She figures you've got about fifteen minutes."

"Alright. Let's call it ten, to be safe. That should give us just enough time to get to one of the troop transports. If you don't hear from us in ten minutes, target the reactor with the EMPs and get the ship to safety. We'll rendezvous with you on the other side of this mess." Static buzzed the comm. "Syd? Do you read?" More static. "I've lost the signal, Dave. I hope he heard me. Come on, mate. We've got a shuttle to steal."

There was only one problem. "The door," said Morrissey, "it's...gone." The main doors leading from the hangar to the station corridor were nothing but a twist of metal crusted into the Frayd flesh, ringed by a throbbing series of swollen blisters. All other access tunnels were scabbed over. "Now what? That shuttle was our only ride off this station. Unless one of those cargo containers contains an escape pod, I think we're stuffed."

Barry sifted through some of the cargo pods that hadn't been absorbed by the Frayd.

"You don't actually expect to find an escape pod in there, do you?" said Morrissey.

"No, but a couple of cheeky spacesuits wouldn't go amiss."

Morrissey joined in the search but the two of them found nothing that might offer hope of escape — no magic transport disc, no portable hyperspace drive, not even a simple rebreather unit to share.

"So, I guess we're stuffed," he said. He had faced all the colours of death these past weeks and had survived every shade. It had given him a new perspective on the universe and a feeling of relative invincibility. To think that it would end with him trapped in the belly of a doomed alien.

Behind them, the Frayd's blisters, now each the size of a human head, bubbled across the skin of the chamber like a virulent cancer. One fluorescent abscess boiled into another, crumpling the remaining cargo pods like egg cartons, folding them into the Frayd's tissue. It was only a matter of time before they, themselves, were swallowed.

Barry checked his comm one last time, hoping against hope but receiving nothing but static. He fell back against the spongy Frayd wall and slid into a sitting position.

Morrissey winced as he plonked down beside him, blasting out a stiff breath of resignation. "So how do you want to spend our last moments?"

"You're not going to hug me, are you?"

Morrissey tried to force a smile. "No hugs. But if this is the end, I'm glad I'm not alone."

"For what it's worth, I'm sorry you got dragged into this fight," said Barry.

"With my family ties, I guess it was inevitable. At least I got to see the universe before I died."

"Hey, we're not dead yet. There's still a chance the EMPs won't fry us."

Morrissey cast a sidelong glance at him. "I appreciate the sentiment, but you don't have to sugar-coat it — I know the chances are slim."

"Slim chances are better than none. Besides, at least you helped rid the galaxy of a mass-murdering a-hole. Maybe even two — unless Vaziil is still alive. But even if he managed to survive, he's trapped here with us."

"Except no one knows but us."

"Yes. Well. There is that. If only there were some way we could at least get that message out."

And then there was. It was faint and distorted by all manner of hyperspace noise, but the voice was unmistakable. *"If you two…finished feeling sorry for yourselves…we've got some rescuing to do. Do you read?"*

Syddyk!

Barry's saucer eyes almost burst out of their sockets. "Yes-yes-yes, Syd! Yes we bloody read you!"

"Give…your location…sensors are erratic…"

"We couldn't make it to the troop shuttle," said Barry. "We're trapped in the main docking bay."

"Stand by…approach…ventral side…no time to mess around…be ready."

Morrissey jumped up, his lungs resisting the urge to burst into flame. He helped Barry climb to his feet. Through the airlock door, he could see the sleek profile of The Briiga lifting from underneath the Frayd station. The ship shivered as it fought to synchronise its tenuous orbit; time dripped like honey as it aligned with the docking tube. Finally, the seals clamped and all systems reported blue. Well, sort of blue-ish.

"What's wrong?" said Morrissey.

Barry thumped the controls. "It's showing a positive lock, but the safeties won't disengage."

"Maybe the mechanisms aren't compatible?"

"These docking tubes have universal seals for just such an occasion. Besides, The Briiga was able to dock at the other bay with no problem."

Then, without warning, the inner airlock doors opened. "Erm…I'm taking this as a good sign," said Morrissey.

Barry gave an awkward smile. "As good as it's going to get."

"You'd better pick up the pace," said Syddyk. *"…don't know how long…maintain our position."*

Morrissey helped Barry into the docking tube, favouring his melted shoulder. At the halfway point a klaxon sounded — never a good sign.

"The seal is failing," said Barry. "Hurry!"

The Frayd trembled violently, its torsional convulsions wrenching the umbilical connection from its housing. The docking tube crumpled like tinfoil; the sudden decompression wave blasting Barry into the Briiga's airlock. Morrissey wasn't so lucky, a conspiracy of forces pumping him back into the Frayd's hangar. Almost instinctively, he pounded the airlock door release, sealing off the vacuum as the last of the tube's debris shimmered like stardust before disappearing into hyperspace. He stared blankly at the chasm between The Frayd and the ALF ship.

"You have got to be shitting me." Freedom was no more than twenty metres from reach but it may as well have been twenty light years away for all the good it did him.

Barry stared through the porthole of *The Briiga*'s airlock door. From his wrist comm, Morrissey heard Barry's tinny and oh so distant voice, a frantic mix of panic and hope. *"Hang on mate, we're coming for you. Syd's going to extend* The Briiga*'s tube. We'll have you out of there in no time."*

Morrissey shook his head. "There's no point. There's not exactly a whole lot to attach to." When The Frayd's docking tube had been torn away, it had taken half the airlock with it.

"Okay, okay," said Barry, trying to inject some optimism into the situation. *"We'll come across in space suits."*

"Erm…I'm no expert, but won't you need to depressurize the Frayd before entering? The outer airlock doors are gone. And even the inner doors are showing signs of stress fractures."

Morrissey could hear the frantic whispers of Syddyk in the background. *"…have to fire those EMPs…the next ten minutes…any hope…saving Morrissey's home…"*

Barry tried to shush him, but Morrissey interrupted. "It's okay, mate. I get it. We're out of options. Syd's right — Earth is the priority. Seven billion humans are worth more than one lone monkey."

There was a long silence before Barry responded. *"You won't be forgotten, Dave. I'll make sure your people know what you've done — what you sacrificed to save them. It's a very…noble gesture."*

"Not so noble that I wouldn't want a statue or two dedicated to me. I mean it, Barry. Screw altruism. I really am pretty shallow by nature. I want people to write epic poems about what went on here. I want them to sing songs about me, to tell my stories to their children around the fire. I want them to make a movie about me — no, a trilogy. Directed by James Gunn."

Even though Morrissey couldn't see him, he knew Barry was flashing his human smile one last time. *"Have no fear, mate. You won't be forgotten."*

A lump caught Morrissey unexpectedly in the throat. Or maybe it was the toxic fumes. "Thanks...*Baz*. It's been...well, it's certainly been an adventure. Say goodbye to the rest of the team for me. And tell Xrrka — well, just tell her. Now get the ship out of here before it's too late." Morrissey's vision began to blur. Toxic fumes — had to be.

CHAPTER 28

As The Briiga began to distance itself from The Frayd, a sinewy tube of muscle lashed out toward it, latching on with a fierce determination. It flexed and pulsed as its girth swelled, smothering the ship's airlock. Morrissey punched his comm unit.

"Barry? Syd? Are you guys okay? What's happening?"

"That creature…getting awfully possessive," said Barry.

"You've got to break free!"

"We're trying but —"

The signal went dead. The last bare patch of airlock porthole had been smothered by the phosphorescent blisters. Morrissey was alone, the fate of his friends unknowable.

Behind him in the hangar, his own situation was no better. Unimaginable pressures mashed him against the Frayd's flesh, squeezing him like a tube of toothpaste. Precious atmosphere screamed through the hairline fissures in the airlock doors. It wouldn't be long before he was sieved through those same cracks, only with infinitely more screaming.

The swollen blisters had bubbled around most of the chamber's surface, pulsing with an almost hungry energy, leaving very little real estate for a safe retreat. They rippled across the failing airlock doors, staunching the leak of valuable air — a small mercy — but souring the existing atmosphere with their sickly stench. At the base of the tendril, an aperture appeared, fist-sized but expanding rapidly. It sucked and snapped, tearing at Morrissey's skin through his clothing, burning his flesh with a searing fire. He tried to buck and roll away from the aperture's maw but the manoeuvre grew less effective with each passing second.

A sudden gush of warm wetness soaked his legs; a quick bladder-check confirmed the fluid wasn't his. Another nearby blister swelled and popped, spurting him with blue phosphorescent goo. It was sticky and viscous with a nauseatingly sweet, almost musky scent. Another blister exploded, this time from above. Then another. One by one, the jellied sacs reached their bursting points, their distended skins erupting with the foul spray, making it that much harder to resist the suction of the Frayd's growing mouth. Ultimately, the combination of air pressure, hydraulic pressure, and Frayd muscle contractions proved too powerful; the rush of current pumped him through the gaping orifice of the throbbing tendril and into darkness.

Morrissey had once ridden the Master Blaster Water Coaster at Alton Towers and found it a refreshingly pleasant diversion on a warm summer's day. This was anything but. It was a harrowing, heart-stopping, flush through a soupy suspension, directly into Hell's toilet. His wet and wild journey came to an end with a skid, a thump, and an unceremonious splash.

A storm of flashing lights raged around him as sirens trumpeted his return to familiar surroundings. He almost choked on the sour mucous as he sloshed to his feet. "Holy shit!" he said to himself as he wiped the muck from his eyes. "I'm back on The Briiga — I'm in the bloody airlock!" Airlock. He punched the controls, cycling the pressure to normal, sealing himself off from the vacillating tendril still holding firm to the ship.

He swiped madly across the bulkhead, finally clearing the comm panel of the Frayd ejaculate. "Barry? Syd? Anyone? It's me — Dave. I made it! Don't ask me how or why — especially why — but I'm back on board. You can fire the EMPs whenever you're ready!"

"Dave? Great to hear you! But I'm afraid that's easier said than done."

Morrissey bounded as fast as he could up the gangway and into the command sphere. The viewscreen was set to panoramic mode, making him feel like he was stepping into dead space; he fought the wave of vertigo and fell into one of the auxiliary jump-seats. Around him the crew almost didn't notice his arrival, each consumed with the ship's survival.

"You're a mess," said Barry. "I'm glad you're back in one piece, though I'm not sure how long that's going to last. Buckle up and hang on tight, and try not to get any of that blue goo on the consoles."

Syddyk looked up from the helm, giving Morrissey a welcome but stern nod. "We can't fire the EMPs yet — with that thing still attached, we'll be fried along with the Frayd."

The Frayd tendril maintained its desperate grip, looking much the same from this end as it had from inside the creature, but the Frayd itself had become something else entirely. The bleak, grey hulk he'd first seen upon his arrival was now a vibrant blob of glowing wonders. The scales, once nothing more than lifeless plates, now shone with a crystalline patina that sparked a kaleidoscope of coloured fire wherever hyperspace touched them. It was intoxicatingly beautiful and hauntingly horrific all at once.

Lillum's eyestalks bobbed upward from the science console. "I estimate the Frayd being will self-destruct in less than five minutes."

"Okay, chums," said Barry, "that's our window. If we can't detach from that tendril in the next couple of minutes, we fire the EMPs and say our goodbyes." He punched the comm unit. "Vintz? What's your status?"

"The dorsal gun is charged and ready to go but I'm having trouble getting a solid lock on the tendril. The targeting array is not optimised for use in hyperspace."

"Take your best shot. It may be your last. Even if we can just loosen its grip."

Morrissey winced, anticipating the worst. "It all seems such a waste, such a tragic loss."

"It'll be a tragic loss for all of us — including seven billion of your people — if we can't fire those EMPs."

From above their field of view, a purple lance of energy streamed toward the Frayd, searing wide of the target. Vintz's second shot struck a glancing blow at the base of the tendril.

"No measurable effect," said Syddyk. "It might have even made it worse."

"The Frayd seems to have developed some sort of oscillating defence shield," said Lillum. "I don't think energy weapons will penetrate."

"Then I guess we're switching to Plan B," said Barry. "Or is it C? I've kind of lost track. Syd, transfer missile control to my station." A pall of death fell over the bridge. "Don't look so glum, Dave." He flipped on the ship-wide comm. "We've still got a shuttle — and I want you all on it in the next minute. That includes you, Vintz. You've earned yourself a ride."

"We're abandoning ship?" said Morrissey.

Barry cast him a solemn glance. "Not all of us."

Morrissey got his meaning. "You don't have to stay. Surely you can fire the missiles on automatic?"

"You saw the trouble Vintz had getting a target lock. We can't take anything for granted."

"And we're not," said Syddyk. "That's why I'm staying."

"We don't have time to argue, Syd, and I'm pulling rank this time."

Syddyk got up slowly from the helm station and placed his small hand on Barry's arm. "Barrek, the ALF has been my home, my salvation. You all have been my friends, my family. But I don't know if I can go on without...without Kheni. If I can't be with my brother in life, then let it be in death. And let it count for something."

"What complete bunk!" said Barry. "I'm hardly likely to let one of my own crew sacrifice themselves while I scurry away to safety. Do you really think I could live with myself?"

Syddyk held up his hand to Barry's protest. "There is no guilt to be felt. It makes sense and you know it, if only from a practical perspective. You know I'm the best shot — literally — that we have. Please...let me do this."

Lillum bristled, her eyestalks bobbing wildly. "I hate to keep bringing up the obvious but if we don't leave soon, we'll all be sacrificing ourselves, and for nothing if we don't fire those EMPs."

But they did not answer her — all eyes turned to Morrissey, his limbs rigid, his eyes rolling back into oblivion. Tremors rippled through his body, soundless words jittering from his mouth. And then the universe swallowed him whole.

Morrissey's nerves danced on a razor's edge as he waited for the inevitable panic to consume him. It never came. Time seemed to stand still as the silence enveloped him. His breathing eased, the thumping of his heart and the pulsing of his blood keeping a gentle rhythm in the black nothingness. *The Briiga* and his ALF friends were gone...yet he did not feel entirely alone. Thoughts. Feelings. Waves of raw, visceral emotions charged around him, over him...through him. None of them were his. The consciousness beckoned and he moved toward it.

The sharp tang of sea breeze assaulted his nostrils as he waded through a pervasive fog, the lonely crunch of gravel underfoot. The sensations were alien yet oddly familiar at the same time. Shadows simmered in his periphery, lunging out toward him, raw animal fear pitted against rage and confusion. A sense of dread and urgency battled with heavy doses of reason and compassion, fracturing Morrissey's brain into a thousand tangents.

Slowly, the shadows merged, forming a single wraith before his eyes. His heart stopped. The figure appeared human, both real and surreal at the same time. A dream? Possibly. Reality? It couldn't be. And yet the two realms seemed to share a common bond that couldn't be severed. His mother, Marion Morrissey. It was her, as a young woman — the mum he remembered. The mum he loved. She reached out to him. There were no words and yet he heard them.

"Hello...Davey."

Tears welled, unbidden. "Mum?" Common sense warned that it wasn't her, that it couldn't be her. And yet, it somehow was, as if no time had passed since that fateful day before she left him. Her eyes. Her smile. Her voice.

"You have to leave, Davey."

She took his hand. It was both cold and electric at the same time. Memories washed over him in melancholy waves, choking all reason from his words. Yet somehow, he found them. "I...I...don't know how."

"You have to leave, Davey."

"Mum, you're not making sense. We're trying to leave but we can't."

"You have to leave, Davey."

Her hand spasmed. Morrissey's bones ached. He felt her suffering, burning with anger, reeling with betrayal, blistering with pain. But amidst the violent rage and searing anguish, he could sense something else smouldering in the darkness, something he could only describe as...hope. The sensation seemed oddly out of place amidst all the physical and emotional turmoil, like discovering a patch of dry land during a hurricane. But it was definitely there: an overwhelming sense of optimism.

"You have to leave, Davey, before it's too late." Her voice was somehow becoming more desperate without changing tone. It was something he felt through her energy rather than heard in her words.

"Mum, you've got to tell us how?"

"You have to...to let go."

The simple answer wrapped in an insoluble problem. If letting go were so easy, he would have done it years ago.

"You have to let go, Davey. It's the only way home. It's the only way home, for both of us."

And there it was. This apparition was his mother. And yet it wasn't. Straddling the chasm between all the worlds at once, he knew this consciousness and he understood it. It was the Frayd, reaching out to him in the only way it knew how. He couldn't define the communication or even make sense of it, but his bond with the creature was palpable. He knew, now, what he had to do. For the Frayd's sake. For his sake. For all their sakes.

Like a diver emerging from the ocean's depths, Morrissey rose from his fugue state, waves of mayhem buffeting his senses and casting him from the calm oasis. He felt like he'd been gone for hours but judging by the situation around him, it had been mere seconds.

"Dave!" It was Barry. "What the hell was that all about?"

The ALF team helped him to his feet as he gasped for air, for speech. "Power...down...weapons."

"What are you talking about? We've got to fire those EMPs before that thing blows."

"The Frayd...it's caught between...self-destruction and...self-preservation. It's trying to fight for both but it's losing the battle."

"Dave, if we don't fire those missiles, your whole planet will be destroyed."

"I don't think he's in his right mind," said Lillum. "We don't have time — "

"For the love of…just trust me! Just…just let go…" And then he was back down to his knees again.

The ALF team looked at one another in thorough bewilderment. Finally, Barry tabbed his comm. "Vintz, power down the plasma cannon."

Vintz's voice crackled over the airwaves. "Say again, Barrek?"

"You heard me." Barry turned to Syddyk. "Go to Yellow Alert. Put the EMPs on standby." Something in his eyes told Syddyk not to argue the point.

Morrissey's voice steamed out in a whisper. "Just let go…"

And just when he thought all hope was lost, the Frayd's tendril quietly and calmly peeled itself from the skin of The Briiga and reeled back into its body mass, flailing gently in the swirling eddies of hyperspace as if waving goodbye. The crew were mesmerised, both by what they'd seen of Morrissey's episode, and of what they were seeing of the Frayd.

A riot of coloured phosphorescence pulsed from between the seams in the Frayd's scales. It throbbed and swelled beyond its limits, burning with a white-hot ferocity. And then, in a shrinking flash, it vanished from their view.

The reaction of unseen energies slingshotted The Briiga with unimaginable force, challenging its inertial compensators to their limits. The ship punched through into normal space like a dog chasing its tail. Even after Syddyk had managed to stabilise their trajectory, it still took Morrissey an eternity of committed prayer to a god he didn't believe in before he could shake himself from the cumulative shock. And just when he thought he'd reclaimed his bearings, he realised that his mind had returned to the Frayd, one last goodbye. Thunder rumbled within him and lightning burned through skin that was not his. His scales were on fire, billowing with one final, brilliant flash before bursting into a billion shards of dying flesh, ablaze with the infinite embers of the universe.

CHAPTER 29

Morrissey sat limply on one of the Med-Pod's diagnostic beds, his clothes stained by fluids he'd rather not contemplate. He sipped half-heartedly from a tall metal flask containing a restorative draught and felt the energy slowly seep back into his body.

Barry sat on the adjacent bed, while Lillum patched his shoulder wound. Surgical lasers flared and dermabonders bonded as his grey complexion slowly flushed to a healthier blue. "Good to see you awake, Dave. We thought we'd lost you," he said.

"*I* thought I'd lost me." Morrissey reflected on his recent out of body experience. He took another sip from the flask and shook his head slowly. "I was there, Barry. I was...talking to the Frayd. The bond we shared during the transfusion — it did more than connect me physically, I was there...inside its head."

"We figured something had happened to you. We just didn't know what."

"It appeared to me as my mum. I think it was trying to frame its communication in a context I could understand. To be honest, I'm not sure that I did."

"Well, I don't know what the two of you talked about in there, but it did the trick — the Frayd set us free and managed to get clear of any planetary bodies before it self-destructed. Long-range scanners report its...remains...were scattered almost four lightyears from here."

"I know. I...saw it." It was a question as much as a declaration.

Lillum sidled up beside him. "After the Frayd let us go, I performed a scan on you. Your brain exhibited a highly unusual level of activity, and wave patterns that did not match your baseline records."

"I don't doubt it. It's difficult to explain. It's like I was seeing the universe through its eyes — or whatever sensory organs Frayd use. I could feel every blistering wave of agony it experienced during its final moments. And yet, the overwhelming emotion that kept bubbling to the surface was one of hope. That's the best way I can describe it."

"Funny thing for a creature about to explode to feel," said Barry.

"There was something else, one other feeling that kept creeping up on me — a sense of...duty. Does that make sense?"

"Mate, not a lot of this makes sense at the moment. The important thing is that whatever you did, it worked."

"So Earth...it's okay?"

"Probably better if I show you." Barry flicked a glance to Lillum. "Am I good to go?"

She waggled her head like a dog shaking off water. "You'll do, but no more heroics for a while."

Morrissey rose tentatively to his feet, catching sight of another of the diagnostic beds. Under a translucent shielding lay the still figure of their reluctant Thuwom ally, Bryndevaan, almost unrecognisable. Absent was his vibrant purple sheen, his skin so dark as to appear almost black. His appendages oozed from his flaccid torso like overcooked noodles. The only discernible sign of life was the slight trembling of his vocal folds visible through the slack opening of his mouth cavity.

Morrissey blanched. "You said he was damaged, but I had no idea how badly."

Lillum's eyestalks bobbed downward. "I had to remove his genetic sensory gland, the part that governs his sensitivity to other lifeforms – to his own kind. It was threatening to permanently destroy his synaptic relays. I don't know what long-term effect this will have on his well-being. I'm not sure whether he will recover at all. For now, he must remain in stasis."

"I'm so sorry. I don't know what to say."

"It's not your fault. He offered himself freely. He just didn't know the toll it would take. None of us did. We weren't to know the lengths he would go to return to his mate's side." Lillum gestured to the next bed where she — or he, or it — lay cocooned in another stasis pod. "Imagine the emotional bond between two such beings that would drive one toward death in order to save the other. The irony is painful: that they are finally reunited, yet he can no longer feel her presence."

Morrissey found a strange comfort in the familiar embrace of the Command Sphere, its concave bulkheads enveloping his beleaguered spirit and weary soul like a security blanket. Syddyk looked up from his diagnostics as they entered, flashing an unexpectedly broad smile.

"I'm glad you survived, Morrissey," he said.

"You and me both, mate." Morrissey didn't know if he should address the elephant in the room. "And how are you? Last I remember, you were all set to sacrifice yourself for the greater good."

Syddyk's smile flattened. "It wasn't necessary in the end."

"I just want to make sure you're not looking for another way out. If there's one thing I've learned on this magical mystery tour, it's that you'll only know if things will get better if you're here to see them get better. Life might just be worth hanging around for."

Syddyk nodded wistfully. "Perhaps," he said, "eventually."

"You've got good people around you. Remember that." Morrissey smiled as reassuringly as he could. "Where's Vintz, by the way? I hope you didn't space him out the airlock."

"Not quite, but I did send him to clean up the river of Frayd fluid you brought with you."

"Yeah, sorry about the mess."

"Never mind that," said Barry as he settled himself in the command chair. "You wanted to know if your homeworld survived?" He punched at his console. "It was tricky identifying our position at first. The Frayd catapulted us out of hyperspace at a very unexpected exit point, creating an entirely new hyperspace conduit."

He expanded the viewscreen to three quarters, revealing a bleak vista of barren grey rock, pitted with craters and shrouded in loneliness. "But it turns out your old dad wasn't lying — we pretty much hit the bullseye as far as being close to your home."

Morrissey gaped at the image on the screen. "Is that what I think it is?"

"If you think it's your moon, you're right."

"We set down on its far side," said Syddyk. "Thought it best to keep out of view of prying eyes."

"Your Earth is as happily ignorant of its imminent demise as it ever was," said Barry. "I sent a tight-beam transmission to Xrrka to apprise her of our status. She's sending a repair ship, which should be here in a couple of days. We just have to sit tight and keep a low profile until then."

Easier said than done. The comm chirped; Vintz's holo-image poured from the node.

"What's up, Vintz?" said Barry.

"I'm in the airlock — I think you'd better get down here. And you might want to bring Lillum."

Barry arched an eyebrow toward Syddyk. "We're on our way."

The airlock smelt as rancid as an abandoned abattoir, thick smears of Frayd slime still clinging to much of the deck and bulkheads. The group arrived to find Vintz keeping an uneasy vigil at the airlock entrance.

"What's going on?" said Barry as he peered over Vintz's shoulder.

"That." Vintz pointed to a watermelon-sized husk sitting on the deck. It looked much like a giant pinecone bound in a tightly woven web of course fibres, dry and brittle, speckled with blue mucous.

Barry was stumped. "What the heck is it?"

"It was my sincerest hope that you could tell me. The bots discovered it lodged under the control console as they began their cleaning cycle."

"Did you touch it?"

"I thought it best not to as it didn't quite look like it belonged on the ship."

"Well spotted," said Syddyk as he reflexively drew his pistol.

"I do not think that will be necessary," said Lillum. She moved in close, waving her scanning wand over the object. Her eyestalks roved hypnotically over the rough curves of the husk. "As I suspected, the object shows the same genetic profile as the Frayd samples I tested earlier."

"What are you saying?" said Barry. "Is this a piece of the Frayd? A fragment of its body?"

"Not as you mean it — it is not Frayd debris. It shows no signs of biological trauma or radioactive damage. Based on what little I've learned of Frayd physiology and what I can divine from its behaviour prior to its destruction, I believe this object to be an offshoot of the larger creature — its…offspring, if you will."

"You mean, this is a Frayd…baby?" said Morrissey.

"More like a seed — an egg, perhaps. I would suggest that the tendril that attached itself to our ship was not a limb, not in the strictest sense. I believe it was an ovipositor, the blue secretion, a form of amniotic fluid."

"So, when I was riding that demented waterslide, the Frayd wasn't trying to save my life, it was trying to save its…child?"

"Maybe a bit of both, mate," said Barry. "You did say that you two bonded. Maybe it took a liking to you."

"Bear in mind that this is only conjecture at this point," said Lillum. "Proof will require a more sophisticated analysis."

"You're not kidding." Barry inched closer, circling the object warily. "I'd like it quarantined."

"We're keeping it?" said Syddyk. "Do you think that's wise? What do we do when it starts growing? You saw the size of its mother. We have no idea how this organism is likely to develop or what its disposition will be when it does."

"We'll monitor it closely. It seems to be in a dormant state." Barry turned to Lillum for confirmation. She waggled her eyestalks in a message that could have been agreement or puzzlement.

Syddyk persisted. "Might I remind you that the adult Frayd was also in a dormant state — at first. Wouldn't it be safer to drop it off in hyperspace where it can live out its normal life cycle?"

"Only we don't know what its normal life cycle is," said Barry.

Morrissey had seen his fair share of movies where mysterious lifeforms grew into ravenous beasts only to devour shiploads of unsuspecting space crews. This scenario had death and destruction written all over it. Yet, his connection to the Frayd had left a mark on his soul that he could not ignore. "Hope," he said, "and duty. Our duty — my duty. That's what the Frayd was trying to tell me in its dying moments, trying to beg me. If this is a Frayd egg, its parent saw fit to deposit it on our ship. If it could've left it in hyperspace, I'm sure it would've. The Frayd went to considerable effort in its last moments of life to protect this...whatever it is. We have to honour its dying wishes."

Barry squatted, frog-like, beside the egg, cautiously nudging it with his index finger. The husk rocked gently but did not stir. "Agreed, but I want it kept in stasis. Lil, do you think you could rig a pod for this thing? That ought to keep it stable until Xrrka can get her people on it."

Lillum shifted awkwardly. "You're suggesting we study it? Might we not be accused of the same crimes against sentient life as Vaziil?"

"The difference is that we would be studying the egg for its own sake, not experimenting on it for ours. It's the ALF's mandate to protect the sentient innocents of the galaxy. If this isn't a case for us then I don't know what is. But this must be kept under the strictest of confidences. We've seen how beings like this can be abused for all manner of nasty reasons. We can't let that happen again. We're the only ones who know this creature exists and it has to stay that way — and in case you haven't noticed, Vintz, I'm looking at you. I know this is a bit after-the-fact, but technically you're still an enemy combatant. You helped Morrissey escape eNdeen's clutches and you helped us escape the Frayd destruction, and that's not nothing, but we've had some...staffing issues lately and we can't take loyalties for granted."

Surprisingly, it was Syddyk who spoke up. "I'll admit I had my doubts about him at first, but he did acquit himself admirably during our subsequent struggles."

"What'll it be, Vintz," said Barry. "If you've got any thoughts about taking this information to the highest bidder, you can just get off the ship right now — and I mean right now." He gestured to the stark moonscape out the porthole.

Vintz's heavy head nodded slowly. "I know I was on the wrong side of this fight and for the wrong reasons. I cannot change my past, but I can shape my future toward better goals — if you'll allow me the honour of offering you my services."

"Well, that's a pretty good start. You'll still need to be thoroughly vetted by Xrrka but if you clear her screens, I'll happily welcome you aboard officially. For now, you can help Lillum and Syddyk secure the egg."

A stifled warble bubbled from the corner of the airlock. All who had weapons drew them, aiming toward the sound. Syddyk was first to probe the chunkier Frayd detritus, yielding more bubbling moans from within. The mass stirred, a portion of it rising. As the Frayd ejaculate dripped clear, they saw what lay beneath.

"You have got to be kidding me," said Morrissey. "Vaziil?"

Like a fish out of water, his body twitched, his slack mouth gulping through the thick mucous. Stunned and confused, Chendra Vaziil tried unsuccessfully to pull himself to his feet, unable to control his own bodily functions.

"Oh no you don't," said Barry. "Vintz, secure him."

"He's going out the airlock," said Syddyk.

"No," said Barry, "he's going into the brig."

"We don't have a brig."

"Then we'll stick him in a cargo pod. We're sending him back with Xrrka and he's going to stand trial for all he's done. There are a lot of species who'll want a piece of him. Syd, you'd better message Xrrka with these latest developments."

Morrissey stared into his biological father's numb eyes. He didn't see his own flesh and blood. He didn't see the malevolence of a genocidal maniac. What he saw was weakness. And it felt good. "So, I guess no exit strategy this time, eh...Dad."

CHAPTER 30

Morrissey sat alone in *The Briiga*'s crew lounge, its observation bubble open, watching intently as Vaziil was loaded aboard the prisoner transport vessel. Xrrka's repair team had come with a Thon Pahl military escort, providing full tactical and medical support. It made sense that they would want their pound of Vaziil's flesh; Morrissey only wished Sha'an were here to see it happen.

The extradition had gone smoothly; Vaziil had been secured in an energy net, much like Morrissey's transport cocoon when he had been eNdeen's captive. An entire squad of Thon Pahl soldiers had escorted him from The Briiga's cargo hold to the heavily armed transport on the moon's surface while a corvette class vessel patrolled from orbit. With such a high-profile prisoner, they were taking no chances.

"That victory is down to you, David." A figure clattered softly behind him.

"Xrrka! I didn't know you were here. You don't know how good it is to see you!" He gave her an awkward hug; she didn't have the cuddliest of physiques. "I was beginning to think I never would." Their last holo-encounter on Chyll seemed oh so long ago.

"I thought it best to oversee matters personally." Her mouthparts vacillated wildly in what Morrissey had come to know as an expression of happiness. "It is good to see you alive and well, also. I understand it was almost not the case — on several occasions. We must celebrate your survival — and our reunion."

Xrrka gestured to the doorway as Barry entered carrying a rather ostentatious bottle of liquor. "I think we could all use a drink about now," he said as he popped the cap. A soft fizz and a generous pour later, the three of them toasted to the end of their long, dark nightmare.

Xrrka raised her glass. "To fallen comrades. The cost has been heavy but the outcome just. They will be remembered, always." She tapped at a place in her chest that may have contained her heart. The sentiment was unmistakable, nonetheless.

"Syddyk is going to need our support," said Barry. "Losing Kheni was like losing his purpose. He's going to need a lot of company on his path."

"And he shall have it," said Xrrka, "always. And we will take care of Bryndevaan and his ailing mate as best we can. I understand he sacrificed much to find his way to you, David, and Vaziil." Another toast. "I also understand that you played a significant role in persuading the Frayd creature to spare us the havoc of its destruction."

"Well, I don't know how much influence I had. It seemed to have an agenda all its own."

"Yes. The Frayd seed. We will analyse it in good time but we must be discreet. JuHu Station is far too centralised to be a safe zone. Such a discovery will need to be examined in a far more...secluded environment — for its own safety as well as ours."

The three watched with no small amount of relief as the Thon Pahl transport lifted from the moon with their very special package.

"Vaziil's capture and eventual trial will be public knowledge in time," said Xrrka. "His punishment will heal a lot of wounds."

Morrissey raised his glass. "I only hope yours will be among them."

"That healing will take more time than I may have." Her mouth tendrils vacillated gently. "But it will help, yes."

They all toasted in silence. Finally, Xrrka nodded to Barry, sharing a glance that suggested a shared secret. Barry fumbled in his tunic, retrieving a small package. He handed it to Morrissey.

"Another present?"

"Thought you might want this," he said.

"I believe you would call it a memento," said Xrrka, "a keepsake, perhaps."

Morrissey unwrapped the package; inside was a small silver frame — Ruth Small's picture frame. His Mum. "Where did you...you got this from Fowler's?"

"Seemed a shame to leave it behind," said Barry.

He stared into the sad woman's eyes, a frozen memory from a happier time. It made him regret, all the more, the decisions she felt she had to make, decisions that drove her down a sad and tragic path, that drove them apart, stealing a lifetime of family from him. And yet, he was glad to have the photo just the same. There was something comforting about it, familiar even. It was as if...

"I remember this photo, or one like it. Except the one I'm thinking of was — hang on." He flipped the frame over and pried open the backing, carefully sliding out the picture. It had been folded in half so that only the side with his mum appeared in the frame. In the other half of the picture was a young boy, maybe four years old, holding her hand. A very familiar young boy. "That's...me."

Both Barry and Xrrka leaned in close. "Well I'll be," said Barry. "Cute kid. What happened to you?" Barry winked a large saucer eye, trying to lighten the mood.

Morrissey smiled wistfully. "I knew I remembered this picture." One of the few happy memories he had of his childhood, one of the few indelible memories he had of his mum. Images and events had faded into pale shadows over the years, ambiguous recollections sharpened by acrid emotions. It was nice to be reminded that it was all real, that he hadn't imagined it. "Thanks, Barry. Both of you. This means more than you could possibly know."

"No problem, mate."

As Morrissey began to reassemble the picture frame, he noticed that there was something else sandwiched between the cardboard inserts. He unfolded the square of yellowed newsprint gingerly, with all the reverence of an ancient Egyptian scroll. It was a voice from the past. His mother's voice. Or at least his mother's voice interpreted by the reporter at The Weekly Titillator, so many years ago.

Sex, Bugs, & UFOs!

It was a headline worthy of the dubious tabloid journal, that much was certain. The subheading didn't help matters much: Close Encounter of the Carnal Kind Turns Tragic. Below that gem was a crudely patched together image of a bug-eyed alien's swollen head superimposed on the body of a man grappling with a cowering young woman. The optics were as embarrassing as the implications.

Morrissey's breath caught in his throat. "This is the article, Barry — the missing exposé covered up by the M.O.D. all those years ago. My mum's story that no one took seriously until it was way beyond too late."

"Holy — your mum certainly was a cunning old devil! Should've figured she would have found a way to keep a copy." Barry leaned in to read alongside Morrissey.

The article, such as it was, asserted that a woman who wished to remain anonymous had gone undercover to expose a network of extraterrestrials hiding out on Earth. The woman, only referred to in the article as RS, had inserted herself into the life of one suspected alien, even feigning a romantic connection and subjecting herself to intimate relations with him to win his confidence." Morrissey felt sickened at the thought but felt a strange sense of pride at her dedication. The story went on to corroborate everything they'd learned about his mum subsequent to her death. Not surprisingly, it intimated heavily of a government conspiracy to cover up the facts. Of course, there were just enough 'allegedlys' and vague references to inside sources to keep the lawyers at arm's length, but the door had been left open wide enough for conspiracy theorists to fill in the gaps with their wild speculations. It was no wonder the M.O.D. wanted the story squashed.

"I can't believe how close she came to unravelling the truth," said Morrissey.

"And the lengths your old boss took to stop her," said Barry. "I guess they couldn't take the chance that someone might go poking around in that can of worms."

Something didn't sit quite right with Morrissey. "Hang on. Smythe had a file on me and my mum in his personal safe, even through her identity changes. He must have known — or at least suspected — that what she reported was true. Or else why would she have been kept on the M.O.D. watchlist? And if she was on the watchlist, then he must have known about me and put two and two together."

"Maybe he did. Maybe he wanted to keep you under close observation."

"But if he suspected that I might be Vaziil's offspring, how come I didn't end up under some government microscope? Surely I would have been of significant scientific value."

Xrrka chirped in. "As an objective observer, might I posit a different theory. It seems clear that the human called Smythe had a familiarity with extraterrestrial threats that no one was aware of. Therefore, it is entirely possible he may have been protecting you. You said the file on your mother was kept in his personal safe — *outside* of your government's watchful eye?" Morrissey nodded. "Then perhaps he was trying to keep you from falling under that microscope. There was no saving your mother. It seems she'd charted a path from which there was no escape. The best he could offer for her salvation was to silence the story that would have exposed her to further alien dangers. As for you, it sounds as if Archibald Smythe was trying to keep you from harm by keeping you close, shielding you from the very trials you ended up facing these past few weeks. And perhaps by mentoring you to investigate things of another world, he was providing you with the tools and skills to one day uncover the truth for all to see, something he didn't have the means — or the courage — to do himself. Something your mother would have wanted."

Morrissey was speechless. He'd been dealing with the fallout of his mother's disappearance on his own for so long now that the concept of an ally in the cause seemed so…alien. Was it possible that he'd become so cynical and jaded that he couldn't even consider that someone else might have his best interests at heart? After all, Smythe had died at QiQi's hands while trying to keep the truth from her. Even if his efforts failed, that had to mean something.

And then there was his Mum. He'd carried the pain and loneliness of her disappearance from his life for so long that he was unable to see the truth for the facts. She hadn't abandoned him for her sake, she'd done it for his. In her mind, leaving was the only way for her to spare him the torment of her life's tragic path. Perhaps that was what the Frayd was trying to tell him by sacrificing itself for the sake of its child. And true to its dying message, the only way forward was for him to let go. At the very least, it gave him a palpable sense of closure.

"You know, Xrrka, I may never know the full truth but it kind of feels good knowing that my mother was looking out for me, in the only way she knew how." He raised his glass to them both. "And maybe now, I've got a couple of more people to watch my back."

Xrrka's mouth-tendrils vacillated in a smile. Barry's temples flushed a deep purple.

"The only question that remains," she said, "is what to do with you now, David. I imagine you'd like very much to see your home again."

"Yeah, Dave," said Barry. "You can almost see the bright lights of London from here!"

"Of course," said Xrrka, "I would like to do a full medical workup on your systems. There's no telling what effect Vaziil's DNA transfusion process may have had on you, not to mention your communion with the Frayd, but if the diagnostic panels show clear I see no reason why you cannot return to Earth. If that is what you truly wish?"

Morrissey found himself torn by the question and didn't quite understand why. Throughout this whole fantastical ordeal, he'd wanted nothing more than for it to be over, to be home again, to taste Earth one more time. Now, with the prospect so close, he felt something churning within him, a feeling that could only be described as...melancholy. Despite every brush with death, every twist of fate, every dance on the knife's edge, he was going to deeply miss his new friends. Tragedy and adversity had rocketed them on an unimaginable journey together and had bonded them more fiercely than he could ever have thought possible. Yet even in the face of such camaraderie, his destiny was inevitable, the pull toward Earth, unstoppable.

"You've all become family to me, Xrrka. More than. But you're right — I need to go home. I need to feel Earth under my feet one more time."

"Of course," she said, "I would expect no less. But you must realise that you will always be part of us, David. And you will always be welcome among us."

CHAPTER 31

The village swelled like a lonely scab crusting the hard face of the northern Scottish coastline. It was as stark and alien a landscape as any Morrissey had seen during his galactic sojourn. Its precise isolation had allowed Syddyk to bring the shuttle down quietly in a nearby clearing for a quick drop and dust-off before any of the local farm life could stir from their evening feed.

Barry had decided to accompany Morrissey on his homecoming tour, taking advantage of the relative lull in the action for some much-needed R&R; during his time stationed on Earth, he'd grown quite fond of its rustic charms and easy pace of life.

Morrissey was glad of the company, for personal and practical reasons. In all the kerfuffle of being punted across the cosmos into every galactic conflict on offer, he'd somehow managed to misplace his wallet. Thankfully, Barry had accumulated an abundance of Earth currency and could think of no better purpose than to see his human friend returned home in style. He owed him that much, at least.

They arrived in the gentle simmer of the evening sun, a sun Morrissey vowed never to take for granted again. Its warm kiss welcomed him home as if he were the prodigal son. The faint rumble of an approaching thunderstorm offered a sharp counterpoint from the distance. It somehow made Morrissey feel quite at home.

From the landing site it had been a brisk four-kilometre trek to the heart of the town where they quickly located a hotel — the only hotel, as it happened. Fortunately there were vacancies, but more importantly there was a pub attached. This was a key point in Morrissey's reorientation plan.

They sat at one of the tables in the generous courtyard, Barry shrouding his alienness in an oversized "I Heart England" hoodie from his collection of Earth souvenirs. The half dozen patrons scattered throughout the yard didn't seem to notice him in any case. In the smatterings of overheard conversations, it suddenly dawned on Morrissey that he was actually hearing their voices — their true voices, not translations fed through the T-Chip implanted in his brain stem. He hadn't realised how used to the device he'd become and found the exposure to pure human speech oddly jarring. He smiled at the irony as he took a long satisfying pull on his pint. "Man, I missed this."

"The beer?"

"Oh, yes." Another gulp. "Simple pleasures, my friend. But not just the beer." Morrissey nodded out toward the silver gash of sea slicing into the ragged cove. Inky smudges dotted an early evening sky studded with the first tiny jewels of starlight peering through the clouds — stars that he'd only recently wandered amongst. He inhaled deeply, drawing fresh Earth air into his starving lungs. "Everything. It just feels like…"

"Home?"

"Yes. Home."

A spider scuttled out from under the lip of the table, mounting Morrissey's forearm, its thin spiky legs tap-dancing across his bare flesh. A few weeks ago, just the thought of such a violation would have given him a severe case of the willies. Now he didn't even flinch. "Even this," he said as he gently palmed the creature back onto the table. "This is the first time in I don't know how long that something with more than two legs has approached me and I haven't feared for my life."

"Being thrown into the deep end of the galaxy isn't for the faint of heart." Barry leaned in close, his human teeth flashing crisp white against his purple and blue skin. "It's not everyone who would have survived, either. You handle yourself pretty well in a fight — for a human." He winked a big saucer eye.

Morrissey was going to miss the big twerp. When he'd first met Human-Barry in the offices of The Weekly Titillator, he wouldn't have trusted him to give the correct time. Now he would trust him with his life, and then some. In a way, his interplanetary adventures made Earth feel that much smaller yet at the same time, that much more precious. Maybe it was just the change in perspective he needed. "I belong here, mate, with my own people. Don't get me wrong — nothing brings people together more than a battle of life and death. It's been an honour fighting alongside you all, but I think I need to be around my own kind, around humans. Maybe to remind me that I am human."

"We all need to belong, mate," said Barry. "Remember though, you've always got a home with the ALF — if you change your mind."

The two of them clinked glasses once more, a toast to their unique bond.

"Of course, there are some humans I could pretty much do without," he said, nodding to their approaching guest — if you could call a rat at the dinner table a guest.

Graham 'Witless' Whitchurch skulked through the courtyard, looking about as comfortable as a vicar in a brothel, his carefully sculpted bespoke blazer as rumpled as his spirits. He sidled up to Morrissey but did not sit.

"Ah, Graham," said Morrissey. "Glad you could make it."

Whitchurch's brittle voice cranked surliness. "Your decidedly cryptic message offered little choice in the matter."

Syddyk had been able to relay a comm signal from The Briiga's shuttle while they were still en route to Earth, giving the impression that Morrissey was calling Whitchurch from a mobile phone within the UK.

Morrissey smirked. "I thought you'd enjoy the change in scenery."

"I've spent the better part of a day in transit and now that I've arrived, I'd hardly call being perched on the rim of Scotland's arsehole 'scenery'."

"I think it's very nice, very serene."

"Nice? I didn't hire you to go on a rambling tour of the Scottish Highlands. I hired you to — "

"Actually, Graham, you didn't hire me at all. I thought we were just two old work chums doing one another a favour. Isn't that how you put it?"

Whitchurch's edge softened somewhat, probably hurting his ego in the process. "Still, I can't imagine how your investigation has brought you so far from home."

Morrissey shook his head slowly. "You have no idea. Look, why don't you have a seat. You're starting to draw a level of attention that doesn't befit our rather private conversation." He tapped a finger to the side of his nose, pandering to Whitchurch's clandestine proclivities. "A little more discretion is required, don't you think?"

Whitchurch grudgingly dusted off one of the wrought iron chairs with his monogrammed handkerchief before sitting. "What is required, David, is a clear and precise explanation as to why you've been incommunicado for over three weeks." He glanced over toward Barry, still carefully shrouded in his hoodie. "And if this is supposed to be a private conversation, who is *this* and what are they doing here?"

"All in good time, Graham. First, I think we should renegotiate our deal."

Whitchurch's confusion lost out to his arrogance. "Our deal is non-negotiable. You agreed to close the Red File on Ruth Small and in return I agreed to remove any roadblocks to your rezoning application. I even threw in a lead on your mother as a bonus. You can't say fairer than that."

"Yes, about that. You didn't exactly provide me with all the facts, now, did you?"

"It was all in the Red File in black and white."

"Mostly black by the amount of redaction. For instance, you neglected to tell me that Ruth Small, the old woman in the nursing home, was actually my mother."

"Your...your mother? Surely you can't be serious." Whitchurch seemed genuinely challenged. "That can't be. But...how?"

"Isn't *that* the question. And Old Archie Smythe had all the answers — he'd been keeping the secret hidden all these years. So either you were in on the conspiracy or you really are as dumb as you look."

Whitchurch twitched in his skin. "I...I really didn't know."

Apparently, he *was* as dumb as he looked. "Yeah, I believe you." For once. If Smythe had been keeping his cards so close to his chest, then maybe his intentions really were born out of kindness rather than malice. But there was still more he needed to answer for. "And you know nothing of Smythe's intergalactic coverup involving the UFO sightings at Rendlesham — and probably countless others? You weren't aware that extraterrestrials have been mining the human population for test subjects for centuries? Or that an alien terrorist masquerading as a human had threatened to destroy the Earth?"

Whitchurch raised a hand in protest. "Come now, David. Obviously, your newfound knowledge of your parentage has caused some emotional distress so I'm willing to give you some latitude — but actual UFOs? Aliens? I think the last few weeks in the northern air has affected your grip on reality."

"On the contrary, Graham. My recent travels have taken me to some very interesting places where I've met some very interesting...people. The simple, if somewhat startling, truth is we are not alone. I know — scary, isn't it. Turns out the galaxy is teeming with life — sentient life. And some of it has made its way to Earth, not all of it friendly. We've been caught with our collective pants down and Smythe's defensive tactic of burying his head under the covers until it blows over isn't going to work anymore. We'd be fools if we didn't start fortifying our intelligence networks to counter any future incursions. So once you've been crowned Prince of All Underhanded Activities, you're going to start the wheels turning. You're going to reinstate the UFO Hotline and assemble a full investigative team to handle the workload."

Whitchurch squinted through pale, slitted eyelids. "You're mad! I think you've been spending too much time with your crackpot abductee friends. If you think I'm going to sully my reputation with such a questionable endeavour, then you don't know me very well. You haven't a shred of proof — "

"Oh, I've got proof."

Whitchurch regained some of his customary smarm. "A faded signature of a dead man on a thirty-odd year-old file isn't proof."

"Maybe not. But my friend, here, is."

Barry leaned forward, reaching out a reedy, blue, four-fingered hand and grabbed his pint. He took a long, hard pull then set the glass down. With overarching drama, he slowly pulled back the cowl of his hoodie, just enough to reveal the pale camouflage of his skin and the dim orange glow of his saucer eyes. He spread a gap-toothed grin as he extended his hand to Whitchurch. "Hello. Barrek, at your service. You can call me Barry. Or Baz. Your choice."

The dark beads of Whitchurch's eyes jittered like Mexican jumping beans. "What the…you…what are you…no…it can't…you can't…" Colour flushed from his already pasty skin and sweat rippled across his furrowed brow as his whole head began to tremble. His eyes rolled slowly back in their sockets as his brain suddenly closed for business. Barry grabbed their pints a split second before Whitchurch's face slammed into the tabletop.

"Okaaaay," said Morrissey. "That didn't exactly go as planned."

"He's not dead, is he?" said Barry.

Morrissey poked Whitchurch in the shoulder. "No such luck. You keep an eye on him. I'll go get him a brandy. He's going to need a drink when he comes to, poor sod. Whatever you do, don't let him leave and don't let him make any calls. We don't want him setting off any alarms."

Morrissey entered the lounge to find the small crowd of patrons gathered around the bar-mounted television, their animated murmurs rising to hubbub levels. The sea of bobbing heads focussed intently on a news broadcast where a young reporter standing outside the Houses of Parliament was looking suitably serious and speaking in carefully measured tones of gravity.

"…reports are coming from all over the globe regarding the mysterious seismic tremors. Cairo, Budapest, Sydney, Mumbai, and Cape Town are the latest in a long list of cities to fall victim to the unexplained quakes. London, itself, is experiencing tremors at a magnitude of 3.2. Though the reports of damage so far are minimal, experts at the British Geological Survey do confirm that the intensity of the tremors has increased over the last hour, as has the number of cities affected."

The reporter went on to detail the lack of history of earthquakes in these regions, but the crowd wanted more current events and less speculation. Many began furiously tapping at their smartphones, searching for answers to questions they didn't understand, or simply reaching out to loved ones. Morrissey moved to the window, scanning the darkening sky, theories about the approaching thunderstorm suddenly falling into serious question. He moved slowly into the courtyard as the remainder of the patrons pushed inside to watch the news report.

Barry flicked him a quizzical glance. "Where's the brandy?"

Morrissey felt the rumblings stronger now, through his feet and into the pit of his stomach. "Not thunder…" he said absently.

"Not…thunder? What are you talking about?"

No storm clouds. No rain. No wind. He should have realised something was amiss. Perhaps he'd been away from home for too long. "Not thunder. Earthquakes. It's earthquakes. All over the world, apparently. Well, tremors so far. Not serious, so they say, but they're getting worse."

Barry leapt to his feet, grabbing Morrissey by the shoulders to shake the cryptic from him. "Look, mate, I don't know what you've been drinking in there, but earthquakes striking all over the planet, all at the same time, are about as likely as — " A chime sounded at his wrist. Barry seemed afraid to answer. "Hello?"

"Barrek, it's Syd. We've got a problem." The shuttle would have made it back to the moon by now and Syddyk would be supervising the repairs.

"What sort of problem?"

"We're picking up a series of massive energy readings bleeding through hyperspace at the precise location where the Frayd ejected us."

"What sort of energy readings, exactly?" said Barry.

"Lillum says the signatures match the Frayd's biometrics. That can't be a coincidence, can it?"

"I wouldn't think so."

"What does that mean?" said Morrissey.

"It means that we've got visitors knocking on our door. How many distinct signatures, Syd? How many entities are we talking about?"

"A half-dozen. Maybe more. They're causing some major seismic activity up here."

Barry eyed Morrissey through a new lens. "We've got the same down here. The hyperspace conduit must have ruptured when the Frayd flung us clear of its blast. Punched a hole where there shouldn't be one."

"If the energy readings are accurate and those really are Frayd, there's no telling what damage they'll do if they break through into normal space."

"Keep me posted, Syd. Let me know if the signals get stronger." Static. "Syd? Do you read?" Still static. "Shit."

"Why would Frayd — if they *are* even Frayd — be showing up now?" said Morrissey. "Are they looking for their friend? Did they detect its scent or whatever passes for pheromones in a Frayd?"

The deep blue of Barry's camouflage drained to a pasty grey as he stumbled back into his chair, grasping for his pint. He downed the remains in one gulp. "I think they're tracking something else — someone else." His burnt orange eyes flickered back and forth like a madman. "We've got to get you out of here, Dave." He nodded vigorously as if he'd just remembered where he'd left the keys to the universe. "Now!"

"What are you talking about? We just got here."

"And now we have to go. But where?" This last bit was mumbled mostly to himself.

"Okay," said Morrissey, "this isn't funny. Now you're starting to creep me out."

"Don't you see? Vaziil used his own DNA as a trigger for the Frayd weapon. What if he passed that trait down to his son — to you? He said it himself — the hyperspace zone around Earth is the perfect resting ground for Frayd. They feel safe here. If they are drawn to your DNA signature and if they breach that rupture in the hyperspace corridor, the damage to your world could be catastrophic — whether it's intended or not." He gestured to the pub TV still playing the news report of the quakes.

Morrissey looked up to the sky as if to see a herd of Frayd tumble from the heavens. He wanted to dispute the logic, but he couldn't. By now, he'd seen enough of the galaxy to realise that the impossible was pretty much the rule rather than the exception. He took a deep breath, feeling the panic well up inside him like a clogged toilet. "Okay. So what do we do?"

"You were able to commune with the Frayd before. Could you do it again?"

"I don't know. I wasn't exactly in control of that. Besides, I had been connected to that specific Frayd. That doesn't mean I have a bond with all of them. What about shielding my genetic signature? Don't you have a forcefield or something you can use?"

Barry made a show of patting himself down. "Sorry, Dave, I must have left it in my other trousers."

"Well, I don't know, do I?"

"No. Sorry. But we do have to remove you from the equation somehow. And fast."

"How? We've lost contact with The Briiga — they could be destroyed for all we know. And even if they aren't, they don't know that I'm the Frayd's main attraction."

Barry's spirits sank. "I doubt they'd make it here in time anyway, before…"

He didn't need to hear Barry spell out the inevitable. "There's got to be another option."

"There may be…but you're not going to like it."

"There's a lot I haven't liked, lately, but I've done it anyway. How bad could it be?"

"This is different. Much different. I can't even bring myself to say it."

"Well, you're going to have to because I'm not a bloody mind reader and we're running out of time." As if to punctuate the threat, another tremor rattled the wrought iron table, the pint glasses slowly dancing around Whitchurch's unconscious head. "Come on, Barry, what exactly do I have to do?"

"You…erm…you have to…sort of…die."

It was Morrissey's turn for silence. "Look, mate, I'm not being funny or anything but didn't we just spend a good deal of time and energy trying to keep me alive? I'd hate to think that was all for nothing."

"Remember what Sha'an said to Vaziil when she confronted him on Earth all those years ago? She figured that if she killed him, the DNA trigger for the Frayd weapon would be silenced and the threat nullified. Vaziil suggested that his death would only accelerate the sequence, but she didn't buy it. She never did forgive herself for letting him escape without testing her theory. What if that same principle were to apply to this situation? We've got Frayd. We've got a genetic signature. It should work…in theory."

"Couldn't we fake my death? Simulate it? Surely there are medical ways to achieve such a state?"

"I'm sure there are, but I'm not equipped to perform them. I'm not a doctor and I'm certainly not an expert in human physiology. I wouldn't know where to begin."

The tremors continued to ripple through Morrissey's soul, growing in strength along with the panic of the pub patrons. He had no problem sacrificing himself for the greater good, if that was what it took, but he had no way of knowing for sure that giving his life would end the threat. If he were wrong, if his sacrifice were in vain, he was going to be well and truly pissed.

On the other hand, he'd skirted death in the past few weeks more than any human ever had a need to. Maybe Death was just finally catching up with him. There were worse ways to go out. At least this way, it was for a damned good cause. "Okay. You'd better do it, then, before I change my mind."

"Do it? You mean…?"

"I mean."

"But…" Barry stuttered. "I — I can't do it."

"Well, you can't expect me to do it. It kind of goes against my programming." There was no time for Barry's reticence. "I know it's not going to be easy, but it doesn't seem we have a choice." Morrissey could scarcely believe his own acceptance.

"Okay…okay, but not here."

Barry was right. It wouldn't do to have an alien kill a human in full view of a bunch of panicked locals. They moved around to the side of the pub, behind a wall of empty ale kegs and liquor crates.

"What about him?" said Morrissey, thumbing to the still figure of Whitchurch.

"I'll take care of him — make sure he pulls the right strings, don't you worry about that."

To be honest, that was the last thing on Morrissey's mind. "How are you going to…you know?"

"I've got my pistol. Heavy stun at close range should do the trick. Quick and clean."

"Oh. That's reassuring."

Barry reached under his hoodie and withdrew his weapon. Morrissey had seen him use it many times in combat but never before had it seemed so lethal. A shiver danced along all his nerves at once.

"Do you want to look away?" said Barry. "It might be easier. And by easier, I mean easier for me."

"If it's all the same, I think I'd prefer to face you."

"I was afraid you were going to say that." Barry thumbed his weapon to active and raised it slowly, gently pressing the muzzle against Morrissey's chest, right over his heart. "Well. It's been a pleasure, Dave."

"Likewise. Well, up until now, that is."

Barry flashed his human smile one last time. It softened the task, some. "So…on three, then?"

"No. No countdowns. I don't think my heart could take it."

"Goodbye, friend."

Morrissey could feel Barry's finger tensing ever so slightly on the firing stud. He wanted to run and hide, to bury his head in the sand. He wanted to be selfish and let the Earth fend for itself. But he knew he couldn't. He didn't have it in him. He waited for each nanosecond to pass, for each microgram of pressure to build on Barry's trigger finger.

The flash came first. Morrissey braced himself for the deadly impact, but it never followed. The fireworks weren't even from Barry's pistol. He opened his eyes, expecting to see Death looking all suave and sophisticated in his smoking jacket. Instead, he found something far more challenging. He couldn't decide whether his life was flashing before his eyes or whether he was already walking amongst the dead. The figure approached, sultry swagger and fierce intent at full throttle. "QiQi?"

His part-time lover and full-time bounty hunter wasted no time on small talk. She thrust her leg out towards Barry's gun hand, sending the weapon clattering across the cobblestones. "What the —
" was all Barry could manage before she struck him hard in the throat. He reeled backwards, stumbling against the ale kegs.

QiQi drew her own pistol and waved it casually toward him. "You don't really want me to shoot you, do you? Again?"

Barry clutched for breath. He shook his head, bewilderment clouding his resolve. "Not so much…no."

"Good. Then let's not waste any more time."

Morrissey had neither the energy nor the mental agility to untangle the twist of events. "Weren't you supposed to be dead?"

"I was supposed to be a great many things, but dead was never one of them."

"But I saw you…flying out the airlock of the Gyrth ship."

"Don't believe everything you see."

The memory was hazy, the power of suggestion had been strong. In retrospect, he'd expected eNdeen's orders to result in QiQi's death. eNdeen had taken great pleasure in describing her grisly demise. But the truth was, he really didn't get a good look at who it was tumbling in the vacuum. "How did you manage it then?"

"The greatest strength in a Gyrth mercenary is his arrogance. It's also his greatest weakness. They tend to underestimate their prey."

"I'll try to keep that in mind for next time."

"Once I'd overpowered them, escape was easy. Teleporters are a necessary risk for someone in my trade." She tapped the disk at her belt. "Since then, I've been on the hunt."

"For me? I'm flattered."

"For eNdeen — where is he? He hired me to track you down and forced me to wear this skin. He's going to pay dearly to get me out of it. And then he's going to pay for betraying me."

Morrissey smirked. "Well, I'm sorry to disappoint you, but you might find it a bit hard calling in that debt. eNdeen is already dead."

QiQi surveyed them both warily. "Dead? How?"

"Funnily enough, ejected out an airlock. Poetic justice, you might say."

"You know this as fact?"

Morrissey wasn't likely to forget. "Yes, QiQi, I know this as fact. I bagged him."

"And I tagged him," said Barry.

"You're absolutely sure he's dead? Because if he still lives..." QiQi left the threat unspoken. "I need you to be certain."

"eNdeen went for a walk in hyperspace without a pressure suit. So unless his species can breathe vacuum, I'd say his fate is pretty certain."

QiQi's beautifully sculpted jaw tightened. Her brow knitted into a complex twist of emotions she probably wasn't used to feeling. "Well...this doesn't mean that I owe you or anything."

"I wouldn't expect that it did. I gave up trying to decipher your moral code when you fed me to that madman." Morrissey tried to look deep into her soul but got bogged down in her shallows. After all she'd done to propel him into danger, he still wondered whether she might be lying to herself. If she'd simply wanted to track down eNdeen, she must have had dozens of contacts she could have plied for intel. But she chose him. Perhaps she had come after him specifically. Maybe she did feel remorse for leaving him to the whims of a butcher. Maybe there was room for compassion in that hard-faced beauty, after all. "Now that you mention it though, there is something you could do for me."

QiQi leaned in close. "I already told you, Dave, what happened between us was just business, pure and simple. And lover, our business is done."

Certainly, Morrissey knew she had to have been cold to have done what she did, that she could not — or would not — betray any sentiment as a matter of principle. But as she said these last words, he was almost sure she let slip the faintest crack of a smile. It was that glimmer of hope mixed with an unhealthy dose of desperation which pushed him. "You have to take me with you."

"You can't be serious."

"Oh yes I bloody can! Take a look around. If I stay here, Earth will be destroyed — all because of me!"

"My...you're a bit full of yourself, aren't you?"

Barry stood, slowly so as not to provoke an attack. "Listen to him. His DNA has attracted a host of Frayd entities and they're playing havoc with the subspace stability. The only way we know to stop them from doing any more damage is to either get him off Earth — or kill him."

"Needless to say, I'd prefer the former," said Morrissey.

"Sorry, Dave, but whatever you've got swimming around in your genetic soup is not my problem."

"Just for once, do you think you could restrain yourself from being a complete bitch? I'm pretty sure you've got a heart in there somewhere. What would it hurt to teleport me away from here? You could drop me off on some mainstream world, let the ALF know where to find me?"

"Maybe you haven't been keeping up with current events but my profession sort of requires that I operate in the shadows of such mainstream worlds, as you put it. You wouldn't survive a minute in those shadows."

"I won't survive much longer on Earth, either. Nobody will." The Earth gave one more urgent rumble, as if to remind them.

"Can't be helped. Besides, even if I wanted to, this teleport disk is only calibrated for one and I don't have a spare. Sorry, lover."

Morrissey was getting nowhere. But even after everything she'd put him through, he still felt the throb of desire, an uncomfortable stirring in parts down under, a yearning for one last... "Kiss. What about a kiss?"

"A what?" said QiQi and Barry in unison.

"One last kiss. Come on. Surely you wouldn't refuse the condemned man his dying wish?"

"Dave, don't you think you've got more important things to worry about at the moment?" said Barry.

"Like what? Where to scatter my ashes? If I'm going to die, I'd at least like a reminder of why I'm doing it — even if she isn't human. What do you say, QiQi? For old time's sake."

She stared long and hard at him, her luscious lips finally stretching into a flat smirk. "Sure. Why not. It's the least I could do, I suppose."

The very least. She pulled him close, fast and hard but Morrissey fought to set his own pace; if he were going to do this, he was going to do it his way. He reached for her slowly, tentatively, cupping her face gently, tracing her upper lip with his tongue. He took a soft nibble of her lower lip and blew a hot breath gently down the length of her neck. She trembled, despite her diamond exterior. His hands stroked her sides, tracing around to the small of her back and rising under the familiar curve of her breasts. Finally, he held her firmly about the waist, leaned deeply into her rich chocolate eyes — and lifted the teleport disk from her belt.

Morrissey pulled away quickly, leaving Barry and QiQi dumbfounded. He fastened the disk to his belt, cursing the treacherous path that had brought him to this point — every beating, every gunfight, every close encounter of the deadliest kind. But if never breathing the air of Earth again was the price to pay for its safety, so be it. He pressed his palm firmly against the teleport device, charging it to action; QiQi lunged, a hair too slow, as Barry knocked her off her feet.

Morrissey shouted to Barry above the mayhem. "Take care, mate! Make sure you keep Whitchurch under control!"

He couldn't tell if Barry heard him or understood. Through the vortex of electric blue chaos, the world began to melt around him as angry spasms churned the ground beneath his feet. Nausea sapped his resolve and his skin burned with a strange yet familiar icy fire. The Earth — his home — spun beneath him in a surreal dance until, once again, the universe went black.

THE END

ACKNOWLEDGEMENTS

It's no secret that writing a book is a lonely journey, one fraught with bouts of nagging self-doubt and crippling insecurity. And while I have spent a good deal of my time alone on this path, I was lucky enough to bump into a kind soul who offered her advice freely and generously. Caro Clarke comes at the publishing industry with some serious street cred, including being an author in her own right. The writing advice she provides on her website is both practical and realistic, offering anyone who takes their craft seriously a fighting chance in their own creative battles. It was this avenue where the connection began. But since that online meeting, Caro has often been there to buttress my flagging confidence, and light my way through the publishing fog. I am proud that I may now call her my peer, but she is also a mentor, a guide, and a trusted friend.

Which brings me to the team at Mirror World Publishing, who rescued this battle-weary author from the lonely wasteland of the submission pile, and actually appreciated my creative voice. Justine and Robert, you've eased me through the process with a gentle, professional touch, while engendering an atmosphere of a caring and nurturing family. Thank you for taking a chance on me. Here's to our future!

ABOUT THE AUTHOR

WARREN A. SHEPHERD was seven when he first realized the world didn't fit him quite right. Two sizes too big or two sizes too small, he couldn't be sure. But having been transported from the streets of London, England to the streets of Toronto, Canada at such a young age left him with a profound sense of alienation — a boy with one foot in each world yet belonging in neither. The experience, however, did sharpen his sense of self-awareness and made him a keen observer of the human (and not-so-human) condition.

When he sees what humankind is capable of, both the good and the bad, he imagines how we would cope amongst the stars and is driven to tell stories of strange new worlds to try to explain the one that he often cannot.

After all, it takes an alien to know an alien…

mirror world
publishing

Why 'Mirror World'?

Mirror World Publishing is a small independent publishing house based in Windsor, Ontario. We publish quality paperbacks and ebooks that feature other worlds, times and versions of reality. Our novels are for all ages and are creative, unique, imaginative and engaging.

We pride ourselves on our originality and 'outside the box' thinking, while taking a good look at the question, 'what if?' Our stories are never ordinary, the dialogue and action engaging, the characters believable, and there will always be some element of romance, adventure, science or magic. We are dedicated to bring our readers novels that will not only entertain them, but also teach them something about the world they live in by showing them one that mirrors it. We hope you'll consider picking up a novel from our collection today so you can see for yourself what we're all about.

You'll find a wide variety of our wonderful titles in our online bookstore and you can also purchase or review them through most major retailers worldwide.To learn more about our authors and our current projects visit: www.mirrorworldpublishing.com or like us at www.facebook.com/mirrorworldpublishing

Keep reading for a sneak peek at *Uncommon*,
Our next release.

Uncommon

By Justine Alley Dowsett
& Murandy Damodred

Chapter 1

When they brought her father's body home, Rhea Saline did not cry. Straight-backed, she put one foot in front of the other in the wake of six men in blue and brown leathers. Their shaved heads were bared with top knots smooth and glistening with oil, their faces held to the sky even though the icy, wet wind cut at them mercilessly as they carried the clan chief's hulking form on a litter up the long winding mountain trail.

Within the deep shadows of her dark blue cloak and shrouded by thick curling strands of her long, dark hair, Rhea was protected from the rain and the wind, but the weather wasn't what concerned her. Through the thick fabric, she felt the stares of her people on her back and knew the entire clan was watching her every movement; scrutinizing her.

But in her mind's eye she was watching not this funeral, but another. The body, wrapped in old, off-white linens, had been smaller then, and her vision blurred by tears, not rain. That day, in the last dying embers of a long summer, her father had stood where she stood now, his shoulders broad and straight, and he had been the one to stare at her, scrutinize her, and find her wanting. She remembered hating him for it.

Now, it was his body they prepared to hoist onto the pyre.

As they reached the sacred plateau where those loved by the clan were sent on, her former position was occupied by her younger brother, Rygal. Technically, he was Rygal Saline the Second, but as the first of his name was two steps from the pyre, the point seemed moot. Tall and lean, and dressed more like a scholar than a warrior, her brother at least knew where to stand by instinct, not like how she had needed to be shown. But he was a man grown, not a child like she had been when their mother passed. However, she could hear him sniffling, fighting back the emotions that threatened to overwhelm him. Without thinking, she wordlessly thrust a handkerchief in his direction, just as her father had done to her all those years ago.

I'm just like him. The thought was as clear and sharp as the cold mountain air. He raised me to be just like him.

Rhea glanced back once more at Rygal, taking in their obvious similarities in his nearly black hair, strong jaw and nose, and the blue of his eyes, while equally noticing his differences: his slight build, the hunch in his posture from too much time spent bent over a desk, and the way he shivered at the chill in the air. He would never take his place among the warriors of their clan, but she also knew that wasn't what he wanted.

Rygal caught her eye and tried to smile encouragingly. She lifted the corners of her mouth to return the gesture, but turned away before the expression could become a grimace.

This clan lost its heart when it lost my mother and it won't regain it with me in my father's place. Rygal's gloved hand slid into her bare one, squeezing it, and Rhea felt the first hint of tears sting her eyes. She fought them, directing her gaze skyward to meet the icy rain head-on. Rygal probably wouldn't agree with me, and the clan certainly wouldn't, but Jaram needs a nurturer like my mother was. She thought about the clan she knew now and the clan of her youth; things had changed, grown harder in many ways.

We've gone too long with only the tough love of my father and it's not enough. As a border nation, Jaram was a clan of warriors, herself included, but in her father's time as chief they had become less focused on just defending the borders and more focused on keeping them closed. They were obsessed with being the best, the strongest, feared. The clan now lived and breathed for the fight, but they no longer fought for the freedom to live and breathe. We've lost our way.

The six clansmen before her parted to allow the clan's resident Priestess of Saegard to join them nearest to the pyre. A petite black-haired young woman barely visible under her thick grey cloak, May was nothing like Rhea had always pictured the sisters of the fabled order she'd read about as a child, but she was what the clan had been sent. May's thin, reedy voice began the funeral dirge, her high pitch in stark contrast to the low, deep voices of the six clansmen who joined her soon after. The sound was low at first, competing with the hush of the rain and the moaning of the wind, but as more and more clanspeople reached the snow-dusted plateau and filled it, they joined in and their voices blended together, growing in strength and number.

The combined sound swelled, rising and lowering in turns, undulating on the wind. There were so many voices now; the clan had grown large and strong. Awed by the sheer force of their song, Rhea turned, looking out over the plateau at the mass of gathered clanspeople. It was as she had feared, they were looking back at her. It was one thing to feel their stares on her back, but another to face them head on and find them not just looking at her but to her, for leadership.

She could see it. See herself leading them into battle. Clan Jaram had become the strongest of all the clans, even larger now than the High Clan of Haldor, the one all the other clans had chosen to represent them to the outside world. If commanded into battle, these trained and disciplined warriors would be an unstoppable force. It was tempting, but in the battlefield of her mind Rhea watched her clanspeople fall as wave after wave of them crashed into the enemy. No, I can't be responsible for that much death. She shuddered.

If father knew what I was considering he would call me weak and selfish. And maybe I am, she thought as she was handed the torch and the six clansmen made way for her to step forward and light the fire. But he is gone and the clan is mine to protect now.

And I will protect it. She stepped back to watch as wood and cloth alike caught fire and the flames spread, consuming everything they could reach. The fire climbed higher, flames licking at the sky despite the rain's attempt to dampen them, and for the first time in Rhea's life she found she no longer cared what her father thought or wanted. Goodbye, Father, may you find peace.

The call went up, a keening howl in sharp contrast to the melodious song from before. This was the sound of thousands of clanspeople voicing their grief the only way they could. The cacophony rose, carried by the wind and echoed by the mountains, until the very ground around them shook with the sound. Then the entire congregation fell silent and the earth followed suit.

We can't go on like this. I won't be responsible for leading the clan to their destruction.

The men and women of Clan Jaram filed back down the mountain the way they'd come, though now they broke into smaller groups to converse amongst themselves. The ceremony was over, the dead at rest, and there was no more need for silence. It was time to live, to move on.

"Are you okay?" Rygal asked, falling in beside her. Rhea shook her head, but more for the question than to give an answer. Earnest as always, he took it at face value. "Do you want to talk about it?"

"Do you think father was a good clan chief?"

Her brother thought the question through before answering, as was his way. "Well, he was strong. He didn't suffer fools and…oh, Rhea, you know father and I never saw eye to eye on anything. He ruled the way he thought he ought to and he demanded obedience."

"And you?" Her words were barely a whisper.

Rygal chuckled, but the sound was bitter. "Me? Since when has what I would do mattered?"

"Humour me," she said. "Father may not have listened to you, but I'm not him…"

I'm just like him, the small voice in the back of her head revealed her words as false.

"The clan wouldn't like it, but I would try and negotiate with the Sheng-Li. We've held them back for almost a decade now and in that time we have grown stronger. We have the advantage and we can use it to sue for peace. As our neighbors, there's so much the Sheng-Li could offer us in terms of trade and knowledge. We could develop a relationship with them, like we have with the other nations. This rivalry doesn't have to continue."

"You're right," she told him, smiling despite herself. "The clan wouldn't like it."

"And you? You'll be named Clan Chief by nightfall, you know. You could do it, approach the Sheng-Li. Is that something you would consider?"

"Stranger things have happened, little brother." She reached out and took his hand, returning the squeeze from earlier. "Mother would have been proud of the man you've become."

Rygal snorted at her tone, but after a moment he added, "I miss her."

"Me too," Rhea admitted. "More than you know."

__Uncommon__ will be available from Mirror World Publishing and all major book retailers September 17th, 2022. Follow our website, blog, or sign up for our newsletter to be kept informed.

CPSIA information can be obtained
at www.ICGtesting.com
Printed in the USA
BVHW041803080722
641669BV00004B/36